Rumours and Repercussions
Stephanie May

Dedicated to my friends from childhood in Toongabbie

"Walking with a friend in the dark is better than walking alone in the light."

Helen Keller

Contents

Prologue

My high school English teacher, Willie Miller, once said a story should always have a beginning, a middle and an end. Well, this story starts at the end, but I've incorporated the beginning and middle along the way. It saved me from wondering where the hell I should begin.

I was planning to title this memoir *Orange*, because Orange is another major 'character' in the story. The town I grew up in played a part in what happened just as much as the people involved. For those who aren't aware, Orange is a country town in New South Wales, Australia. I guess not much has changed there since I was a teen in the late '70s. Even decades after leaving Orange, I can still picture the bicycle-tyre tracks left by my friends and me on the dirt roads. I can still remember Ralph Ferguson squirting peaks of Reddi-Wip cream onto sundaes at his parlour, Lickety-Split.

Our interests back then were simple: heartthrobs, rock 'n' roll, and riding over to Lake Canobolas on our bicycles. We had no internet or mobile phones; our neighbourhood didn't even have fast-food restaurants. Growing up in the '70s was akin to having unprotected sex with strangers. God, the things we used to get up to back then would make a mother of today want to wrap her precious daughter in cotton wool, *lest she be damned for all eternity.*

Shit. I can't very well tell my story if you don't know who I am, can I? You'll have to forgive me; I'm not a 'professional' storyteller. Even so, this story needs to be told, and for anyone who stumbles across it, think of it as a confession. Some parts should make you laugh, while other parts will do the opposite. By the end, you might even hate me. But I promise one thing: I will not lie, even if there are parts where you think I've gone overboard with my honesty.

Let's backtrack. My name is Kylie Romano, née Gardner. A woman in her fifties who is on a lonesome journey back to her hometown of Orange. I wish I didn't have to go. The memories ... *my God*, the things I'm about to tell you. But first, I need to get something off my chest: I regret nothing. Remember that later on, and perhaps those involved would say the same thing. It's been a while since I spoke to anyone from my childhood. My parents have both passed on and, after I got married and had a family of my own, there was no reason to go back there.

Until now.

For a funeral.

There were four of us, you see. Four high school girlfriends. We called ourselves The Sunsets. I can't remember who came up with that genius name, but I know it was because we lived in Orange. Orange ... Sunsets ... Get it?

Sharon O'Rourke and I were the oldest in our group – and at fourteen, we thought we fucking rocked! Tahlia Ashcroft and Helen Baldwin were both thirteen. I don't know why friendship circles seem to comprise four. But it's a nice round number, don't you think? We had other friends, of course, but our group was like no other foursome I've ever come across.

No doubt you'll want to know which one of The Sunsets passed away. I promise I'll tell you; I'm still coming to terms with it myself.

If you're wondering what made our little group so different, well, it's because we murdered someone.

And not just any old someone. We killed a policeman.

Chapter One

Monday, 29 October 1979. Eight weeks of term left before the six-week summer break.

Our high school was Orange West. I have to make this clear as there was also Orange East. The only two high schools in town. No prizes for guessing their locations.

As I mentioned, our English teacher was Willie Miller. Of all the characters I will tell you about, Willie is in the top three of those from whom I learned a great deal. He wasn't as cool as Ralph Ferguson over at Lickety-Split, but he had a kind nature and lived to impart his wisdom to a bunch of ungrateful kids. That's how I think of us back then. Ungrateful. We had great parents, great teachers, a great education system, but when we were at school all we could think of was hanging out at Lake Canobolas or riding our bicycles. We'd often gaze out of the classroom window in a reverie as Willie spoke passionately about metaphors, similes and alliteration.

It seems to me every group has a stereotypical label. Ever wonder why labels are stereotypical? Because there's a ring of truth to them; it's so people don't have to stretch their imagination because they know *exactly* what you mean. That was true of the school we attended. We had the class clown, the goody two-shoes, the smelly kid who everyone picked on, the pale kid who was allergic to everything under the sun, the blonde who the boys drooled over, the athletes, the no-hoper who only turned up to avoid the flogging his dad would give him, and then you had the punks who thought smoking weed was about the coolest thing since Sammy Davis Jr.

Outsiders dubbed our group 'The Misfits' – no explanation needed, really – and I can still remember my first interactions with the other three Sunset girls:

Tahlia Ashcroft, Helen Baldwin and Sharon O'Rourke. The latter was easy enough: Sharon lived on the same street as me – Sycamore Avenue.

She was the blonde who every male (including teachers) wanted to ball. And she loved the attention; for her, attention was like a flower needing water to thrive. She was the first one in our group to lose her virginity. The 'relationship' with that guy lasted about as long as her menstrual cycle, but she found a replacement soon enough. I don't actually remember meeting Sharon the first time, but I have memories of us together at Trinity Preschool. Our mothers gave birth around the same time, so for as long as I can remember, Sharon was there. It felt as though we were sisters early on because she was always around, but along the way someone must have told me otherwise. When I was fourteen, though, I couldn't imagine a future without her.

But life is never stagnant.

As Willie Miller waffled on, I fixated on things of interest around me. I glanced up from my doodling on the lined page and looked to my right. Tahlia sat next to me, hands clasped together on the scuffed desk, spine as straight as a ruler, brown eyes fixated on Willie. The sunlight through the window beside me illuminated every speck of colour in her orange hair. I marvelled at it; it was like the embodiment of autumn, with hues of red, blonde and brown. It looked so darn squeaky clean, I wanted to reach out and stroke it.

If I'm honest, it's because of Tahlia that I'm even telling this story at all. I'm not the type to lay blame or pass the buck, so I hope you believe me when I say again: I do *not* regret a thing. But if it weren't for dear, sweet, innocent Tahlia Ashcroft, there wouldn't be a story to tell.

Tahlia was a mixed bag, a hybrid. She was so damn pretty, with her flowing orange hair that reminded me of those vitamin C tablets my mother used to force down my throat during winter. She had an appetite for life the way a gluttonous person demolishes a buffet. Tahlia didn't have a boyfriend, nor had she been kissed. She showed no desire for male attention, even though her father had buggered off a year prior to the incident I'm about to divulge. Tahlia's school marks were the best out of any of us, and people couldn't help but fall in love with who she was as a person.

She smiled as often as Willie Miller, always seeing the good in things, always looking for that rainbow.

She truly was a beautiful human being.

Tearing my eyes away from Tahlia's fiery mane, I looked towards Sharon, who was leaning to one side of her chair, making goo-goo eyes with the boy next to her. Sharon held a pencil and stuck the rubber end of it between her lips – not all the way, just enough to tease the hell out of the cow-eyed guy named – who knew? If she didn't know it before mimicking fellatio to him, then I certainly wasn't going to remember, even if he was in my class.

I sniggered and looked behind me at Helen, who was paying Willie close attention, but when she sensed me looking, her focus broke and she offered a tiny smile. Helen Baldwin matched her hairstyle to Stevie Nicks' latest coif, and she loved fashion, always wearing bright tops and flared pants. But to be clear: Helen was not vain. That gold trophy had to go to Sharon. Helen's school marks were enough to keep her strict parents happy, and she devoured books just like I collected vinyl records. Helen believed she was going to be the next Agatha Christie. But as we all know, seldom do childhood dreams turn into reality.

'Kylie Gardner?'

As everyone turned to look at me, I sat straighter and faced Willie, the plump, middle-aged guy who wore suede-patch jackets as often as he wore a smile: every single damn day. He squinted at me behind his glasses and took a step away from the blackboard. He leaned on his desk using his fists, the pose making him resemble a lowland gorilla. 'Well? Do you have an answer?'

The class fell silent.

Sucking in my lips, I glanced at the blackboard, hoping for clues. His doctor-like handwriting was illegible from any distance, but thankfully I could make out *Jay Gatsby, Daisy Buchanan, Nick Carraway* and *Green Light*.

A student behind me tittered as I kept Willie waiting, the second hand of the wall clock ramping up my anxiety with each tick.

'Sorry, Sir, what was the question again?'

The corners of Willie's mouth dimpled in an attempt to stop himself from grinning. 'What was the green light used for in *The Great Gatsby*?'

I side-glanced Tahlia and, God bless her soul, she was chomping at the bit to answer, her neck taut, her hand twitching to shoot up, and her eager expression making me hide a smirk. I may have been a mind wanderer in class, but that didn't mean I couldn't hear snippets of what was being said. I'm female, aren't I? I *can* multitask.

After clearing my throat, my eyes settled on Willie once more. 'The green light is a metaphor, Sir.'

Willie tilted his head. 'How? For what?'

The surrounding students craned their necks, wide-eyed, waiting for me to answer the question, which they obviously didn't know the answer to, judging by their expressions of relief.

'Because the green light is always out of reach for Jay Gatsby. It always seems just that little bit too far away, that little bit too bright. His world is centred around that green light shining on the other side.'

Willie stood straighter, pursing his lips like a bullfrog as he stared at me. 'And what does the light represent?'

'Jay's doomed love for Daisy. He always seems to want what he can't have. The green light was not meant for him, and neither was Daisy Buchanan.'

He grinned and adjusted his glasses. 'If I had a gold star to give you, I certainly would, Miss Gardner.'

Tahlia dipped her head towards me as if to say: *Well done.* I giggled and turned to look at the windows on my left, where prior students had fingertipped love hearts or initials in the film of dust. I always tried to sit near a window so I could gaze at the maple trees outside. In autumn and spring, they were just about the prettiest sight I ever saw.

But that morning, I saw something other than the swaying trees and the other dove-grey block of classrooms parallel to ours. Something that made my insides flutter exactly as the short love stories in *Cosmopolitan* described it. In the quadrangle, a tall boy with the most hypnotising swagger you could imagine had piqued my interest. All I could glimpse was the back of him, but his unkempt dark-brown hair, lean stature and the way he walked as if he didn't give a *fuck*, made my heart beat faster.

Willie's voice faded away again like the end of a song as I stared, mesmerised. I craned my neck as far as I could to see who he was and where he was going, but someone's fat head blocked my view. We were only in Year 9, but still, I was certain I would have remembered seeing him around school. And he wore the same uniform as us: white short-sleeved shirt with dark pants (navy-blue skirts for the girls). Simple. But back then, everything was.

I confess at the time I was head over heels in love with David Cassidy (from a TV show called *The Partridge Family* for you young'uns). A poster of him had pride of place on the wall behind my bed. I won't say I had sexual fantasies about David, no way in hell. But I did think about kissing him. I used to blush when I thought of him kissing me back and, to be frank, I smooched his poster often. I was also of the firm belief that the song from the show – 'I Think I Love You' – was written with yours truly in mind. That said, I didn't experience any weird sensations over David. But seeing that hip guy wearing our school uniform, I touched my face as though I'd never felt it before, feeling how strangely hot and tingly my flesh became just by seeing the back of him. How crazy is that?

The cause of my craziness turned out to be Trix. Or, as the teachers and authorities called him, Tristan Douglas Walker. His friends called him Trix for short, because he was about the coolest thing since the Rubik's Cube and he never took anything too seriously. Upon first glance, I couldn't have foreseen that he would become the green light to my Jay Gatsby.

Chapter Two

WHEN THE SCHOOL BELL trilled, we picked up our backpacks as excited chatter bounced off the walls like a squash ball in play, and we headed outside in single file. Tahlia walked ahead of me, and as we shuffled out the door she turned to me and grinned.

'Great save with that answer!'

Sharon draped an arm around my shoulder. 'Couldn't have said it better myself.'

I laughed hard. 'I totally saw you looking at that boy.'

Sharon's eyebrows rose in mock confusion. 'What boy? Be specific. I look at them all.'

When Helen joined us, we moseyed down the bustling corridors until we were out of everyone's way.

'So, who wants to go to the lake this arvo?' Sharon asked, flicking her lustrous blonde hair behind her shoulder. 'We need to discuss our summer plans, bitches.'

Helen removed her orange-and-yellow headband and used comb-fingers to rake through her light-brown hair. It was similar to mine, only her hair was shorter and thicker – like Stevie Nicks'.

'I wish I could,' Tahlia said, her brow wrinkling, 'but Mum's new boyfriend is coming over and she wants us to have a "family night".'

'Eww,' Sharon said, then eyed a handsome boy passing by. 'Who'd wanna do that? Families are overrated.'

'What's his name again?' Helen asked, replacing her headband.

'Clyde. I don't even really like him.'

Sharon draped her other arm around Tahlia's shoulders. 'Then fuck him. Come with us.'

Tahlia looked at the boot-scuffed linoleum floor as students rushed past us. 'I can't. Mum wants to play some board game that'll bring us "closer together".'

'Still no word from your dad, then?' I asked. I always felt sorry for Tahlia that she'd had little to no contact with her father since he'd left about twelve months ago. I came from a great family and wondered how I would feel if I didn't have Dad around. I also had a brother. Sure, sometimes Keith was a stinkarse who loved his Monaro more than anything else, but it was nice to have that stability. Tahlia was an only child and back then, divorced parents were about as rare as blue roses. It was something people didn't speak openly about, seen as taboo, and others would question it: 'Why would anybody get divorced and bring shame on the family?'

Tahlia's mother was a piece of work, but this made me admire Tahlia *that* much more. To come from a home where your mother chose her boyfriends over you ... I couldn't imagine it. But Lorraine Ashcroft was meek, used to being submissive. She always viewed family as hierarchical: man goes to work while the woman stays home and cleans and cooks, then spreads her legs for him when he so demands. That worked fine for Lorraine. It was all she'd known.

Tahlia shook her head as slowly as her shoulders slumped. 'No. My sperm donor has his own family now.'

'Your *what?*' Helen said, her nose wrinkled. Sharon chuckled, shaking her head at her naivety. I was also scratching my head, but no way did I let on.

'Sperm donor. That's what Mum calls him. I think I know what it means.'

We all stood silent for a moment, Sharon wincing and me looking at Helen for suggestions on what to say.

'Come to the lake for a while,' Helen said to Tahlia, adjusting her backpack. 'We can go straight after school, or we can get ice cream.'

The thought of seeing Ralph Ferguson made me smile. I could have seen him any day of the week, whether I was happy or sad; he was like that favourite uncle you only ever saw at Christmastime. He'd tell dirty jokes and cuss – the things my parents would cringe at.

Sharon's hazel eyes lit up. 'Yes! Let's get Coke spiders instead; I still have money left over from Mum's pokies win. My shout.'

Tahlia's head shot up. The smile the rest of us had all grown to love resurfaced. 'Okay. Sure.'

'Totally rad,' Sharon said, grinning. 'So, what time will we ...?'

As the girls discussed plans, I felt a sensation so palpable I could have sworn fingertips were caressing me. I looked to my right towards the building's exit just as that mysterious boy I'd seen in the quadrangle walked through and towards me. I knew it was him: his dark hair with its wild, abandoned look, and his overall cool manner ... God, I'd never seen a guy walk with so much confidence and self-assuredness. Girls around him stared, stopping mid-sentence and hiding blushing faces behind textbooks; guys observed his devil-may-care swagger, wondering if they could mimic it. But he seemed blithely unaware of his magnetic pull.

His confident gait had me spellbound and for a moment, I thought my rubbery knees would give way. When his chocolate-brown eyes met mine, a jolt of electricity shot through me, my hot flesh breaking out in goose pimples. My mouth flung open and my cheeks burned. To him, I must have seemed like the dorkiest kid in school with my mouth agape, but I could not turn away from him for the life of me – my eyes were like suction caps on a glass door. During our prolonged staring match, he gave me the most breathtaking, lopsided grin before breezing straight by us – his tantalising cologne following like his shadow under the midday sun.

Moments later, Sharon shook my shoulder. I turned to her and saw the other two girls also staring at me.

'Earth to Kylie, heelllloooo!' Sharon said, waving both arms in criss-crosses before my eyes.

Shaking my head, I said, 'W-what did you say?'

They turned and looked at the demigod, who was now halfway down the corridor.

'You were staring at him!' Tahlia said, giggling.

'No, I wasn't!'

Sharon turned back to me, grinning. 'You want to suck his dick, don't you?'

Helen wheeze-gasped. 'Sha-*ron*!'

If I hadn't felt like fainting before, then I sure as hell did right now. I barely understood what blowjobs and vibrators were; I was still smooching David Cassidy's poster at bedtime.

Most of my 'birds and the bees' talks and masturbation advice I'd learned from Sharon – not that she was using sex toys at that time, but she *was* more advanced about these things – things I would die of shame talking to my mother about.

Helen shook her head. 'Nope, don't go there, Kylie.' She pointed after him. 'Don't you know who that is?'

God, I was thankful to have another excuse to stare at him. 'No; who?'

'Tristan Walker, but everyone calls him Trix. He's in my sister's year and, from what I hear, he's naughty.'

'Great!' Sharon said, laughing. 'Give him to me!'

Helen shoved her shoulder. 'Not like *that*. They sent him away for misbehaviour. It doesn't look like that time away did his behaviour any good. Look at him! He needs a haircut.'

How I disagreed. His untamed hair suited his bohemian manner well, and most of the boys wore their hair as short as my late grandfather's front lawn – talk about boring. Trix stood out above the rest. A hip-gyrating Elvis among wholesome choirboys. But I still didn't understand how he could have slipped my attention before. If he was in Melinda Baldwin's year – Year 12 – that meant he was also in my brother's year.

'How come I've never seen him before?' I asked, eyes still on him as he rounded a corner and disappeared out of sight. Two brunette girls standing at a bubbler tiptoed around the corner to watch him stroll on, one of them biting her lower lip. No boy at our school had ever appeared more aloof, more laid-back. He gave me the sense of being far superior to our adolescent selves, a leader among disciples.

'He comes and goes as he pleases,' Helen said. 'Ever since they released him from a correctional school, he's morphed. Like a tadpole into a frog – at least, that's what Melinda says. He used to be in the chess club and the maths club, but something must have happened recently. You should see his picture in the school yearbook from just last year – you wouldn't believe it was Tristan. It's only him and his dad living at home, from what Melinda told me. And she also said he's had s-e-x with girls from this school.' She then fixed me with a serious expression. 'Kylie, he's no good. Stay away from Trix.'

But, of course, when we hear those words, it makes us want the forbidden fruit *so* much more. What is it about girls who think they can change the natural behaviour of a guy? It's like trying to transform a lion into a kitten. They say 'Nice guys finish last' and you know what? I'm sorry, fellas, but it is true. Girls want the bad boy. Girls want to fight for a boy and his affections, because it means they've earned it. Who wants it all to come easily on a silver platter? No drama means no story. Girls want the drama. Girls want boys like Trix. Do we see ourselves as superglue, as fixers of the broken? Is it the natural motherly instinct in us, to protect and pamper? I still can't figure that out myself. All I knew to be true then was that I'd never felt such potent emotions by just looking at someone.

To this day, I'm not sure if I believe in love at first sight, but I can tell you there is such a thing as lust at first sight. And when I laid eyes on Trix, he was all I could see in the world around me, and Helen's words of caution were obscured like a blinking neon light on a foggy night.

Chapter Three

Sharon, Helen, Tahlia and I strolled inside Lickety-Split after parking our bicycles in the dirt car park. My focus went straight to the front counter, where Ralph Ferguson was scratching his bald head, conversing with a middle-aged woman in a white jumpsuit and wide-brimmed beige hat, holding her son's hand.

At fourteen, I didn't have a proper job yet. No way, eww, I'd rather have kissed a boy; work sounded like the worst thing in the world. Instead, I would do menial jobs around town, including cleaning shifts at Lickety-Split. Ralph was about the coolest cat I'd ever met, and he paid me in cash when I worked there. It wasn't much and it wasn't many hours, but it was easy labour and gave me spending money for the school canteen, or to buy new tie-dye shirts or albums. That was my thing: music. God, those twelve-inch vinyl records and the music of that era ... To save up enough money to buy a new LP was the best feeling in the world; better than getting straight A's – not that that ever happened.

When Ralph saw us, he flashed us his trademark smile: warm, honest, infectious. He raised a hand and waved, prompting the lady to turn to look at us. We all waved back and took a seat in one of the booths.

Lickety-Split wasn't as fancy as those ice-cream parlours over in the US, but it was our safe haven. There was also the Cherry Inn, where they served the meanest hot dogs on hamburger buns, but it didn't have the same laid-back vibe. The booths inside Lickety-Split weren't made of plush leather, but it was comfortable enough. Ralph loved music and it would always be blaring from the jukebox. Some customers complained about this, saying the music was so loud they couldn't hear their own thoughts. Well, who'd want to do that, anyway? Why would you come to an ice-cream shack just to hear what your brain had to say?

Ralph preferred soul music and the blues. Sometimes we'd be sitting in a booth, listening to Ralph jamming away to Otis Redding while he scooped ice cream or squirted whipped cream. He was hands down the happiest person in Orange.

'In the Summertime' by Mungo Jerry boomed from the jukebox, but even that wasn't enough to drown out the cacophony of chatter and laughter from the abundance of schoolkids; we were lucky to have found a place to sit. When Ralph finished the lady's order, he instructed Laverne DuBois to take over at the counter while he came over to greet us.

He wiped his slick hands over his apron and grinned, bending down to hear us. 'How are my favourite girls in all of Orange?'

Sharon played with her blonde hair, smoothing it over yet again. 'School was pretty shit.'

He raised a finger in the air. 'Ah, they are the best times of your lives, girls; if only I could go back. You should be happy! Being a kid is easy. Wait till you become adults, then you'll be wishing you were still in school.'

Sharon's eyelids flickered and she smiled. 'Can we just have our usual?'

He laughed and shook his head. 'For you lot, anything.' He turned to me. 'Kylie, when will I see you back here? You want any shifts Fridee or Sat'dy night?'

'I can probably do some hours this Friday night, if Keith can drive me.'

Ralph winked as a blob of sweat slid down his chrome dome, cutting a path to his chin. 'I'd consider it an honour. Anyway, four Coke spiders coming right up!'

Ralph took off behind the counter and Sharon retrieved her purse to count the change to pay for our order. A bunch of girls in the booth behind us squealed – naturally! My eardrums bore the brunt of their ear-piercing noises.

'Any of you girls going away for the summer break?' Helen asked.

Tahlia shook her head. 'No. I think Mum and Clyde are going away, though.'

Sharon looked up from counting her coins, her lips forming a perfect O. 'You're shitting me? You mean, your place is going to be free during the break?'

Tahlia shrugged. 'I don't know for sure; they'll probably be broken up by then. I'm surprised it's lasted this long.'

Sharon took Tahlia's hands in hers. 'Babe, we need to organise a party!'

'But I don't even know if—'

'Think of all the cute boys we can invite.' Sharon squealed louder than the girls behind me.

'Do you ever think of anything else?' Helen asked, rolling her blue eyes but grinning.

Sharon poked out her tongue. 'Maybe this summer we can actually get you to French kiss a boy.'

Helen's head reeled back. 'Eww, gross! Who wants a boy's tongue in their mouth?' Her body spasmed and her tongue protruded. 'Yeee-uck!'

Sharon's left eyebrow rose. 'You think that's bad? How are you going to handle a penis in there?'

Helen mimicked being physically ill and we all laughed. Sharon then flicked a clump of hair behind her shoulder and, as she glanced towards the back of the parlour, her face lit up. Helen and I craned our necks around to see what had captivated Sharon.

'No fucking way! This is just too grouse!' Sharon leaned towards us and we huddled forward. Thanks to all the schoolkids roaming around, I hadn't seen diddly-squat.

'What?' Helen said, eyeing Sharon's infectious grin. 'Who is it?'

Sharon focused her attention on me, wide-eyed with excitement. 'Trix is back there with his mates.'

At the mention of *his* name, my heart raced like a sprinter near the finish line. I was so confused why I felt like this ... a *hotness* sweeping through me. My brain was telling me I was being silly, but my body was speaking a different language: one I needed an interpreter for.

'D'ya want me to invite him over here?' Sharon grinned again, wiggling her eyebrows.

Helen, who was next to me, shook her head. 'No! Kylie can do better than Trix!'

Sharon gasped and leaned back with a straight spine, shushing us. 'Bonzer! Here he comes.'

Blood drained from my burning cheeks, leaving them cold at the thought of him heading our way. But he had to in order to reach the counter, and already I could hear the peals of laughter from those boys Sharon said he mingled with. Somehow, their baritone laughter floated above the surrounding girls' chatter, like trombones in an orchestra of violins.

'Kylie, fix your hair; he's walking this way,' Sharon whispered out of motionless lips.

My toes and fingers clenched simultaneously. I sat back, eyes focused on the Formica table as my chest expanded and deflated like bellows.

'Hey, you!' Sharon said, one hand cupped to her mouth as she beckoned him over with the other.

Beneath my lashes, I glared at the traitor opposite, scrunching my lips. On my periphery to the right I saw him approach, and heard more boisterous cackling from the group he'd come with. As he loomed over our table, I thought I was going to pass out. I nose-breathed in and out trying to calm myself, while Helen's steel-like talons gripped my right knee bouncing under my navy-blue skirt.

'You're Trix, right?' Sharon said.

'Who wants to know?'

I wasn't looking at him, but could hear amusement in his voice. He no doubt thought we were nothing but a bunch of uncool little schoolgirls who had no right to be speaking to someone like him.

Sharon laughed. 'You go to Orange West High, right? Same as us.'

'Oh, yeah? How do you know my name?'

She scoffed good-naturedly. 'Everyone at school knows your name.'

'Is that right?' Again, amusement laced his voice.

'Yeah ...' she purred.

Oh God, she's flirting with him! Was she doing this for me, or for *herself*?

'And who are you?' he asked.

'I'm Sharon. This is Tahlia, that there is Helen and in the corner, looking away, is Kylie.'

Save for 'April Sun in Cuba' by Dragon now playing on the jukebox, utter silence followed – or so it seemed. Then I heard the front door opening and closing, and the girls in the booth behind us squealed louder. *Gosh, hurry up, Ralph!*

'Hey, girls,' Trix said, and that's when Sharon kicked my shin under the table. I glanced up, scowling, and her stern expression translated to: *Look at him! Don't be rude.*

There was a moment of awkward silence until one of his friends called out: 'Yo, Trix, come on! Stop playing wiv yourself, man.'

I closed my eyes and focused on steadying my erratic breathing. Helen clutched my knee harder.

'Your friend there ...' he said. And I *knew* he was referring to me, so I opened my eyes but focused on the chrome napkin dispenser while my heart thwacked against my tight sternum. 'Is she okay?'

Sharon kicked me again but harder, so that's when I turned to him and *oh, God*, a strange, prickly sensation rippled through my belly. He was so achingly beautiful I wanted to break down and cry. I believed his dark, untamed hair and piercing brown eyes would have made even a heterosexual male go wobbly at the knees. His crisp white collar was turned up (not down like the other boys), and his shirt open at the second button revealed tanned skin beneath. His complexion was flawless and his chiselled cheeks made me wonder if there was Cherokee Indian somewhere in his lineage.

'You all right?' he asked.

Everyone faced me, so I nodded, but underneath the table my hands were clasped into one giant sweaty fist in my lap.

He stared at me a while longer before eyeing Sharon. 'What are you doing after this?'

Sharon leaned forward on the table, an elbow scattering her coins as she propped her chin on a fist. 'Nothing. Why?'

A sandy-blond–haired boy approached and draped an arm over Trix's shoulder, his hand showing the telltale signs of fresh canings. He looked around the table, settling on Sharon. 'You girls wanna come to the lake wiv the boys?'

Sharon's face lit up like she'd just won the lottery, plus a yacht, a Corvette, and an island in the Caribbean. 'Groovy!'

Trix turned towards him with a set mouth.

'Nah, it's cool, man; they'll love it!' Blondie grinned. 'Forget about what hap—'

'Wait,' Tahlia said, holding up a hand and eyeing Sharon. 'I can't; remember?'

Sharon scoffed. 'Babe, forget about your mum – the way she forgets about you.'

Tahlia's mouth flung open. 'Hey!'

Sharon laughed that laugh that made you forget what you were mad at her about. She could wrap pretty much anyone around her finger. She then focused on Helen. 'What are you doing this arvo?'

Helen twisted her lips. 'I *was* going to go clothes shopping with Melinda—'

'Sweet; you're in too.' Sharon eyed me and cocked a brow. 'You in?'

For the life of me, I couldn't think up an excuse. But let's cut the shit; did I really want to?

'I'm not doing anything,' I heard myself mumble.

This time Sharon used both her hands to flick her hair behind either shoulder. 'Then it's sorted.' She faced the blond-haired boy. 'Oh!' She smacked her forehead. 'We just ordered spiders, though.'

'No wukkas.' Blondie grinned again. 'Meet us down by the lake when you're ready.'

Trix focused on me and oh, sweet baby Jesus, those chocolate-brown eyes made my insides jittery, all right. 'See you soon.' He gave me another lopsided grin before he took off.

Helen leaned forward, her face redder than a drunk's. 'Sha-*ron*! Are you crazy?'

Sharon went back to her coins, having to recount them. 'It's just a bit of fun; don't have a spaz.' One by one, she slid the coins across the table with a metallic scrape towards an open palm.

Helen squinted. 'Those boys are older than us.'

Sharon looked up, a fingertip on a silver twenty-cent coin. 'Exactly.' She grinned, then looked at me. 'He's a deadset spunk! I think he digs you; didja see the way he looked at you?'

'Shut up!' My cheeks burned and sweat gathered at my throbbing temples. 'Anyway, the blond one was looking at *you*.'

Ralph Ferguson bounced over with a tray in one hand carrying our drinks, picking up the first glass and swinging it in an arc before placing it in front of Sharon. 'Here we go. Four Sunset Specials.'

We each said thank you as he placed our Coke spiders before us, then he popped the black tray under an armpit, revealing a sweat patch on his shirt. The door burst open as more kids in school uniforms piled in, one with a skateboard under his skinny arm.

'I wish I could stay for a chinwag, girls' – he waved an arm about the place – 'but we are busier than a streetwalker on truckie payday!' None of us knew what the hell he was on about.

'No sweat; we have to leave soon, anyway,' Sharon said, handing her coins to Ralph.

'You're not gonna be messin' with those boys now, are you?' He fish-hooked an eyebrow as he collected her coins.

She played with her hair, lips holding back a grin. 'Maybe.'

He closed his eyes and shook his head. 'Don't be playing with no fire, girls.' He then looked at each of us. 'Working in customer service, I hear all the gossip. Already dipping their quills into all the inkwells they can find. I can practically see those boys folding bed linen now.'

Helen squinted, twirling her spoon around in the glass of ice cream and Coke, making it resemble a brown tornado. 'Bed linen?'

He tapped the side of his noggin while clutching the coins. 'They've all got a few roos loose in the top paddock, is what I'm getting at.' He then glanced around the room as more students piled inside the shop. 'My dears, I'm off – like smelly sneakers. Enjoy your spiders.'

Sharon broke the seal cap on her glass bottle of Coke and poured the dark liquid over her scoop of vanilla ice cream, watching it fizzle and bubble before it settled down. 'We'd better hurry with these; I don't want the boys to think we've ditched them.'

'I can't stay for long,' Tahlia said, grabbing her straw and sipping.

Sharon shrugged, licking her wet lips. 'No sweat; I need to go home before dinner too.'

I remained silent while slurping on my creamy Coke and man, the ice-cold drink dampened my flushed body, but my mind raced with wild ideas about Trix and his group of friends, despite having heard how Trix was a raving delinquent.

Little did I know he would come in handy when we needed him the most.

Chapter Four

WE RODE OUR BIKES over to Lake Canobolas before the spiders had had time to settle in our stomachs. Sometimes Sharon embarrassed the hell out of me, but other times she knew what I wanted and acted accordingly. I *could* pretend to be mad at her, but secretly I thanked her for her brazenness. Sharon treated life how she treated boys: she grabbed it by the balls. She believed in making her own destiny, to be an active participant and not just a bystander letting things happen to her.

That afternoon, I stowed my ham radio in my basket as 'Dream Weaver' by Gary Wright played on 2JJ FM radio. All four of us loved music – not just me. The Grundig portable transistor was mine, but we shared it and looked after it, and would take turns carrying it in our bicycle baskets wherever we went. Some lazy afternoons, all we did was ride our bikes around town and listen to music.

On Saturdays, we would gather at Lake Canobolas – a man-made reservoir featuring a boardwalk, paths lined with blue gums, and frayed ropes tied to overhanging branches so kids could swing across and jump into the water. Late at night, the main car park was a popular spot for teens and turned into lovers' lane. Sometimes we would ride past as Ford Falcons and Holden panel vans rocked like they had hydraulics. Usually, the windows were so foggy we couldn't see a thing, but we could hear girls breathlessly professing their love of God. Late one night after riding back from Helen's, I'd spotted Keith's Monaro bouncing and I stopped in my tracks, shuddering. I never knew my brother's girlfriend was so religious.

Sharon rode in the lead, as always, and Tahlia was bringing up the rear. I almost stacked my bicycle twice because my legs seemed to be made of Play-Doh, and my sweaty hands kept slipping off the handlebars. We had to pass creeks, paddocks and vineyards to reach the lake, but the quicker we rode, the longer it seemed to take.

A row of bicycles already lay sprawled in the dust by the time we arrived, our calves screaming, our hair wind-blasted. Sharon had jumped off her seat before the wheels had stopped turning. At the time, I didn't understand why Sharon had such a zest for boys. The only thing that came to mind was that she'd had a brother who'd died in Vietnam. Lonnie had been much older than Sharon, but she still kept a black-and-white photo on her nightstand of the two of them together – a photo of Lonnie dressed in his greens, smiling proudly while holding his younger sister in the air on the day he'd departed for 'Nam. But apart from Lonnie, she lived with both her parents and from what I gathered, it was a happy home life. But do we ever really know what goes on behind closed doors? As I've discovered over the years, the answer is often no, and sometimes I think it's those who smile the widest who need the most checking up on. We fail to ask the happy ones if they're okay because we assume they are, well, happy. It's a common misperception.

'*C'mon!*' Sharon said as Tahlia parked her bicycle next to ours. Tahlia shot her a sharp look, but soon joined the rest of us to travel along the narrow path that led to the lake. The dark-blue water reminded me of the denim straight-legged Levi's Helen loved to wear.

That afternoon, the lake was chockers; people everywhere. We were used to seeing other schoolkids around, and sometimes the smell of dope wafted in the air, overriding the menthol scent of the blue gums.

'Where are they?' Sharon said, her neck outstretched, scanning the sea of heads.

Kids were already frolicking in the water, splashing around and creating white frothy scars on the surface. Teen girls had placed blankets around the bank; bare, glossy backs lathered with baby oil absorbing the blazing sun's heat. Some older, tanned guys with terry-towelling bucket hats and short shorts were gathered around a portable radio, drinking VB and smoking either grass or tobacco.

This time I stood at the back of the group, where I felt safest. We were walking past a group of teen boys flipping through *Vampirella* comics when I felt something brush up behind me. When I turned around, my breath caught in my throat as I stared directly into Trix's eyes. He wore that lopsided grin, and I felt like being this close to him was a health hazard.

'Enjoy your spider?'

My lips were superglued shut, but Sharon spun around and smiled. 'There you are!'

His eyes darted to hers. 'We're over here.' He pointed to the left. His group of friends were positioned away from the water, among a collection of grey gums near a smaller car park. Four boys were laughing, punching each other's shoulders, mock tackling.

A black car was parked facing them with its doors open, and 'Don't Fall in Love' by the Ferrets blasted from the speakers.

'Sweet!' Sharon said. 'C'mon, let's go.'

Trix looked at me, then headed off through the trees, fingers of sunlight filtering through as we stepped over rocks and fallen branches, and dead leaves crunching under our feet along the way.

Tahlia squeezed my arm. 'I can't stay for long.'

'Same.' But boy, I wanted to be out all night. We lived in a quiet neighbourhood, so we often had to come up with our own devices to get our kicks. We'd never done *this* before; this was as about as exciting as Orange got.

When we reached the group, Trix's friends stopped mucking around and stared at us in silent regard. The sandy-blond–haired boy who'd invited us along stepped in front of the others and eyed Sharon. His lips curled into a grin. 'What'd ya catch, Trix? How old are they?'

Trix turned back to us. 'I don't know. How old *are* you girls?'

'Thirteen,' Helen and Tahlia said in unison.

Trix eyed me. 'You?'

Sharon stepped forward, beaming. 'Me and Kylie are fourteen, but I'm the eldest.'

Blondie walked in a circle around Sharon, looking her up and down. 'Is that so? A little too young to be hanging wiv us dudes.'

She tilted her chin in defiance. 'Well, how old are *you*? We all go to the same school.'

He stopped in front of her. 'We're all seventeen, but age ain't nothin' but a number.' He outstretched his hand. 'I'm Bobby Dean.'

She grinned and shook his hand. 'Sharon O'Rourke.'

Trix blocked my view of them by standing before me. My eyeline levelled with his Adam's apple. A faint trickle of sweat slid down his slender neck, resting in the hollow of his collarbone. 'Kylie, right?' He extended his hand and I shook it. 'Tristan Walker. But call me Trix.' His touch felt warm and, for a so-called delinquent, his grip was surprisingly gentle.

'You girls wanna hang wiv us for a while?' Bobby said, looking at each of us. 'Listen to some tunes, drink a little, smoke some weed?'

'Sure.' I tried to smile nonchalantly, but damned if I could remember how. 'Wait!' I shook my head as if suddenly remembering one important caveat. 'We don't drink or smoke.'

'Good,' Trix said softly. 'I like that in a girl.' He turned away from me to look at Helen and Tahlia as Sharon flirted with Bobby, cackling at everything he said. 'Come over; I want you to meet my friends.'

Tahlia held Helen's hand as they ambled over, their faces so pale they could have passed for vampires low on blood.

Trix pointed to a black-haired boy – the shortest of their group, but only by a few inches.

'That there is Ed Rickard.'

Ed folded his arms over his chest and gave one nod, eyeing Helen. 'G'day, girls. I'm Ed ... and I'm sweet and I'm single.'

We all chuckled. There was something irresistibly charming about that little guy; nothing cheesy or creepy about him. I liked Ed from the minute I saw him.

Trix directed our attention to a guy with a gold earring next to Ed. 'That's Mike Perkins.'

With a forefinger, Mike lowered his black sunglasses to the tip of his nose. Like Trix, he also had an aura of mystique with his dark, shoulder-length curly hair. He reminded me of Jim Morrison – lead singer of the Doors. *Ex*-lead singer; it'd been years since Jim's untimely passing.

'And the bald-headed dude is Rodney Saliba.'

Despite also wearing our school uniform, Rodney could have passed for being in his late twenties, or even early thirties – hence why out of all of them, he was the only boy I recalled seeing a few times at school. The angry scar on his left cheek looked like the result of a knife wound; I wasn't sure whether he was going for the Neo-Nazi look with his shaved head, but it didn't do his image any favours. He seemed like the type of guy who had a chip on one of his broad shoulders, and his default emotional state would be angry. Seemed like he was pissed off about everything – life most of all. He didn't smile or offer us a wave; he didn't acknowledge we were there any more than Sharon did at that point. All I could hear was Bobby making jokes and her giggling at them.

After the brief introductions, Bobby told us all to gather around before he clapped once. 'Who wants a beer?'

Sharon's hand shot up so fast I swear I heard a whip crack. 'Me!'

Still holding hands, Tahlia and Helen shook their heads. The other boys nodded or said yes, and that's when Trix faced me.

'Do you want to come to the car with me?' He pointed towards the black car with its open doors. 'Day After Day' by Badfinger now played from the speakers.

'That's *your* car?'

He flashed me that heart-stops-pumping lopsided grin and grabbed my hand, lacing his fingers through mine as he headed towards the car. I turned to look at Helen and she shook her head the way my mother did when she disapproved of something. Tahlia's lower jaw unhinged as she stared at our entwined fingers, and Sharon flashed me a huge grin and gave me the thumbs-up. I didn't know what was happening any more than anyone else. This gorgeous boy was holding *my* sweaty hand and leading me towards *his* car. Delectable chills ran through my wired body and made me feel giddy to the point I had to suppress a squeal, the way one forces down a burp in the company of others. I glanced down at our joined hands and noticed a simple silver band wrapped around the perfect thumb of his left hand.

For the life of me, I didn't have a clue what to say as we walked, so I picked the first thing I spotted. 'Um, what type of car is this?'

He flashed a devastating grin over his shoulder. 'Pontiac Phoenix.'

'It's a nice car. Nice and … shiny.' God. I'm palm-hitting my forehead now thinking about it, but I was fourteen then – what was I supposed to do; talk about the carburettor or the transmission? He chuckled, which I translated to 'How cute', but I was more focused on staying upright, because holding his hand and walking normally was not easy. In fact, my wobbling kneecaps could have been mistaken for Aeroplane Jelly.

Trix opened the boot of his car, revealing a lidless esky full of ice and cans of beer. I didn't want to know how a seventeen-year-old could acquire beer, and he probably wouldn't have told me if I'd asked.

He leaned over, digging out cans of VB as ice fell out and onto the black carpet of his boot. 'Wanna help me carry them over?'

'Sure.' I reached out while he handed me three ice-cold cans and he grabbed the rest. 'Um, what if the cops come around? Aren't you worried?'

He stood close enough that I had to tilt my head back to peer into his eyes. 'The cops around here are more corrupt than a bunch of underaged kids drinking beer.' He reached up with one hand, grabbed the boot lid and shut it. When it slammed down, I jolted, and looked at the sunlight bouncing off its slick surface, to tear my focus away from him. I still didn't understand the emotions coursing through me. I'd never felt like this before; it seemed I had lost the ability to control my body. If my brain was the control panel, why wasn't it listening when I tried to tell it something? Don't laugh, don't cry, don't blush, don't shake like a vibrator in the presence of attractive boys …

'Don't worry,' he said, 'you won't get into trouble.'

Some mechanical part of my brain opened my mouth before I could think. 'Is that why you went away? Because you keep getting in trouble?'

Something flickered in his eyes. It was momentary, like a shooting star, but I caught it, regardless. I honestly didn't know how he was going to react. Would my directness anger him? Would he tell me to piss off? With his reputation I thought he could be kind of dangerous; someone who could turn from civilised into a raging beast at the slightest provocation. But he leaned forward, close enough that for a quick, hopeful split second, I thought this was going to be my first kiss.

'Don't believe everything you hear.' He trailed off, leaving me to follow, not knowing if he was mad, sad or indifferent. Looking back, I realise the kids were the only ones who kept it real; my friends were the only ones who told me the truth. Adults routinely lie to kids; it's their job. And as a mother myself, I understand why. But when I was fourteen, I had no idea how many adults' lies I'd have to sort through like a deck of playing cards. If there were a TRUTH pile and a LIE pile, most of what my friends told me that year ended up in the former.

Chapter Five

WHEN TRIX AND I re-joined the group, we handed out the cans of beer. Sharon took hers, peeled back the tab so it clicked and created froth, and raised it to her puckered lips. The fact she didn't wince, even as a thin trail of brown liquid spilled down her jawline and neck, told me this wasn't her debut with alcohol. Looking at Helen and Tahlia sent waves of guilt slamming against the wall of my stomach, and I felt sorry for them as it was as obvious as heck they felt uncomfortable. I don't think they even spoke to each other.

In retrospect, I should have stepped up and been a better friend, but the selfish, curious part of me wanted to stay. This was the first time we'd ever done anything remotely similar. For Sharon, this was probably a normal Monday night out, but for the rest of us, hanging with older boys while drinking beer and listening to rock ... hell no! I'd either be listening to vinyls in my bedroom or watching *The Paul Hogan Show* with Mum, Dad and Keith (if he wasn't driving around in his Monaro). So I pretended not to notice their worried expressions and faced Trix once the beers were distributed. He looked at me while he cracked open his VB and threw it back, stretching his neck taut and I watched, fascinated as his Adam's apple bobbed up and down his tanned throat.

When he lowered his can, he used a knuckle to swipe along his lower lip. He looked at the can and back to me. 'Want a sip?'

I shook my head.

Sharon yelled out: 'Go on, Kylie! Don't be a pussy.'

Frowning, I turned to her, but then she laughed, and Bobby Dean stared at her as though he'd never seen a chick before in all his seventeen years.

'Try some,' she said, grinning. 'It won't hurt you. You might even like it.'

Buckling under pressure, I grabbed the chilly can and studied it. Through the small opening, tiny bubbles rose to the surface of the dark liquid and I raised it to my nose to take a whiff. *Phew*! It smelled like mephitic piss, so I lowered the can, wrinkling my nose.

Sharon raised her can and swallowed from it, so I wanted to match what she could do. Blocking my nostrils, I raised it to my lips and sipped. The taste ... bugger me dead, it was rank. I didn't throw up, but I struggled to comprehend how people could drink that. How was that tasty? How did people get pleasure or satisfaction from drinking it? For the life of me ... who invented beer? Sucking on the exhaust pipe of a pickup truck would have had more appeal.

Most of the guys laughed at my disgusted expression, but Mike Perkins stood to the side, beer in hand, peering at us from behind his black sunglasses.

Trix wasn't laughing, either, and he took the can off me as 'Werewolves of London' came on his car radio. He reached into his pants pocket and pulled out a doobie. Between clamped lips, he lit it, inhaled, and blew out a plume of smoke from the corner of his mouth – his intense eyes never leaving mine. I thought he was going to offer me a drag, but he surprised me instead.

'You should go see your friends; they looked scared.' He turned around and approached Rodney, offering him the doobie. Rodney took it between thumb and index finger, raised it to his lips and sucked while squinting. He held the smoke in for a second, then blew it out in a column. Personally, I thought weed smelled like cow dung. That, too, was something of a mystery to me: how people could smoke that stuff.

Turning away from the boys, I trudged over to Helen and Tahlia. They no longer held hands, but they still looked as comfortable as two rabbits amid a pack of salivating wolves.

'Are you girls okay?'

Helen shot me another disapproving-mother stare. 'What do *you* think? If we get busted by the police, we're in trouble.'

Trying to make light of it, I shrugged. 'We aren't doing anything, though. *We* haven't smoked weed.'

'Don't be silly, Kylie,' Helen said before giving the boys the stink eye.

'Yes, I think I'll have to leave now,' Tahlia said. The boys behind me continued goofing around, cackling. 'Anyway, we all have homework to do by tomorrow.'

Clarity washed over me when I looked into Tahlia's brown eyes. What was I doing? They were my best friends and I knew they weren't having a good time. It wasn't in my nature to be cruel, but Trix had me spellbound. 'You're totally right; we said we'd only be here for a little bit. C'mon, let's tell Sharon we're going home.'

Helen snorted. 'Yeah, right – look at her! I'll bet you five bucks her and Bobby end up kissing before we leave.'

Tahlia shook her head, orange hair flying out behind her shoulders. 'No way, I don't want to lose that much money.'

The three of us laughed and Helen wrapped an arm around Tahlia's shoulders, then mine, before we headed over to the others.

By now, Sharon's hand was toying with Bobby's school tie, laughing a little too hard at something he'd said. Trix leaned against one of the horizontal wooden logs that acted as a barrier between the grass and the car park. He eyed me as we came closer, raising the doobie to his lips and inhaling.

Helen cleared her throat loudly above the music. 'We're heading back now.'

Sharon turned to us, gasping. 'No, stay!'

Helen shook her head. 'You can if you want, but we're going.'

Sharon eyed me for backup. Even though she was the eldest, it was only by a couple of months, then after me was Helen, then Tahlia. But because Sharon and I were both fourteen, she somehow believed we had the casting vote. If we said 'yes', then Helen and Tahlia would have to put up with it. But it didn't work like that; I'd tried to tell her this a hundred times before.

Tucking a loose hair behind my ear, I said, 'It's your choice, but we have to jet.'

Sharon rolled her eyes in a melodramatic way that would have impressed a soap opera director, but she faced Bobby and handed him her beer can. 'I better scat.'

Bobby dipped his head, bending his knees to look into her eyes. 'Can I have a kiss before you do?'

A look of delighted surprise transformed her face. 'Hell yeah!' She wrapped her arms around his neck, pulling him down as their tongues battled it out for dominance.

Trix used the heel of his right foot to push himself off the log barrier and approached me, standing inches away. 'It was nice to meet you.' He extended a hand, the afternoon sun hitting his silver thumb ring. 'Take care.'

Was he going to ask me for a kiss? And if he did, what would I do? Gazing into his spellbinding eyes, I took his hand. 'Ditto.'

'See you around.' He released my hand too soon for my liking before saying his goodbyes to Helen and Tahlia.

'Nice to meet you all,' Ed yelled, a hand cupped to his mouth. 'And don't forget, girls ... I'm single!'

Helen actually giggled at this, and Tahlia shook Trix's hand with a pleasant smile. I looked towards Sharon, Bobby's hands cupping her bum as they pashed.

As I turned back to Helen and Tahlia, someone called out: 'Yo, Trix.'

I swung around again to see Rodney Saliba with his back to us, facing the car park.

Trix let go of Tahlia's hand and walked over to stand beside Rodney. Helen, Tahlia and I swapped frowns, wondering what was going on. Because of the music from Trix's Pontiac, we couldn't hear a thing they were whispering, but when Mike and Ed also hurried over to Rodney, I got the sense that whatever this was, it wasn't good.

Mike turned to Bobby and called him over. Sharon pouted when Bobby freed himself from her arms, and we watched as the five boys stood shoulder to shoulder, their backs to us, with Trix standing tallest out of the lot.

Helen grabbed my arm and led Tahlia and me over to behind where the boys stood. My heartbeat stalled when Rodney reached into his pants pocket and pulled out a switchblade. Tahlia cupped her open mouth, and Helen tried to make us both stop and turn the other way, but I *had* to see, and so did Sharon. She and I gave each other blank stares as we crept forward to see what had riled the boys, while Helen and Tahlia retreated a little way. Without turning his head, Trix grabbed Rodney's left bicep as if to tell him not to react, to just be cool.

Sharon and I couldn't see anything while standing behind them, so we tiptoed to the side but stayed behind their defensive line. As we got a clearer view, a red Holden VB Commodore with five boys inside grabbed our attention. Their scowling faces made my heart hammer like a tribal drum, my whole body going taut. They wore the school uniform of Orange East High, the only other high school in town. What they were doing here on 'our' side I had no idea, but whatever the heck was happening before our eyes looked like more than lingering hostility between feuding neighbours.

'Do we settle this now?' Ed said. The song on the radio faded out, and Doug Mulray's voice came on air.

They all faced Trix. He squinted but shook his head.

When he turned to the right to look at Rodney, his eyes then bounced to mine. I felt like I'd been busted, intruding on something I shouldn't have been privy to.

'Put it away,' Trix said to Rodney.

Rodney's shoulders relaxed and he shoved the switchblade back into his pants pocket, but Trix turned back to the Commodore. The car idled at the exit of the car park. No traffic travelled in either direction on the road, so they weren't waiting for a safe moment to leave. They were waiting for something. Or someone.

I tore my focus away as Trix walked over to Sharon and me. 'You better go home.'

'What just happened?' I said, my heart rate slowing at last.

'Don't sweat it.' He shook Sharon's hand as a goodbye and re-joined the boys, who were huddled like footy players discussing pre-game strategy.

Sharon grabbed my upper arm, grinning but exhaling with relief. 'Oh my God, that was intense.' She led me away, back to where Helen and Tahlia waited, but not before I glimpsed Trix looking back at me over his shoulder.

Chapter Six

Sycamore Avenue was a typically uneventful street where everyone knew everyone. It was not uncommon for me to ride home from school and see neighbours leaning over one another's fences having a yarn, or a stay-at-home wife wearing oven mitts dropping off a crock-pot casserole at a friend's place. Even though I was glad to see the back of Orange when I left years later, I missed the familiarities of living in a tree-lined street where everyone was respectful and looked out for one another.

When I arrived home that evening, I parked my bicycle on our front porch, praying with everything I had that Mum and Dad wouldn't smell the weed permeating my uniform. I wasn't too concerned about the nip of beer, but weed has an unmistakable, pungent aroma.

My older brother, Keith, was usually in our front yard working on his Warwick Yellow Holden HK Monaro GTS 327. When Mum would call him in for supper, his face would typically be covered in grease so thick it could have filled potholes.

Keith delivered weekend newspapers for a quick buck and, at seventeen, he didn't have to worry about a mortgage or bills, so he'd blow all his money on the Monaro. I can still remember my mother, mug of coffee in hand, peering out of the lace curtains in the lounge room, shaking her head as Keith smeared polish over every nook and cranny of his pride and joy parked on the front lawn.

'I swear Keith spends more time with that car than he does with his girlfriend.' Then Mum would shake her head in the disapproving manner she always did and resume watching her beloved *Laverne & Shirley*.

However, that particular evening, Keith wasn't outside with his head under the bonnet of his car, as the sunlight faded and the smell of Mum's dinner wafted throughout the fibro house – we always ate dinner early.

As I shut the front door, Mum called out to me from the kitchen. *Shit*! I wouldn't even be able to change clothes.

I bypassed our lounge room on my right and entered the kitchen as Mum pulled out a baking dish from the whirring avocado-green oven. Elizabeth Gardner was just about the best cook in the neighbourhood. A tray of garlic bread sprinkled with parsley flakes already lay on the table.

'Where have you been?' Her tone was light; she wasn't as strict as Helen's parents, but she did like to stickybeak, because that's all she had to do. She'd been a stay-at-home mother for as long as I could remember and was popular in our street. Sometimes I'd come home from school and she'd be cross-legged on the couch, flipping through a Margaret Fulton cookbook while speaking on the phone to someone else in the street, gossiping about what one of the other neighbours had done. She liked to know everything that was going on, and sometimes used to spy out of the curtains, which she called 'keeping a watchful eye on the neighbours'.

My family wasn't rich, but we weren't slugging it, either. My dad, Jeffrey, was in between jobs. It wasn't that he didn't *like* working, but by the late '70s, as the population in Orange grew, gaining employment became harder. He'd never attended university or college, but he was smart. He seldom watched the 'boob tube' unless it was the news; he preferred to have his head in a book, or play with his model train. Yes, I'm not kidding. In his 'playpen' he'd built a train track and surrounds that filled almost the whole damn room. The track rose, then it dipped down, then it went through all seasons of the year in different climates: snow, ice, wind, sunshine. I'm selling it short; it was actually pretty rad.

My father seldom asked questions and generally kept to himself. Out of the two, Mum was stricter, but there was never any hitting or cussing towards my brother or me. She'd usually ground us or take away privileges. For me, she'd ban me from listening to my vinyls, which was about the cruellest thing I could conceive. For Keith, she'd take away the keys to his precious car and hide them until the ban was lifted. I was as open to my parents as any other teenager trying to discover themself and work out where they belonged in the world: not yet an adult, but still needing care and supervision. I was selective about what I told Mum, but, of course, if she didn't hear it from me, she'd hear it from some other nosey parker in the street, including Sharon's mother, Cheryl.

As I stood before Mum, Keith emerged from his bedroom and brushed past me, rubber thongs flapping, while he adjusted his white puka-shell necklace. 'Hiya, dork.'

'Hey, bumface,' I said as he opened the fridge door. He took out a carton of milk, opened the flaps outward to form a beak, and raised it to his lips.

'Keith!' Mum said, the hot dish still in her mitted hands. 'Don't even think about it.'

He shrugged, arm still raised. 'What? What'd I do?'

Mum gave him one of her disapproving glances, so he lowered the carton, exhaled, and opened the cupboards to find a glass. Mum turned back to me, one eyebrow raised. 'Where were you, love?'

'Just with the girls.'

'The Sunsets!' Keith mocked and laughed as he poured the milk. 'Ooooh, The Sunsets – cool name.'

'At least I have friends; you only have that stupid car.'

'That's not true,' Mum said, placing the dish on a wooden block on the table. Pasta bake. 'He has Amy.' She removed her yellow oven mitts and ran a hand through her shoulder-length feathered brown hair.

'Yeah, right! His car *is* his girlfriend – Amy is just a cover-up.'

Keith grinned and flipped me the bird.

'Keith!' Mum said, closing the oven door and turning the knob. She then directed her attention at me. 'Kylie, go get your father – dinner's ready.'

How I thanked the good Lord she didn't question me further. I headed left up the carpeted hallway to Dad's den on the right at the end. Using a fist, I pounded on the door to be heard over his train going *chugga-chugga-chugga* as it raced round and round.

'Come in!' Dad yelled above the various noises. I twisted the handle and entered the stuffy den. He smiled softly, putting his remote control down on a bench. He didn't have a grand old smile like Willie Miller or Ralph Ferguson, but it was good enough for me. Any scraps of affection my father afforded me were worth more than my entire vinyl record collection. 'Hi, love.'

'Hey, Dad, dinner's ready.'

He hopped off his stool. 'Righto. Thanks.' Despite being home all day, he still wore work attire as though anticipating an emergency call from a desperate employer: white short-sleeved shirt, brown corduroy pants and shiny black shoes. At the power board, he flipped a few switches, and the lights, sounds, the falling snow and the sunshine faded to oblivion. His black-over-red Distler G-scale model train had studded lights along its body, bright headlights, and even smoke rising from its smokestack. Dad had built the whole scenery from scratch; it'd taken him years and cost I didn't even want to know how much dough. I used to love sitting on Dad's knee, watching the train go round and round, through tunnels, crossing over railroad trestles, ploughing through icy mountainsides before finishing at Sycamore Station (Sycamore – the name of the street which we lived on). He'd added miniature benches, and there were little people in uniforms or normal attire, and trees and dogs. I don't think I ever fully appreciated how meticulous he'd made everything, right down to different shades of grass for hot and cold climates. And then, of course, I became a teenager, and the thought of playing with trains was as uncool as listening to anything from the '50s. But Dad never tired of it. He could sit there for hours, just watching the train take more of a journey than his life ever did.

Dad adjusted his glasses and then patted down his comb-over. 'I'll just wash my hands.'

When I returned to the kitchen, Keith was already at the table, using a long-handled black nylon spoon to scoop steaming penne pasta. The top layer where the melted cheese ended had a brownish band around the circumference of the baking dish. Keith slopped a dollop of creamy sauce onto the white lace tablecloth, and Mum once again berated him.

'Oh, fair dinkum, Keith. Look at the mess you made – a toddler is cleaner than you.'

He banged the spoon onto his plate and the tubed pasta tumbled off. Grinning, he passed the spoon to Mum, a string of cheese as thin as a spider's web dangling from it, and she scooped some herself, giving him the eye. All the while, my mind was fixated on the events of that afternoon. So many questions about the elusive Tristan Walker and his friends. What had happened between them and the carload of boys from Orange East High? Our school versed them in sports, and we had a huge annual event where the boys' footy club met at the only sports ground in Orange – Wade Park. The footy final was a big event; it drew in hundreds of citizens. The Sunsets attended every year to cheer on our school, and most times our boys won the trophy, but other than sports, I couldn't see a connection between Orange East and Orange West High.

I knew Rodney Saliba was trouble the moment I laid eyes on him. Sometimes just by looking at kids your own age, you can tell right off the bat their future is going to be nothing but violence and drugs, going in and out of the revolving door of the prison system, until one day the judge has had enough of seeing their face and gives them life without parole. But at seventeen, I didn't understand why he'd need to carry a switchblade, and did that mean Tristan did too? I couldn't see why he'd be any different, and I remembered the way Rodney had called out to Trix as though he was their leader. Every group had to have a leader, and if ours was Sharon, then Trix was theirs.

Now, at the dinner table, I could picture the red Commodore idling, waiting; I could smell the hot oil belching from the rumbling exhaust pipe. Perhaps if we girls hadn't been there, something violent might have happened. I'd heard of bad blood between East and West beforehand, but nothing to warrant an all-out fight. It was always about footy, just as New South Wales and Queensland folk are rivals in the State of Origin series. But we'd won the inter-school trophy almost a year ago – in fact, the next annual final was only weeks away. So why come now; why wait this long for retribution? And I was *sure* none of those five boys were even on the footy team. No. This was something bigger than sport. This was personal. And the boys had been expecting it.

Speaking of expecting it, I cupped both hands over my mouth to hide a giggle when I thought of how brazen Sharon was. Not knowing Bobby for more than thirty minutes before she stuck her tongue down his throat. Of course, people like her usually go far in life; they know what they want and they go for it, regardless of what those around them think about it. Sharon was adaptable to any situation – you could have thrust her into a Guatemalan tribe and she'd end up being Chief before too long – running the show as her devotees carved her face into totem poles in her honour.

The sound of Dad washing his hands under the running faucet in the bathroom broke my musings, and I looked over as Mum stared at me with a raised eyebrow, holding out the nylon spoon, waiting for me to take it.

'What are you thinking about, boofhead?' Keith asked, grinning like an idiot.

'Shut up.' I snatched the spoon off Mum.

Dad ambled into the kitchen and sat down, the wooden chair legs scraping across the bumpy linoleum as he moved closer to the edge. 'Looks good, Liz.'

'Thanks.' She picked up her fork and impaled three pasta tubes on the tines. 'So ... how was everyone's day?' Mum glanced between my brother and me.

Keith tore off a chunk of crispy garlic bread with his teeth, golden flakes drifting onto his plate as some stuck to the corners of his mouth. 'Shit.'

'Keith!'

Dad grabbed a piece of steaming garlic bread off the tray. 'Why's that, mate?'

In between chewing, Keith said, 'Monaro needs a new battery; the thing's rooted.'

Dad placed the garlic bread on his plate before taking the spoon off me. 'Do you need any money?'

Keith opened his mouth, but Mum put up a hand.

'He's old enough to pay for things on his own.'

Keith sat back in his chair hard, swallowing. '*Yeeeaaaah*, but—'

'No "buts", young man; if you want something in this life you work hard for it, and pay using your own money. Lord knows your father and I didn't get any handouts when we were younger – did we, Jeff?'

Dad shook his head. 'No, dear.'

'See? Everything we have now is from hard yakka.'

'*Yeeeeeah*, but this thing chews up more than I'm puttin' into it, Ma.'

She licked the corner of her mouth before chewing again. 'Doesn't matter. The agreement was it's your responsibility; you pay for it, remember?' She pointed her fork at him. 'If you and Amy were to have a baby, should your father and me have to pay for the child's welfare?'

Keith smirked, then shovelled pasta into his wide gob. 'Nup – Amy's folks are loaded!' He grinned as he chewed.

Mum gave him a disapproving look and turned to me. 'Kylie, let this be a lesson for you: in life, you have to own up to your responsibilities.'

In retrospect, I had no idea about the prophetic nature of her words. Although at the time I thought Mum was being totally uncool, it makes perfect sense now. In life, we have to own what is ours; what belongs to us. The good, the bad, and the burdens we bring upon ourselves.

Even at fifty-nine years old, that's the one thing in life I've struggled to do: own my mistakes. But back then, I didn't know how heavy burdens could be.

Chapter Seven

The next day at school, I found Sharon and Helen sitting together on one of the aluminium benches near a dove-grey classroom block. We typically met there before school, then again at recess and lunchtime. It was ideal because it was at the rear of the quadrangle, so we could see students enter from the car park or the front gates, and the concrete set of steps leading to the classrooms on our right kept us out of sight of the headmistress's office at the front.

Sharon waved at me, her ice-pink lipstick sparkling.

'Who's the lipstick for; Bobby?' I asked, giggling.

She flicked a lock of blonde hair behind her shoulder. I swear she played with her hair more than teen boys played with themselves. 'Shut your gob; I look perf.'

I sat down next to Helen, who was munching a Jupiter bar, and surveyed the other students. 'Where's Tahlia?'

'Don't know, Eskimo,' Sharon said. 'Haven't seen her.'

'Hmm. She's usually the first one here.'

'Not today.' Sharon craned her neck to look about the other students – no surprise who she was looking for – as I also searched for someone. Trix had been on my mind throughout the night; so much so, I'd forgotten to kiss David Cassidy's poster goodnight.

'There he is!' Sharon shouted and squealed.

I looked to where she pointed and saw the group of five boys walk through the gate together from the opposite side – Tristan had parked his Pontiac in the student car park; that's why I hadn't seen him.

'Oh my God,' Sharon said, clutching her navy-blue skirt. 'D'ya think I should go over and say hello to Bobby?'

Helen shook her head. 'Don't be silly! He's probably forgotten all about you.'

Sharon scoffed. 'As if! I'm a great pasher.'

Trix strolled in the lead with that mesmeric gait, white shirt collar up. His dark hair looked clean but like he'd raked two hands through either side of it. Rodney and little Ed were on his left, and Mike and Bobby were on his right. Even with those five boys wearing high school uniforms, their persona and energy still projected bad-boy vibes. Students stopped what they were doing to ogle them passing by; I didn't think they could have an enemy at this school the way people seemed to idolise them. To me, Trix had the charisma of Reverend Jim Jones – well, except without the whole mass murder-suicide and religion part. And those black sunnies ... You know what? Forget Jim Jones.

Sharon rose from the bench, but Helen yanked her arm and she sat down with a *clunk*! It got me thinking hard. Was Rodney carrying his switchblade today? Would my brother or his girlfriend catch us mingling with these older guys?

'Maybe he hasn't seen me,' Sharon said, eyeing Bobby with a downturned mouth.

For the life of me, I didn't understand how I'd never noticed these boys before – except for Rodney. I guess we see what we want to see. Also, I recalled Helen telling me her sister had said Trix had been sent away for a while. They say prison can turn a boy into a man, and although he wouldn't have been old enough to be sent to an actual prison, there were reform schools for boys under the age of eighteen. I decided if I ever got the chance, I would ask him about that.

Sharon cupped the side of her mouth. 'Yo, Bobby!'

Helen squealed, a scowl crinkling her forehead. 'Sha-*ron*! Oh *great*, here they come.'

Thank God I was sitting down, because my whole body shook and my clammy hands left sweat stains on the covers of the books I clutched in front of my heaving chest.

'Bobby looks even hotter today!' Sharon said, and Helen cupped her flushed face in both hands, leaning forward while groaning.

When the five boys reached us, Sharon jumped up. Without a word, Bobby grabbed her hand and led her behind a set of concrete steps, his lips already on hers before she could wrap her arms around his neck.

'Morning, Kylie,' Trix said, his eyes boring into mine. No smile. No insight into his thoughts – he was harder to read than a French menu.

'Hi, guys.' I tried to look at each of them, to appear indifferent.

Trix's eyes trailed to Helen. 'Are you all right?' He looked at me. 'What's her name again?'

Helen lowered her hands from her flushed face. 'It's Helen!'

Trix's lips twisted and he rubbed his jaw as the wind ruffled his white shirt. 'That's right. Helen.'

From that height, he appeared devilish; the morning sunlight making his chocolate-brown eyes appear a different shade altogether.

'Only three of you today?' Mike Perkins said. Thanks to the sunlight streaming from behind me, I could see the outline of his eyes and dark brows behind his black sunnies.

'I'm not sure where Tahlia is,' I said, observing more students piling in through the gates, sucking on Red Skins or sipping on chocolate-flavoured Mooves. Due to Tristan's presence, my best friend had been pushed from my mind. I wasn't too worried, because Tahlia was a straight-A pupil. She'd arrive soon. Instead, I focused on the surrounding students: boys playing handball; pigtailed girls flipping through glossy pages of *RAM* (*Rock Australia Magazine*); some students were taping flyers to poles around the quadrangle; others were gorging on steaming, tomato-sauce-sodden meat pies – the breakfast of champions.

'What're they for?'

I turned back as Ed pointed at the flyers, but Trix was still staring at me.

'The football final,' Helen said, then pointed to a brunette girl. 'That's my sister over there – Melinda.'

Trix watched Melinda Baldwin patting down a flyer she'd taped to a brick wall. 'That's your sister?' He faced Helen again. 'She's cool; I like her. Melinda's in some of my classes.'

Helen's face relaxed at his compliment; she even smiled. Inhaling, I turned away from Helen and looked past her head, over towards Bobby and Sharon.

'Bobby!' Ed said, grinning. 'Get your tongue outta there, man.'

Bobby kept pashing Sharon, but raised his left arm and stuck his middle finger up.

The boys laughed, except Trix, and Rodney kept looking around as if to see where people were and what they were up to. *Only those paranoid about what's around them act like that*, I thought. Surveying their surroundings, making sure no-one sneaks up on them.

'Oh, fuck *me*,' Mike said, his gold earring glimmering in the sunlight.

We all turned to where Mike was looking and saw our headmistress approach, high heels scraping against the concrete as she marched over. Headmistress Pamela McCarthy always wore a two-piece suit, no matter what season. The only variation was the shade, and today's was plum purple.

Trix turned back to Bobby and Sharon, and said, 'Zeppelin.'

Bobby broke free so fast it was like an invisible man had yanked on the back of his shirt collar. Later, Trix explained to me that 'Zeppelin' was a code word to let someone in their group know something bad was about to happen, or to stop what they were doing without having to explain why. Bobby wiped his glistening mouth with the back of his hand, straightened his tie and whispered something to Sharon. She smoothed over her skirt and hair. They walked out from behind the concrete steps and joined us just in time as the headmistress stopped before us, eyeing Trix. Her auburn hair looked like a blazing red star in the sunlight.

'What do we have here?' Headmistress McCarthy said, hands clasped before her, her smoker's lips pursed.

'Nuffin',' Ed said, shrugging, looking around as if this authority figure wasn't there.

Her grey eyes zeroed in on Rodney. 'And what might you be doing, cavorting with these younger students?'

Rodney gave a watery snort of derision.

Headmistress McCarthy's eyes narrowed, her head tilted. 'Something funny, young man?'

Trix placed the palm of his left hand over Rodney's chest. 'We were talking to Helen about the footy final coming up.'

'What would you need to talk to her about it for?'

'Her sister, Melinda, was putting up flyers but she ran out. We thought we'd help spread the good word, and Melinda wanted to know if Helen had more flyers.'

Headmistress McCarthy stared, and I could almost see her brain cells compartmentalising the information. She then eyed Helen on the bench. 'Really? Is that true, Miss Baldwin?'

All eyes were on Helen. She nodded with gusto. 'Yes, Miss McCarthy; Melinda and I made copies this morning, but unfortunately I have no more in my schoolbag.'

'She'd just finished telling us that before you interrupted us,' Mike said, biting back a grin.

Headmistress McCarthy faced him. 'Take off those sunglasses. And fix your tie.'

Mike's grin burst free. 'It's sunny out, but.'

Her shoulders tensed underneath her blazer. 'I do not care, young man; this is *my* school and you will follow *my* orders. You are lucky I don't have you take out that piece of shrapnel in your ear.'

Mike placed a fingertip on his earlobe and wiggled it back and forth. 'What, this?'

She closed her eyes and breathed in. 'I will be so pleased when you lot finally graduate in several weeks' time. My days will become much easier.' She opened her eyes to focus on Trix. 'Now that you have your answer, move along. School starts in' – she consulted her wristwatch – 'exactly thirty seconds.' She then clapped twice. *Clap-clap*! 'Pronto!'

Trix and I locked eyes. There was nothing left to be said and by the time the bell rang *exactly* thirty seconds later, we were scattered like autumn leaves by a leaf blower. And I'd forgotten all about the absence of Tahlia Ashcroft.

Chapter Eight

First period was Science with Mr Evans. He was a weird one, always looking at the girls longer than necessary and, from what I understood, he wasn't married nor did he have kids. Like every school, students spread rumours about teachers as much as they did about their fellow classmates. The rumour surrounding Mr Evans was that he got his rocks off to kiddie porn. Don't ask me how or why this rumour began, but he *was* weird – there was no denying it. Whenever he invited someone up front to help him perform an experiment, ninety per cent of the time he'd choose a girl. Sometimes he kept girls back in class after the bell rang because he needed to 'chat' with them. There was no way for any of us to know if the rumours about him were true, but they spread like wildfire through dry leaves. I felt bad for him in a way because he would have had no clue what the students whispered behind his back, but rumours usually held a ring of truth; trees don't grow if there aren't seedlings in place.

The rumour about Headmistress McCarthy was that she was a closet lesbian – not that I thought there was anything wrong with that; that's just what people said – and that she and the PE teacher, Miss Abrams, did 'things' to each other during recess and lunch in the groundskeeper's shed.

Another rumour was about Mr Willie Miller, our English teacher; that his wife had left him for a History teacher over at Orange East High. Apparently, the teacher was ten years her junior and hung like a horse.

But the thing about rumours is they can lead to irrevocable repercussions, and people ought to fact-check before they open their mouths. And sometimes, rumours from this school leaked into Orange East and vice versa, but I'll get back to that later. It would play a pivotal part in what came about.

That morning, Mr Evans spoke about the development of fungi and bacteria. Once again he asked for a volunteer, and although half the boys raised their hands, he chose Julie Stone. We all watched, fascinated as Julie kissed a Petri dish of gelled agar. He explained that in a few days, we would see colonies of fungi, moulds and bacteria spread across the agar, and then he rambled on about haloes and something called a 'kill zone'. It was kind of gross, so my thoughts again deviated to Trix. What class was he at now? Was he thinking of me? There was no way anything could come from this schoolgirl infatuation. I could not picture me introducing him to my parents, so whatever I felt for the boy had to stop posthaste. But the more you tell yourself not to do something, the more that thing becomes your forbidden fruit.

I also thought about the way Rodney Saliba had scanned the quadrangle earlier on, like a lion in the savannah eyeing who was around and what they were doing. Something toxic was brewing, but I had no idea what connection these five boys could possibly have with Orange East High. As I said, these boys didn't even play footy, so they wouldn't be versing them in the annual clash, but it was a known fact our school had claimed the trophy more times than Orange East had; it sat in our school right now – guarded by a thick glass cabinet. Only time would tell if we got to keep the gleaming trophy for another year.

When class finished, I had collected my belongings and headed out the door, when I sensed someone walking close behind me. I looked to my right and saw Trix stroll up next to me, but he faced straight ahead as we fell into step down the corridor, shoulder to shoulder.

'Oh … hi,' I said as casually as I could muster, heart rate speeding up, flesh tingling. Was this a coincidence?

'How was your class?' Still not looking at me.

I gripped my textbooks tighter as we cut through a throng of students checking their timetables. 'Boring. What'd you have?'

'Geography. It was stimulating.'

I laughed at his sarcasm. We rounded a corner, passing a dog-eared poster about the etiquette of washing your hands after going to the dunny, then descended a flight of stairs. 'What do you have now?'

'Don't know.'

Grinning, I eyed him. 'What do you mean?'

'I don't know what subject I have.'

I grabbed the peeling dark-green paint of the steel handrail until we reached the bottom of the stairs, and then let go as we kept walking past rows of empty classrooms. 'Then where are you going?'

'Walking you to your next lesson, which is ...?' He turned to me.

I stopped next to a bubbler and faced him, eyeing him as my heart thwacked against my buzzing chest. 'Maths.'

He grinned. 'Groovy. My forte. Which room?'

'Why are you walking me to my class?'

He waited until a group of giggling girls riddled with acne passed by us before he spoke. 'To make sure you get there safely.'

Chuckling, I adjusted the strap of my backpack. 'No, for real – what's your next lesson?'

He leaned in closer. Held the eye contact. 'For real, I do not know.'

My cheeks turned from blushing to all-out blazing; I wished I knew how to control it. The English language suddenly seemed lost to me, so I cleared my parched throat to stall for time. Where was Sharon when I needed her to take the lead? Students and teachers rushed by us, but for me it felt like time had slowed down and everything, including sounds, sights and smells, had evaporated into a black hole.

'You girls going to Lickety-Split after school?'

'Maybe.' We had no plans, but I was pretty sure Sharon would be keen for the idea. I didn't know about the other two. Speaking of which, I realised I still hadn't seen Tahlia yet.

'I'll see you there.' He took off, leaving me to stare at his captivating gait as other girls' eyes dreamily followed his back. He really, truly didn't give a fuck.

And I hoped that maybe, just *maybe*, he was falling for me the way I was falling for him.

English was the last class of the day. Willie Miller continued with *The Great Gatsby*, discussing how author F. Scott Fitzgerald used foreshadowing as a technique in his prose. Willie spoke from the heart, and passion hijacked his voice when reciting poetry or Shakespeare. Of course, the school board had its own ideas about what to teach us kids, but like a rebellious teen, Willie hated following rules and taking orders as much as we did. I've forgotten most of the advice Willie imparted during our school years, but some titbits wormed their way permanently into my memory: 'You'll never be as young as you are now' is one example.

We laughed when he said that, naively thinking we'd be young forever. As I soon learned, nothing ever stays the same, and the way life robs us of our youth is almost criminal. When I was younger, I couldn't wait to get older. Yet, when I reached adulthood, all I could think of was my youth.

Everything during that afternoon's class seemed the same, except for one major difference: Tahlia Ashcroft looked gnarly. When we'd seen her at recess, the poor girl had told us she had a headache, and although we'd urged her to skip the rest of the day, she'd declined.

But now, her face was paper-pale and her eyes had lost their vibrant shine. At recess she'd said she woke up feeling like she'd been hit by a Mac truck, but bless her soul, she'd pushed through and now we had less than thirty minutes to go before school ended.

As predicted, Sharon was thrilled by the idea of going to Lickety-Split. I didn't tell them Trix had asked me, nor that he'd waited for me outside of my classroom. Anyway, suggesting we go to the ice-cream parlour wasn't out of character for me; we often used to hang out there, even on weeknights. What did surprise me, though, was when Tahlia also agreed to go. I thought she'd hurry home to sleep off her headache, but she'd said a cold ice cream was just what her throbbing head needed.

Ralph's booming jukebox came to mind, but I'd pushed that visual aside as I was glad to have her join us. Helen had also agreed to come, on account that her sister, Melinda, was going out with her girlfriends that night to watch *The Amityville Horror*, so Helen had nothing else to do – the book she'd just bought wasn't up to her standards, she said. Helen was the one who'd suggested we go to the lake and hang out afterwards.

As Willie picked up his tattered paperback of *The Great Gatsby*, I glanced through the finger-smudged windows on my left. It was weird to think how yesterday morning Trix wasn't part of my life, nor had I seen him at this school before. Now we were making plans revolving around him and those boys, and I'd sworn never to be the type to put boys before my girlfriends, but it was also true I'd never felt anything for any boy in real life and now that I did, I was putting my morals and principles on the backburner. When something or someone comes along that makes you feel alive, you grab the opportunity with both hands and don't let go, right? That's not to say it'll turn out all peaches and cream, but take it from this fuddy-duddy: there won't be too many people who come into your life who'll make you feel like your insides are carbonated.

I knew Tristan Walker would be most girls' parents' idea of their worst nightmare. But for me, Trix was like smoking a cigarette for the first time: you know it's bad for your health, but you *have* to see what the fuss is all about. Bugger the warning signs – isn't that the standard teenage mantra? Needless to say, I couldn't wait to hang out with him again at the lake, away from prying eyes.

Besides, Lake Canobolas was about the only outdoor location available to hang out near Orange. Now, the thought of that damned lake makes my stomach lurch. But before it all turned to shit, I probably spent more time there than at school or at home.

It was also the place where we would dump a body.

Chapter Nine

Sharon rushed ahead of us to open the door at Lickety-Split, jamming a few P.K chewies into her gob. I was right behind her, so I held the door wide as Helen and Tahlia bounded through.

'My Sharona' blasted from the jukebox, and the place appeared as full as yesterday. All the tables were occupied; students in uniforms stood in groups, stuffing their faces with ice-cream cones, or monopolising the arcade video games lined against the back wall: Space Invaders, Lunar Lander, Space Wars, Pong.

Eileen Bradbury and Ralph Ferguson threw us a warm smile and a wave from behind the counter. I returned the wave as Sharon hurried to the back of the parlour, heading for Bobby's booth. No cool kids ever sat up the front, and that included in classrooms and on school buses. When Ralph saw who Sharon was headed towards, he shot me a look of confusion. I shrugged as if to say: *You know Sharon* ... and followed my friends over to the group of five boys.

Laverne DuBois pinballed throughout the tables, collecting empty milkshake cups, juggling glass sundae boats, but when she saw me, she smiled. Her brown bob seemed superglued to her sweaty temples, and dark patches stained the armpits of her canary-yellow swing dress.

'Hey, darlin'!' She scrambled off, past the rowdy students and occupied tables to head to the side door next to the cash register, leading to the kitchen.

When I locked eyes with Trix, my stomach heaved. Overtaken by the others, I was happy to be at the back of The Sunsets so I'd be able to turn and run to the bathroom, or out the front door.

Trix rose from the booth as we made our way over. There was no way nine of us could slide in one booth – eight at most, if we *really* sucked it in. But we wouldn't be here for long; this was just the starting point before the lake. Sharon pecked Trix on the cheek before she slid in next to Bobby Dean. Trix said hello to Helen, but he frowned when he looked at Tahlia.

'What's the matter with you?'

'Headache.'

His dark brows rose. 'You sure you want to be here, then? The music's loud – even *I'm* saying that.'

I stared at the back of her orange hair, watching her head bob up and down. 'I'll be fine.'

He stepped aside so she could slide in next to Rodney on the other side of Sharon.

When I stepped forward, Trix raised a hand. 'It's too full now.' He grabbed my wrist and led me towards a two-seater in the corner – the only vacant table left – but something told me he'd been monitoring it. After taking a seat, I looked at the booth as Helen rose and peered at me over the back ledge.

I smiled and waved to affirm I'd be okay. When she nodded and sat down, I turned to face Trix. He sat back in his chair, fingertips at the side edges of the table. Relaxed. Cool. Calm. We stared at one another as we heard girls screeching with laughter; the front door opening and closing as kids ran in and out; and teen boys just about jizzing in their undies over winning the arcade games – slapping buttons, shoving the joystick up and down, then left and right. *Pew-pew-pew*!

For a moment, I thought Trix wasn't going to say anything as he just stared at me, until finally he wet his lower lip by running the tip of his tongue along it. 'How was school?'

'School's school.' I smiled and shrugged. 'How was your day?'

He looked around the place before his eyes found mine. Why did Trix always want me to lead the conversation? With all his confidence, I'd assumed he'd want to take charge, but apparently I was wrong. Speaking to boys did not come naturally to me like it did with Sharon. She believed God had created them for her alone, but I was a novice. I'd never kissed a boy before or gone on a date. I didn't have a clue what boys liked either; the only boy I interacted with was Keith, so from that I only knew two things: boys loved cars, and boys loved their mama's cooking. Didn't Helen say Trix lived with his father? Did his mother split town or something? I couldn't remember, as the Knack jamming it from the jukebox made it impossible to string two coherent thoughts together. However, as I eyed the empty space between us, I found an opening.

'What are you going to get? Or did you guys order already?'

'I was waiting for you.'

Act cool; don't blow it! 'We usually just get Coke spiders.'

'Then I'll order five.' He rose and walked away. While he stood at the back of the queue, I let out a rush of hot air, slinking into my chair as I glanced at the booth. Only the tops of four heads were visible above the back ledge, but I could tell Bobby and Sharon were facing each other – his sandy-blond hair melded with her blonde hair. God, were they pashing *again*? I felt bad about leaving Helen and Tahlia by themselves, because they weren't good conversationalists either, especially with people they didn't know well.

By the time Trix returned, 'Pop Muzik' by M was playing on the jukebox.

Trix faced me without a word, but we both turned to eye the row of arcade games when a redheaded boy with a constellation of freckles let out an almighty '*Yeeessssss!*', pumped his fist in the air and gave a high-five to his oily-faced friends jumping for joy around him.

Once again, I struggled to find words. 'So ... um, where do you live?'

'Not far from here.'

I bobbed my head. 'Cool. Who do you live with?'

'My father.'

'Rad. Totally rad.' I swear he never blinked; he just stared with that penetrable gaze, probing the darkest labyrinths of my mind. 'What do you wanna be when you grow up?'

He leaned forward the way someone does when they want to tell you a secret, so I leaned forward too. 'Why don't you ask me what you really want to know?'

Sucking my lips inwards, I sat back as my mind recalibrated. *What the heck is he on about?*

'You want to know if the rumours about me are true.'

My shoulders involuntarily shot up to my ears and I shook my head. My mouth flew open, but I didn't know what to say. He could see right through me, and I'd never experienced that invasiveness before; something that made me feel as naked and defenceless as a newborn. It wasn't as though I was *dying* to ask him about the rumours, and I hadn't even been thinking much about it. But since he mentioned it, yeah, sure, I *did* want to know.

'The jacks sent me away to a reform school after they busted me with drugs. It's not the first time I've been in trouble with those corrupt pigs, but my age is my scapegoat – they know it, and I know it. They sent me to Bathurst School for Boys. It took longer than expected to get released because I wouldn't back down on the inside.' He leaned forward further, close enough for me to smell the residual cologne on his shirt collar. 'So yes, you should stay away from me. But I am glad we could clear things up face-to-face.'

Flames burned from my belly up to my cheeks. Where had this come from? 'I-I wasn't asking.'

'But you wanted to know, yes?'

I licked my lips, shrugging as my throat clicked. 'It wasn't on my mind.'

'So, there's nothing else you want to ask me?'

That seemed like a double-edged sword. As much as I was intrigued by what I saw, I had the feeling that if I asked him anything, he would tell the truth. Trix had a way of making me believe he was an open book. Not just because he was so laid-back and cool, but also I think he wanted people to know. He'd never come out and spill his guts, but if anyone asked, he'd tell them straight. So there, as he sat before me, did I *really* want to know what mischief he had got up to? The only thing I'd heard about him was that he was 'naughty' – I remembered Helen saying that. A sudden visual of my brother's face popped into my whirling thoughts. *Keith*! Keith was in Trix's year at school; if anyone knew more about Trix then it'd be him – assuming they had classes together. There was also Melinda Baldwin, but I wasn't game enough to ask her – we'd barely spoken in all the years Helen and I had been besties.

'No?' He inclined his head. 'You don't want to address any other rumours? Are you sure?'

Jeez, how many other rumours were out there? Something about the way he said it implied he was referring to one rumour in particular. Wait, was there a connection between this and the Orange East High boys?

Ralph approached with five spiders on a black tray, and I was so thrilled for the interruption I could have jumped up and kissed his sweaty, bald head. As he stood before us, he eyed me. 'How ya doing, Kylie?'

'Not bad. What about you?'

'You know me – running around like a blue-arsed fly! Hey, are you gonna give me a helping hand on Fridee?' He placed our glasses of ice cream on the table, followed by the glass Coke bottles.

I winced and sucked back air on a hiss. 'Oh, err, I forgot to ask Keith if he could drive me here. It's only because my parents don't like me riding my bike home after nine o'clock—'

'I'll drive you.'

Both Ralph and I turned to look at Trix. He stared at me with a blank expression until Ralph patted my shoulder, drawing my attention. 'My dear, how about you check with Keith first?'

'Sure thing.' I offered Ralph my most convincing smile.

Ralph focused on Trix and lifted his now-lighter tray higher in the air, the spoons inside the glasses tinkling. 'Son, where are the rest of these spiders going?'

Trix jerked his chin towards the booth. 'The other girls.'

Ralph bobbed his head. 'Right on! Take care, now. See ya round like a rissole.' He took off.

Grabbing my Coke bottle, I looked at Trix. 'Thank you for—'

'Don't want Mummy and Daddy to see me?' He cocked a brow, his eyes pinning mine.

The Coke bottle slipped from my fingers and banged onto the table, causing three boys to tear their gazes away from the arcade games and snigger, as brown liquid fizzled and overflowed down the sides of the bottle. Gee, talk about a chip on the shoulder. What was his problem, anyway?

'Trix,' I whispered, shaking my head and lifting my shoulders, 'I-I don't even know you.'

He stared at me for what seemed like until tomorrow. 'You will.'

Chapter Ten

Turned out we did part ways after our spiders. Trix had told me he and the boys had something to take care of, but didn't elaborate. Near Trix's Pontiac in the dirt car park, Bobby and Sharon had made out like he was a soldier leaving for overseas duty. Trix had offered me a measly handshake as a way of goodbye. I was left more confused by the end of our weird interaction and pedalled home with more questions than answers.

After a Vegemite sandwich and a quick chat with Mum in the kitchen, I went to my room and switched on the telly. It was only a black thirteen-inch Zenith portable, but it had a built-in carry handle, and I'd positioned it on a chair near my white chest of drawers. My room was like any other teen's back in the '70s: posters of heartthrobs dominated my tacky wallpaper. You know about the David Cassidy one that took pride of place overlooking my bed, but I had others: John Travolta as Danny Zuko; Kurt Russell; Donny Osmond; and Michael Gray from *Shazam!*

I've also told you about my love for music. My jam was Skyhooks, the Rolling Stones, Supertramp, Kiss. Then there was Suzi Quatro. Man, I wished I could have been like that black-leather-wearing, cool-arse chick. She was smashing it here in the Australian charts, with number one hit after hit; she'd even been to Melbourne – in '74, I believe. My favourite song of hers was 'Devil Gate Drive', and how I wished I had gravelly vocal chops like hers, and to be able to strum a guitar like the devil possessed my fingers. I wasn't into glamour models like Sharon was; I was into rock 'n' roll chicks and glam rockers – Marc Bolan, David Bowie, Joan Jett. Some days when I felt blue, I used to spin an album, and all my worries melted away like frost when the sun rises. Not that I'd had too many sad days; they were more soap-opera-dramatic, as everything is when you're a teen.

My bedsheets were nothing to write home about: floral designs, which thankfully never made a comeback, and the wallpaper was the colour of diluted sunshine. My Ariston RD11S turntable was the coolest thing since Fonzie – the tonearm even had shock absorbers! Beside my turntable, a stack of vinyls took up an entire row on my bookshelf – practically every record ever pressed: *Sgt. Pepper's Lonely Hearts Club Band*, *Tommy*, *Wish You Were Here*, *Electric Ladyland*, *Dreamboat Annie* – just to name a few.

On my bedside table were a digital alarm clock and a framed photo of The Sunsets. The Polaroid had been taken only a year prior on the front steps of Sharon's house. I was seated on the far left with my arm around Sharon's shoulders, Sharon had her arm resting on Helen's head, and Helen was leaning an elbow on Tahlia's shoulder. That photo was snapped in medias res: in the middle of us laughing. There was nothing artificial about it, just a group of teens with flared jeans, tops brighter than the sun, with our loose hair blowing in the wind. Sharon's mother could be a lot of things, but she sure knew how to snap a pic when the time called for it. Beside that frame was a pastel-pink Princess phone that I used to gabber on when I wasn't listening to music.

Still wearing my shiny black school shoes, I propped myself against my pillow, legs stretched out, and settled down to watch *Wombat*. Yes, it was a kids' show, but there wasn't much else on considering we had few channel options, and I loved that cranky little puppet, Agro. He'd make me laugh until I almost peed my pants. My beloved show *Countdown* didn't air until six p.m. on Sundays, so this would have to suffice. A bag of chocolate-chip bickies lay open and ready to go beside me, but just as I reached inside the packet, I felt something trickle down south. And it wasn't pee; I hadn't even started laughing at Agro yet. I lurched forward, frowned, and cocked my head as if to listen when I should be feeling. Then more hot 'stuff' oozed out of me. I jumped up off the bed as my fingers stiffened. I remembered I'd just peed after eating my Vegemite sandwich; it was a ritual because I wanted as few distractions as possible while watching the boob tube. So ... what the heck?

Then it hit me: my first period. Don't ask me why, but I had the urge to cry. I hadn't yet taken off my school uniform, so it was a matter of spinning my navy-blue skirt around and undoing the button, then yanking the zipper down. But once I understood what was going on, my stomach started cramping – a psychosomatic reaction to this realisation. It felt like hot poker tips pressing into my belly, so I stripped off my skirt as though it was now made of snakes. I threw it on the bed and stared at my white undies until a hot trickle seeped out of me again. Using my thumb and index finger from each hand, I grabbed at the elastic and peeled the fabric away, millimetre by millimetre so I could peak inside. I couldn't see much because my legs were pressed together so tight they could have busted a watermelon. So, I winced and moaned as my eyes filled with warm tears, and spread my legs wider to reveal a pool of crimson. And then I screamed bloody murder – pardon the pun. Seeing it for the first time, knowing that my own blood was flowing out of me when I wasn't even injured, it scared me. It seemed like an anatomical anomaly and besides, it was dark red, so the contrast against my white knickers made the situation scarier.

Someone pounded on my door. *Bam-Bam-Bam*! 'Kylie? You okay?'

The elastic snapped back in place as I grabbed my skirt. 'Yes, Mum.'

'I thought I heard you screaming?'

'No; that was Keith.'

A leaden pause followed. 'Ahhh, Keith's jogged over to Amy's for dinner.'

Crap. 'Okay, it was me. Maybe can you ... come in?'

The door swung open as if she was planning to barge in anyway. She looked at the skirt covering my privates, then back to me.

A sceptical eyebrow rose. 'Why are you crying, and why are you half-naked?' She then eyed David Cassidy with overt suspicion. 'What were you doing to yourself in here?'

Then the floodgates opened and Niagara now had a competitor. 'I ... got my ... p-period.'

Her eyes widened and she clutched her cheeks. 'I've been waiting for this.'

Squinting, I said, 'You have?'

'When Cheryl told me Sharon started dripping, I've been waiting, wondering when it'll be your turn.'

I stood there snivelling and crying as more warm, sticky blood flowed from me. Was I dying? 'I need to get those things girls use – the cloths.'

'No. Pads. Or tampons.' Her left brow fish-hooked. 'Do you ... know how tampons work?'

I wrinkled my nose. Bile tickled my throat. Discussing with my mother about inserting objects into my vagina was not how I'd pictured spending the evening. 'Of course!'

She held up her hands. 'Okay-okay.' She leaned forward. 'Lucky for you I have both.'

'Huh?' Using the back of my hand, I wiped my dripping nostrils.

'I knew that when Sharon started, you'd be next. So, I stocked up for this moment. Think of it like stockpiling food for the fallout shelter.' She raised an index finger. 'I'll be back in a jiffy.'

When I glanced at the TV, I cried even harder. And I mean, ugly, snot-nosed crying. Not only was I bleeding from my fanny, I was also missing the funniest parts of the show. When Mum returned, she held out both hands like she was offering a sweet deal on a game show. In one hand lay a tampon, the other a Modess pad.

'Your pick.'

I grabbed both, turning away from her. Mortified! Absolutely mortified!

'Good. Yes. You don't have to stick to one. Maybe use a pad for now, then tampon later on.'

''Kay. Thanks, Mum.'

She hugged me tight. Her baby girl had passed a rite of passage. 'This makes me happy.' She leaned back, holding me at arm's length. 'You're a woman now.'

As soon as she left, I studied both pad and tampon – foreign objects. I wanted this to be over and done with, so I grabbed the tampon and used as little of my fingers as possible. I used my other free hand to open my knickers as I closed my eyes and placed it under my hole. Wincing, I bared my teeth. Then my eyes popped open: David Cassidy was staring at me with his trademark boyish grin. That wouldn't do, so I turned my back on him and repeated the process; little by little inserting the tampon. There was nothing pleasant about this task, and of course, I was still bleeding. After I shoved it all the way up, I looked at my bloodied fingers and sniffled again. I moved like I had rickets, left leg first, then the right, until I reached my white chest of drawers. I grabbed a bunch of tissues and wiped my fingers, then I blotted in between my legs and bloodied thighs. After chucking it all in my bin, I removed my soiled panties and tossed them in the bin, too, before getting a fresh pair.

Glancing in the mirror, sniffling, I said, 'There. That wasn't so bad.'

And it wouldn't have been, except I never knew until Sharon told me later on that I had to remove the plastic wrapping first.

Chapter Eleven

I DIDN'T SEE TRIX or the other boys for the rest of that school week. It seemed they came and went as they pleased. How would they graduate Year 12 if they didn't pass their HSC? But it occurred to me perhaps they didn't give a rat's arse.

Nothing too eventful happened with The Sunsets either. Tahlia had returned to school the day after her headache and appeared somewhat better, but was not her usual cheerful self. Sharon had written I <3 Bobby on her school folder until there was no more pink left to be seen. We told her she was a lovesick puppy and needed to stop being silly, but you know what teenage girls are like when they have a crush. That's exactly why it's called as such – inevitably, someone ends up crushed; it's a given. But Sharon didn't care. She kept wearing that pinky-white lipstick, looking out for Bobby every morning before school started, while I searched faces for Trix. I told myself it was stupid; I didn't even know the boy. It was like my brain had become a petulant teen: *I can do what I want!*

When Friday night rolled around, Keith dropped me off at Lickety-Split, as he planned on picking up Amy and sneaking into the new R-rated movie *Alien* showing at the Coronet Theatre on Summer Street – the Village Orange Drive-In was undergoing renovations. Thankfully, Amy's folks had coughed up the money to help Keith fix his Monaro – a fact my parents knew nothing about. I loved my older brother as much as any sister would, but he could be a selfish dude. He seldom went out of his way for anyone, and Mum always pulled him up on it. If he didn't reap some benefit from helping you, then you could kiss the idea of Keith's involvement goodbye.

I waved at Keith as his yellow Monaro screeched out of the dirt car park, narrowly avoiding hitting a tree. Either he was keen for Sigourney Weaver, or he was keen for Amy to start praising God at lovers' lane.

Friday nights at the Lickety were as busy as hell's kitchen, so it was no surprise to see a long queue at the counter. Two people were serving: Ralph and Eileen. Because it was so raucous, I could barely hear 'Friday on my Mind' by the Easybeats on the jukebox. I slipped in through the door beside the counter and made my way over to the back storeroom to stow my bag. My role was cleaning up, or grabbing stuff those out the front called for me to get – whipped cream, ice-cream tubs and so on. Plates and milkshake glasses with remnants of toppings around the inner rim sat on the drainer for me to wash up. Ralph liked to squirt toppings inside the frosted glass before pouring in the milkshake – it looked awesome, but it didn't always come off easily. I donned yellow rubber gloves and began filling a sink with hot water, squirting green dishwashing liquid into the running stream. I'm sure other establishments had fancy dishwashers, but Lickety-Split kept it simple.

'Kylie, ya back there?' Eileen yelled above the noise.

'Yes!'

'Hello! And also, get me some strawberry ice cream, please!'

Removing my gloves, I yelled, 'Coming!' I raced to the freezer, slid the door on its hinges, and pulled out a tub of ice cream. We had any flavour you could conceive: chocolate, rainbow, boysenberry ... Oh yeah, baby, Ralph only stocked the good stuff! I slid the door back on its hinges, then ran out the front and observed the queue. It was bananas – reminding me of those merchandise marquees at rock concerts, how everyone lines up to buy a T-shirt. I wasn't old enough or experienced enough to serve out the front, but Ralph and Eileen worked in tandem, and no matter how busy it was, Ralph kept humming as he scooped and squirted whipped cream and plopped maraschino cherries on top of sundaes.

'Anything else?' I asked, turning to Eileen.

Eileen shook her head, jamming a chilled silver milkshake jug under the spinner until strawberry-flavoured milk spilled over the sides. 'No, honey – but thank you.'

'Where's Laverne?'

She rolled her eyes, scooping powdered malt and plopping it into a jug of milk. 'She called in sick. Again. Useless as tits on a bull, that one.' She squirted caramel topping into the jug of malted milk. 'You go on back, honey; I'll find a way to clear those dishes.'

I looked around the seating area. Dirty plates had been stacked onto a Formica table in the middle of the room. Either one person had done it, or everyone had assumed that's where they should stack their empty plates and glasses.

'Hey, hurry up!' some dickhead at the back of the queue yelled. I looked towards the swinging front door as Bobby, Sharon and Trix waltzed in.

Sharon squealed and waved at me as though she hadn't just seen me a few hours ago at school. My cheeks already burned from the sight of Trix in tight Levi's, his intense eyes on me.

With a flapping hand, Sharon beckoned for me to come over.

I side-glanced Ralph, who hummed away as he sprinkled crushed peanuts onto a chocolate-fudge sundae. Seeing I was in the all-clear, I scooted away from Eileen and Ralph to open the side door that led to the seating area.

'Hey, Sunset!' Sharon wrapped her arms around me, and so did her mum's perfume.

Leaning back, I rubbed my sweaty hands over my apron, eyeing the hickies on her neck. 'What are you guys doing here?'

'Hangin' out,' Sharon said, 'which is what you should be doing.'

'But I just started.' I motioned behind me to the sink.

'Spewin',' she said, her breath smelling of Minties, 'but I s'pose one of us has gotta earn the dough. Unless you wanna chuck a sickie and have some fun?'

Wait! I didn't tell her I had a shift here tonig— I looked at Trix. Excitement raced through my veins upon realisation.

He proffered a hand. 'Hello again.'

'Hi.' I shook his hand, peering into eyes like pools that a girl would happily drown in. I was about to ask him where he and his friends had been all week, but that would mean I'd *noticed*; that I'd been looking out for him. 'How are you, Trix?'

'Well. You?'

'Busy.' I swung an arm to indicate the queue of customers. 'See that table over there?' He nodded when he saw where I pointed. 'I haven't had a chance to pick the plates up. One of the other workers, Laverne, called in sick—'

He took off. I looked over at Bobby and Sharon, not surprised to find them trading spit again. Shaking my head, I stepped out further and watched Trix bending over the table to grab the dirty dishes and cups. Seeing that made me feel embarrassed as heck. I wasn't ashamed to work at an ice-cream joint – most kids my age didn't even *have* a job – but seeing Trix helping remove customers' dirty dishes bummed me out.

I yelled out his name, but above the jovial clamour and 'Eagle Rock' on the jukebox, it would have barely constituted a whisper. Still, I held out a hand when he came back with crockery and cups, expecting him to give them to me.

'Where do you want them? Am I allowed back there?' He jerked his head towards the kitchen.

'Um ...'

'Go ask Mr Ferguson if it's all right.'

Frowning, I turned around. Jeez, I'd half-expected Trix to waltz out the back, but he'd asked me to ask first. But before I did, I ran to the sink to turn the tap off. Then I sprinted over to Ralph out the front, slipping past Eileen as she scooped 'Strawberry Fields Forever' ice cream.

'Ralph?'

He was bopping away to Daddy Cool's song, handing a young girl with braces and pigtails her choc-vanilla cone. 'There you go, little miss.'

'Gee, thanks, Mr Fergie!' She grabbed the base, licked the hardened chocolate on top, and rushed off.

He turned to me with the patience of a man who has nothing but time to offer, as though there weren't people lined up waiting to give him their money. 'Yes, my dear?'

'Is it okay for my friend to help me out with the dishes for a minute?'

Ralph peered past my shoulder to where Trix stood with plates in either hand. Then he looked back at me. 'You know I don't like you messin' with those older boys. They're all a coupl'a sangas short of a picnic, if you ask me – that blond one is as mad as a cut snake. Friggin' hell, Kylie, you're like another daughter to me.'

Sweaty fingers interlacing, I said, 'I know, but I just thought since Laverne called in sick, he could help me. I guess you wouldn't have to pay him nothing—'

'Hey, c'mon,' a man with mutton-chop sideburns in the queue yelled. 'We're starving here!'

Ralph paid him no mind and Eileen grabbed me from behind, mumbled an 'Excuse me', then rushed past. He inhaled deeply and made sure I saw it too.

'Please, Ralph?'

He waved a dismissive hand. 'I don't want to know nothin' about it, but he'll get paid in sugar, not cash.'

'Sugar?'

He motioned towards the ice cream display, every dentist's nightmare – or money-maker, depending on how one looked at it.

'Ripper; you're the best, Ralph!' I said, just as someone else yelled out about the slow service and the irony of the establishment being called 'lickety-split'.

When Ralph turned away, I approached Trix. 'He said it's cool for you to help me. He can't pay you in cash, but you can have ice cream.'

The corner of his mouth twitched. 'I don't need money.' He strolled into the kitchen to place the dishes beside the already-mountainous pile.

'You really don't have to—'

'I'll be back with more.' He brushed by me and out the side door, leaving it open, exposing Bobby and Sharon pashing like kissing was going to be outlawed tomorrow. God, they literally couldn't keep their hands off each other. Trix hadn't so much as pecked my cheek, but I told myself I didn't care. Not one single bit. Nope. Not me. No way, José.

I got to work, placing the same-sized plates into the soapy water. See, I had a routine: all of the same things in at once, and the most-used ones needed to be washed first. By the time I'd placed the last plate into the hot, sudsy water, Trix was standing beside me with more crockery.

'Trix, I can do this—'

'Are you always this way when people try to help?' He deposited his loot onto the drainer and trailed off while glancing over his shoulder. 'There's still more.'

I stood there, blushing like the silly teen I was, and then pulled the gloves onto my hands. When Trix returned, he stayed and helped me scrape plates and sort their sizes in order.

'I thought you were supposed to be hanging with Bobby and Sharon?'

'What fun is that when their tongues are tied?'

Laughing, I went back to scrubbing the dishes and placing them on a tray to drip-dry. 'You don't have to hang out here.' Which, of course, was female for: *Please stay; I don't want you to go.*

'What are you and the girls doing on the weekend?' he asked, picking a striped milkshake straw out from a glass and throwing it in the bin.

That he included my friends in this question impressed me. I came as a package deal, and it made me fall for him even more. He was the most paradoxical boy I'd ever met. So much for a bad boy – there he was, helping me scrape dirty plates. And sure, I was only fourteen, but he was only seventeen. What was three years between teens? Although sometimes, mere months made the biggest difference – Sharon never let me forget she was older than me by just that. Still. Older boy with 'delinquent' tattooed on his tanned forehead ... yes, please!

Trix understanding that wherever I went, my girlfriends went too, showed he was vigilant. He was the type of person who was quiet only so he could observe. And sure, it wouldn't take a genius to see that the four of us were inseparable, but there were other things too. Trix didn't just look at something; he *saw* it. He saw the layers beneath; he saw the hidden meaning; he viewed the world the way a philosopher does, always questioning everything but keeping his observations to himself.

And how I interacted with the other Sunsets would surely be the same as Trix did with his friends. Only ... it was just Bobby here now. I didn't know how those three had organised this hangout date, but it had happened, and now Bobby and Sharon were at it again. How did they get here? The thought of Sharon riding in Trix's Pontiac filled me with jealousy. Had she been talking to Bobby on the phone? I didn't even know she had his number. Trix hadn't asked for mine.

'Well?' Trix said, staring at me.

'Oh! What are we doing on the weekend? We go to the lake on Saturdays and swim.'

He bobbed his head, giving me a close-lipped smile. 'Groovy.'

'W-what about you guys?'

'We will be going to the lake to swim.'

Blushing harder, I turned away to hide a goofy grin just as Eileen yelled out again: 'Honey, gimme banana ice cream! And more caramel fudge!'

'Sure thing, Eileen!'

When I handed Eileen the tub and caramel fudge, I caught sight of a group of boys up the back near the flashing arcade games, still wearing Orange East High uniforms. They glared at Bobby with narrowed eyes. Something bad was brewing, and someone was going to get hurt. Not only did I not want the boys to get into a fight, I also didn't want Ralph to lose customers over an incident. For my own peace of mind, I had to ask Trix – nothing was going to stop me. I rushed out the back to find Trix wiping the inside of a sundae glass with a white cloth.

'Trix ...' He turned to me, the wet glass producing squeaky sounds as his hand turned inside it. 'What's going on between you and the Orange East boys?'

He looked back to the glass. *Eeek-eeek-eeek*. 'What makes you think something's going on?'

'You don't need to lie to me.'

He looked up, his hand stilling.

'There are boys from Orange East High in here right now, staring down Bobby.'

He placed the glass down on a bench with the cloth still inside it and hurried over, opening the side door and glancing around until he spotted them. Heart rate spiking, I watched from the sink, too fearful to get caught up in any trouble. Bobby broke free from Sharon and spun around to look towards the back of the shop. His body tensed, like he wanted to charge over to the Orange East boys, but Trix held his arm, pulling him back, speaking close to his face. Bobby's nostrils flared. He then nodded curtly once, grabbed Sharon by the arm, and dragged her out the front door.

Trix eyed me as he strode over. 'We're leaving. There won't be any drama.'

I clenched my hands, unnerved by the idea of him keeping secrets from me. 'You said I could ask you anything.'

His jaw tightened as he looked away to safer ground. 'See you tomorrow.' He turned and left me alone with my plethora of questions.

Chapter Twelve

SATURDAYS WERE MY FAVOURITE day of the week. I expect for most people it would be Friday, but considering we had little pocket money and weren't old enough to get into M-rated double features at the Coronet Theatre, we had few options. But on Saturdays, The Sunsets made it a ritual to meet at the lake for a swim. Of course, the lake was out during winter thanks to the snowfall, but even then we would still catch up somewhere – typically at the Cherry Inn. To us it became known as Sunset Saturdays, and the greatest thing was we didn't need our parents to drive us over there. Saturday nights were also when the ABC would do re-runs of last week's episode of *Countdown*.

When I arrived at the lake at around two in the afternoon, the car park had not one vacant spot; the bike rack also chockers. It appeared every man and his dog had rocked up. Families loved to gather lakeside as there was play equipment for the kids, and enough grass that we weren't all packed in like sardines. The lake also housed picnic areas with gazebos and benches, plus gas barbeques for those who brought along their own food. As I biked along a path, the usual aromas associated with the lake clung to the humid air: fried onions, sunscreen, grilled sausages. The usual sights and sounds too: kids squealing in delight; teenage girls marinated in baby oil sunbathing; boys in rubber thongs walking dogs on leashes. Various portable radios were playing – not always on the same station, but that meant I had a decent variety to listen to as I pedalled down to our usual spot. Sometimes the area would be taken, and us girls would have to move elsewhere, but we'd chosen a spot that most families didn't desire because it had little shade for the young ones, and it was farthest away from the car park, which meant lugging eskies and heavy picnic baskets a good distance. But we could ride our bikes all the way down to the area near a huge charcoal-grey rock, which we used to dry our wet towels on. Typically, by the time we were packed up and ready to leave, our towels would be as dry as a Pommy's bath mat.

That afternoon, the sky was the richest turquoise-blue I had ever seen. Not one cloud had made an appearance, and the canvas was the same shade all the way across; it looked as if God had grabbed His paint roller and gone from one side of the sky to the other. Unbeknown to me then, it would be one of the few perfect afternoons we had left before the incident. Our days of innocence were drawing in; our days as The Sunsets had an expiry date, but none of us could have predicted it. As kids, we assumed everything would stay the same: that we'd always be friends, that our parents would always be together, that we'd always live in our childhood home. Poor, naive girls.

By the time I reached our spot, all five of the boys were present: Mike, Ed, Trix, Rodney. Bobby and Sharon were ... do I even need to say it? Sharon's yellow wedge platforms gave her that extra boost, and a pink-and-white scarf pulled her blonde hair back so she could pash without impediments. Her baby-pink halter-neck top exposed her bare shoulders to the harsh rays, and I swear her boobs looked fuller. Maybe the old 'bundled socks' trick? I wondered.

Behind round transparent purple-tinted sunnies, Helen lay flat on a picnic blanket reading a paperback version of *Flowers in the Attic*. Tahlia sat beside her, gazing out at the glistening water where parents held their kids in floaties, and girls dressed in bright bikinis along the bank used the tree ropes provided to go swinging through the air to see who could make the biggest splash. To my right, towards the entrance, identical twin boys were trying to lift their inflatable Puffer Kite in the air.

Trix's Pontiac couldn't access these parts, but a Philips transistor radio on the rock played 'Horror Movie' by Skyhooks over 2JJ.

Trix walked over to me as soon as I laid my bike down beside the others in the warm grass. 'You finally made it.'

'Yes; I had to help my mum with something.'

'Just in time for lunch.' He turned around as Rodney approached carrying a blue esky, the scar on his left cheek more pronounced under the blazing sun. No smile, no wave. He was about as welcoming as an STD.

'What's in there?' I asked Trix, referring to the esky.

Trix faced me again. 'Everything. Hope you're not a vegetarian.'

'Hey, Kylie!'

I spun around and Helen waved to me from her blanket, open book in the other hand.

'Hey!' I made my way over. 'How are you guys?'

'Starving.' Helen rolled on her side. 'The boys are putting on a barbie.'

'Cool!' I sat beside her and removed my backpack to retrieve a Rolling Stones beach towel featuring their famous red tongue and lips logo. I spread it out before me and eyed Tahlia as I climbed on. 'How are you?'

Tahlia gave me a close-lipped smile. 'Okay.'

Frowning, I stared at her profile. Peals of laughter rose from the bank. 'Are you sure?'

She nodded, but her fingers fidgeted with the edge of her blue-and-orange crochet blanket. It was obvious she wasn't okay, but what else could I say? Maybe the headache had returned? If she didn't want to talk about it, I couldn't force her. She'd loosen up soon enough.

'Okay, girls, I hope you're hungry?'

We all peered up at Mike. He stood before us, a wink of sunlight bouncing off his black sunnies. 'If there are any preferences ... Ah, shit, who cares; you get what you're given!' He laughed, clapping his hands once, and took off to help Rodney carry the esky over to an unoccupied barbeque pit.

I turned to Helen, who had resumed reading her book. 'Who brought all this food along?'

Helen brushed a strand of brown hair from her sun-kissed face. With those transparent purple sunnies, all I could picture was the late Janis Joplin. 'Sharon told me Trix paid for everything, but it's Rodney's esky.'

Trix paid for all the food? I glanced over my shoulder to see Trix looking at me. He stood by little Ed, who cracked open a VB can and slurped the overflowing bubbles that coated his hand. I gave Trix a tiny smile, which I hoped translated to gratitude for buying all the food, and turned back to watch those in the water, splashing, wrestling, seeing who could hold their breath the longest.

Leaning over, I said again, 'Tahlia, is everything okay?'

Gazing at nothing apparent, she sucked her lips inwards and bobbed her head twice.

I placed my arm around her shoulders, her warm orange hair brushing against my forearm. It felt comforting, like sitting in front of the fireplace with a cup of hot cocoa during winter.

'Are You Old Enough' by Dragon came on the radio as I peered into that gorgeous sky, watching magpies dipping and careening, wondering how nice it would feel to be as free as that. One day, maybe ...

'D'you girls want any drinks?'

Helen peered over her shoulder at little Ed. 'We don't drink beer.'

'Who said anything about beer?' He spread his arms like the wings of the birds above us. 'I am your drink master. We've got creaming soda, Coke, UDLs and ... oh shit, I actually think that's it – but still ... your wish is my command.'

Helen giggled, lowering her paperback. It was groovy to see her warming up to the boys, but as much as I enjoyed having them around, I didn't want us to combine forces. Call me selfish, but I loved my alone time with the girls, and wanted to keep it separate. I didn't want our talks from now on to only revolve around those boys and what they were doing. I wanted to continue our sleepover dates, I wanted to continue riding our bikes and listening to the music from my transistor radio, and I wanted us to still be 'us'.

'Hmm ... can I have a creaming soda, please?' Helen said, placing a hand to her pinkish forehead to shield the sun's glare.

Ed winked. 'You got it, doll!' He looked between Tahlia and me. 'Girls? Drink?'

Tahlia shrugged meekly. 'Same, I guess.'

'Three creaming sodas, please,' I said, smiling.

He snapped his fingers, then pointed an index at us in a gun and trigger pose. 'Coming right up.' He fired the 'gun' and then blew imaginary smoke from the tip.

Ed may have been the shortest of the five boys, but he made up for it with his sense of humour. And it occurred to me, while watching Rodney and Trix flipping sizzling steaks and rotating spitting sausages, that beneath our personas we projected to the world, underneath all the rubble, we really were just a bunch of kids. Trying to figure out who we were and our place in society. Considering we girls were in Year 9, we had a rough idea by now of what we wanted to be when we got older. Helen Baldwin dreamed of becoming a mystery writer, and in case it isn't obvious, Sharon O'Rourke longed to be the next Farrah Fawcett. She had the beauty for it, and I reckon she could have chopped off her cascading blonde hair and sold it for a million dollars. As for me, I had a hankering to become a music producer; that's all I'd ever wanted to do, associate with music – to live and breathe it. And dear, sweet Tahlia Ashcroft, she wanted to become a schoolteacher.

It's a shame we never got to find out.

Chapter Thirteen

When lunch was ready, Mike cupped either side of his mouth. 'Oi! Come and get yer grub!'

We all rose and shuffled towards the barbeque as the warm grass tickled our bare feet. Steaks, sausages, bacon and lamb chops sizzled on the hotplate.

'Oh, wow!' Helen said, ogling the feast. Usually, we asked our mothers to make us some devon and tomato sauce sangas, and pack a few snacks like Cheezels and Curly Wurlys – if we were lucky. This seemed more like a banquet for royals.

'Nice work, man!' Ed said, grabbing Mike's hand and jumping up to bump shoulders.

Mike jerked a thumb towards Trix. 'Thank this dickhead for buyin' all this shit.'

Trix shook his head, unsmiling. 'It was nothing.'

The boys laughed.

Rodney cracked open a beer and used a rag to mop the sweat off his bald head. I still had a hard time believing he was only in Year 12. Maybe he'd repeated a few years? Which would make perfect sense, but I was not about to ask, as he had a demeanour worse than a junkyard dog. I wouldn't have been game to ask him for directions to the nearest bathroom. It occurred to me that in the few times I'd met Rodney, he'd barely said three words. But as my late grandmother once said, 'It's the quiet ones you have to watch out for.'

'Thanks, Trix,' Sharon said, moseying over to the shaded gazebo with Bobby in hand.

'You're welcome. Eat up, girls.' Trix looked at Mike. 'The girls go first.'

Mike raised both hands in the air, the tongs dangling from a thumb. 'Never thought otherwise, dude. Here y'ar, Kylie.'

I grabbed the tongs first but handed them to Tahlia. She still didn't look well, so I believed if we piled her with food, she'd perk up and colour would return to her pale cheeks.

With drooping jowls, she took the tongs off me and grabbed one sausage. 'Thank you, Trix.'

He looked at her plate, then into her eyes. 'You're allowed more than one snag.'

Tahlia shook her head, brown eyes downcast. 'Not very hungry.' She handed the tongs to the next in line. Trix gave me a quizzical look.

My shoulder shrug translated to: *I don't know what's eating her.*

Helen grabbed a plastic plate and piled food on top.

Ed clapped once, then backhanded Mike's chest and grinned. 'I love this chick! Finally, a girl who knows how to eat!'

Helen gave a close-lipped smile. 'I haven't had much to eat all day.'

'Maybe if you got your head out of those books, you'd take better care of yourself,' Sharon said, adjusting her orange hot pants at the thigh before grabbing a plate for her and Bobby.

'Maybe you should *try* reading a book.' Helen picked up the tomato sauce bottle and squirted it over her food.

Sharon flicked her hair behind her bronzed shoulder. 'Yuck; I only read when I have to.'

Ed approached Helen, sucking back a gutful of air. 'So, ah, you like books? I read a bit of *Blinky Bill* back in the day.'

Helen handed the tongs to Sharon, licked her thumb free from sauce, and I turned to watch her and Ed stroll off together – it seemed Ed had forgotten all about lunch. Next was my turn as I grabbed the tongs from Sharon after she'd stocked up.

'Thanks heaps, Trix; this looks yummy.' I didn't look at him as I said this, still thinking about the previous night at Lickety-Split, how he and Bobby had left as soon as I'd told him a bunch of boys from Orange East High were in the parlour. They'd left faster than the snap of fingers, and I had no idea why. Yes, I was probably being cold to him this afternoon, but I wanted to keep my distance until I received more answers.

'There won't be any drama' he'd said before walking off. That told me there *could* have been if he and Bobby hadn't left. The mystery bugged me, like an itch I couldn't reach to scratch.

Trix stepped beside me, grabbing a plate as I decided what to eat. It all looked so inviting – char-grilled meat, glistening with juices.

'You're welcome,' Trix said. 'I'm sorry for leaving you the way I did last night.'

Using the tongs, I snagged a plump snag and plopped it on my white plate, which smeared it with brown grease. I was aware Mike and Rodney were staring at me, probably wishing I'd hurry up so they could eat the food they themselves had cooked.

'No sweat,' I said, grabbing a lamb chop lying in its opaque fat.

'Maybe next time you and I can hang out for real at the Cherry Inn. And for longer.'

The pulse in my neck throbbed as I struggled for oxygen. *Breathe! Just Breathe!* 'Groovy. We'll see.' He took the outstretched tongs off me, but made no move to take any food. I put the plate on the small foldout table, grabbed a doughy bread roll as soft as air, and tore it apart through the centre with my fingers. Then I squirted tomato sauce over my food, watching from the corner of my eye as Trix observed me. When I was done, I gave a smile to the boys watching with silent regard, and headed over to Helen and Tahlia, just as little Ed made his way back to the barbeque.

After our bellies had expanded to twice their size, Ed approached us. Even though we were together, the boys ate away from us – but to be fair, I think we girls started the segregation by banding together. Anyway, I was more than happy to sit with Helen and Tahlia ... you can guess where Sharon sat.

Ed clapped once and dipped his head. 'Who wants to come swimming with Eddy-boy?'

Helen raised a hand, placing her empty plate with its smeared tomato sauce and a crumpled greasy napkin in front of her with the other. 'I do!'

He grinned. 'All riiiiight! You got sunscreen, doll? Don't wanna look like beef jerky after this.'

Helen giggled and pulled out a bottle of Coppertone QT suntan lotion from her backpack, but when she handed it to him, he frowned.

'Ain't ya gonna rub it on me?'

Trix hurried over, grabbed the bottle and handed it to Ed. With a frown, Ed took it and watched Trix storm off.

Helen stood up on her towel and began removing her flared denim jeans and rainbow-striped top to reveal light-purple swimmers underneath. That's what we usually did – it saved having to trudge all the way to the public dunny blocks just to change into swimmers, then walk all the way back, which was a pain in our teeny tushies!

'All riiiiight!' Ed said again, grinning as he ripped off his high-waisted jeans to reveal black swimming trunks. Mike sauntered over, ripped off his blue polo T-shirt and peeled his dacks off to reveal budgie smugglers, and then plunged into the water – sunnies and all. He bounced to the surface and spat out water.

'Fuck *me*, this is beautiful!' Mike flicked water off his shades using an index finger, glistening dark hair plastered to his forehead and temples. 'Deadset unreal. Girls! You coming?'

'I know I sure am!' Ed yelled back, laughing. He turned to Helen as excited screams arose all around, and a group of young kids behind him tossed around a large inflatable beach ball. 'You ready, or you want to put sunscreen on?'

'I always put it on before I leave home because Mum makes me—'

Ed grabbed her hand and led her in, where they gasped and hissed as the cold water lapped at their shins.

'Yowzah!' Ed yelled, wading through until it was waist high. 'Aww man! Whooooo!'

Turning to Tahlia, I nudged her shoulder as we both watched a brown-and-white kelpie with a large stick in its mouth sprint by. 'You going in?'

She shook her head and I side-glanced her half-eaten sausage. 'I think I'll pass.'

'Why? What's the matter?'

'I feel sick again today.' She clutched her stomach, her eyelids at half-mast.

'Then that's the perfect time. The cold water will make you feel better. Plus, your face is getting red.'

'It's because I have such pale skin; I get this way just from stepping out of the house.'

I laughed and nudged her again. 'Go on.' I grabbed her hand. 'I can't go in, but you should.'

'Why not? You're asking *me* to.'

That's when I told her about my rags, and how much it sucked that I couldn't join the boys and girls this fine afternoon; it seemed the fulgent sun and the clear blue sky mocked me for having two X chromosomes.

'You should go, though, Tahlia; I can dip my feet in the water. The Sunsets, remember? All of us. Together.'

She snapped blades of grass in half, then let the pieces fall. 'You mean us and the boys.'

'Is that why you're not yourself?'

She shook her head, the sunlight bouncing off different shades of her autumn-es-que hair. 'No. They're nice boys, I guess. Although we don't really know them.'

'Then what's the matter? If you don't tell me' – I poked her shoulder – 'I'll keep bugging you.'

She turned to me, unsmiling. 'Okay. I'll go in the water.'

I sat up straighter, extending my spine. 'Really?'

She nodded, the corner of her lips forming a half-hearted smile. Because she wore a light-green wrap dress, she unfastened it around the waist to reveal red swimmers underneath, but her knees were in line with my face. Angry-looking bruises on her kneecaps stared back. Blackish-purple, aggravated bruises that made one nauseous just by looking at them, and I couldn't help but wheeze-gasp.

'Tahlia, what *happened*?'

She looked at where I was referring. 'I fell.'

I scrambled to my feet to look into her dull eyes. 'You *fell*?'

Then I glanced at her ribs. How was it possible she'd lost weight since last week? How sick *was* she?

'I think the cool water will do me good.' She looked behind me at the sound of footsteps approaching.

'Coming?'

I turned around to find Trix facing me with a blank expression.

'Err, no.' I didn't need to ask if Trix was going for a swim or not; he stood there in nothing but black trunks. Most of the boys wore black trunks, come to think of it. His smooth, tanned chest and long legs stole my focus, making it hard to turn away. 'N-no, I'll have to watch.' I'd never hated being a girl more in my life than in that moment. My period stole away an opportunity to swim semi-naked with Trix as water dripped off our bodies. My God. How life can be so damn fucking cruel.

Trix eyed me as jovial screams rose from those in the water. 'You said yesterday you were going swimming.'

'Yes, I did say that. But I can't.' Would he stay and keep me company? I counted the heads in the chalky-blue water and they were short four: Tahlia, Rodney, Trix and me. I didn't want to be left alone with Rodney, who by this point I wasn't even sure could speak. How did his voice sound? Baritone? Trombone? Tenor? Anybody but him, please; he gave me the heebie-jeebies.

'Suit yourself.' Trix eyed Tahlia and held out his elbow. At first, I thought she'd smack him away, but she smiled softly and held on, letting him lead her down to the embankment.

Rejection to a teen is heartbreak, no matter how big or small. Instead of indulging my weak emotions, I blinked the stinging tears away and climbed on top of the hot rock that protruded over the water. It wasn't huge like Ayers Rock, but it gave me a good vantage point from a few metres above the water, the sunlight bouncing off the surface shining like diamonds. I had to take my Rolling Stones beach towel because this rock could fry an egg if it grew hot enough. I splayed it out before me and perched on it, gazing at the towering cliffs opposite. They were so high it was forbidden to jump. Besides, from what I understood, you couldn't even drive up there – private property.

'Strange Magic' by Electric Light Orchestra bled from the radio, and I moved it to the side so the speakers could face the others while I watched everyone frolicking in the delicious water. Despite not being able to jump in, the sight made me smile, and it filled me with such a sense of familiarity, of happiness, of calmness. Sharon making out with Bobby; Helen and Ed floating a few inches away from each other while chatting about who knew what; and Trix, Mike and Tahlia huddled together. Ed then shot up in the air, held his breath, and went under. Helen gave me a wave as iridescent droplets ran off her wiggling fingers. I smiled and waved back before closing my eyes as a soothing breeze blew over me like a sigh of relief. The sun scorched my unprotected head and shoulders, the air redolent with smells that spoke to me of family togetherness, jovial shouts ringing around my ears. Boy, I may not have been able to take part that afternoon, but I tell you what ... it proved to be a memory that I would revisit many times over the years. There wasn't a worry in the world that fine afternoon. Everything was the way it should be.

We hadn't a clue it was the calm before the storm.

Chapter Fourteen

When I arrived home that Saturday evening, I parked my bike out the front, entered the house, and sniffed Mum's pleasant cooking that permeated the air.

'That you, Kylie?' Mum yelled out.

'Yes.' I bypassed the lounge room and entered the kitchen to find Mum mashing spuds in a yellow pot. Bright-orange Tupperware containers cluttered the wood-panelled benches, one containing those God-awful tinned peas Mum used to cook to within an inch of their life.

'How was your afternoon?' She poured a dash of milk into the pot and went to work again.

'Good! Yours?' I appraised the dinner table. Mum had already set it with plates, salt and pepper shakers, cutlery, and eggshell-blue plastic cups with floral designs.

Mum flicked a free hand in the air. 'The usual. Can you call your father for supper?'

I turned around, trailed down the carpeted hallway and knocked on the door. 'Dad?'

'Yeah?' The comforting sound of his train running on its tracks made me smile.

'Dinner's ready.'

'Righto.'

I smiled wider and turned away to head back to the kitchen. 'Mum?'

'Mmm?' she murmured, not looking up from whipping the mash with a wooden spoon. That was her secret: she didn't just mash it then plop it on a plate; no, she whipped it until it was like butter afterwards.

'Where's Keith?' I pulled out a bottle of Coke from the fridge to place on the table.

She sighed theatrically and shook her head in that disapproving manner, her feathered brown hair swaying. 'He *should* be out looking for a better job.'

Dad ambled into the kitchen and took his place at the head of the table, removing his glasses to clean them with the hem of his white shirt. 'Smells good, Liz; what's on the menu?'

'Beef, veg and red wine stew – I know it's not exactly a springtime dish, but I needed to use up the beef.'

'Sounds good.' Dad smiled. Well ... lifted the corners of his lips, anyway.

Taking my place at the table, I looked at Dad while unscrewing the lid off the Coke bottle. 'Any luck with a job?'

He shook his head, patting down his comb-over. 'No. But something will come up.'

Mum approached the table with the pot of steaming, buttery mashed potatoes. Dad and I watched her stroll to the stove and then bring over a large, forest-green dish and place it on a corkboard in the middle of the table. She lifted the clear lid, inhaling deeply as aromatic steam escaped. 'Dig in.'

'Shouldn't we wait for Keith?' Dad said.

She slammed the lid on the table. 'That friggin' boy is a lost cause!'

As if on cue, we heard the familiar sound of his car pull into the driveway. Not one minute later and the front door burst open then slammed shut, rattling the windows.

All three of us swapped frowns, but no-one dared speak. Keith stormed into the kitchen, raking a jittery hand through his brown hair, avoiding eye contact.

'Son?' Dad said a moment later, frowning. 'You all right?'

Keith headed straight for the fridge, his rubber thongs flapping. 'Yeah. Nah. I dunno.'

Mum placed her hands on her hips, over her paisley dress. 'What did you do now?'

Keith yanked the fridge door open, bent forward, his head bobbing as he searched the shelves. 'Dad, can I've a beer?'

'Sure thing—'

'Jeffrey!' Mum said, then faced Keith again. 'Young man, no, you cannot have a beer.'

Keith raised a hand in the air, his back to her. 'Ma! I need one!'

We all watched Keith grab one of Dad's Carlton Draughts before he snatched a silver bottle top opener from a drawer near the sink. When Keith upended the bottle to his lips and swallowed three gulps, Mum and Dad glanced at each other, communicating via telepathy, then back to Keith.

'You're not in any trouble, are you, mate?'

Keith laughed a maniacal laugh. 'Well ... I think Amy is the one in trouble.' He laughed again and took another swig of beer before wiping his lips with the back of his other quaky hand.

'Where have you been?' Mum asked.

'With Amy, at her place.'

Mum raised a brow, shrugging. 'And?'

Keith laughed nervously again, took another swig. He lowered the bottle, swallowed, and closed his eyes. 'She's pregnant.'

Mum placed a hand over her chest and wheezed. '*Pregnant?*'

'That's what I said.'

Her lips flapped before she settled on a bunch of rudimentary words. 'How? When? Why?'

Keith flashed Mum one of those looks that said: *Are you stupid?* 'How? Because we had sex, that's how.'

When Dad chuckled close-mouthed behind his balled fist, Mum turned her anger towards him. Dad raised his hands in a conciliatory manner and soon lost his smile as he cleared his throat.

Mum's head swivelled back to Keith, gritting her teeth. 'How dare you?!'

Keith threw an arm in the air, his cheeks flushing scarlet. 'It's not like I planned it!'

She tilted her head, folding her arms over her chest. 'Did you use protection?'

'Nah ...'

'Then you planned it.' She plonked on her chair, cupping her forehead with both hands. 'Fair dinkum, Keith. How could you be so reckless?'

'I don't need this shit from you, Ma! In case you hadn't noticed, I'm freaking out about this.'

Her head snapped up. 'You should be! You two are only seventeen!' She closed her eyes, gasping. 'How could you be so stupid and naive?'

Dad leaned forward, reaching out a hand to Mum. 'Liz, the boy's obviously—'

She pointed at Dad. 'Don't you side with him on this.'

Dad lowered his head, retracted his arm and looked at his empty dinner plate.

Mum turned to Keith and shook her head. 'This is *unbelievable.*'

'Don't get all troppo. It's not like I killed someone, Ma. Calm down!'

Even at fourteen, I knew telling a woman to calm down was like poking a sleeping bear and expecting it to stay asleep. Mum's chest expanded and her eyes held that crazy look she got right before she exploded, and then grounded me or confiscated my prized possessions. It didn't happen often, but when it did – boy ... look out. Dad was usually on the receiving end of that crazed look; me ... once or twice but tonight, it was all about Keith. Call me biased, but I felt bad for my brother. It was clear he was packing shit over this. He would become a father before his eighteenth birthday, and although I knew he was smitten with Amy Jung, I didn't see them getting married and living happily ever after until they were both grey-haired and wrinkly. Who, as a teen, wants to miss out on all the fun? That was how I assumed boys thought, anyway. Keith was now white-lipped with anger, or anxiety, or animosity. Perhaps like Neapolitan ice cream: a little bit of all three.

'How did her parents take it?' Mum asked, pinning him with her best disapproving stare.

Keith shook his head, his jawline rigid. 'They don't know.'

She looked about the room as if she had an audience, including them as well. 'Well, I can't imagine they'll be too pleased.' She breathed deeply through her flared nostrils. 'We need to call the Jungs and have them over here for a family meeting.'

Dad raised an index finger. 'Liz, let's not spit the dummy—'

'No way!' Keith yelled. 'Are you off your rocker?'

She held up a palm. 'Don't you *dare* talk to me like that, Keith David Gardner.' Keith scoffed and his head lolled back. 'You made your bed, now you have to sleep in it.'

He glared at Mum, teeth bared. 'I already slept in it – with Amy – that's why we're in this mess!'

'I've had just about enough of your bad attitude towards me! I'm not the one who's knocked someone up before the age of eighteen. Do you realise this is going to ruin the rest of your life?'

Dad held up a hand. 'Liz, come on—'

'Don't be coming to your father and me for money – your father hasn't got any.'

'Did I *say* I was going to ask you for money?' Keith yelled, his mottled neck the colour of old bricks, making his white puka-shell necklace stand out even more. 'Did I?!'

Mum still had her palm raised at Keith. 'Stop using that tone of voice with me. Amy's parents and your father and me will have to have a serious discussion about this before the baby is born. You are *not* going to run out on Amy while she's carrying your seed.' She banged a fist into the flat palm of her other hand. 'You are going to be a responsible man and be there for your child – even if it means selling the Monaro.'

Keith downed the rest of his beer, plonked the bottle on the bench behind him, and turned to Dad. 'Can I have another one?'

'Sure, mate. Get one for me while you're at it.'

'No! Don't you dare have another beer!' Mum's elbows slid on the table, knocking over a pepper shaker as she cupped her head. 'Oh, Christ, who in their right mind would get knocked up while they're still in school?'

'Heaps of people!'

Mum shot Keith a sharp look and her face wrinkled, accentuating an abundance of hidden lines. 'Name *one*.'

What I thought she meant was: *How come I haven't heard about this from my girlfriends around town?*

Keith opened the fridge door and pulled out two bottles of beer. 'I forget her *name*, but there's a chick at Orange East High. She's preggo to someone from our school.'

'Who?' I blurted abruptly, realising this was the first and only thing I'd said during this heated argument.

Keith shrugged and took the caps off both beer bottles. 'Some drongo called Tristan Walker.'

Chapter Fifteen

Monday rolled around with the swiftness of a three-legged tortoise. I hadn't told the girls about what Keith had divulged regarding Trix. I didn't want it to be true. Keith hadn't disclosed any more information, and I hadn't asked any more questions in case it'd look suspicious to Mum and Dad. Keith had left before eating a bite of dinner. Mum, Dad and I had eaten in silence, but Mum's face remained the same deep-red hue throughout. I'd asked to be excused before I finished what was on my plate and rushed to my bedroom, switched on *Countdown*, and wept uncontrollably into a pillow until I fell asleep. I cried over feeling stupid; I cried over the ring of truth to what Mum said to Keith: 'This will ruin your life'. Maybe not completely to where he couldn't make something of himself, but that child was his forever, and he barely had money as it was. I also cried over the way my heart ached for a boy who obviously didn't care about me or my feelings. How could Trix not have told me he had a pregnant girlfriend over at Orange East High?

When I finally ambled into the school grounds, the five boys were already congregated with Helen and Sharon, but I couldn't see Tahlia. I tried to avoid them, having vowed not to speak to Trix again, but Sharon called out my name and waved me over. As soon as Trix spun around and we locked eyes, my heart leapt into my throat. With Milo and Weet-Bix travelling up my tight oesophagus, I turned and ran the other way, leaving them looking at me with confusion and Sharon yelling my name once more. I hid inside a toilet cubicle until the school bell rang. First period was English, and I was happy to see Willie Miller, but knew I'd have to answer Sharon's questions about why I'd ditched them.

When I reached the classroom, Bobby and Sharon stood by the door, facing each other. Sharon was giggling; Bobby was looking her up and down with a cheeky grin, whispering sweet nothings.

Trix stood next to them, glancing around the throng of heads and, when he spotted me, he hurried over, frowning. 'What was with this morning?'

Shrugging, I swallowed past the heart-shaped obstruction lodged in my aching throat. 'I needed to use the bathroom.'

'You didn't even wave or smile back at Sharon. What's wrong?'

'Hey, Fred, heads-up!' some kid yelled before throwing a black-and-purple Frisbee.

Eyes fixated on the floor, I said, 'Nothing. I need to go inside now.'

I brushed past Brutus and walked straight by Bobby and Sharon, who didn't even know I'd been standing there. That morning, I took my seat up the front; I had no interest in peering out the windows to watch the world go by. I retrieved my textbooks as other kids piled inside the room, some laughing at a joke, some looking like this was the last place on earth they wanted to be. On the blackboard, Willie had scribbled some illegible words with white chalk, but I had a feeling one said 'prepositions'.

Sharon sauntered inside and approached me, her lips red and swollen. 'You okay?'

Teeth grinding together, I nodded.

'Honest? 'Cause you don't look good.'

Helen ambled in behind her, her short brown hair pulled into ponytails on either side of her ears. 'Hi, Kylie – what happened this morning?'

'Nothing.'

'Why are you sitting up the front?' Helen asked. 'You *never* sit up the—'

Willie cleared his throat. 'Miss Baldwin, Miss O'Rourke, please take your seats; there will be plenty of time for cavorting at recess and lunch.'

'*Okaaaaay,*' Sharon said, flicking her gleaming hair behind her shoulder and strolling towards the back with Helen. I glanced out of the doorway and spotted Trix leaning against the far wall of the corridor, eyes narrowed on me, his forehead pinched.

He looked as hurt as I felt.

Willie Miller grabbed a stick of white chalk and opened his paperback copy of *Sophie's Choice*.

'Allrightyroo, boys and girls, take out your books if you haven't already done so.' He raised the hand holding the chalk and started singling out people – his usual ritual before class. 'Chad Hogg, spit out your gum; Ian Younie, fix your collar and tie so you don't look like a drunken Hemingway; and Nathan Leslie … where is your book?'

'My dog ate it, Sir.'

The class erupted into guffaws. Well, the rest of the students howled; my chaotic thoughts still immobilised me. Trix had taken off about a minute before the last student rushed in, his wounded expression making me want to run to him and console him, despite my newfound knowledge. Helen *had* tried to warn me: *'He's naughty.'*

Willie used the back of his hand holding the chalk to rub his chin. 'What breed is it, Leslie?'

'German shepherd, Sir.'

'German? Well, that explains why he ate it – considering *Sophie's Choice* references the Holocaust. He's probably ashamed of his own heritage.'

Although I think this went over most of the class's heads, some students laughed all the same.

'Righto. Who can tell me what parallels are drawn between—' Willie stopped and turned to the door as it opened.

His back straightened and his grey-brown eyebrows rose. 'Ahhh, Miss Ashcroft. How lovely of you to grace us with your presence. Did you also have trouble with your pooch eating your paperback?'

Everyone laughed again, but I gripped the edge of my desk hard. I'm surprised still to this day, that Willie didn't pick up on anything regarding Tahlia's demeanour that morning. Then again, we were the ones who hung around her every day; we'd noticed her shift in mood.

Tahlia shook her pasty-white head, glancing at the floor. 'No, Sir. I forgot to set my alarm.'

Willie hissed back air, making his potbelly swell. 'I swear … you kids have made me lose my marbles.'

'I'll find 'em, Sir!'

I turned around to see Ian Younie drop to his knees, searching the floor, looking under the shoes of his fellow classmates for the 'missing marbles'. Everyone laughed harder, but the sad thing was … Ian was for real.

Stifling a laugh, Willie said, 'No, Younie, it's an idiom.'

'Ha! Sucked in!' Aaron Downes said, pointing at Ian. 'The teacher called you an idiot!'

All the students cackled; even Willie joined in, pinching the bridge of his nose after removing his glasses.

'No, Mr Downes, an *idiom* – as in a common expression.' He turned to Ian. 'On your feet, Younie; I'll find my marbles on my own time.' He pawed the air and grinned, and Ian rose to his feet, cheeks as red as poppies. Chad Hogg punched Ian in the arm playfully, but Ian flicked him away, scowling.

Willie repositioned his glasses and grinned. 'Miss Ashcroft' – he motioned towards a vacant table – 'please take a seat.'

With my mouth agape, I eyed Tahlia as she shuffled past my desk. Her head drooped as she trudged along, clutching her folder and textbooks to her chest. My heart ached just looking at her. Her orange hair appeared limp and thin. It wasn't oily, but it looked deflated, which seemed to match Tahlia's energy. Gone was her beaming smile that made me believe everything really *was* going to be okay in life, gone was the sparkle in her brown eyes, and gone was her zest for life. It damn near made me cry all over again looking at her that day. How was I to know the truth, though? When she'd told us everything was fine, we'd let her be, assuming she didn't want to talk about it. We all behaved like that – hell, I'd reacted the same way that morning when Sharon and Helen had asked me what was wrong. I'd brushed them off, hiding what hurt me the most. I hadn't told them about Keith and Amy's situation, nor had I told them about Trix's pregnant girlfriend at Orange East High.

We all kept secrets; it wasn't like I hadn't *tried* to find out what was going on. So with Tahlia, we sort of let her be, believing she'd tell us when she was ready. No harm in that, right?

Chapter Sixteen

When English class finished, the students rose and packed their bags. I spotted someone's red apple fall to the floor and roll in between stampeding feet. Zipping up my Cheap Trick pencil case, I glanced back at Tahlia, wondering what had prompted her demeanour. Was it her no-good father? Sharon and Helen approached her, but Tahlia kept shaking her head, jerking her shoulder back when either of them touched her. Sharon soon found my eyes and she shrugged: *What should we do?*

Swallowing, I shook my head. Tahlia wanted to be left alone, and who could argue with that? I felt another hot trickle seep out down below. God, it'd already been six days – how much longer did a period last? Was this normal?

The way Tahlia reacted to Sharon and Helen, it was clear she did not want to reveal why she looked so terrible. There was nothing I could do except turn away and head towards the girls' bathroom to change my 'gadget' yet again. As I exited the building block, someone grabbed my arm and swung me to the side, away from the steps, away from other students. My heart already thwacked before I knew what was going on, or who'd grabbed me.

Trix stared at me but let go of my arm. He looked neither angry nor sad. It was so difficult to read his blank expression, it drove me nuts. Why couldn't he be like a flashing neon light with his emotions?

'What happened to you?' he asked.

I shrugged, shaking my head as heat rose to my cheeks. 'Nothing.'

'Why are you colder than ice this morning? Did I do something wrong?'

'I don't know; did you?'

He took a step back, staring at me with keen interest.

Shit. Do I ask him? Even if I did, would he tell me the truth? If he did confess, how would I be able to handle this nauseating feeling of betrayal for the rest of the day? I didn't see how I could cope.

'Just forget it,' I said, turning away.

He grabbed my shoulder, spinning me around. 'Kylie, I don't want to keep grabbing you, but you need to tell me what I did wrong.'

'No.'

He squinted, head cocked to the side. 'I don't deserve to know what I did wrong?'

I glanced over at the kids descending the steps, some of them leapfrogging from the top landing to the ground. No-one seemed to notice us. 'I mean ... I don't want to talk about it.'

'Why?' he whispered, dark brows knitting together. 'Are you afraid of me?'

'I'm afraid I won't want to hang around you anymore.'

His jaw clenched and his eyes lowered to my folder. 'Another rumour.'

It wasn't a question. *Shit. I went too far.* Sucking back air, I said, 'Maybe.'

'What is it this time?' His eyes met mine and I saw their hue change right before me like a mood ring. 'Just say it.'

'I heard you' – I drew back oxygen – 'got some girl from Orange E—'

'Orange East pregnant ...'

My heart shattered. The rumour was true; he didn't even try to deny it. My brother was right after all, but how I wished it wasn't so. Trix was not my boyfriend; he owed me nothing (not even an explanation). But despite that mantra, searing vomit crept up my throat.

He inhaled deeply and closed his eyes.

'S-so it's true, then?' A chasm of silence stretched out between us. 'Hello? Trix ... it's true? Is that why those boys want to bash you? Did you get someone's girlfriend or sister pregnant?'

Damn. It all made perfect sense. Of *course* that's what it was: he'd gotten some poor teenage girl pregnant, and now he refused to acknowledge the baby. With that thought, I had to admit, if I had been the boyfriend or the brother of the girl, I'd probably have wanted to fight for her honour too. We may have drifted away from the conservative '50s, but knocking up a teenage girl and then abandoning her has been frowned upon in pretty much every culture throughout the ages. The lowest of the lows, and now Trix was faced with being a father before the age of eighteen (depending on when his birthday was – I still didn't know). The same situation Keith now faced. Ironic how my brother had called Trix a drongo, but Keith was literally no better. And it was only when I confronted Trix that I understood why Mum had flipped her lid. She was angry because she *loved* Keith and wanted him to succeed in life. Now I felt how Mum had on Saturday night. You're angry because you care; because you're frightened for that person's future and wellbeing. But how could I be so foolish to have thought Trix would be any different from the other troubled boys; that he'd magically be the exception to the cautionary tale?

I touched Trix's arm. His stony eyes were pinpointed on a eucalyptus tree with carved-out initials on its trunk. 'What's her n—?'

I heard the high heels on the concrete before I heard the voice.

'What do we have here?' I spun around to see Headmistress McCarthy behind us at the top of the steps, her hand on the green guardrail. 'What are you two doing together?'

'Nothing, Miss McCarthy,' I said, clutching my folder hard. Trix kept his back to us.

Just then, the wind picked up and carried the smell of tobacco that impregnated her teal-coloured two-piece suit.

Headmistress McCarthy's lips twitched and I noticed her red lipstick had bled into her smoker's lines. 'Well, then, may I suggest you get to your next class? And young Mr Walker, stop hanging around buildings you don't belong in.' She paused, inclining her head. 'Tristan? Can you hear me?'

She knew he could, of course, but what else was there to say to a rebellious teenage boy with his back to you: *Turn the fuck around*?

Headmistress McCarthy breathed in and then out, her grey eyes popping open. 'I will be so thrilled when the summer break is here.' All I could do was smile meekly in response, but there was nothing humorous about it. 'Tristan Walker, are we going to have trouble this morning?'

I grabbed Trix's stiff arm, jerking him. He finally turned around and glared at her.

Headmistress McCarthy's broad shoulders squared. 'Well?'

'No.'

'Good. Then get to your next class.' She then eyed me. 'Same goes for you, young lady.'

'Yes, Miss McCarthy.' Clutching my folder, I brushed past her, but then turned around and saw Trix's stormy eyes on me. This couldn't wait; the anxiety would dissolve my insides like caustic soda – I already felt light-headed. 'Wait!' Headmistress McCarthy turned and faced me as I stared at Trix, walking back over to him on numb legs. 'Is it true?'

Headmistress McCarthy chuckled behind a closed mouth, then inhaled and said, 'I can save you time, young lady, if it's pertaining to this boy here, then the odds are yes, it's true.'

Gripping my folder tighter, I licked my dry lips. 'Trix! Is it true?'

His steely eyes held mine for a silent moment until his shrivelled lips finally parted. 'Yes.'

Chapter Seventeen

On Saturday night, Helen, Tahlia and I gathered inside Sharon's bedroom. I hadn't seen Trix for the rest of that week. No idea where he was or what he was doing, but I did see the rest of the boys, although I tried to avoid them. By now, the rumour of the older Bobby and younger Sharon being an item had spread like staph through a hospital, and I'd overheard students referring to her as Sharon the Skank. Boys would walk by us and shout, 'Show us yer map of Tassie, Shazza!', or sniff the air in her presence and say they smelled fish. I didn't like it, but she *was* putting on a display at school without a care in the world. Sharon rarely gave a fuck what others thought, and I admired that about her. Things that would have made me cry only seemed to strengthen her. She knew who she was, so why should she waste her time worrying about what others said behind her back, especially those who didn't know her? That Bobby was seventeen seemed to be the main reason for the name-calling but, as I said, when we were younger, three years' difference seemed like the difference between a gopher's mound and Mount Everest.

Helen, Tahlia and I lay on our stomachs, leaning on our elbows, each thumbing through a copy of *Dolly* while 'I Like It Both Ways' by Supernaut spun on Sharon's Luxman turntable.

What the hell, I confess: I wasn't flipping through *Dolly*; it was the August 1971 print of *Tiger Beat*, as David Cassidy was featured on the front cover and it was the same magazine I'd nabbed his wall-sized colour poster from. And yes, my crush on him developed when I was six.

Sharon's room also displayed posters, but they were of celebrities she aspired to imitate: Christie Brinkley, Debbie Harry, Goldie Hawn – and, of course, the famous photo of Farrah Fawcett in her red swimsuit.

The bedroom door opened and we glanced up as Sharon and her mother carried drinks and nibbles over. Cheryl O'Rourke was the archetypal woman who couldn't let her youth go. Her peroxide-blonde curls were supported by about a can of hairspray, she drew on pencil-thin eyebrows, and her long acrylic nails made it hard for me to believe she could function properly in her normal, day-to-day life. I even wondered how she could wipe herself down below with nails that long. Her enormous boobs were always pushed up high as if to say: *Check out these headlights.* I'd never seen Cheryl have an 'off' day with her appearance. Not once did she open the front door wearing sweats or a baggy grey jumper. She'd rather have died of embarrassment.

Her maroon leather miniskirt hugged her slim thighs like an extra layer of skin. But back then, we thought she was the 'Cool Mum'.

'Here we are, girls,' Cheryl said, slinking into the room on her four-inch-high beige leather heels. She placed a tray of snacks in front of us, all the cool things we loved: a pot of melted chocolate, plump strawberries, sliced bananas, pink and white marshmallows.

She straightened, placing her manicured hands on her Barbie-sized waist. 'If you girls need anything, let me know.'

'Thank you, Cheryl,' we said in unison. That's the other thing about Cheryl O'Rourke: she loathed to be called 'Mrs' or 'Ma'am'. I think she would have even preferred for her own daughter to call her Cheryl. She was the antithesis of Helen's mother, who would probably have slapped us if we'd dare try to address her by her first name. That's why we loved hanging out at Sharon's; we could crank up the tunes, eat whatever the hell we wanted, and stay up late.

I looked over at Tahlia, hoping she'd eat something. We must have asked her what was wrong a thousand times this past week alone, and each time she'd given a brusque response.

Cheryl pecked Sharon's cheek before she headed for the door and shut it behind her.

'Your mum is the coolest,' Helen said, pushing her magazine towards the mountainous pile. Sharon owned more magazines than a newsagency, and loved getting her hands on her version of the micro-Bibles: *Cosmopolitan*, *Vogue*, and *Teen* – cutting out photos of women she idolised and sticking them to her heart-shaped mirror.

'You say that every time you're here,' Sharon said, laughing. She placed a tray of Cheryl's homemade cherry sodas on the carpet. Years later, I worked out that it was only lemonade, grenadine, wedges of lime and maraschino cherries, but it tasted like the bomb, especially on sticky summer nights. The chilled glass was always chock-a-block with ice too.

When the song finished, Sharon went to her turntable and moved the tonearm away before replacing the record. The 12-inch spun, and 'The Real Thing' by Russell Morris pleasured our ears. Sharon raised her hands above her head and started swaying, eyes closed, grooving to the psychedelic riff.

'I swear,' Sharon said in a dreamlike tone, eyes still closed, face to the ceiling as her blonde hair shimmied behind her, 'when I smoke weed for the first time, it'll be to this song.'

'Only losers take drugs,' Helen said, swiping a strawberry through the glossy melted chocolate before looking at our gaped expressions. 'What? That's what my mum says.'

'I wanna get taken away ...' Sharon whispered, dropping her hands as her hips undulated. In that moment, she transfixed me as she was transported to another realm, forgetting about everything. That's the power of music, baby, and we had an abundance of songs in the '70s to help us with that existential journey. I didn't see why we'd need weed to chaperone us there. Sharon stepped lightly, turning, hips tilting from side to side as Russell Morris took her on a trip and we remained voyeurs.

When the song finished, Sharon dropped to her knees like nothing had happened before using the tip of a strawberry to scoop up some velvety chocolate. 'Who wants to play Truth or Dare?'

Helen scowled. 'Sha-*ron*! We played that last time!'

'So? Let's play it again.' Sharon stuck the strawberry into her mouth, smearing her lips with dripping chocolate.

Helen picked up a pretzel and dunked it into the chocolate, its colour reminding me of Trix's eyes. He was everywhere. As omnipresent as God. 'Fine. Who starts?'

Sharon leaned under her bed and brought out an empty glass Coke bottle. 'I'll spin.'

We all sat and watched as Sharon spun the bottle and it landed on me. *Oh great!*

Sharon beamed. 'Kylie, Truth or Dare?'

'Truth,' I grumbled.

'Is it true you have the biggest crush ever on Trix?'

My stupid burning cheeks drew pointing and laughing from the others. 'No.'

Sharon slapped her thighs, laughing harder. 'You're such a liar!'

I grabbed a pillow and threw it at Sharon's arm. 'I don't want to talk about Trix.'

'Babe!' Sharon said, eyeing me and grinning. 'What happened between you guys this week? Bobby says he hasn't seen him, either.'

Reaching for the banana slices, I said, 'Ask Trix, not me.'

Sharon rolled her hazel eyes. 'Fine. Don't tell us.' She folded her arms over her chest.

I grabbed the bottle and spun it, watching it settle on Sharon. We all tittered – what were the odds? Of course she said Truth. She always chose Truth. Something I don't think she ever received much of, especially from Cheryl.

Now it was my turn to grin like a jester. 'Sharon, have you done more than kissing with Bobby?'

She covered her flushed face with both hands and squealed as she lay back on the carpet. We all giggled and I glanced at Tahlia, who joined in on the fun too. Whatever problems she had were forgotten. For now.

Sharon kicked her legs out in front of her, stamping the carpet with her bare feet and laughing. Finally, she lowered her hands and grinned. 'I sucked his dick.'

We all squealed, but her flushed face turned into a frown and she sat up. 'Shh! My mum will hear.'

Like she will care, I wanted to say. Instead, I pointed at her red face. 'I totally knew it!'

Sharon flicked her shiny hair behind her shoulders and shrugged. 'Oh well ... I was going to tell you guys, but it only happened last night.'

I wrinkled my nose. *'Last night?'*

'Yeah! He picked me up and we went for a drive to Cook Park. He's also asked me to be his date to the Year 12 formal – finally! I'm totally stoked, deadset. It's gonna be at the Amoco Hall.'

Helen's blue eyes widened. 'He picked you up from *here*?'

'Yeah, why?'

Helen clutched the carpet. 'My mum would have *kittens* if a boy came to my house.'

Sharon shrugged, grabbing a marshmallow. 'My mum's totally fine with it; she likes Bobby.'

'What about your dad?' I asked. 'Does he like Bobby?'

Sharon turned away, her smile fading. 'He wasn't home.' She swallowed the marshmallow and reached for the Coke bottle. 'My turn again.'

Helen held up a hand. 'Wait! How ... how *was* it?'

Sharon grinned, using a knuckle to wipe the corner of her mouth. 'He's big.' Her eyes expanded, which caused us to laugh. 'Like, so big. But it was good. He said I was the best at it.'

We all giggled like mad and Sharon fell on her back, smiling like a teen swooning over Mick Jagger. My eyes travelled to the black-and-white photo of her and her deceased brother, Lonnie, sitting on her nightstand.

'Do you love him?' Tahlia asked.

Sharon lifted her head, craning her neck. 'It wasn't your turn with the bottle.'

Tahlia tittered and shoved Sharon, and Sharon lowered her head to the floor to gaze towards the ceiling. I sprang to my feet and changed the record to David Bowie's *Pin Ups* vinyl, and we were all silent for a moment, consumed with our own private thoughts.

'Sharon?' Helen said after I sat down. 'What's going on with your dad? Why isn't he here anymore when we come around?'

I watched the slow roll of Sharon's throat before she spoke. 'I dunno. Neither does Mum.'

'But does he live here?' Tahlia asked, frowning.

'When he feels like it.'

Helen moved into a sitting position. 'What's that supposed to mean?'

Sharon swallowed again, her unblinking eyes trained on the ceiling. 'He comes and goes as he pleases.'

'How does your mum feel about that?' I asked. To me, Cheryl didn't seem the least bit fazed; perhaps she was thrilled to have the house to herself. Something told me she wouldn't stay single for long. She was a good-looking lady; it wouldn't be long before someone else warmed her bedsheets.

'She's fine. All they did was argue, anyway. She still blames him for allowing Lonnie to enlist in 'Nam.'

'But doesn't your mother care that he's not here?' Helen asked, staring at Sharon. 'Because if he's not here, then he's sleeping somewhere else.'

'Ding-ding-ding!' Sharon said, cheeks rouging.

Helen, Tahlia and I looked at each other, none of us knowing what to say. I may have been naive in some aspects of my youth (like not knowing I had to remove the plastic wrapping from a tampon before inserting it), but this seemed as obvious as skywriting. Bruce O'Rourke had a mistress on the side. And instead of Cheryl wallowing in grief and pity, she acted like it'd been the best thing in the world, which showed how far their relationship had bombed since their wedding day.

'You wanna talk about it?' Tahlia said, sliding over on the carpet, her hand on Sharon's shoulder.

'What is there to talk about? Shit happens. Life is just shit sometimes.'

'Are you ... *sad*?' Helen whispered, staring at Sharon, who lay still on the floor, gazing at the ceiling.

'What can I do about it? Sit here and cry because my father doesn't love us anymore?'

I soothed Sharon's leg. 'He does. Maybe not your mother so much, but he will always love you.'

She raised her head to stare at me, her lips a thin slash. 'You want to know what my *father* said to me the last time I saw him?'

I nodded hesitantly; I wasn't sure I wanted to know because I didn't have many more positive affirmations to give her after this. It's true that in life, some people never should have been fathers or mothers to begin with. I was beginning to think both her folks fell into the category of 'deadbeat parents'.

We all focused on Sharon, waiting for her to tell us what Bruce had said. We listened patiently, but then the song faded and another came on and we were still looking at her.

'What did he say?' Helen finally whispered.

And we waited again, staring at her staring at us, and then it clicked.

'What?' Tahlia said, leaning forward. 'Was it *that* bad?'

'No.' I shook my head. 'He ignored her. Bruce didn't say anything.'

'Ding-ding-ding.' Sharon lay her head flat against the carpet again and covered her eyes with her forearm.

Misty-eyed, I turned to the others. 'Come on, let's play some more.'

'Someone spin for me,' Sharon mumbled.

Clearing my throat, I eyed Tahlia. 'You go.'

Tahlia grabbed the bottle and spun it. This time it landed in front of Helen. She looked mighty pleased and extended her spine, waiting to be asked. *So much for not wanting to play in the first place*, I thought.

'Helen Baldwin – Truth or Dare?'

'Truth!'

Tahlia sat back, ruminating. 'Hmm ... is it true you have a thing for Ed?'

Helen cupped her blushing cheeks. 'I'm not telling!'

Tahlia giggled, pointing at her. 'Go on.'

Helen turned her body away from us, folding her arms over her chest in defiance. 'No!'

Tahlia faced me, her eyebrows puckered. 'She has to answer; it's the rule!'

A knock on the door diverted our attention and, to be honest, I was thankful for it.

'Come in, Mum!' Sharon yelled, removing her forearm from her flushed face.

The door swung open and Bobby Dean stood there, grinning. When Sharon saw him, she jumped to her feet, stepping over the food and drinks in our circle and captured him about the face in both hands, kissing him.

Cheryl stood behind them, smiling like a proud mother watching her daughter graduate from university. There was no way in hell my mother would have let this happen, but who was I to question Cheryl's parental choices? I was fourteen; she was forty!

'What are you doing here, babe?' Sharon said, seemingly forgetting all about her dad.

'Came to see ya.' Bobby peered inside the room at us. Raised a hand. 'Hey, girls.'

All three of us waved back.

Cheryl took his face between her hands. 'Baby, can I get you a drink?'

'Sure! Thanks, Cheryl. You're the best.'

She chuckled and placed a hand over one of her round melons. 'I know.' She winked, then sauntered away.

Sharon led Bobby by the hand into the room, his tight-fitting charcoal bell-bottoms doing little to conceal his ... um, package.

'What you girls doin'?' He plonked down on the side of Sharon's bed, the springs creaking.

'Not much, just playing silly games,' Sharon said, beholding him through dreamy eyes.

Bobby bobbed his head, gazing about the room, looking at the posters, eyeing the turntable that'd switched to 'Sorrow'. 'That's a dope song; Bowie's madhouse. Got any Sex Pistols?'

Sharon giggled and kissed his cheek.

Bobby locked eyes with me. 'What'd you do to Trix?'

Everyone turned to look at me, and it felt like my skin shrivelled under the accusatory stares. 'Nothing.'

He hooked a brow. 'Oh, yeah? Then why the hell hasn't he returned my calls?'

'I don't know – ask *him*.'

Bobby slapped his thigh. 'I was thinking of doing it. Wanna come wiv?'

Sharon gasped. 'Yeah, let's go!' She then looked at each of us. 'Wanna see Trix? It'll be fun!'

Helen and Tahlia eyed me as if to see if we should. I wanted to say no, because I was still hurt over something I wasn't really sure I had a right to be hurt over. Trix was not my boyfriend, nor would he ever be. He was free to do whatever he pleased, but try telling my aching heart that.

'Come on,' Sharon said, pleading more with her eyes than her tone. 'Let's go for a drive.'

'I don't think so.'

'Mum! Hey, Mum!' Sharon shouted, a hand cupped to the side of her mouth. No-one thought to turn down the music – to do so would be sacrilege to Ziggy Stardust.

Cheryl shimmied into the bedroom. It seemed she'd applied more lipstick and her boobs sat higher. Call me loco, but I *swear* she'd pushed them up. Was she expecting company? Somehow, I didn't think so. I snuck a glance at Bobby, who was staring at Cheryl's bazookas.

'We're gonna go for a drive now – if that's cool?' Sharon said, already slipping into her yellow wedge platforms.

Cheryl looked at us in turn. 'It's not up to me; it's up to your friends.'

'They said yes.'

'Whose car are you driving, baby?' Cheryl said to Bobby.

'My old man's.'

She raised a thin eyebrow. 'Does he know you're driving it?'

Bobby grinned and turned his face away, the biggest display of mischief I'd ever seen.

Cheryl licked her lips, glossing them. 'You kids.' Her eyes flickered, but the grin splitting her face in two said she was loving being the cool parent in this situation.

'Can we, Mum, please?' Sharon asked, her face a mask of desperation.

Cheryl grazed the sides of her bouncy blonde curls with her fingernails – not that her hair moved much, thanks to the lacquer. 'Oh ... well ... I guess so.' Then she pointed a talon at each of us. 'Be careful, girls. I don't want any angry phone calls from your parents tomorrow.' She gave us a close-lipped smirk as her head dipped and a conspiratorial eyebrow rose.

We all assured Cheryl we'd be on our best behaviour.

'Can we grab our drinks in takeaway cups?' Sharon asked, her arm draped over Bobby's shoulder.

Cheryl's head reeled back. 'What am I; your maid?'

Sharon frowned and pursed her lips. 'Mum!'

Cheryl threw a hand in the air and ran her rosy tongue across her top lip. 'Okay-okay, don't get in a tizzy.' When she bent down, Cheryl squeezed her boobs together with her upper arms as she collected the glasses from the floor. I snuck a glance at Bobby, who was receiving kisses on the cheek and neck from Sharon, but he was staring at Cheryl's breasts while discreetly adjusting his crotch.

Chapter Eighteen

Bobby pulled up to Trix's house and killed the engine, cutting off Mi-Sex halfway through 'Computer Games'. My sweaty hands were clenched together in my lap and it was on the tip of my dry tongue to tell Bobby to turn around.

'Right,' Bobby said, craning his neck to look at Helen, Tahlia and me in the back seat, 'everybody out.'

'Wait.' I leaned forward, clutching his shoulder. 'What if he doesn't want to see us?'

'Yeah,' Helen said, fingers twisting together in her lap. 'What if he isn't home, or he's in bed?'

Bobby snorted and pointed to the house. 'The lights are on, and his car is right there.'

That was true. Trix's Pontiac Phoenix sat in the driveway, and I wondered why he was at home on a Saturday night by himself. Or did he have company?

'Come on.' Bobby opened the squeaky car door first, and we followed suit, hopping out into the springtime breeze and making our way over to the one-storey brick house.

'Where's his father?' I asked, my kneecaps gelatinous.

Bobby turned around. He led the pack, holding hands with Sharon as he walked backwards. 'His old man's probably at the pub again.'

My jittery fingers caused the ice cubes in my takeaway cup of cherry soda to rattle, and as I stole a glance at Trix's house, the cup slipped from my grasp. As soon as it hit the concrete, the lid popped off and ice hit my legs, but worse, sticky red liquid splashed against the driver's side door of the Pontiac.

'I'm so sorry,' I said to no-one in particular, watching the dark liquid run down the driveway. *I'm such a moron!*

'Meh, don't worry about it, babe,' Bobby said, walking back over to me and kicking the empty cup into a nearby bush. 'The next rain will clean the car.'

'Spewin',' Sharon said. 'What a mess.'

Keep your shit together, Kylie! Just relax and breathe! He's only a boy.

'You can have some of mine,' Helen said, holding out her cup to me.

'It's all good,' I mumbled, watching Bobby hurry back over to Sharon. 'But thanks.' *Breathe!*

Helen, Tahlia and I linked arms as we followed the others to the front door. Through the vertical glass panel on one side of the door, I peered inside with a thundering heartbeat and could see Trix sitting on a moss-green leather couch, with what looked like homework spread out in front of him on a wicker-and-glass table. The rubber end of a pencil pushed his upper lip up as he stared at the papers, with deep concentration lines across his pinched brow. Then he punched in a few numbers on a calculator and scribbled something down on a piece of paper.

With a fist, Bobby hammered on the door. 'Open up, motherfucker.'

My breath quickened, perspiration gathered on my upper lip and my lungs seemed to reject any air I attempted to breathe in.

Trix looked up and frowned, then hopped off the couch, neck outstretched to see who it was through the panel before opening the door.

'Surprise, dickfacc!' Bobby said, holding out his arms on either side of him: *Ta-da!* Trix's eyes diverted straight to mine at the back of the group.

'What is this?' Trix asked, neither smiling nor frowning. I came to accept that was who he was – giving nothing away. He'd make a superb poker player.

Bobby turned and pointed right at me. 'She wanted to see ya.'

Everyone faced me and Sharon laughed as my cheeks burned. My stomach tightened as I held up my hands. 'Th-that's not true.'

Trix held my gaze, but his impassive disposition never faltered.

'Can we come in, man?' Bobby said. 'I need to piss.'

Sharon whacked his arm. 'You were at my house a few minutes ago.'

'*Yeeeaaaah*, but Cheryl put whisky in my drink, and the piss always makes me need *to* piss.'

Sharon threw her head back and laughed. 'Pussy.'

'How about it, man? I'm *busting*.'

Trix eyed Bobby for a moment and then opened the door wider, letting Sharon and Bobby pass. We all shuffled forward, and in the bottleneck Helen and Tahlia squeezed in before me, passing Trix. When I stepped to the threshold with what felt like hollow legs, Trix stood in front of me.

'Not you.'

Searing tears blurred my vision as I whirled around and hurried away. I had just reached the boot of his car, holding back the vomit threatening to erupt like Regan in *The Exorcist* when he grabbed my shoulders and forced me to face him.

'You and I need to talk.'

Hot tears cascaded down my burning cheeks as I struggled against his grip. 'Leave me alone.'

He released me and took a step back. 'I will. I promise I'm going to leave you alone, but you need to hear me out first.'

Wiping my face with both hands, I nodded. ''Kay. What do you want to talk about?'

'Not here.' Trix hurried back to the front door. He leaned inside, said something to those in the house, and then closed the door. Within seconds, he had strolled ahead of me – but not before he gave the dark spillage in his driveway the once-over. 'Come on.'

Like a dutiful puppy, I followed my master. Talk about embarrassing; it hadn't even been my idea to visit Trix in the first place. At the end of his driveway, he turned right and walked along the street, under the diluted light of the streetlamps. He sauntered with his hands in the front pockets of his flared blue pants, not with that confident gait I had grown to adore, but not dragging his feet, either.

'How have you been?' he asked, facing forward, eyes on the road as he dodged a parked panel van with purple curtains concealing the back windows.

I've missed you so much. 'Okay, I guess.'

'How has school been?'

'Why weren't you at school?'

He continued walking, but I could hear him breathing through his nostrils.

'Trix … I don't know why you're mad at me.'

He spun around, standing an inch away from me. 'I told you right at the beginning when we first met: don't always believe everything you hear.'

A fresh wave of tears flowed down my hot face. 'I didn't say I believed it.'

He narrowed his eyes. 'But you do.'

'You said it was true.'

He sneered. 'It'd be easier for you to believe that about me, huh?'

Shaking my head, I sniffled and swallowed past a knot in my tight throat. It felt like sucking a golf ball through a drinking straw. 'I don't know what the right answer is.'

'I do. I know how you feel about me and what you believe to be true.'

I balled my clammy hands, looking at the road through blurred vision. 'I'm confused. Is it true or not?'

'You heard Headmistress McCarthy the other day: if it's about me, then it *must* be true.'

I chanced a look at him again. 'Trix, I didn't say I believed it; I just wanted the truth!'

'But if you even had to *ask* it …' He spun around and continued walking. 'Forget it. You'll never understand.'

I raced after him, my neck pulse throbbing. 'But I want to understand.'

'No. You need to stay away from me.'

Heart constricting, trying to keep up with his stride, I said, 'I don't want to!'

'You need to. For your own good. You're too young to understand anything.'

Who the hell was he to tell me I was too young? Raw emotion grabbed hold of me as I halted and then punched him in the back. Lord knows why; I had never even hit Keith before, not even growing up and messing about as kids. But I was brimming with emotions, my mind whirling like a cyclical washing machine spinning one way, then the other. I no longer knew what was right, nor what was wrong; I neither knew what I believed, nor whom I could trust.

The punch stopped him in his tracks, though; that was a bonus. I retracted my fist and held it to my wired body. When he turned around, I thought he would strike me, or at least push me. But he stared at me, with neither hatred nor irritation.

'Why'd you do that?' he whispered.

The soft tone of his delivery made me cry harder. 'I-I don't know. I'm sorry, I guess you want to hit me back now, but—'

'Hit you? I've never hit a girl in my life. But, of course, if that's what the rumours state, then hey, I guess it to be true.'

'I just want the truth. There are so many rumours going on right now I don't know what to believe, and I still don't even know you.'

'You are *exactly* right. You do not know me; you'll never know me; you and I are not cut from the same cloth.'

'What does that mean?'

'You'll never belong in the dumps where I am. You're too good for that shit.'

I licked my lips, tasting salty tears. 'Can you give me a straight answer, please? I'm confused and I don't know what to say or do, and you're mad at me, but I don't know why.'

He turned and walked away.

'Do you want me to ... go?' I wiped my wet nostrils and sniffled again.

'No. I want you to come with me.'

Without another word, I followed him, making sure I stayed just a step behind him. Fear flashed across my mind. I didn't know which part of Orange we were at, nor did I take notice of what street I was in. We strolled in silence until the end of his street, then we hooked a right and within a few yards we faced a kids' playground. He stepped over the horizontal log barrier with ease and headed for the swings. He plonked down on one, causing the chains to jangle and bounce – the metallic sound prompting a dog to bark: *YABBA-YABBA-ROW-ROW*.

I followed and sat on a swing beside him, gazing skyward. Grey clouds drifted across the full moon, marring its excellence.

'There's this girl, Nicole Sullivan, over at Orange East High, and she's in the same year as us – Year 12, I mean, not your year.' He breathed in deeply through his mouth, then exhaled through his nose. 'She's this pretty blonde girl who was dating the footy captain, but a few months back this guy broke up with her for another chick. Nicole got upset about it and said she would take revenge on him and the new bird. So, she went out that night. It was a Friday and I was with the boys, driving around, doing stupid shit and smoking weed. But we had a deal to make with some boys from Orange East High.'

'Drugs, you mean?' I whispered, staring at his profile.

'Yes. Weed.'

'How do you know the boys from that school?'

Trix turned to me. 'I know lots of people in this town. Not just those from our school.' He clutched the chains on either side of him. 'Anyway, we pulled up to our arranged location and made the deal. We gave the guys some drugs, we got the cash, and they left. We stayed around and smoked a bit of weed, listened to some music, drank some beer—'

'Where were you?'

The leaden pause suggested he was wondering whether to tell me. 'At the Wade Park sports ground.'

''Kay.'

'Then we see this blonde chick staggering towards us. It was clear she was off her chops; she was all over the place, wearing this slutty miniskirt and white leather thigh boots. Yeah, sure, some of the boys made jokes about doing things to her. But it was only shit-talk – you know the boys – Ed and Mike are still virgins. When she reached us, she flirted with every one of us, touching us on the chest or bicep, giggling, making a fool of herself. I think it was Mike – no, Ed – *Ed* asked her what she was doing out by herself at night. And that's when she told us what had happened. Her boyfriend had picked her up from her house, told her he was dumping her, so she got out of his car, went to score alcohol from someplace, then she took off, staggering towards home blind drunk.

'Mike offered her some weed to calm her down, and after she drank more of our beer and smoked a lot of our weed, I told her I was taking her home. She didn't want to go. But I said she was done for the night, and I grabbed her wrist and led her to my car. I told the boys I'd be back after dropping her home. She was kicking and screaming and calling me a motherfucker because she wanted to stay and party. But I wasn't having any of it. I managed to strap her in my car, but she wouldn't tell me where she lived – as if I knew; I'd only just met her.

'So, I drove around, begging for her to tell me where she lived so I could get back to the boys. She then said I should ... fuck her.' He cleared his throat. 'Sorry about all the language, Kylie, but that's what she said. Instead of being angry, she turned slutty, and then pulled her top down and grabbed her boobs, trying to get me going. I told her if she didn't pull up her top, I'd drop her off on the side of the road and leave her there. Nicole thought I was playing hard to get, so she reached over and grabbed my ... she grabbed me, if you know what I mean?'

I nodded, clinging onto the chains of the swing. I was young, but not *that* young. I'd learned about penises and vaginas in school. Or, as my Sex-Ed teacher called them, holes and poles.

Trix turned to me as I remained immobile and silent. 'I smacked her hand away, okay? I didn't punch her or anything, but I was still driving and she kept reaching for me ... so I smacked her hand away again after she squeezed me tight, and pulled over to the kerb. I told her to get out; I even undid her seatbelt. And I *truly* didn't want to leave her there by herself in her state; anything could have happened – she could have thrown up and choked on her own vomit – but I wasn't going to drive around with her groping me. I gave her one last chance. I said to her, "Tell me where you live or get out – it's your choice." She spat in my face, called me a faggot, and then she got out, slamming the door so hard my whole car shook.

'I sped off and left her there on the side of the road, under a streetlamp, in the middle of the night, watching her give me the bird through my rear-view mirror as I wiped her spit from my face. I thought that'd be the end of it, but of course, I wouldn't be talking to you if it had been.

'Couple of days later, I heard through local gossip someone from Orange East High had been raped. And in my gut I *knew* it'd be Nicole spreading rumours. As you know, some rumours are jumbled like Chinese whispers; it's not the same as from the front of the line to the back, right?'

He waited for me to nod.

'At first, I heard Nicole was gang-raped by boys from our school. Then I overheard someone say *I* had raped her before dropping her off at her house.' He captured his lower lip between his teeth and then released it. 'I only knew one thing: *none* of us there that night touched her. Though the thing is, Nicole became pregnant, but there's no way in hell it could be mine. I never laid a hand on her.'

Taking a minute to fuse thoughts together, I said, 'How do you know she's pregnant, then?'

'The doctor's report. It confirmed everything. I never saw it myself, of course, but others did.'

I remained silent until I could trust my own voice. 'But why do people think it's yours?'

'I told you: she made up a story about me raping her.'

'No, I mean, if she really is having a baby, then why couldn't it be anyone else's?'

'Because the timing matches up to the night I met her, and ... she hadn't had sex before.' He hooked oxygen through his nostrils, focusing on his thigh. 'She was a virgin, Kylie. That's why her boyfriend broke up with her – he'd been sleeping with the new chick because Nicole wasn't putting out. I know it sounds unbelievable, a virgin begging for sex from a stranger, but I guess when she was dumped for being frigid, something inside her snapped – no more Miss Nice Girl – either that or she desperately needed to feel something other than the betrayal of a cheating boyfriend. And according to gossip, Nicole also did a rape exam at the hospital and they found blood on her – whoever did it was as rough as guts.' He cleared his throat and pounded his chest once. 'Vaginal tearing.'

I cupped my mouth, not wanting to scream and wake up those in the surrounding houses. I had no idea what time it was, but I guessed it to be close to midnight.

Oh God, that poor girl! The visuals of what a vaginal tearing looked like caused my tight guts to constrict harder.

Trix held my gaze and, in the moonlight, pain swam across his glinting eyes. 'Someone raped her. But it wasn't me.'

'What did you do after you dropped her off?' I whispered, trying to breathe through the anguish.

He held up a hand as if swearing before a court. 'I drove straight back to the boys. I told them what happened and yes, one of them made a joke about me having sex with her – "You rooted her first, didn't you?" one of them said – I can't remember who – probably Mike. I was so pissed off by the time I arrived back – and don't forget: I didn't know where I'd taken her; I'd driven around blind while asking her where she lived – so I told the boys the night was over. Everyone piled into my car and that was the end of our night. I dropped each of them home before I went to bed. I never saw Nicole again after that.'

Hand to my tingling chest, I said, 'So, someone raped her *after* you dropped her off?'

'Yes.'

'Does that have anything to do with you taking time off from school?'

His back stiffened and his chest expanded. 'A formal investigation was done. I was suspended.'

I furrowed my brow; things were not making sense! 'But they let you back into school?'

'Nicole miscarried.'

'She—?' My breath caught in my throat; I couldn't utter a sound.

'She lost the baby. Now we'll never know whose it was. But I was waiting for that day when they did a blood test to prove I'm not the father. I was counting on it to save my arse.'

Fingernails digging into my thighs, I said, 'I-I don't know what to say.'

'What *can* you say?'

I couldn't gather my scattered thoughts into anything coherent, so I stared at Trix, watching how the moonlight played on his hair, birthing shades of dark blue; it reminded me of a raven's sleek coat after the rain.

'They only let me back into the school because my father threatened to sue both them and Orange East High, and without proof of what happened, the school had no choice but to let me back after I did a reform course – to cover all bases, I guess. There are only two schools in Orange, so it's not like I had much of a choice; they couldn't force my father and me to leave town over what someone said happened with no proof. The only physical evidence I had to back my innocence disappeared. But as you know, rumours stick around. Just look at our school; how many teachers do you know have had rumours spread about them?'

Truer words had never been spoken. I could think of a rumour for nearly all of them. Our headmistress being a closet lesbian; Mr Evans (my Science teacher) jerking off to kiddie porn ... so many more. Right then, I felt as low as pond algae for entertaining the thoughts. Some of those faculty rumours dated back years. Whoever started them was long gone, probably had families of their own. But it made me rethink everything, because when I looked into Trix's drooping eyes, I saw the hurt. Even in the moonlight, I saw the same look he'd given me when I'd confronted him about it at school. No wonder he'd said 'yes'. It all made sense now, why he was rebellious and acted out. One time a girl in my History class lied that I had nits and man, that hurt like a bitch. This was about *rape* – just about the worst thing there was. I would have to think of a way to let Keith know he was wrong and shouldn't say things he didn't know were true.

'Nicole has a twin brother, Nicholas – yes, I'm not kidding – who goes to Orange East High, too, and he and his mates have been causing me and the boys problems ever since. A part of me believes this has something to do with the footy final coming up, as her brother's on the footy team. The boys and I have been getting prank phone calls, threatening notes in the letterbox, dog shit thrown at our windows ... you name it.'

'Trix, you're not going to the footy match, are you?'

'Try and stop me.'

I reached out and grabbed his arm, almost toppling off the swing in my haste. 'No! Don't be silly. They'll probably kill you.'

'So your advice is to walk around town with my head hanging low over something I didn't do? If I hide my face, then it says I'm guilty; if I go out in town, I'm asking for trouble.' He scoffed softly. 'I can't win. But I will not let *them* win.'

'What do you mean?'

He fixed me with a stern look. My heart thumped with anxiety over the unknown horrors that lay ahead. 'The boys and I are going to the footy match. No matter what.'

Chapter Nineteen

On Monday at school, I met with Helen and Sharon at our favourite spot before the bell rang. I thought of school as like the African savannah: everyone had their own place in the kingdom – breach it and enter someone else's territory, and you ask for trouble. Those two aluminium benches facing each other had been our turf for as long as I could remember.

'Where's Tahlia?' I said, swinging a leg over the bench and placing my backpack between my thighs.

Sharon was holding up a compact mirror, inspecting a suspicious-looking red dot on her chin. A plastic bag of Milkos lay in her lap. 'Dunno.'

My eyes searched the grounds, not just for Tahlia, but for one person in particular. 'So weird; Tahlia is still not looking like herself these days.'

'I know,' Sharon said, still inspecting the red area. 'Even my mum said Tahlia looks thinner and sadder, but we've all asked her what is going on.' She glanced up from the mirror. 'She won't tell us.'

'What do you think, Helen?' I asked, eyeing people chasing their mates around the quadrangle, leafing through magazines or playing handball. Tahlia was nowhere in sight, so I turned back around to face Helen.

Helen shrugged and bit into her half-eaten green apple. 'Beats me.' She chewed, then swallowed as a trickle of juice slipped from her shiny lips. 'I tried calling her on the phone last night to discuss our music performance, and Lorraine answered and said Tahlia wasn't well. That she couldn't come to the phone because she was sleeping. At six o'clock at night!'

After Sharon had placed her stash of lollies inside her schoolbag, she pulled out her ice-pink lipstick and began applying it while looking in the mirror. 'We don't have much choice, girls. If she doesn't want to open up, we can't force her.'

'She's hiding something, though,' Helen said. 'I just don't know what.' She ate the last of her apple and left the bench to dump the core in the bin.

Sharon snapped her mirror shut and shuffled over to me, grinning. 'Now that Helen's gone, tell me the truth.'

'What?' I squinted, hugging my bag to my chest, the curious look in her eyes like a magnifying glass.

'You sucked Trix off, didn't you?'

Cheeks aflame at the mere thought, I pushed her shoulders away. 'You're gross.'

She pointed a finger at my face about a centimetre away from my nose. 'Okay, maybe not a blowie or even a handy, but you totally kissed him.'

'I've told you a thousand times: we never kissed.'

'Then why did you guys disappear for yonks?' She raised an eyebrow as if to say: *Ha! Got ya*!

I rolled my eyes. 'I already told you girls. It was about Nicole Sullivan.'

'Tell me the story again so I can pick up on your lies.'

When I laughed, she leaned forward and kissed my burning cheek. 'Love you.'

Even though Sharon could be an annoying, embarrassing pain in my arse, I really loved her. She was loyal to those who loved her back, but she relied on boomerang love: the love and affection she threw out needed to be returned. Sharon O'Rourke *needed* to be loved, the way a kid needs to impress his billionaire father before taking over the family business. As I explained earlier, Cheryl wasn't like a mother; she viewed herself as another one of her daughter's young, hipster friends ... just with bigger boobs. Bruce was an absent father, ignoring his own daughter now he'd found a hussy to shack up with.

I've learned that in life there are things people want, but then there are things they *need*. And that can be as contrasting as onions and oranges. There's a constant struggle between internal and external. We all have vices, and we all have certain motivations. For some it's love, but for others it could be sex, money, praise, adoration.

For many, it's success in terms of what makes them happy, as opposed to riches and jewels.

I stared at Sharon, who so overtly *craved* attention, but she *needed* love. And that was a fine line to skate between. Attracting attention for a girl who looked like Sharon was easy, but when you get that kind of attention, it's harder to earn respect.

I wrapped an arm around her shoulders and planted a kiss on her cheek. 'Love you, too, Sunset.'

She pulled away from me, smiling, then her hazel eyes darted to the left of me. 'Oh, hell yes, here comes my beau!' She peered over my shoulder and I turned to see Helen returning from the toilet block after washing her hands, and behind her were the five boys, who were becoming closer to us as the days and weeks passed, headed our way.

I wanted to talk to Sharon about Bobby on a deeper level and ask her what she *really* knew about him – apart from the fact he had sandy-blond hair and knew how to use his tongue. I was having a hard time forgetting how Bobby had ogled Cheryl when she'd bent down in front of him, but Sharon's mum had been laying it on thick. What teenage boy would turn away from an attractive older lady with impressive knockers, especially one who cups his face, looks him in the eye and calls him 'baby'? I was beginning to like Cheryl a lot less as time drew on.

Was I being too harsh about Bobby Dean? He sure seemed to dig Sharon. Apart from them sucking face at every chance, he seemed keen to spend time with her whenever he could. Then again, what the hell did I know about boys, really? I was still smooching David Cassidy's poster.

'Where's my baby?' Bobby said, jogging over, arms outstretched. Sharon grabbed his hands and pulled him behind the concrete block of steps before shoving her tongue into his mouth.

Then little Ed approached, gripping a finger bun smothered in coconut icing. He winked at Helen. 'The stealer of hearts! The girl invading my dreams! The one who—'

Trix smacked Ed's chest with the back of his hand, but kept his eyes on me. 'Morning, Kylie.'

I rose from the bench. 'Hi.' Then I looked behind him to the rest of the boys. 'Hey, guys.'

Mike lifted his black sunnies and peered around. 'Where's Tahlia?'

'We don't know,' Helen said, her residual blush from Ed's declarations fading. 'She's late again.'

'She looked ill the other night,' Trix said, still looking at me.

Ed grabbed Trix's shoulder. 'You mean to tell me you guys hung out without me?'

Mike turned to Trix. 'And me?'

Rodney stood at the back, acting like a guard dog, making sure no-one snuck up on them.

Helen tittered. 'No, you guys, it happened by accident.'

'Was Bobby there?' Ed asked her, feigning puppy-dog eyes.

Helen looked at Trix as if to say he should explain.

'They came to my house. It was Kylie's idea.' He flashed me a lopsided grin, the same one that had stolen my breath the day he'd breezed past me in the corridor. The one that made me blush and giggle, and turn my flaming cheeks away.

The bell rang, right on time.

'Yay! Learning time!' Ed said as he and Mike smacked hands and laughed like loons.

'Have a good day at school, girls,' Trix said before looking at Bobby. 'Let's go, Romeo.'

Bobby leaned back as Sharon panted and clutched his face. He kissed her hard once more and broke away, wiping his lips before running to catch up with the others. Sharon smoothed over her hair and reapplied her lipstick before zipping up her schoolbag.

'Man, what a kisser!' she said, grinning, then threw a peppermint Life Saver into her gob.

I smiled, turned around to look at the boys as they sauntered off while other students gave them a wide berth, and wondered what it would feel like to have Trix kiss me senseless. Giggling to myself, I stole another glance around the quadrangle to try to locate Tahlia – but to no avail.

Chapter Twenty

I searched the grounds for Tahlia Ashcroft during recess and in between classes, and when I went to Period 4 Maths in – a class she also attended – and saw she was absent, I knew she hadn't come to school at all.

Trix and the boys didn't eat lunch with us that day, and I was more than fine with that. As much as I enjoyed their company, I still didn't want to share my friendship group with the boys. Not every minute of every day, anyway. Besides, they had friends their own age, and the girls and I could get back to being our typical, dorky selves – discussing TV shows, talking about music. But the vibe wasn't the same without Tahlia.

When we met for lunch, I suggested we go over to Tahlia's house that afternoon, but Helen said her sister, Melinda, wanted to buy new clothes to wear to the big game on Saturday, and Sharon said her aunt was coming over.

I didn't know it at the time, but her 'aunt' had been an alias for her father. I don't know why I didn't pick up on it back then, because Sharon being my best friend and all, I should have remembered Cheryl didn't have any sisters. But I didn't know whether Bruce did. So, I figured maybe the 'aunt' was *his* sister who wanted to come to see them. I did wonder why Sharon's expression had turned serious when she'd said she couldn't come with me to Tahlia's house.

Sharon told me the real story much later on in private, that Bruce had called Cheryl to organise a time to collect the last of his stuff. Sharon wanted to be there when he came home; she wanted to have one last look at him – for him to see his own flesh-and-blood daughter before he took off to live with the mistress he'd had on the side for God knew how long. Sharon told me the mistress was pregnant, and as far as Bruce was concerned, that new baby of his was the only child he'd acknowledge. Cheryl had had another man in her bed that same night. He'd been half her age. Sharon saw him leave early in the morning when she got up for school, shoes in hand as he tiptoed out the front door, never to return. He was one of a long list of faceless, nameless men who came, *came*, and then vanished. Sharon told me that in the end Cheryl stopped giving a fuck about who might hear her in bed. And it was clear the men cared even less, forcing Sharon to place a pillow over her ears so she could get to sleep at night.

So instead of going to Tahlia's, I rode home, plonked onto my bed and picked up the phone. I spun the numbers for Tahlia's house on my pink Princess phone (I knew Sharon's and Helen's numbers off by heart too) and stared at my Gene Simmons poster while I listened to the phone ring at the other end.

When Tahlia's mother, Lorraine, picked up, I said who it was and asked if I could speak with Tahlia. But this time I said I had an urgent message to give to her from our English teacher, Willie Miller; that he was becoming more than concerned about her absence. When Lorraine heard the urgency in my voice, I assume that's what pushed her to get Tahlia to come to the phone.

A minute later, Tahlia picked up the receiver. 'Kylie? Is that really you?'

Her voice was quivering and I sensed raw emotion, which made me sit up straighter and clutch the phone harder. 'Yes, it's me.'

She sniffled first, then I heard her crying.

My heart throbbed, hot tears stung my eyes. 'Tahlia. Please tell me what is going on.'

'I can't – yes, okay, Mum; I won't be a minute – sorry, Kylie. I love you.'

My throat constricted. I believed she was trying to send me a message, an encrypted code I was meant to decipher. She wanted to tell me, but couldn't because our conversation was being listened to – at least from her end. Why was her mother eavesdropping on Tahlia's conversation?

'You can't speak right now, can you?' I asked, fingering the telephone cord.

'No.'

'But you want to?'

'Yes.'

'Are you going to come to school tomorrow?'

'I don't know – okay, yes, Mum.' She exhaled and sniffled. 'I miss you, Kylie. I love you.'

I wiped my stinging eyes, then shut them. 'I love you, too. *Please* come to school tomorrow.'

'Maybe.'

'Well, I have some of your homework with me—'

'No, Mum, don't—'

The line went dead. Clutching the receiver, I stared at it, picturing Tahlia's face. We were light-years away from FaceTime, but I could see her. I stared hard as if anticipating the answer would appear. Why would her mother hang up on me? What didn't she want Tahlia to tell me?

Chapter Twenty-One

The rest of the week rolled on without anything too eventful happening; however, my anxiety metastasised, as did my heartsickness. Tahlia had returned to school the next day after I'd phoned her, but she'd closed up on us like a clamshell, not willing to talk about a thing. And it hadn't been just us asking about her welfare; other friends were too. A few had approached me in the corridors or at a bubbler, even in the canteen line, and asked me why Tahlia kept missing so many days. I'd told them she was feeling sick, and that was the end of that. Either way, I was happy to see her and be with her again, even if she was only giving us fifty per cent of what she used to be – a meagre decoy meant to throw us off the scent.

Aside from Tahlia and her secrets, my mind was fixated on the fact that tomorrow was the dreaded footy final. Orange West versus Orange East High and, like a storm cloud brewing overhead, I knew in my fluttering stomach that something bad was going to happen. You couldn't have this much testosterone gathered in one place without someone trying to start something. Banners had been placed all up and down Summer Street, tickets were sold out, and Helen and her sister, Melinda, even bought new tie-dye jumpsuits for the occasion. The Wade Park sports ground seated up to one thousand spectators. This was going to be huge. Our town was, in some ways, divided by east and west – and not just because of the footy teams, but for other reasons too. Whatever the reasons, put simply it was about a bunch of passionate families supporting their kid from whichever school, or people like us girls just wanting to show support and have a groovy time.

We'd had punch-ups over it before. Oh, yeah. And they'd found soiled condoms behind the toilet blocks, as well as needles and joints – I'm not kidding. It got wild.

One time, some kid's dad from Orange East kept hectoring the ref, so another dad from Orange West stuck up for the ref, told the guy to calm the hell down or he'd give him a clip round the ear. You can guess how that one turned out.

The footy final was also a way for boys and girls to meet one another. Back in the '70s, if you wanted to meet the opposite sex, you had to put effort into it – get dressed in your Sunday best, do your hair and make-up, iron your favourite pair of Levi's.

I was dreading this match the way an adult might dread getting a mysterious lump checked out by a doctor. Every molecule in my wired body was screaming 'Don't go!' and to just forget about it. But I had to go. Besides, The Sunsets always went; it was another annual thing we did and we looked forward to it, not because we loved footy, but because it was another chance for us to socialise and pretend to be adults for the night. The one thing about the match, though, was there was no designated seating. The organisers had tried that once before, but people ended up complaining – don't ask me why. So that meant we girls were free to hang with the boys, and when I found out that Orange East High wanted blood from our side, well … mingling with the targets was like putting your hand in a lion's mouth and not expecting him to have a little taste.

Don't forget: this was Orange. And while I assume it's still just that quiet, country town it once was, with maybe a new shop or two, and I'm guessing a Starbucks and a Guzman y Gomez, it wasn't like it is now at footy stadium matches, with metal detectors and barcode scanners. Hell no, we all stood in two huge-arse snaking lines on either side of the oval – one on the east-side and one on the … you get the drift. Both sides of the oval would fill up like water flooding into a ship from both port and starboard, as people ran to grab their favourite spot. Sometimes people lined up for hours, waiting to get a decent seat. If you knew you wanted the grassy area on top of the hill, then you could pay a cheaper ticket price and bring your own foldout chairs. That ended up being a popular idea for people who weren't too passionate about the match, but didn't want to miss out on all the fun, either. I had a sneaking suspicion the nine of us – five boys and four girls – would end up on the grassy knoll. Anyone could walk in and around our group from up there. Anyone from the west, anyone from the east. Shit was about to go down. Little did I know how bad it was going to be.

Chapter Twenty-Two

LATER THAT FRIDAY AFTERNOON, the day before the big game, the nine of us met at Lake Canobolas. Because the annual footy final was such a huge event, people were already waving flags around in support of either team – orange shading for us with a purple W in the middle, or black shading with a white E.

I rode my bicycle down to our favourite area, grabbed my transistor radio while it played 'Fox on the Run' by Sweet, and rushed off to greet the rest of them.

'It's about time, babe!' Sharon said, her arm around Bobby's shoulders. He was shirtless, of course – why wouldn't he be?

Trix made his way over, sucking on a joint. 'Glad you could make it.'

'Hey, Trix,' I said, smiling before walking off to mingle with Helen and Tahlia. Helen sat on her mauve blanket with *Bridge to Terabithia* in hand, wearing her transparent purple sunnies. A pack of half-melted chocolate Royals lay beside her.

I stopped in front of Helen as an arid gush of wind brought with it the heady scent of menthol from the nearby blue gums. 'Hey—'

Helen raised an index finger, continued reading, then put the book down and smiled. 'Sorry. I liked that chapter.' She picked up the pack of Royals and raised them. 'Bickie?'

Tahlia walked the few steps over and hugged me. Tight. There was a hidden message behind it, but damned if I knew what it meant. 'Love you,' she whispered in my ear.

Closing my eyes, I hugged her tighter. 'Love you, too, Sunset. Always.'

'Get a room, girls!' We broke free to see Ed beside the giant charcoal-grey rock, grinning. He held out his arms on either side of him. 'Or ... if you get a room, can I join in?'

Trix flashed him a warning glance, not that Ed noticed – he was still grinning.

Helen poked out her tongue at him. 'Shut up, Ed – where are our drinks?'

Ed mocked being offended, his mouth forming an O. 'Is that all this little guy is good for?'

Helen placed a finger to her chin, eyes darting skyward. 'Hmm ... yes.'

Ed clutched his chest as though he'd been shot with an arrow; he staggered around on wobbly legs, making us laugh.

Then something tickled my arm. I turned to see Trix staring at me with a blank expression, his fingertips still lingering on my skin.

'Don't go to the game,' I whispered, my breath catching in my aching throat. Where did that come from? The footy match wasn't even on my mind at that point! No, but it was lurking in my subconscious.

He held my gaze, once again giving nothing away. 'You know I will be there.'

'Be where, bro?' Mike said, coming up to drape an arm around Trix's shoulders.

'The footy final tomorrow night,' Trix said, still looking at me.

'Oh *that*? Fuckin' oath; up the west! Whooo!' Mike screamed, fist-pumping the air, his neck a purply red. Those around him who supported the west cheered along with him, raising their little flags higher. 'And if the faggots at Orange East don't like it, they can suck my dick!'

'See?' Trix said to me. 'The boys are keen to go.'

I shook my head, ready to grab his arms and shake sense into him. 'I don't want you to.'

'I have to.'

I flared my nostrils in an attempt to stop the tears before they embarrassed me again. God, why was I always emotional around this guy? 'Why, Trix? Let's do something else – let's go to the Cherry Inn instead. Who cares about footy?'

'The town doesn't belong to them.'

'It doesn't belong to you, either!' I stormed off, passing Sharon, who was rubbing sunscreen into Bobby's sun-kissed shoulders and neck.

'Oh yeah; that's it, babe.' Bobby rolled his neck around with his eyes closed.

Ed carried our drinks over and Helen handed me a creaming soda. As I took the chilled can from Helen, I heard footsteps rustling on the dry grass behind me.

'Can I talk to you for a minute, please?'

I spun around to face Trix. Everyone looked at us, even Rodney. I gave Helen back the can and followed Trix like a balloon tethered to his wrist by string as everyone eyed us.

Even though it was Friday afternoon, it wasn't as packed as the weekends and also, given this was the night before the big event, people were either at home baking those extra slices of cakes and treats to sell at stalls, or colonising Summer Street, making side bets on who would win the footy match. So it wasn't difficult for Trix to find a shaded, secluded spot among a copse of silver birches, away from prying eyes.

He turned around and pulled me in for a hug. At first I stiffened, as he'd caught me off guard, but within seconds I wrapped my arms around his waist and pressed the side of my head against his chest.

'What worries you so much about tomorrow?' he whispered.

Gosh, these damn tears! I was going to have to do something about them – I didn't want him to think it was my constant state of being. His beautiful heart thumped against the side of my cheek as I said, 'I'm afraid you'll get hurt.'

He moved a hand up and down my back, causing my flesh to tingle. 'Don't worry about it.'

'I am worried about it!' As much as I loved being in his arms – and this was our first hug – I was too full of raw emotion, as I had been when I'd punched him in the back. I pulled away from his comforting embrace, but only stepped back a few inches. 'I'm very worried about it. Maybe I'm just a silly girl who doesn't know about boys, but I can feel something inside me.' My stomach heaved as if on cue, pushing out more tears.

He didn't laugh at my tears or break away, but he raised a hand and grabbed a thick horizontal tree branch, leaning forward. His eyes studied mine.

'I think you're asking for something to happen by going tomorrow,' I said.

'Maybe.'

My eyebrows shot north. 'Maybe? Maybe?!' I shook my head, briny eyes roaming the dry grass as birds twittered around us – giving us their two bob's worth. 'I don't understand your way of thinking.'

'You wouldn't.'

My head shot up and we held the eye contact. 'What's that supposed to mean?'

'Thank you for caring enough about me to cry.' The soft tone of his delivery made me sob even more. Did anyone in his life care about him? Where the heck was his so-called mother, anyway? 'But it's something you'll never have to deal with. You do not know what it feels like to be accused of something so vile and disgusting it makes you feel physically ill. And did you ever stop to think that the person who *actually* raped Nicole Sullivan might be out there, watching me trying to get on with my life while they get on with theirs?'

Admittedly, I hadn't. The person who'd raped Nicole was parading around this town right now, loving life, knowing he'd got away with rape because someone else got the blame – someone innocent. No matter what Trix wanted me, or us, or the students and teachers to believe, he was still just a kid at the end of the day. A mature one, well beyond his years in thinking, but he wasn't even old enough to vote yet.

'But ... I don't want you to get hurt.'

Trix shrugged languidly, rubbing his cheek against the raised arm still touching the branch. 'Maybe nothing will happen.'

'I hope so. I'm trying to think of good things, to be positive.'

The lips smiled, but the eyes did not. 'Good.'

'But, Trix?' I heard Sharon's high-pitched laughter rise above everything and everyone else in the distance. At least they were having a good time. 'What if the boys from Orange East do attack?'

'Then we retaliate.'

'Would you ever run away from it?' He stared at me as I rubbed away the hot tears tickling my chin. 'Trix?'

He hadn't blinked this whole time; I swear he hardly ever did. Maybe he was afraid he'd miss something.

'Are you scared of what they could do to you?'

'Yes.' His hand slid down from the branch and he opened his arms. I fell into his embrace, loving the comfort of him, of the warmth, of listening to his heartbeat. But something else, something new stirred in my belly, and a wave of heat rolled through my entire body like smoke trapped in a glass jar, enough to make me break into a sweat. Hearing Sharon's laughter did something to me; it made me want to be like her in that moment. A girl who knew what she wanted and went for it; a girl who took the reins of her own life and steered the way. If I hadn't heard Sharon's carefree laugh, I probably wouldn't have had the guts to ask my next question.

'Trix ...?' I said, my face still pressed against his chest as a burst of laughter exploded from our group in the foreground.

'Yes, Kylie?' he whispered.

'Are you going to kiss me now?'

His body tensed against mine. I held my breath. Then: 'No.'

My chest heaved and I broke free from his embrace, wiping my flaming wet cheeks. I'd misread everything! How could I be so foolish? I really was just a silly, stupid, naive teenage girl who'd misread all the signs I thought he'd been putting out. 'B-but ... don't you want to?'

Trix averted his gaze and took his sweet-arse time before answering my question. 'I've thought about it more than I probably should have.'

'But you won't.' It wasn't a question. I understood now – having an allegation of raping a girl had scarred him. That's why he took extra-special care regarding The Sunsets; the reason Trix gave Ed and Mike looks of caution if they joked around with us, or said something Trix thought was inappropriate. And Bobby Dean ... well, Bobby was a lost cause. Good luck getting him and Sharon to quit playing tonsil hockey.

'No.' With delicate hands he cupped my face, the beaming sun behind his head bathing him in a celestial, tangerine glow. I parted my lips and took a shallow breath of anticipation despite the word 'no' still ringing in my ears. He stared into my eyes and I thought he was going to kiss me; I believed he would; his chivalry meant shit! His eyes roamed over my lips, but when he peered into my eyes again, I saw tears. He blinked them away and released me, turning his back to me. The safeguard erected once again. 'Come on. Let's go for a dip before it gets too cold.'

I had no choice but to follow him, and the entire afternoon passed in a daze. However, I have some interspersed memories: Mike setting up my radio on the charcoal-grey rock and blasting 'Baby It's You' by Promises; Ed doing a cannonball from the rock I was sitting on into the leaf-dappled water; Bobby and Sharon holding hands and taking a run up the rock before jumping off. I remember Trix throwing me glances now and then. I remember Helen scolding one of the boys who'd dive-bombed into the water and splashed her paperback as she lay on her blanket, and Rodney cooking us a barbeque dinner – simple but tasty: butterflied sausages on buttered bread rolls, with fried onion and tomato sauce. We talked, we laughed. The boys and Sharon downed UDLs, while Helen, Tahlia and I drank creaming sodas as the sunlight dwindled.

Then Mike held up a hand and told us to be quiet. Conversation stopped. A slow smile spread across Mike's face. He turned up the radio and out boomed 'You'll Never Walk Alone' by Gerry and the Pacemakers. The boys all looked at one another as their circle closed. Ed motioned for us girls to bring it in as the boys began singing along to the song. The nine of us soon stood with our arms around each other, belting out along with Gerry's voice. Our circle swayed from left to right, with our arms still draped around one another. I remember looking at Ed going for gold, singing so hard-out his neck and face turned as red as a cardinal; Helen sang with her eyes closed; Sharon made eyes at Bobby (what a surprise); Rodney actually got into the song for a bit, and for the first time in weeks, Tahlia's face lit up the way it used to. Whatever was ailing her was forgotten in that moment as we all let loose, belting out an absolute ripper of a song. Trix eyed me from across the huddle, and it seemed he was singing to me, and me alone.

We sang our hearts out to the point that those surrounding us tuned their radios in to 2JJ and joined in, and for a moment I believed everyone at the lake, from one end to the other, was united like one harmonious choir. I've never experienced anything like it since: a complete moment of togetherness, all our worries nothing but a drop in the ocean. When the song finished, some people clapped to us, but Mike went to the radio, turned down the volume, and then came back and we all hugged each other. We didn't say a word; we just looked at the person either side of us, embraced them, then broke free and hugged the others. Maybe it was a divine power foreshadowing what was to come. Because I sure didn't have a clue.

I had no idea it would be the last time all nine of us would ever be together again.

Chapter Twenty-Three

We lined up outside the Wade Park sports ground just after six p.m., ready for the seven-p.m. kick-off. Trix had driven the boys – except Mike, who'd injured himself that day while helping his brother move out of home. Apparently, a chest of drawers had come down on Mike when he was walking backwards down the stairs.

The girls and I found one another soon enough, and stood in line while the boys located us. Sharon's tongue plunged into Bobby's mouth before the rest of us had a chance to say hi to him. Trix hugged each of us and we stood around, laughing, making bets on what the score would be. People wore colours representative of their team. Orange for the west; black for the east. Towering floodlights saturated the oval and when we reached the front of the queue, a frizzy-haired woman used a hole puncher on each of our tickets, muttered a grunt followed by an abrupt 'Move along!' My apprehension and anxiety increased as we shuffled inside the grounds.

The footy pitch lay to the right-hand side of us, and up ahead I looked at the flood of spectators wearing black for the east-side boys. They filed inside, waving homemade banners and yelling out, stirring up the crowd. The canteen to our left sold everything from Big Ben meat pies to sausage rolls. Customers were already lined up in rows of four, and it only grew as more people arrived and wanted a tea or coffee before kick-off.

'Where are we going to sit?' Helen asked, shouting above the chatter.

'Let's go up here!' Ed said, pointing to our right, behind the seating area. A grassy hill wrapped around the circumference of the oval, overlooking the seats and pitch. Spectators were already seated on foldout chairs or blankets, but most were standing and talking to those around them. Some took photos of the pitch, even though the players weren't there yet.

'Yeah, good idea, Ed!' Helen shouted back, adjusting her yellow headscarf, her eyelids caked in blue eyeshadow.

Trix grabbed my elbow and we all trudged up the sloping hill towards the top, walking past adults blowing steam off their Styrofoam cups of bitter-smelling instant coffee, and kids running around everywhere. Litter already defaced the greenery: crumpled beer cans, Wizz Fizz packets, Polly Waffle wrappers.

Trix's hand on my elbow felt as comforting as a hot lavender bath after a stressful day, but that didn't mean it settled my queasy stomach. I kept glancing over to the far left at the droves of people dressed in black, dotting the grass. Any one of them could have been friends with Nicole and Nicholas Sullivan. Would they search for Trix and the boys? I knew that no matter what, our boys were going to come to the game, so if drama unfolded, I couldn't turn around and say I was surprised. When we found a swathe of grass big enough for the eight of us, we began spotting things about the pitch: 'That green grass looks good enough to eat' – trivial stuff.

Trix leaned down to my ear just before the organisers blasted 'Immigrant Song' by Led Zeppelin to liven up the crowd. 'Do you want a Chiko Roll?'

Mum had already made sure Keith and I ate her special apricot chicken before we came, so I shook my head. Lord knows where Keith and Amy were; I'd ridden my bike here while he'd driven over to Amy's house to pick her up. My oldies never attended these things, but I was sure Cheryl O'Rourke was lurking around somewhere, probably checking out the footy teams, wondering who she could seduce. Helen's older sister, Melinda, was already here too, but I had yet to see her.

'You sure?' Trix said. 'I'll go down and buy us dinner.'

'I'm fine. But thank you!'

'I'll be back.'

When he turned, I grabbed his arm, spinning him around. 'I should go with you!'

'No, you stay here. I'll be fine.' He left and I watched him weaving in and out of people on the grassy hill until he disappeared.

Tahlia faced me, a paisley-print scarf wrapped around her orange hair. 'I hope we can win the trophy again this year.'

I turned back to the oval and had to refrain from telling her I didn't agree. I did not want Orange West High to win it that year. That would be the worst thing to happen.

Chapter Twenty-Four

After twenty minutes had passed, the gnawing worry inside my stomach had just about dissolved my organs. Fearful something had happened to Trix, I was about to tell the girls I was going to search for him when, moments before the footy teams emerged on the field, he made his way past the now even bigger crowd. In one hand lay a Chiko Roll with tomato sauce cradled in a white napkin, in the other he clutched a glass bottle of Coke.

I sprinted to him, hugging him about the waist so he had to lift his arms up and to the side so he didn't drop his stuff. 'Wow, you were ages!'

'The line was crazy,' he shouted above some squealing kids playing tag. 'There were only three people serving at the canteen.'

Heart rate steadying, I released him and smiled, and we made our way back to the group. A few of the boys had brought along collapsible chairs, but the girls hadn't; we preferred to stand during these games.

Trix and I strode towards a svelte woman and a barrel-chested man. The woman eyed the man and said, 'Did you see that boy and girl kissing like that?'

'Blame the parents,' he said, shaking his bald head.

I side-glanced Trix and he offered a little shoulder shrug. When we approached our group, sure enough, Bobby and Sharon were going at it, seeing who could asphyxiate the other first.

'Do they *ever* stop?' Tahlia said as we came to stand beside her and Helen.

'It's nauseating.' Helen made a disgusted face, poking out her tongue.

'I'll open it for you,' I said to Trix, taking his Coke and twisting the cap.

He looked me in the eye and gave me a devastating, close-mouthed smile. 'Thank you.'

'Welcome.' I handed him back the bottle just as 'We Will Rock You' blared from the speakers positioned around the oval. It was super loud, as those on the hill were closest to the speakers, but I didn't want to say anything and seem like a wuss; that's what you got when you were right at the back. The hundreds of 'fans' – I use the word loosely – roared as the two footy teams spilled out of entrances on either side of the oval. It was in perfect tandem: to our left came the boys in orange shirts, to the right-hand side came the boys in black.

As soon as we saw the Orange East High team, Sharon booed with two thumbs down. 'Poofters!' she yelled.

Bobby laughed and kissed her cheek, and I turned to Trix and rolled my eyes. Helen and Tahlia cheered and clapped for our boys in orange, and that's when flashes erupted from Polaroids and Kodaks as the teams stood opposite each other on the pitch in two straight lines.

'Ladies and gentlemen,' a male voice echoed through the speakers, 'please stand for the national anthem.'

Spectators groaned and grunted before rising to their feet, and soon 'God Save the Queen' drowned out everything else. Some people stood with their hands over their hearts, eyes closed, giving it their all. When the anthem finished, onlookers hollered and whistled.

'Fuck them east-side boys up!' a burly guy yelled, a can of Tooheys New dwarfed by his chubby hand.

I observed the crowds on the other side of the hill, hoping, praying with all I had that this would be a smooth, clean game, and we could all go home safely. But it seemed God was on sabbatical that night.

By the end of the first half, it was neck-and-neck – sixteen apiece. The adults on both sides of the oval were growing rowdy and aggro, some blaming the ref for bad calls, some blaming dodgy players from the other team.

'Did you *see* Wilson push my son?!' a woman in an emerald kaftan yelled.

'How much are they paying the ref to fix the game?' another woman shouted over the caterwauling and booing.

During half-time Sharon needed to pee, so she made me tag along and wait. The line at the entrance snaked for metres outside the block and I longed to be back on the hill, standing beside Trix. Would he ever kiss me? Not in the way Bobby kissed Sharon, but just *one* kiss to see what it would feel like for real. As much as I enjoyed smooching David Cassidy's poster, I was certain that kissing Trix would be a little different and less carbon-tasting.

While I stood outside the dunny block waiting for Sharon to hurry up, I observed the spectators wearing black. To me, they looked no different; they all had hair, two eyes, a mouth and a nose. So, why were people always fighting? We were different sides of one town, not different nations with opposing ideals and customs. But like an African savannah, people fight tooth and nail over their own territory; they are loyal to invisible barriers. Just like kids at school; there are no borderlines divvying up property, but we believe they are there just the same. Even ants have all-out creed wars – reds versus blacks – why can't everyone get along, no matter where they're from, no matter what side of town they live? Why should geography make us targets, and vice versa?

But I digress ...

I finally spotted Keith: in the canteen line, with his arm around Amy's petite shoulders. I waved and shouted their names, but it was hard to hear even the person *next* to you, let alone from metres away. Parents were riled up, and the tied score was all they could talk about during half-time.

Sharon finally emerged from the toilets and wiped her wet hands on my forearms. 'Forgot to wash my hands!'

I swiped my arms. 'Eww! Sharon!'

She flicked a clump of hair behind her shoulder, releasing the ambrosial smell of raspberries, and cracked up laughing. She took my hand and we made our way in and around adults yabbering. We could feel the tension in the air like static hovering around us before an electrical storm. Each side wanted that damned trophy – us, because we didn't like the thought of handing it over, and, of course, the east-side because they believed they were due; they'd worked hard enough for it.

When the siren sounded to signal the second half was about to commence, we shuffled through the snaking canteen lines and trudged up the sloping hill.

'Who d'you reckon is going to win?' Helen shouted to Sharon once we re-joined them.

'How am I s'posed to know? I haven't been watching it!'

Wasn't that the truth. You'd think she and Bobby thought people were here for *them*. At one point while they were French kissing, I saw some people tap the person they were with, drawing their attention to it. Some laughed, while others turned away in disgust and shook their heads.

Trix approached me without a smile. 'Thought you got lost.'

'No; Sharon had to do a poo.'

Sharon shrieked and pushed me as I laughed. 'You're a big moll-faced liar!'

Trix slid his arms around me to bring me in for a cuddle. Sharon stared and grinned. He let go as the two footy teams once again emerged onto the field, the players jumping up and down on the spot, stretching their calf muscles, arms raised in the air as they leaned over to stretch their sides. Soon the two teams were in place, a whistle was blown, the ball kicked, fans turned wild, and scores were added. Ultimately, Orange West High ended up winning by two points thanks to a penalty kick: 24–22. When the ref blew the final whistle, both sides in the seating area rose collectively and got verbal – for different reasons.

'Too fuckin' close for my liking! We didn't come for a dogfight; we came for an arse-whoopin'!'

'Johnston, we know you is bein' paid to fix the game!'

Soon, parents from both sides were pointing at each other in threatening manners. Spittle flew from enraged people's mouths, middle fingers were raised in the air, wives restrained their husbands by pushing their chests. I don't know why the Orange West side was as crazed as it was considering we'd won, but there were always bones of contention.

'Your boy tripped my boy!'

'Your son should stick to ballet!'

It was over pretty much as soon as it had started, though; this was about as wild as it got. After tonight, the citizens of Orange would settle down and revert to their mundane lives. At the exit gates, there was a bottleneck on both sides, and people were still hectoring the 'other side' as they waited to leave. Trix stood beside me and we were at the front of our group. After a moment, Sharon shrieked – a louder and more unusual shriek than normal. Trix and I both spun around at the same time. My heart seized up like a charley horse.

Standing behind our group of eight were about twenty boys dressed in black, all of them glaring at Trix. One of them had tripped Sharon over and Bobby was bending to help her up. For all his bravado, I could see the fear in Bobby's eyes when he realised we were severely outnumbered.

I grabbed Trix's arm, and then turned around with the hope of running away, but the line heading out the front gate was too long. As my heart tried to burst through my rib cage, I looked all around us; I even thought about running down the back of the hill, but there was a brick wall, so unless Trix knew how to pole-vault, we had nowhere to run. The Orange East boys had waited until this exact moment when we would be blocked in from all around. A crowd to the back of us, those in front, the rows of seats to the left of us, a high brick wall to the right. Rodney shot Trix a look, which to me said: *You say the word and let's rumble.*

Trix tried to free his arm from mine, but I squeezed it with everything I had. 'Don't go!'

He turned to me, released his arm with a slight everything's-going-to-be-okay smile, and walked through the middle of our circle to face the snarling guy standing in front. 'Leave the girls out of this.'

Helen and Tahlia gripped me, their fingernails breaking my goosepimpled skin as we stood, frozen, petrified at what was to come.

'We're gonna fuck you up!' a red-haired kid yelled from the back of their posse, pointing at Trix.

'Why don't you just *fuck* off?!' Sharon yelled, holding her grazed elbow while giving them the stink eye.

A brawny bloke with pockmarked skin sneered. 'Which one of you are we going to put in the hospital first?' He then revealed a smuggled-in cricket bat from behind his back and started smacking his other palm with it – the varnished wood dented and chipped in various places. It reminded me of one particularly violent scene in that movie Keith loved, *The Warriors*. The dull thwack of a wooden bat hitting flesh. Sickness cramped my stomach like a fist; I couldn't believe my eyes.

Tahlia turned to me, her eyes wide and full of panic. 'What do we do, Kylie?'

'Why do they want to fight for?' Helen whispered, her hot breath tickling my other ear. 'Is this because of that girl you told us about?'

'Let the girls go first,' Trix said. If he was scared shitless, his steady voice didn't reflect it.

The pockmarked guy hacked up a golly and spat it in Trix's face, who used a forearm to wipe the phlegm from his cheek. Rodney went to move, but Ed pulled him back by his arm.

'Not until he says so,' Ed whispered through clenched teeth. The sad thing was no-one else seemed to notice what was happening. Parents were enmeshed in their own little world, revelling or sulking, but mostly just wanting to get home, and it was still loud with the angry chatter floating throughout the oval.

'I thought you liked playing with girls?' the pockmarked bloke said to Trix. 'You *fuck*! Why don't you rape a girl now, you pussy chickenshit?!' Then he raised the bat behind his shoulder and swung it around, aiming for Trix's head.

Chapter Twenty-Five

Trix ducked and avoided the bat, then lunged forward, tackling the guy to the grass. What happened next was all-out war. The east-side boys began kicking Trix, throwing punches at his back and ribs. Sharon screeched, and Bobby started swinging at whoever he saw as the enemy. Rodney and Ed raced forward, their fists connecting with jaws as heads snapped back, and cries of pain echoed from all around. Boys from both sides raged, throwing blind punches, trying to connect with whomever they could. The cricket bat fell to the ground and somehow, thanks to our boys jumping in to help, Trix scrambled to his feet, clutching cricket-bat guy around his shirt collar. Trix headbutted the bloke, and as a result, the guy's nose split open. Dark blood poured down his mouth and chin like a macabre water feature. Helen and Tahlia screamed and began whimpering as I stood there, shuddering and transfixed. Spectators waiting in the exit line heard the commotion, and then a scrum of men tried to make their way over.

'Hey! Stop that!'

'Break it up!'

'Get off him, ya maggot!'

People pushed past me and when a guy with landing-strip sideburns suckered Bobby in his jaw, that's when Sharon joined in. She kicked and bit and screamed, and then onlookers from the other side of the hill turned around and raced over. At first, the men behind me went in to break it up, but when the adults from the east-side arrived, it turned into an even bigger clusterfuck. Yells, ear-splitting screams and screeches erupted all around. Trix was fighting three guys at once, ducking, copping blows to the head from behind.

And then I looked at Rodney, who'd just knocked someone unconscious. In the blink of an eye, he reached into his pants pocket and pulled out his switchblade. He pressed the button. Out swung the blade. In the sodium floodlights, the tip glittered, and I wanted to yell out that he should stop, just put it away before he caused serious damage, but the rage in his soulless black eyes ... it would have fallen on deaf ears.

Helen squealed and tried to flee the other way, but my feet were planted to the ground, spellbound by violence like I'd never seen it. The sharp blade pierced one guy's belly, and he yelled out in surprise, clutching his oozing stomach as he went down like a sack of potatoes.

'You want some of this?' Rodney roared, beckoning with the fingers of his free hand to ask if anyone else dare tried to take him on. When a boy twice as big as Sharon punched her in the head, that's when I lost all sense of control. Heart thumping, mouth as dry as chalk, I raced forward and started pushing people, pummelling them. Out of the corner of my eye, Trix was in a chokehold as someone else punched him in the gut. His brow was pissing out blood and his bottom lip was faring no better, but he clenched his teeth and kicked out at those who tried to sock him. Trix threw his head back, connecting with the guy who was choking him, splitting his cheek open, and then Trix turned around and clobbered him in the eye.

Bobby swung left and right, crash-tackling anyone before him. Ed also kicked out, connecting with shins and kneecaps, sending boys toppling backwards. I scratched the face of the one who'd hit Sharon, blood dotting the torn skin. He blocked me on my second attempt and slapped me hard across the cheek with his other hand. When Trix saw this, he took care of the two blokes who were hitting him, raced over to me, grabbed the beefy guy by the back of his shaggy brown hair, and punched him in the side of the face before fatso went bye-byes.

Sharon scraped her fingernails down the man who had Bobby in a bearhug and when his cheek bled, he let go of Bobby and grabbed her by the throat. That's when a foldout chair rose in the air and came crashing down onto the guy's back, sending him flying forward. When I looked at the chair-thrower, my mouth fell open at the sight of Helen. She was blubbering and shaking, but no doubt courage had taken over when she couldn't stand the thought of any of the boys or girls on our side getting hurt.

By now, it seemed everyone was flogging someone else. No longer were citizens concerned about getting home; the tension had built up all year in anticipation of this main event. Tahlia also tried to join in, but was she pulling people off of one another, she wasn't throwing punches.

As Trix staggered towards me, chest heaving and one eye clenched to keep out the blood pouring from his eyebrow, someone kicked his lower back and he went sprawling before me. I tried to catch him, but he fell to his knees with a grunt. A split second later, Rodney came charging over and stabbed the guy who'd kicked Trix. As blood began to pour from the guy's ribs, he cried out and hit the deck, his body going into spasms as it flapped about like a landed trout. I looked at Rodney and didn't recognise him. Blood coated his hand clutching the switchblade, blood was smeared on his face and his teeth were bared. His eyes were a crazy black, like a shark's during a feeding frenzy, scanning for his next victim.

Then someone grabbed me from behind and bit my shoulder. No clue who she was, but I screamed as the blonde girl dressed in black held me, sinking her chompers into me. My fist connected with the top of her head and I heard Helen scream, 'Get off her!' and down came a chair on Blondie's back. She screeched and dropped to the ground, then crawled on her hands and knees in between people's legs to locate sanctuary.

I spun around to help Trix, but both boys and grown men were pummelling him left and right. Bobby also copped a thrashing from a group of guys; one fist connected with his mouth, another with his ear, and a boot heel found his groin. He tried to protect himself down there, but he was no match for the four boys. They wanted blood, and they were doing everything to achieve it.

'Kylie, run!' Trix yelled in a strangled voice, but as long as he was here, and if Sharon was doing her best too, there was no way I was leaving. I ran into the thick of it again as my shoulder throbbed, swinging at anyone who was causing my friends harm. Ed lay flat on the ground. Blood trickled from his open mouth, and people trampled his body during the fight – one guy even tripped over it.

Rodney ran up behind someone who laid into Bobby's bloodied face, and stabbed the guy in the back. The boy threw up his hands like an evangelist, his face a mask of pure agony before he collapsed. Bobby leaned forward, scuffed hands on his kneecaps, spitting out globules of blood in between wheezing. But his respite wasn't for long; some tattooed knob charged over and smashed a beer bottle on top of Bobby's head. Sharon screamed, trying to make her way over to him, but Bobby was out cold, blood leaking into his sandy-blond hair as shards of amber-coloured glass stuck out of his scalp.

Sharon slapped and kicked anyone in her way, and I also tried to make my way over, but bodies were piling up around me.

'Kylie, run!' Trix yelled again. Blood covered his face like a Halloween mask, his left eye so swollen he couldn't open it.

'Leave her alone!' I yelled to one moustachioed guy who slapped Sharon across both red cheeks, left and right, and I rammed into him with my good shoulder. He toppled to the ground, and I was about to kick him in the Crown Jewels, but someone knocked into me, sending me flying back. My shoulder hit the ground, jolting it and connecting with my jaw, and then came a sickening *crack*! The sound of a thunderbolt striking a tree, splitting it in two comes to mind. The pain was immense – I felt as though molten lava had been poured over me. I heard Trix scream my name, but I was too dazed to see where he was or what was happening to him. My eyes closed involuntarily. All I could hear was screaming, yelping, swearing, the tinkling of glass bottles smashing, some people even cheering. Then the unmistakable sound of police sirens floated above it. It was faint, but still piercing through the surrounding cacophony. The sirens grew louder, but it didn't seem to deter anyone from fighting; if anything, I think it egged them on, knowing this would be cut short and they'd have to bottle their emotions for another year.

'Kylie! Kylie, can you hear me?'

My eyelids twitched and fluttered open. Tahlia was kneeling above me, crying.

'Are you okay?' Her hot tears dripped onto my cheeks and she sniffled, then someone bumped into her from behind, but she kept looking at me.

I heard Sharon shout, 'Fuck off and leave him alone!' – I could only assume it was about Bobby, even though he was out cold.

'Fuck you, motherfucker!' someone else yelled. It sounded like Rodney.

'You're fuckin' dead, cunt! You're *fuckin'* dead!' No idea who that was – not one of ours.

Tahlia shook me. 'Kylie! Are you hurt bad?'

Even though I shook my head, she sobbed harder, wiping her florid face with one hand and holding me with the other.

'The police are here now.' She snivelled and wailed, but then stopped to take a shuddering breath. 'This will be over soon, 'kay? Hang in there; I'll get you h-help.'

'Kylie!' Trix yelled from somewhere in the distance; it sounded like he was on the other side of the oval.

Someone bumped into Tahlia again, knocking her body forward, but she stayed with me, never letting me go. I closed my eyes. Pain slammed into me from all over, but Tahlia's reassuring hand remained on me the whole time.

The noise died down when the coppers finally made their way up the hill, using their batons to knock people out of the way and club those who were still fighting. By the time people cleared out, bodies were sprawled on the grass like discarded mannequins, and blood seeped into the soil. The jacks tackled Rodney to the ground for refusing to let go of his bloodied switchblade, and they jammed handcuffs over his wrists while he squirmed and bellowed, 'Fuck off, ya dogs!'

The last thing I saw before I passed out was Trix on his wobbly legs, in handcuffs, swollen eyelids closed as blood jetted from the gash on his eyebrow.

Chapter Twenty-Six

My eyelids fluttered open. It took a while for my brain to register that I was lying in a hospital bed. As my vision focused, I could make out my mother standing by the closed blue curtains, tissues in hand, dabbing her leaking eyes. Dad stood beside her, concern lines carved on his pale forehead. Keith's arm was draped around Amy's shoulders, and they both stared at me with drawn faces. A young brunette nurse with chart in hand conversed with an older police officer, who held his hat in front of him. Her nametag read 'Lucy'.

'Where's Sharon?' I asked. My mouth felt as dry as desert sand and my throat had that scratchy feeling when the flu is taking hold of my body.

'Oh!' Mum said, throwing a hand in the air. 'Who cares?! They're nothing but troublemakers! Look at you! What happened?'

Dad gave Mum a sidelong glance. 'Liz ... let's give her some room.'

'Oh, shut up, Jeffrey! Just shut *up*!'

Keith and Amy turned to Mum, but she glared at me. 'Explain yourself.'

'It wasn't our fault.'

'Then whose was it? Huh? It's always someone else's fault, isn't it?'

The young nurse eyed her. 'Mrs Gardner, perhaps you should let her rest for a while. She's free to go home now, but she'll need plenty of fluids and—'

'Actually,' the policeman said, 'we need statements from everyone. And the sooner the better.'

Lucy tilted her chin. 'Then perhaps you should do it at the station, sir?'

He folded his hairy arms over his chest. 'Do you know how many people we arrested tonight? The station is chockers; there's no goddamn room left.'

Lucy stiffened, hooked the chart on the end of my bedframe, then exited through the gap in the curtains. During the awkward silence following her departure, I heard people outside: someone shouting in agony, women sobbing, one male telling a nurse where he was going to shove his foot. Machines beeped, people ran back and forth across the linoleum floor. It was total madness; I'll bet the hospital hadn't been that busy since the 1968 flu pandemic when the global H3N2 virus broke out.

The policeman eyed me. 'We need to hear it from you what happened. Right now, I got blokes passed out, teenagers under arrest, sheilas outside bawling their eyes out … And to think it turned into bloodshed over a footy match.' He shook his head solemnly. 'What is the world coming to?'

'It wasn't our fault; the east-side boys started it. They came at *us* as we were leaving.'

Mum shot me a poisonous look. 'Who were you there with? And don't lie!'

Dad looked on with an expression that said he'd like to help me, but couldn't.

'Just some boys from our school, and the girls.'

'Which boys?' Mum spat out.

'Just … like, Trix, and Ed, and—'

'Trix?' Keith said, his eyes wide. 'You went with *that* drongo?'

I gave him my best evil glare. 'He's not a drongo! You don't know him; none of you do!'

'Even *I* know of his reputation,' Mum said. 'And it's no wonder; his father's on the turps just about every night of the bloody week. He's a no-good boy who'll end up in prison, believe you me.'

'Yeah,' Keith added, 'he knocked up some chick from Orange East High.'

'No, he didn't!' My outburst prompted a cough and my chest constricted, but I was so full of anger. Not only over what happened to us at the oval, but also because I was now being frowned upon for being there at all. 'That was a lie; Trix never touched her. Nicole made it up to get back at her boyfriend for dumping her.'

'But she *was* pregnant,' Amy whispered. 'You can't deny that; there are doctors' reports.'

As much as I liked Amy Jung, and she was a stunning girl with the silkiest black hair I'd ever seen, her words only fired me up more. My bedsheet suddenly seemed stifling, incubating my flaming body.

'She was,' I mumbled, 'but she lost it.'

'Oh, I didn't know that part,' Keith said, his bottom lip protruding.

'This is such a friggin' mess,' Mum said, fingertips at her sweat-slicked temples, tissues still in hand. 'Why would you want to fraternise with older boys?'

'Only by three years; it's not like he's thirty.'

Mum pointed at me. 'That's enough! I knew Sharon was a troublemaker – believe you me, I'm going to have a word to Cheryl about this.'

It was on the tip of my dry tongue to say I doubted very much if Cheryl would even care; that she'd let Bobby into her house and let even younger boys into her bed. But if I wanted to keep my relationship with Sharon alive, then I needed to keep quiet and let Mum assume Cheryl was as strict as her and Helen's folks when it came to dishing out punishments.

'It wasn't Sharon's fault! And it's not our fault the east-side boys came over to our side with a cricket bat!'

'You shouldn't be mixing with older boys with bad reputations.' Mum stood straighter and looked from Dad to Keith and held up her hands. 'That's it! I can't deal with this family anymore!'

I figured she was about to mention Keith knocking up Amy, but she held her tongue. What a bombshell for my mother, huh? In just a short space of time, she'd learned her seventeen-year-old son had given his girlfriend a bun in her oven, and now her daughter was hanging out with older misfits. I could almost see the grey hairs sprouting through the brown.

Mum placed the back of her hand to her mouth, shed a few tears, then removed her hand, shaking her head. 'We've all lost the plot.'

The policeman sucked in air, making his stomach expand. His shirt looked like a mainsail that'd picked up a good wind. He clicked his tongue. 'So, your story is *they* started the biffo?'

Why was nobody *effing* believing me? 'Yes, it's the truth.'

He annoyed the heck out of me when he scratched the greyish stubble along his jawline, taking his time, even though he'd said he was pressed for it. 'Well, I got half the injured saying that wasn't the case.'

I didn't try to hide inhaling through my flared nostrils. I wanted them to leave me the heck in peace; their bad energy alone was siphoning my oxygen. All I could see was Trix's bloodied and battered face as he'd swayed on his feet before the police led him away in handcuffs. Despite people sniffling and talking outside my cubicle, I could still hear the sound of the slapping when someone had laid into Sharon. My shoulder blade and jaw ached. If only I could close my weary eyes and make it all disappear.

Glaring at the policeman, I said, 'Whose side were they on when the fight broke out?'

'There isn't a side at Wade Park; people from both sides can sit wherever they please. There's nothing to say east and west can't mingle together.'

'But one guy had a cricket bat!'

He cocked a brow in the most arrogant way and said, 'And one of your friends had a switchblade.'

Mum clutched her chest and wheezed. 'Disgraceful! It was only a friendly footy match.'

My boiling flesh tingled with agitation. 'This wasn't about footy.'

'Kylie's right; it's because Trix made someone's twin sister preggo after raping her,' Keith said, shaking his head.

'He didn't!' I punched the bed beside my thigh – a substitute for my brother's face. 'He didn't! Nicole made it up.'

'And how would *you* know?' Mum said, glaring at me.

'Because Trix told me.'

Keith, Amy and Mum chuckled as if to say: *Oh, you poor, naive girl.*

Tears sprung to my eyes, hot, thick and stinging. 'Shut up! Just shut up, all of you! You don't know Trix like I do.'

'I know he's been arrested before, young miss,' the policeman said, bending forward. 'Dealing drugs, causin' blues, tearing up the streets in that Pontiac Phoenix of his as though he's at Mount Panorama …'

Mum leaned against Dad for support; her kneecaps had buckled. 'And you find this attractive, do you?'

Tears clung to my chin, tickling my boiling flesh – I'm surprised they didn't evaporate. 'Just leave me alone.'

The policeman turned to Mum, clutching her left shoulder. 'Liz, she'll need some rest now. Seeing as the nurse has given her the all-clear, if you could manage it, perhaps tomorrow or the next day – if I haven't cleared things up – then I'd like for Kylie to visit the station and give a formal statement.'

'Is that necessary?' Dad said in a thin voice. 'She's just a fourteen-year-old girl mingling with some older kids from school. She wouldn't have done anything wrong.'

Mum clenched her hands in front of her chest. 'Shut *up*, Jeffrey!'

The policeman removed his hand from Mum's shoulder. 'It's not about whether to arrest her; this is about getting a story straight. People have got broken bones, internal bleeding; some are still unconscious. The only reason I'm here now is to keep an eye on things; the tension is thick enough to lay foundations on. People are going to be charged over this and will have to face court. We need to know we're doing the right thing by charging the right people.'

'He knows what he's doing, *Jeffrey!*'

I wanted to ask Mum whose side was she on, and I had to wrestle the urge to call her 'Hanoi Jane', but the fear of what she was already going to do to me – as in what privileges would she take away – already circulated in my mind like vultures around a potential meal. 'Where's Sharon and Trix?' I asked, thinking that was a safer option.

Keith pointed to the left of us. I heard a pair of sneakers skid across the linoleum from outside the closed blue curtains. 'Sharon is in another ward up that way, and Trix is at the cop shop.'

Cupping my eyes and cheeks, I cried, gasping for air. 'But he didn't d-do anything w-wrong.'

'That remains to be seen,' the policeman said.

'Your other friends are outside waiting to see you,' Dad said gently. He didn't say much, but when he did, he made every word seem valuable.

I uncovered my eyes and looked at him, sniffling hard. 'Who?'

'Helen and Tahlia,' Mum said. 'And Helen's parents are *furious*. Can't say I blame them.'

'Are they okay?' I asked, wiping my wet chin with the back of my quaking hand.

Mum shook her head. 'Tahlia keeps crying, saying she doesn't want to leave, and Helen is still in shock – and it's no bloody wonder; poor girl.'

The officer clapped once, a little too loud for my liking, but he said something that put a kink in my leaking tear ducts. 'You folks should take Kylie home; make sure she gets some rest.'

'I'm sorry to cause you so much trouble, Barry,' Mum said, clutching his arm with one hand, clasping her chest with the other as bits of tissue drifted to the floor.

Hopping off the bed, I glared at her. And I *wanted* her to see it. I wanted her to know I was in worse pain than my aching shoulder and jaw, because of her lack of support and her disappointment in me over something I did not instigate. Perhaps I *had* been asking for it by being there with Trix and the boys – I got that. But as I've said before: I didn't regret a thing.

Not even the events that followed.

Chapter Twenty-Seven

By the time I shuffled outside the blue curtains, Helen and Tahlia had been picked up and taken home. The townsfolk waiting on plastic chairs stared at me as I ambled past – some with looks of sympathy, some with anger. The ward hadn't been divided into two factions, of course, so I came face-to-face with those from Orange East. With blood-smeared faces, they sat holding bruised elbows or had bandaged ankles, others just sat with a thousand-yard stare. It was my walk of shame, and for what? I'd gone to the final to have a good time with my girlfriends, and now Mum glared at me like I was an ogre pretending to be her daughter.

When we piled into Dad's station wagon, I half-expected Mum to wait until we arrived home before she ripped me a new one, but I was kidding myself. I hadn't even clicked my seatbelt in when, looking back over her shoulder, her fusillade of verbal attacks started.

'How *could* you?!'

'Liz … she's been through enough toni—'

'This is a disgrace to the family!'

I should have sat behind her, but no, I'd chosen to sit behind Dad because being near him felt comforting, like he was in my corner. I placed my throbbing temple against the window as Dad drove away from the hospital. I'd asked if I could go home with Keith, but Mum had said over her dead body – then she'd added: 'And with the way things are going, it'll be sooner than later!' Gee, didn't that make me feel good. At least Keith and Amy had promised to go back to Wade Park and bring my bike home.

'What are the neighbours going to say? Huh? What about when this gets around town?'

'Liz ... let her get some rest.'

'Would you just shut up?! You never say a goddamn thing and when you do, it's utterly useless. Are we co-parenting here, or am I to look like the bad guy every time? You don't even have a job!'

I wanted to point out that neither did she, but I believed my mother was ropable enough to slap me across the face, and I'd had enough violence for one night.

Mum placed the back of her fist to her mouth again and cried. 'Where did we go wrong?'

Dad drove on, probably consumed by a longer list than Santa's of answers to that question.

She turned to him, the moon's hue shining a subdued light into her glistening eyes. 'Huh? You make me seem like the strict parent, but look what happens. Keith ... knocking up a nice young girl before he's an adult; Kylie ... running around with older boys, participating in bloodied fights. Is this what you want for your children?'

As the car wobbled while travelling over the uneven roads, I stared at the back of Dad's comb-over through the gap in the headrest.

'Well?' she whispered, voice breaking. 'Am I alone in the car, Jeff?'

He shook his head and continued driving. 'Lightnin' Strikes' by Lou Christie played softly on the 'Classics' radio station.

My eyes volleyed between Dad and Mum, watching her crying her heart out, and Dad driving in awkward silence save for the song.

Mum turned to me, her anger resurfacing. 'You're grounded, young lady. I'm confiscating your turntable, phone, and your TV. No more music, no more *Countdown*, no more sleepovers until I say so – is that understood?'

There was nothing left in me to break down and cry. My heart was broken over the fallout of that stupid footy match. No more *Countdown* ... one of the things that had helped me through puberty was now to be taken away from me. Next she'd be ripping down my David Cassidy poster – for what? What did I do to make her hate me so much? I had a fleeting thought of running away – Trix and me, grabbing what we loved most and getting the hell out of Orange – a town that now seemed tainted. The vivid thought of escaping, of hitting the Mitchell Highway and driving until the wheels fell off, made me smile serenely.

'Something's funny, is it?'

I opened my eyes to discover Mum staring at me. Her tears had made tracks in her foundation, and her mascara was smudged in the hollows of her eye sockets.

'No, Mum.'

'Good. I didn't bloody think so. Because if that's not enough, there's a lot more I can take away from you. No more sleepovers, no more hanging with your friends – it's school, and that's it!'

'She's got work as well, remember?' Dad said in a thin voice.

Her lips shrivelled. 'Fine. You'll go to work, but that is it. If I find out you've been hanging out with the girls, or *especially* those boys, you'll be in a world of trouble. I might even pull you out of school and send you to Orange East High. How would you like that?'

'Liz, don't go overboard.'

'Would you shut up, you stupid old man?!'

When Dad drove down Tahlia's tree-lined street, I sat straighter as we neared her house. But I squinted and frowned when something unusual caught my eye; something that didn't belong at her place.

I sucked in air and pointed at the driveway, and as much as I did not want to speak to my mother, I knew darn well she loved to gossip. A person couldn't have diarrhoea in this town without my mum finding out about it, so she'd be the best person to ask.

'Why is there a police car in Tahlia's driveway?'

Mum ducked her head, eyed the house and scoffed. 'I'm surprised you didn't already know – considering Tahlia is your best friend.'

'Know what?' Man, I was confused as hell. Had a copper picked up Tahlia from the hospital and taken her home? But where were they now? The car was parked behind Lorraine Ashcroft's Ford Capri; there was no-one at the front door (plus the porch light was off). That didn't sit well with me – my insides swirling like a tornado and dredging up sharp debris.

Dad slowed down as we passed Tahlia's one-storey house on the right. The front living-room light shone behind the lace curtains, but I couldn't see any shadows moving around inside.

'You didn't know that Lorraine is dating a walloper?' Her flat tone like I was some kind of halfwit.

Frowning, I turned back to face Mum as Tahlia's house left us in the distance. 'What? *Huh*?'

Mum rolled her eyes. 'Lorraine's new boyfriend – Clyde? Yeah? Well, he's a policeman.'

Chapter Twenty-Eight

THAT SUNDAY WAS THE worst day of my teen years. I sat in my room, my turntable and TV taken away, Mum and I avoiding eye contact when we passed each other in the house. Dinner had been a quiet affair. Keith and Amy had joined us for the succulent roast pork and trimmings, and Amy tried to make conversation, but everyone was suffering their own private turmoil. By now, Amy's parents knew of the pregnancy and although they were displeased, they'd said they'd do anything they could to help with midwives, medical bills and baby supplies. Mum and Dad had hardly spoken a word to each other. Not that that was anything out of the ordinary, but the tension in the air was so thick I felt like I needed an oxygen mask to breathe. Dad had escaped to his den to watch his train going round and round, no doubt absorbed in the distraction from the reality of his life. I'd gone to bed straight after dinner and cried into my pillow, too consumed with a sickness of longing to see Trix. What made my situation worse was I could hear the introduction to *Countdown* from my bedroom. Mum, Keith and Amy had gathered in the lounge room, watching my favourite show as I'd been stuck in my room like a prisoner! Dramatic, I know. Tell that to my fourteen-year-old self.

Trix's battered face was all I could picture, and I had no idea what would happen to him – no idea if they'd send him away to another reform school. Although I didn't see why; he had just been standing up for himself. I was convinced Rodney Saliba would end up doing time, though – the police didn't muck about where switchblades were concerned.

Sharon tried to see me on the Sunday morning, but Mum told her I was grounded. Sharon pleaded with Mum, but Mum ended up giving her a lecture on the front doorstep. I wasn't too concerned because I knew I would see Sharon at school the next day.

In a small town like Orange, the news and gossip of the brawl spread as fast as head lice during summer camp. By the time Monday arrived, it made front headlines of the *Central Western Daily*, and the students as well as teachers spoke non-stop about it. Could I blame them? The ground had resembled a battlefield by the time everyone had jumped in.

Before I'd left for school, Mum said only three words to me – and they weren't 'I love you', but 'Straight home afterwards'. I left the house, hopped on my bike with the weight of the world on my shoulders, and pedalled to school, crying. Sharon and Helen were seated on the aluminium benches and watched me plod over. Sharon was a bit battered, but nothing her make-up couldn't conceal. Helen told us her oldies had also gated her for two weeks, but all Cheryl had said to Sharon was, 'Don't do it again'.

Sharon was okay, physically, but her emotions were all over the shop and, once again, Tahlia was not at school. We all guessed she'd been gated, and when I'd asked the others if they knew Clyde was a policeman, they were just as mystified as me. Why hadn't Tahlia told us? Was she embarrassed; scared the cool kids would tease her?

The assembly bell shrieked and soon we were sitting on the rough concrete, listening to our headmistress talk about how disgusted and hurt she was over what had happened. Sharon began crying. Headmistress McCarthy spoke about her disappointment that her own students had been involved. She told us those students had been suspended, and that criminal charges were pending. She did not name names, but every single person knew. It wasn't hard to guess, considering the boys in question were not present – including Mike Perkins.

Even though both schools knew who'd started the brawl, our headmistress did not budge, and she suspended those involved. Trix couldn't have attended school even if he'd been well enough.

Students gossiped about it in the corridors, in bathroom cubicles, during recess and lunch too. A few girls approached us during our lunch break to ask how Bobby was, but Sharon just told them to nick off. It was the biggest brawl the town had seen. Orange was usually peaceful and quiet, and parents were outraged at what they perceived to be the kids usurping control.

I never ended up going to the police station to give a statement. With the grace of God, after statements from spectator witnesses and the staff, who'd cleaned up the mess everyone had made, the police concluded the east-side boys had started it. A cleaner, who'd been weaving through the seating area with a garbage bag collecting trash, corroborated our story of the pockmarked bloke – I didn't know his name – approaching us with a cricket bat. He also said in his witness statement there had been about twenty of them.

Not knowing what had happened to Trix hurt like a bitch, but on Tuesday I received some answers. Because Mike had hurt himself while helping his brother move out of the house, he'd missed it all. But when he'd heard about it, he'd headed straight to Trix's house. Trix was still detained at that point, but Mike spoke to Trix's dad. His dad had said they'd given Trix medical attention after he was arrested, and they'd only allowed Mr Walker in to see his son on the Monday morning. Mike didn't come to school that day as he'd made the rounds to the other boys' houses instead, but he came to the schoolyard on Tuesday.

Mike, dressed in school uniform to avoid suspicion, had turned up just to see us girls. He'd hobbled over to us, limping from his own injury, hiding his face behind black sunnies. When Sharon spotted him, she jumped up and hugged him tight. He told us to gather around the concrete steps so no-one up the front could see us. We collected our bags and textbooks and hid behind the block of steps. Some students heading into the grounds saw us, but I felt certain they wouldn't rat us out.

Tahlia was still not at school and because my phone had been confiscated, I had no way of calling her to see how she was. Sharon was the only one of us who had escaped any punishment, so she'd called once to see how Tahlia was, and her mother told Sharon she was gated, and that also included coming to school. That was the end of that. But why would Lorraine let her daughter's education suffer? Tahlia hadn't hit anyone, hadn't even pushed anyone; she'd tried to pry people apart.

'Shh,' Mike said to Sharon, who was already crying after he'd informed us what had happened. 'Bobby's all right, so calm down.'

'I hate them, Mike!' Her face turning a purply red. '*They* fucking started this!'

'I know,' he said, holding her shoulders. 'They'll release the boys soon, but. The cops have enough witnesses to back their story up.'

'What's going to happen to Rodney?' Helen asked.

Mike shook his head, then glanced around to make sure no teachers approached. 'It's not good, eh. I think he will go away for a while.'

'Go away?' Helen whispered.

'Yeah ... as in, like, juvie prison.'

Helen fell against the wall, her eyes wide open.

'This is so totally unfair!' Sharon said, wrapping her arms around her waist.

'Fuckin' oath. It's total bullshit. You wanna know what else is fucked? McCarthy, the dumb slut, suspended the boys and she's already told them they can't go to our Year 12 formal.'

'What?!' Sharon screeched. 'But I already picked out my dress and four-inch platforms!'

Mike jerked his chin towards our headmistress's office. 'Tell *her* that, babe. That moll reckons bad shit will happen if they come.'

A fresh wave of tears escaped my stinging eyes. 'So not fair.'

'I know. It's fucked up, man.'

'How's Trix?' I asked, using a palm to wipe away my tears.

Mike adjusted his dark sunglasses, his forehead rumpling. 'He's pretty beat up. The fuckers got him good. But the jacks should release him either today or tomorrow. They won't charge him. Lucky he didn't carry any weapons.'

'I want to see him, but I'm gated.'

'I can tell him that.'

'Thanks, Mike.'

'Are you going to your classes?' Helen asked.

Mike shook his head. 'That old bitch won't let the others, so I'm not, either.'

'But you only have a few weeks to go before school finishes.'

'Helen, I don't give a shit. This means war. You know that, don't you? Those *fuckers* are gonna pay for what they did.'

'They deserve it!' Sharon said through clenched teeth.

'This isn't going to end,' I said, picturing the ongoing war for years to come. A constant tit-for-tat. The Vietnam War ended in '75, yet people were still suffering from the aftermath. Would the North and South – who'd since joined as the Socialist Republic of Vietnam – put their differences aside and forget about what had happened? I didn't see how they could; I didn't see how people could forget their anger and push their beliefs aside. Would our situation be any different?

'No-one is going to win,' I whispered, spotting Keith and Amy strolling hand-in-hand behind Mike – too distracted being lovey-dovey to notice any of us.

Mike gave a watery snort. 'Yeah, but we can get even.'

'What are you going to do now?' Helen asked.

Mike winced when he leaned on his bad ankle. 'Gonna go see Bobby.'

Sharon's hazel eyes lit up. 'Give him a kiss for me!'

Mike grinned. 'I don't think my tongue down his throat is going to mean the same thing.'

We all laughed. For the first time in three days, I had something to laugh about.

'How long is the suspension for?' Helen asked.

Mike glanced all around, then faced us again. 'Two weeks.'

'School will be almost over by then.' Helen's eyes grew wild and large. 'She can't do this!'

No doubt, the thought of *her* not being allowed to attend school would be like hell on earth. She wanted to graduate university with a Bachelor of Arts; she'd dreamed of becoming a writer since she was an embryo. But it was clear Mike thought school was something to do to kill time, to socialise. He didn't take it as seriously as Helen, or even Tahlia.

'I can come back now if I want to, but fuck it. I've already failed my year. I don't want to go to uni, anyway; I got a mechanic apprenticeship lined up – I'll be working with my brother. School don't always mean shit, and the adults don't always know what they're talking about.'

'So true,' Sharon said, her eyes fixed on the ground.

Mike then looked around as if suddenly noticing something. 'Where's Tahlia?'

'Hasn't been to school since last week,' I said.

'Is she okay? Did she get hurt?'

'No,' Sharon said. 'But *I* did.' She pointed to the Beatles' Band-Aid on her elbow.

Mike shook his head. 'I'm sorry you girls got caught up in it.'

'I want them to pay for what they did to Bobby! Did you see his face?'

'Yeah ... I'm not gonna lie, it sounds like Trix and Bobby copped the worst of it.'

To prevent myself from crying again, I mashed my lips together. I could only imagine how Trix felt, and how his face looked after taking that kind of savage beating.

When the bell rang, Sharon moaned. 'I don't want to go; I wanna see Bobby!'

Mike grabbed her arm. 'He's not out yet, anyway – by lunchtime, I believe.'

She clutched his bicep. 'Tell him I love him.'

That was news to me, but I was not surprised.

Mike nodded and Sharon released her grip. 'I will. But take care of yourself in the meantime, yeah? I better get going before anyone sees me.'

Helen leaned in and gave him a hug. 'Tell Ed I hope he gets better.'

'Yeah,' I added, 'tell Trix I ... I, um, hope to see him soon.'

'I will. He wants to see you; he was asking about you – according to his old man.'

Students rose from green wooden benches or off the ground to shuffle inside the classrooms. I could already hear trampling footsteps behind us on the concrete steps, which led to the Science block.

Mike said his goodbyes and Helen leaned back to watch him shuffling away as best he could with a busted ankle, out past the school gates.

'Do you really, truly love Bobby?' she asked Sharon as we strode through the quadrangle.

'Yes. And I know he loves me.'

Helen continued eyeing Sharon while walking. 'Has he said it?'

Sharon shook her head while smiling, dreamlike. 'No, but he will. He will. Mum already gave him a spare key, so he can come over whenever he likes.'

Suspicion rolled through me as we pressed on. *Did Cheryl do that for you, or for her?*

Chapter Twenty-Nine

Later that night, I was sitting on my bed, knees to my chest, when there was a knock on my bedroom door. How I prayed it wouldn't be my mother. We still weren't talking, and that was more than fine with me.

'Come in,' I mumbled, looking at the door with dread.

The door opened slowly. Keith stuck his head in. 'Hey, bumface, how are you feeling?'

Shrugging, I turned away from him to stare at my kneecaps.

He entered and closed the door, then sat at the end of my bed, the mattress squeaking under his weight. 'Any news about your boyfriend?'

I jerked my head up and glared at him. 'He's not my boyfriend.'

Keith laughed and held up his hands. 'If you say so. Nah, for real – how is he?'

I played with my nails, my heavy eyelids felt like they were weighing down my head. 'Don't know.'

He slapped his thighs and sucked in air. 'Fair enough.'

'What do you want, Keith?'

'Just to see how you are.'

'I'm fine, so can you bugger off?'

He frowned and leaned back. 'Whoa, who pissed in your Froot Loops this morning?'

'Just leave me alone.'

He pointed a thumb at his white puka-shell necklace. 'I'm not the one who grounded you; why you givin' *me* shit?'

'Just go back to your room where you have a phone, and music, and a TV.'

'Why d'you need a phone, dorkface?'

'Because I have friends!'

'How are they?' His face was serious now.

'I haven't seen Tahlia; I don't know what happened to her.'

'Why don't you call her?'

It took all my inner strength not to throttle him. 'My phone got taken away, idiotbrain!'

'Well, why don't you use *my* phone, bumface?'

I sat up straighter on the bed, hope soaring through me. 'Huh?'

'I'll bring my phone in here, you dial Tahlia, and I'll distract Ma.'

The thought of him going out of his way made me smile; for the first time probably ever, I appreciated having an older brother. Keith was usually the type to do things only if he reaped some benefit from it, but I guess he couldn't stand me moping about the house. Dinner had been awkward as hell, the four of us chewing, then swallowing, then back to cutting meat on our plate while Mum eyed us all from under her lashes – knives screeching against bone china ringing through our ears.

'Where's Mum now?' I asked, my heart rate on a steady incline.

He jerked a thumb behind his shoulder, indicating the front of the house. 'In the lounge room, filing her nails.'

'Dad?'

'Guess.' I nodded: *Got you ... his den.* Keith swiped the air. 'He wouldn't give a shit, anyway; Mum wears the pants around here.'

My spirits lifted at the thought of hearing Tahlia's sweet voice. Of course, Lorraine would most likely shoot me down faster than Bonnie Parker practising on tin cans, but if I didn't try, I wouldn't know.

Clutching my quilt cover, I said, 'Okay, Keith, let's do it.'

'All right, but don't go yabbering for yonks. Make it quick. I don't want Ma to rip my balls off.'

'Hurry up, idiotbrain!'

Keith jumped up off my bed and opened the door a crack, peering down towards the kitchen on the right. He then opened it all the way and tiptoed out. My heart galloped in leaps and bounds as I clutched the quilt cover, thinking how sometimes, just *some*times, my selfish brother could be thoughtful and nice when he wanted to be. Thirty seconds later, he rushed into my room and closed the door as quietly as he could, wincing when the doorjamb clicked.

'Hurry!' I stage whispered, watching him plug his phone cable into the baseboard jack near my bedside table as my pulse hastened. There was nothing more thrilling than outsmarting an adult – *especially* if it was a parent.

'Yeah, but if Ma picks up the phone to dial someone, she'll hear you on this end.'

'I'll be quick!'

Keith placed his black Bakelite phone in my clammy hands. 'You've got five minutes.'

'What are you going to do?'

Keith raked a hand through his brown hair. 'I'm gonna sit down beside Ma and talk to her about baby shit.'

I snorted. '*Really?*'

'She secretly loves the thought of being a grandmother while she's still so young.' He slapped my knee softly and turned for the door.

'Hey, Keith?'

He spun around, one eyebrow raised. 'Yeah?'

'Thank you.'

He gave me a tender, close-lipped smile. 'You owe me one, boofhead.' He turned the handle, peered out, then stepped into the hallway and closed the door behind him.

As fast as I could, I spun the numbers on the rotary dial and held the receiver to my ear. Four agonising rings later, Lorraine answered.

'Hello, Mrs Ashcroft, it's Kylie Gardner. Is Tahlia in?'

'She's in the shower.' Her tone wasn't one of anger, or sadness, or happiness. It was automated like a robot; how could I pick up on anything with that kind of attitude?

'Oh.' Cue the crickets chirping. 'Err, will she be coming to school tomorrow?'

'Her stepfather and I have decided she will be taking a few days off.'

'But … she didn't do anything wrong, Mrs Ashcroft, honest to God. None of this was our fault.'

Then I heard Tahlia in the background: 'Who's that on the phone?'

'Tahlia!' I yelled, gripping the receiver tighter. Hearing her voice when her mum had said she was in the shower sent anger racing through me at being lied to. But then I realised my mother might have heard me from the lounge room, and not only would *I* get in trouble, but also Keith. Wincing, I smacked my forehead.

'Thanks for calling,' Lorraine said, then hung up.

I was so sick of this; sick and tired of being told lies and of being confused, of being angry, of being misguided. I promised myself then that no matter what, the next time I saw Tahlia, I was going to get to the bottom of what was happening with her. No more bullshit, no more lies, no more covering up whatever was going on at home. This was it. She *would* tell me the truth, even if I had to slap it out of her.

Chapter Thirty

Tahlia hadn't turned up to school on Wednesday, and it was now Thursday. I approached Sharon and Helen, who sat together in our usual spot. Sharon was finger-combing her blonde hair, and Helen was reading a Scholastic brochure while pulling up one of her calf-length white socks with her other hand.

'Morning,' I said, stopping in front of them.

Sharon grinned. 'Hey, Sunset!' Didn't she look peppier all of a sudden.

'Hello, Kylie,' Helen mumbled, still assessing the sleek brochure.

'No Tahlia again, huh?' I swung my leg over the bench, plonking my schoolbag in between my thighs.

Sharon shook her head, her lipstick sparkling in the sunlight. 'Nope, but Bobby slept over at mine last night.'

Helen looked up, her mouth wide enough to fit an apple. 'Really?'

Sharon nodded, still combing her hair. 'Yep. We had sex.'

Helen dropped the brochure and clutched her red face, pulling her cheeks down so she resembled a Greek tragedy mask. 'What?! Sha-*ron*! Are you serious?'

Sharon shrugged as if to say: *No biggie*. 'Yeah! I had to lose my virginity some time.'

'But you're so *young*!' Helen's wild eyes roamed the ground near her shiny black shoes. 'I haven't even kissed anybody.'

'And you won't if your head is always stuck in a book.'

'I can't believe it,' I said. Although, to be fair, I could. What I meant was, I couldn't believe it took them so long. 'How *was* it?'

Sharon bobbed her head, but her wrinkled nose suggested something was amiss. 'Yeah ... it was okay.'

Helen and I both leaned in closer.

'Just okay?' I said, hooking an eyebrow.

Sharon inhaled and focused on the other side of her mane to finger-brush it. 'Well, I thought it was supposed to go longer. Like ... you go through a lot of pain, then it's over in, like, two minutes.'

'Two minutes? That's all?' Helen said, squinting. 'Maggi noodles take two minutes.'

Sharon breathed in through her nostrils. 'Yeah, like, I'm sure it was just because he was nervous and, like, I have pretty nice tits, which probably made him spoof quicker. We'll do it again soon; I'm sure it'll be better next time.'

Helen shook her head so hard she had to readjust her sky-blue headband. 'I still can't believe you did it! You must be the first one in our year!'

Sharon shrugged again, grinning. 'He said he loves me.'

Helen's brow wrinkled and her mouth widened. 'So, you let him ...?'

Sharon rolled her hazel eyes. 'I didn't *let* him, Helen; I wanted to. Didn't even need to use any Vaso; it was like we were made for each other.'

Helen leaned forward further. 'Did he use one of those rubber things?'

'A frenchie? Of course!' *Scoff*. 'What kind of girl do you think I am?'

Now it was my turn in this game of twenty-one questions. 'How is his face? How are the rest of the boys? How's—?'

'Trix?' Sharon said for me.

Lips pressed together, I bobbed my head.

Sharon pointed beyond my shoulder, towards the car park. 'He's right behind you.'

I spun around so fast I almost lost my balance on the bench. Trix was leaning against the bonnet of his Pontiac Phoenix. Despite his black shades, it was clear he was looking our way and man ... the sight of him. My heart thumped and my flesh tingled, and I conceded I wanted to be with him. As his girlfriend. I knew that as sure as I knew my own name and date of birth.

'Oh my gosh,' I whispered, dreamlike, rising from the bench.

'Go and talk to him,' Sharon said. 'I told Bobby last night that you were gated, and I asked him to tell Trix just in case Mike forgot.'

Sharon O'Rourke, loyal to a tee. Even though it had been her first sexual experience with a boy, she'd still thought enough of me to tell Bobby to tell Trix about my imprisonment. I loved her more than anyone in that moment.

'Keep an eye out for me,' I said over my shoulder before I sprinted across the ground, darting past a cluster of students devouring Choo-Choo Bars. Everything zoomed past me in a kaleidoscopic blur: the maple trees, boys playing handball, skipping ropes twirling, games of hopscotch. My ears blocked out the sound of shoes scuffing the concrete, of schoolbag zippers opening, of a plane flying overhead, of laughter and chatter.

Before I reached Trix, I dropped my bag and folder in the dirt and then wrapped my arms around him. My tears started before his hands had even circled around my waist. Oh, his poor face! It looked as black and brown as an old banana – the soft ones my mum used to make banana bread with; the ones she'd said were better for that type of recipe. Seeing the three stitches in his bottom lip caused my stomach to plummet.

'Oh my God,' I said, clinging to him, trying to bring him closer even though we were hip to hip.

'It's okay,' he whispered before dry swallowing, his throat clicking.

Shaking my head, I said, 'No, Trix, it's not okay.' I leaned back, too afraid to touch his face. 'Look at you.'

'It'll get better.'

I cupped my face, shaking my head as I cried into my trembling hands. 'This is so unfair.' I sniffed back tears and lowered my hands to dare another look at his sickening injuries.

He reached into his pants pocket and pulled out a folded piece of yellow paper. 'Bobby told me Sharon said your oldies gated you.'

'Yeah ...'

'I didn't want you mixed up in that fight.'

'I tried to warn you!'

'We stood up for ourselves. I'm not going to miss out on enjoying life because some girl got pregnant and is too afraid to say who the real father is.' His eyes dropped. 'Or, *was*, rather.'

'You're totally right; we don't even know if she was actually raped. I'm sorry, Trix.'

He placed the paper in my flat palm and folded my fingers around it. 'If you ever need me. Night or day. Don't hesitate, okay?'

'I'm gated until I don't know when – my phone's been taken away too.'

'I wish you hadn't been involved; that's the only thing I regret.' His battered fingers caressed my cheek, turning my stomach to soup. 'Are you hurting now?'

'Only a hurt shoulder and jaw. Nothing broken. What about you?' God, that was a stupid question, looking at his stomach-churning injuries. Black on purple, it was nauseating eyeing them.

'Don't worry about it.'

'Of course I worry! How can you say that?' I cupped my face again, heaving as the piece of paper crinkled in my hand.

He slipped his arms around me. 'I don't want you to get in trouble at school.'

'How much trouble are you in?'

'None. But Rodney's foster parents have already hired a lawyer for him. He carved up some people pretty good.'

Snivelling, I lowered my hands and wrapped my arms around his waist. 'But no-one died, and *they* started it!'

'Doesn't matter. He's a troubled guy who carried a switchblade – that's all the cops see. They'll see him as problematic; a loose cannon who needs to be off the streets to protect civilians.'

The bell rang and I leaned back to clutch his warm shirt. 'I don't want you to go.' I could just make out his black eyelashes behind the dark sunnies.

'I have to,' he said, his voice as tender as a lover's caress.

'Why?'

God, I knew the question was dumb. He'd been suspended, of course, but it was the broader 'why'. Why did this boy have such bad luck? Why should he – and the rest – miss out on school and their Year 12 formal for standing up for themselves during a fight? What else was Trix supposed to do; have his brains bashed in with a cricket bat so he could still come to school the following Monday? He wouldn't have had any brain cells left to learn with if that bat had clobbered him – the guy's swing would have impressed Don Bradman.

'Because we're a bad influence on the rest of you.'

'But the cleaner saved your arse, didn't he?'

'That doesn't matter to McCarthy. She hates us; probably saw this as a blessing.' He looked past my shoulder to where Sharon and Helen mingled. 'Still no Tahlia?'

'She hasn't been here all week.'

He turned back to me. How I longed to stare into those desirable chocolate-brown eyes – eyes that could turn a saint into a sinner. 'Gated for what happened at the oval?'

'Don't know. But when I see her next, I am going to force her to tell me what's going on. Her mum's dating a cop. But she never told us he was one; my mum told me.'

His forehead rumpled. 'Who?'

'Clyde something.'

'Hmm.'

I waited for him to explain, but realised bread would turn to penicillin by the time he chose to, and the bell had ceased ringing. Such a closed book. 'What, Trix? What do you know?'

'Nothing. You need to get to your class now. No sense in all of us missing out on an education.'

After hugging him with everything I had, I broke free. He walked me to where my stuff had scattered on the ground and helped me brush the dirt off my papers and books. When he handed them to me, I leaned up and kissed him on the cheek. Just a quick peck; I didn't want to hurt him, and I seriously wondered if that soft graze would. Before he could say anything, I turned and raced to class, believing Trix knew way more about Clyde than he let on.

Chapter Thirty-One

When Saturday rolled around, we received a blessing: it was student–teacher night, when parents would go to the school and speak to teachers about their child's improvement (or lack thereof) during the school year. As soon as Mum and Dad were out the front door, I told Keith I was heading off. He seemed more than okay with that considering Amy was coming over, and it was rare that both oldies would be out of the house together for a few hours. I suspected he wanted to test the bedsprings of his new mattress. Of course, during lunch on Friday, The Sunsets had already pre-planned a clandestine meet-up. Helen had said yes, she could sneak out, but unfortunately Tahlia had been a no-show all week, so we couldn't extend the invitation to her.

I biked straight over to Sharon's as soon as the sound of Dad's station wagon faded into the distance. Sharon only lived down the street, but my folks would be gone for two hours – three at max if they stopped off to get petrol and do a grocery shop at Coles, or something – and when Mum grabbed the ear of a friend, she could yabber for hours. I told myself two hours to be on the safe side, so I didn't want to waste spare seconds walking.

Mum had left plates of ham steaks and grilled pineapple wrapped in cling film for Keith and me. Little did I know that by the time I arrived back from Sharon's, I would feel too sick to want to eat a thing for the next few days.

I parked my bike on the lawn and then pounded on the front door. Sharon opened it and smiled. 'Come in. Helen's already here.' We hugged and I looked down at her dark-blue flared pants, her bare feet revealing red toenail polish.

I stepped inside to hear 'You're My Best Friend' by Queen playing on Sharon's turntable. We entered her bedroom, where Helen was lying on her stomach on the floor flipping through *Dolly*, her rainbow-striped bell-bottom-covered legs bent up behind her. She'd read anything, even the TV guide, but now she jumped to her feet, brushed aside her thick brown hair and hugged me.

'How are you?' she asked, leaning back to look at me.

'I'm okay.'

'Nervous about what our teachers will say?'

'I'm packing shit, but even if it's bad, my mum can't hate me any more than she does now.' I turned to the doorway. 'Sharon, where's Bobby?'

'Told him not to come; I wanted to spend time with you girls.' She walked over and hugged me tight again. 'Have you spoken to Trix?'

'Not since I saw him at school a few days ago. He left me his number and address, but I can't see him.' *But I've stared at his phone number long enough to memorise it.*

Sharon broke free and grimaced. 'You still don't have your things back?'

'Nope. No TV, no phone, no turntable.'

Her eyes expanded to twice their size. 'Deadset, your oldies are totally uncool!'

'Tell me about it ...'

Sharon clutched my shoulder, then Helen's. 'What do you girls wanna do? We only have a short time.'

Helen smiled, raising a hand. 'I'm thinking we should play—'

A rapid knock at the front door stole our attention. Sharon frowned at the urgency of it. She made her way out of the bedroom and rushed down the carpeted hallway. When Helen and I heard Sharon gasp (even above the music), we both hurried out. Tahlia stood at the threshold, and for a split second I had to do a double-take to make sure it was in fact *her*. Her limp orange hair looked like it'd been falling out and gnawed on by rodents, and her red-rimmed eyes were dull and droopy.

'What *happened* to you?' Sharon said in a breathless whisper, taking Tahlia in her arms after closing the door. Tahlia wept in Sharon's embrace. The sight of her dishevelled appearance alone made me want to break down and cry.

'Shhhhh,' Sharon whispered, rubbing Tahlia's back. 'It's okay. You're here with us now.' Sharon looked back at us through watery eyes. Tahlia continued weeping – her profound sorrow infectious.

'Come into the bedroom,' I said softly. Helen and I walked over to Tahlia and rubbed her back with calming strokes. Tears of agony spilled out as though she'd been bottling it all in and the dam wall had burst. She let us lead her into the bedroom. Sharon spun her around and helped her sit on the edge of the bed as I went to the turntable and lifted the tonearm off the spinning *A Night at the Opera* vinyl.

We all stepped back, giving Tahlia room to breathe. She cupped her head in shaky hands and continued bawling.

After a lull in Tahlia's sobs, Helen whispered, 'What happened to you?'

Tahlia shook her head, lowering her hands. 'I can't keep it in anymore, I just *can't!*'

'You don't have to,' I whispered, dropping to my knees then shuffling forward, pushing the *Dolly* magazine out of the way, but my eyes never left hers. 'We're here for you when you're ready.'

Helen and Sharon also joined me on the floor, crossing their ankles together and hugging their knees. We all stared at Tahlia patiently as she calmed her breaths. I'm sure we were all consumed with our own theories as to what had brought this on. Was she dying of cancer? Did her nan have another stroke? Was it to do with her estranged father?

Tahlia finally looked up. For now, the tears had abated. 'Clyde ... he raped me.' She whimpered, but didn't break down again.

'Y-your mum's new boyfriend?' Sharon whispered, frowning deeply, nostrils flaring as she fought to control the shock and disbelief.

Tahlia bobbed her head once and sniffled back tears as her lips mashed together. 'He's been t-t-touching me for the past few weeks.'

Helen cupped her ashen face with both hands, mouth frozen wide.

The instant I heard 'Clyde' and 'rape' in the same sentence, my tears spilled. Hot and heavy, pouring down my face in endless streams; torrents of anger and sadness flowing freely as I sat and stared. I didn't blink. I didn't move. I don't even think I breathed.

'Oh my God!' Sharon said, cupping her mouth as she too became teary-eyed. Then added: 'Does your mum know?'

'I *tried* to tell her! I tried to say he was touching me, but she said I was making it up! She said I was spending too much time with bad influencers at the school – she's trying to blame you guys.' She brought her knuckles to her chin and heaved. 'That's why she hates it when you girls call me.'

'Oh fuck,' Sharon whispered, staring at nothing in particular as her mind raced behind vacant eyes.

Helen's face had turned paper-pale, like a victim who'd gone through trauma but had no tears left to shed.

'I told her I would never lie about a thing like this, but she thinks it's all in my mind! My own mother doesn't believe me!' She clutched her stomach, whimpering.

'I can't believe it,' I whispered – not that I thought she was lying, but that her mother could treat her own daughter in such a way. But not only that – Clyde was a *policeman*; he was supposed to protect people!

'How did this all begin?' Sharon whispered, swallowing deeply.

'Y-you girls remember that family night we had a few weeks ago?' She wiped her dripping red nose with the heel of a jittery hand.

We all bobbed our heads simultaneously – it was the one she'd been dreading; yes, we remembered.

Tahlia nodded, her eyes squinting like she was trying to read the fine print at the bottom of a contract. 'It started then, when we played a board game. Clyde got mad that I beat him. *The Game of Life* was supposed to bring us all closer together, but when I won, he lost it. His face went all red and he said I cheated. Anyway, things c-calmed down and I went to bed that night feeling sad about what had happened. I don't know what time it was, but later on I woke up to find him in my bedroom. He was s-s-standing there, looking at me with this weird look in his eyes – even in the moonlight I saw it. His eyes were like ... like a beast's. I tried to scream because he scared me, but he knew I would, so he put his hand over my mouth so that when

I screamed it was muffled.' She stopped and wiped her eyes, heaving back a lungful. 'I was so scared, but I didn't know what to do. He then dropped to his knees beside the bed' – *sniffle* – 'and his face came close to mine. He just … *stared* at me. And my whole body froze with fear.' She looked at us, squinting. 'Has that ever happened to you? When you've been so scared you can't move, you can't even blink?'

We all nodded, transfixed by her story. Not that it was a good story, but I'll bet none of us had heard anything like it. And I'm glad I only had to listen to this once; I was at the point of heaving my guts up over Sharon's carpet.

Tahlia wiped her puffy eyes with her halter-neck top. 'Yes, exactly, so that was me. Then I saw my bedsheets move. His other hand – the one that wasn't on my mouth – came under the sheet. At first, he touched my belly, but then he … he …' She cupped her face and wailed, shaking her head violently as if to expel the visceral memory. 'His fingers went into my underpants. He started … t-t-touching me where he shouldn't have been, and th-then he began whispering in my ear.' She choked on her sobs, whimpering, snot flowing from her nostrils, running over her quaking lips. 'He asked me if I liked it, and if I'd done it before.' She clutched her top at the hem. 'But I couldn't move! I was so scared! I just kept looking at him, wondering why, wondering when my mum would come in and save me. But no-one came. So he kept t-t-touching me. I was so frozen with fear, I don't think I blinked the entire time.'

She palmed away more tears as the three of us stared at her, also frozen with fear. 'This went on a few more times – and he got rougher; he kept hurting me by pinning me down and causing bruises. At first, I didn't know what to do, or who to tell. I wished for it to go away, but it didn't, and Clyde kept coming back when Mum was asleep and I thought it was my fault. That it was something I did or said and he was punishing me for being a bad girl – because he said that to me once – that I was a bad girl, and I didn't know what he meant because I was good; I am a *good* student, so I didn't understand. I was so *confused*.'

She bawled again, eyes clenched, before working up the courage to resume the sickening story. 'Then one night he went further than before. When I woke up, he was kneeling next to my bed with no clothes on. Each time I would open my mouth to scream, he would cover it to stop me. Then this time when he touched me, he was doing things to ... himself ... you know? I could hear ... wet sounds; I could see his arm moving up and down very fast, and I could see his face changing as he made weird noises. I closed my eyes and waited for it to pass, for him to just go away and leave me alone, and when he finished touching me, he wiped his other hand on the mattress and left. I cried myself to sleep like I always did, wondering what I was being punished for. Then I knew I had to tell Mum. I was losing sleep, I was sick in the tummy, I couldn't concentrate at school. Even if I had been bad somehow, I needed to tell her, no matter what.' She sucked back air, throat clicking while her leaden eyes trailed to the ceiling as if seeking strength from God. 'One afternoon when I came home from school, I did. I told Mum. And she ... she *slapped* me across the face!' Tahlia's body crumpled forward as she clutched her stomach. She released a wail so high-pitched I thought it was going to shatter the windowpane.

My heart couldn't take any more; streams of tears flowed faster than my heartbeat. I shuffled over and wrapped my arms around her waist in a bear hug. The sound of wailing and suffering echoed throughout the room.

Tahlia punched her own thighs with tight fists as she bent forward. A line of saliva dangled from her bottom lip, her puffy eyelids clenched tight as tear after tear squeezed their way through. 'My mum *slapped* me!'

'I'm so sorry,' Sharon said, her face as red as the pits of hell while she heaved. 'I'm so sorry we didn't catch on.'

Tahlia shook her head, sniffling back mucus. Her teeth chattered incessantly. 'I couldn't t-t-tell you. My own mother slapped me and t-told me I was making it up. She said, "A policeman who spends his days protecting Orange would never do such a vile thing". I said, "Why would I make this up?" And she blamed you girls – said you're bad for me and it was my immature mind. She didn't even *talk* to him about it, didn't even ask! And she *still* lets him stay over.' She inhaled, closing her bloodshot eyes. 'How? How c-c-could she not have felt him getting off the bed in the middle of the night?'

'She fuckin' knew,' Sharon said, wiping her dripping nose and wet chin on her forearm. 'She fucking knew but chose to ignore it – the cruel bitch.'

I didn't want to say it aloud – mainly because I couldn't physically utter a word for the life of me – but I agreed with Sharon with every fibre of my being. There was no way Lorraine could not have known what was going on inside her house. The fact she didn't even ask him implied she was aware. But if she knew, then she'd have to kick him out – because what type of mother would allow this to happen? Yes, how could a mother let their new boyfriend get away with it? I later learned this happens surprisingly often. Some women just cannot be without a man and will forfeit their own child rather than be alone.

Tahlia shook her head, gasping for breath in the airless sauna. Needing a break from the heart-wrenching sight of her before I passed out, I glanced towards the fogged-up window. The air had become so thick with moisture, I thought it had to be from the rage each of us was emitting into the room.

Tahlia used her top again to help absorb her never-ending tears, gulping before she continued. 'He raped me the night of the footy match. He'd been called in to break up the fight, so he knew who was involved and he knew I was there. When he finished taking the arrested ones back to the station, he came and picked me up from the hospital.' She turned to me with eyes brimming with tears. 'I was waiting with Helen to see if you and Sharon were okay, but he came for me, so I had to go with him. Hours later, I woke up to find him climbing on my bed. He covered my mouth, and again he pulled down the sheets, but this time he … he … t-took my underwear off, and—'

Sharon soothed Tahlia's back. 'You don't need to tell us if it's too hard.'

Tahlia clung to Sharon's right arm and rocked back and forth. 'He kept whispering in my ear the whole time, telling me this was all my fault, and that he had to punish me for being a naughty girl.' She shook her head, tears spurting out sideways. 'But I wasn't bad; I was a good student!' Moans escaped her quivering lips through suppressed hiccups.

Helen, who was still sitting on the floor, hugged Tahlia's legs to her chest, sobbing the hardest and loudest now. My tangled mind whirled with thoughts as dark as a winter night. All I could see or think of, was red. The pain emanating from my best friend would have shattered anyone who felt it. The endless tears each of us took turns in wiping from her eyes were enough to drown a cat. I was sad, yes, but mainly, I was livid. I wanted to hurt Lorraine, I wanted to hurt Clyde; I wanted them to feel the agony they had both inflicted on my best friend. I was angry with myself for not pressing Tahlia more when we'd seen her at school; I was angry we were being punished by the adults who were supposed to be running the show, and I was angry I couldn't see Trix, because now I needed him more than ever. But I *would* see Trix tonight; if I ever needed a reason to sneak out of my house, this was it.

'Sharon,' I managed through an aching throat, wiping my wet face using both tremulous hands, 'can I please use your phone?'

She frowned deeply. 'It's not to call the cops, is it?'

I fixed her with a *Get real* stare. 'No, silly.' *Someone even better.*

Chapter Thirty-Two

By the time the clock showed one a.m., I was still trembling with rage. I wished I could have seen Trix earlier, but in case my parents were still awake, I needed to make sure we would not be disturbed. When I saw his black Pontiac creeping along my street without its headlights on (I guessed he was looking at the house numbers), I snuck out of my open window. As soon as I'd returned to my house from Sharon's, I had my game plan. I'd stormed into my bedroom and opened the window halfway so I wouldn't need to when I snuck out later on. I'd heard Keith's bedsprings, all right; they'd obviously heard me come through the door – as the squeaking had stopped abruptly. When Mum and Dad returned from the teachers' meeting, they'd called both of us into the lounge room for a pep talk (Amy stayed in Keith's bedroom). Mum had a lot to say about Keith, but he'd asked her what the big deal was, considering he was graduating soon. My school marks had impressed them, but a few teachers said I had a tendency to let my mind wander. Ain't that the truth. My mind had been wandering ever since I'd kissed Tahlia goodbye on her wet cheek. I hadn't said a word to the girls about my plans, although they did ask me who I'd called. I'd told them it was Keith – just to make sure Mum and Dad hadn't come home yet.

We'd stayed, cried, held Tahlia's wracking body and told her everything would be okay. Helen had said, 'Why don't we go to the police and tell them?' Sharon had echoed my exact thoughts: because they stick up for their own. There is no way a policeman would charge his fellow mate. They would make up some bullshit story and say they couldn't find any evidence, that it was all a misunderstanding. I didn't know how raping a young girl could be a misunderstanding, but okay … You do you; we'll take the law into our own hands, buddy.

When Trix pulled over to the kerb and waited, I tiptoed along the front lawn, ducking low, and climbed into his idling car. He took one look at my crumpled face and leaned over to hug me, but I pushed him away, wiped my tears and told him to drive until it was safe to talk. He was unfamiliar with the streets, so I pointed towards a cul-de-sac, which gave way to grassland at the end. Once he'd turned off the ignition, he pulled me close. Silver moonlight pooled inside the windows.

'What's happened?' His breath was warm against my ear.

It took a long time for me to be able to speak. I shivered in his arms as my tears soaked into his black T-shirt, but when I finally composed myself, I told him what Tahlia had told us, sparing no detail.

When I was done speaking, Trix sat back, faced forward and gazed out of the windscreen.

I clenched my hands into fists and bared my teeth. 'I want him to pay for this, Trix! I want to hurt him real bad!'

'Where is Tahlia now?' he whispered, staring straight ahead, unblinking.

'She's staying the night at Sharon's; her mum doesn't know where she is.'

He closed his eyes, his nostrils flared. I cried harder.

'She was in so much *pain*, Trix. I want them both to pay for what they've done! She doesn't deserve this; she's a good girl.'

'No-one deserves this.' With a rigid jawline, he opened his eyes and gazed out of the windscreen again.

'I know, but she is a beautiful person and my heart is broken for her. Helen said we should go to the police—'

'No. They won't give a shit.'

'That's what *I* said.'

'They'd probably interview him, then her, then turn around and say, "Well, Clyde said he didn't do it", then Clyde would say, "She's a troublesome child", and with what happened at the oval, they'd believe him. They'd probably send Tahlia home with him too.'

Nodding, I wiped my stinging eyes. 'I agree. But what do we do?'

'I need to think for a moment.'

'She can't go back home; even her own mother says she's a liar.'

'She's not. I know Clyde Hanratty. He already has a wife.'

My head jolted around and my mouth flung open. '*What*?!'

He chewed the corner of his bottom lip and stared at the steering wheel. 'In another town. They're probably separated – but still, he has a wife and son.'

Blinking several times while trying to process this, I said, 'How do you know this?'

'Clyde and I know each other. He's arrested me before. I hear things when I'm around other officers. They talk about their families, or how shit work is, or how they're not being paid enough for what they do.' He turned to me. 'But yes, he has a wife and son.'

'Oh my God; maybe if we tell Lorraine—?'

He shook his head. 'She wouldn't give a shit. She'd probably blame the wife for being "the other woman". If she can slap her own daughter over that piece of shit, telling her about the wife and son won't mean a thing. And you're right' – he faced the front again, his jawline tensing – 'he deserves to be punished.'

He punched the steering wheel three times in quick succession and hopped out of his car. I jumped out without bothering to close my door and followed him. He stormed away from me into the grassland, raking his hands through his hair and breathing deeply.

I stood behind him, staring at his tense shoulders. 'What are we going to do?'

'Fuck him up.' He said it so quietly I barely heard him.

I took a step closer, aware that houses were just metres away. 'How?'

'I don't know. I don't know ... I need to think about this.'

'The way I feel, I could kill him with my bare hands.' I watched on in silence as he walked forwards, further away from the houses, but I could see his back expanding as he breathed heavier. Did he really care this much for Tahlia? Or did this run deeper?

'Trix?' I whispered, as a dry wind ruffled the leaves of the surrounding trees. I felt the anger shimmering off him like a heat haze on a tarred road. That's when I understood, and goosebumps dotted my flesh from head to toe upon realisation. 'It happened to you too … didn't it?'

Every time I tried to face him he turned away, but then I grabbed him tight and forced him to look at me. In the moon's hue, I saw tears gleaming in his eyes. His lips thinned. He struggled to breathe through his nostrils.

'It happened to you,' I whispered again, but this time it wasn't a question; not even a suggestion. I'd come to believe he cared for all of us – maybe it was nothing more than a brotherly type of love, but I couldn't see him reacting like this over Tahlia unless …

He'd only met us a few weeks ago, and had had only a handful of conversations with her. This was personal; this went deeper than sympathy.

'Yes,' he finally whispered in a strangled voice, the tendons in his neck stretched taut. 'My mother's father.'

Stepping backwards as if taking a hit to the gut, I said, 'Wait, what? *Huh*?! That means he was your—'

His expression calcified as his stony eyes met mine. 'Yes, Kylie. My grandfather.'

Chapter Thirty-Three

Trix dropped me back at the front of my house at around one forty-five a.m. He'd said he needed time to think about Clyde's punishment. Going from being a small-time drug dealer was a vast difference to murdering someone, which even at the time I had an inkling was where this was headed; what I'd insinuated when I'd called upon him. But I wanted and *needed* Clyde to pay for what he'd done. Even if the cops arrested Clyde for counts of child rape and molestation – did any pedo ever go away for life? Not even murderers went away for life. Most times kiddie diddlers served a few years – tops. Then they'd be back out on the streets with access to more services for healing and rehabilitation than the actual victims themselves.

No, an evil mind like that doesn't just reset itself after doing time. I knew it was a sickness, a disease that crept in and grabbed a stronghold. It takes a 'special' kind of monster to do this to a child and then go about their day as if nothing happened. They don't care, and they don't change. I loathed the squeamish thought of any more harm coming to Tahlia, but I would have to wait until Trix got back to me with a plan. It was the only time I ever saw him come close to sobbing. And when he'd confessed, everything fell into place. The rebellion, the attitude towards his elders and those in authority, the reason he drank and smoked weed, to numb the pain of his existence. It could be argued some people who are victims of abuse go down a different path, but we have no right to judge someone for how they deal with their turmoil. I've seen the psychological effects of what this can do to a person. Like with the vile predators who do this, I believe it also never leaves the mind of a victim. They can carry on and have a family of their own, but it's like a physical wound that never heals. The gap is closed but the wound remains, and no amount of oils or lotion or therapy will ever make scars go away.

Trix and I had said nothing to each other when he dropped me back. I knew by talking to me about it, it had opened old wounds. He'd said to leave the planning with him, and that was sufficient for me. As I watched him cruise down the road and then flip his headlights on, another pair of headlights materialised from the other end of Sycamore Avenue. Then, like a black silhouette against the horizon, I saw the bubble lights on top of the police car. I don't claim to be psychic, but I have intuition, and I *knew* it was Clyde, searching for Tahlia. Without thinking of anything else but Tahlia's welfare, I raced up the street towards Sharon's house. To hell with my parents and the grounding, to hell with the adults of this town, to hell with what the neighbours would say when I caused a scene. I sprinted across lawns and concrete driveways, dodging parked cars as the warm air brushed against my sweaty forehead and wet cheeks. I should have taken my bike, because by the time I arrived, Clyde was at Sharon's door, pounding on it. The absence of Cheryl's car told me she'd either picked up, or *been* picked up, by someone at the parent–teacher night, which meant Sharon and Tahlia were alone in that house.

Before I saw her face, I heard Sharon telling Clyde to go away. As I got closer, I saw she was dressed in a baby-pink nightie. I tiptoed beside a bush to observe Clyde; it was the first time I'd seen him. Sharon had to crane her neck back to look up at him; he was built like a brick shithouse. His broad back faced me, the living-room light illuminating his silhouette.

'I ain't leaving until Tahlia comes home,' Clyde said, his voice as gravelly as Bon Scott's. 'Her mother's frantic.'

That's when I stepped up behind him, panting. 'She's not here.'

He spun around, hands on his broad hips. The first thing I saw, thanks to the moonlight, was his thick black moustache, and his lips twitched when he trailed down the steps towards me with heavy footsteps. 'And what do we have here? Another troublemaker? How would you like for me to handcuff you and take you down to the station? How'd'ya think your folks would like that?'

The smell of beer and cigarette smoke on his breath almost made me gag, especially when thinking about what this vile pig had done to my best friend; his policeman's uniform meant nothing more to me than a trick-or-treat getup.

'Why?' I asked, gasping and clutching my side where a stitch held it hostage. 'We haven't done anything wrong.'

'Little late to be out walking around, isn't it?' He made a *Tissssstt* sound through his front teeth. 'Troublemakers. The lot of you.'

'*You're* the troublemaker!' My confident tone was the antithesis of how I felt. My knees were quivering like telephone wires during a storm.

He threw his head back and chuckled. It took all my inner strength not to jump up and punch him in the throat. 'Ahhh, you kids crack me up.' His laughter abated and he turned to face Sharon. 'Get Tahlia for me and I'll leave you be. It's as simple as that.' He spread his hands out beside him.

Simple? Get your friend so I can rape her at home, and all will be well again. Simple!

'I told you,' Sharon said, pushing out the words through clenched teeth. 'She's not here.'

'Then let me check the house.'

'No!' Sharon yelled. 'Go away!'

He ascended the steps one by one until the tips of his boots nudged the edge of the WELCOME mat. 'You've got a big mouth, just like your mother … if you know what I mean, but you wouldn't, because you're just another fuckin' kid who thinks she's an adult. If you don't let me in, I'll barge in and drag Tahlia out kicking and screaming. The choice is yours.'

Sharon glared at him, her fingernails embedded into the wooden doorframe.

'She's not here!' I yelled again, shaking all over, bile coating the back of my tight throat. Somewhere in the distance a dog barked, and I had a suspicion we were being spied on by the neighbours, who'd be peeking through their venetian blinds. Usually, if something like this happened, people would burst out the front doors, ready to render aid to their fellow neighbour. But this was no ordinary situation, and I assumed as soon as Sharon's neighbours saw the police car, it had put a dampener on them wanting to rush out and be a hero.

'Go away!' Sharon yelled again.

His back expanded and he shook his head. 'I tried to warn you.' He then raised his right leg and kicked the door wide open using his heel. With a shriek, Sharon stumbled backwards, the back of her head slamming against a pointed edge of the glass coffee table. What frightened me the most was how Clyde seemed to know his way about the place. Had he been spying on us? Sharon's bedroom window faced the street, so it was plausible. I raced in after him, eyeing Sharon clutching her head, writhing in pain on the shag pile rug. I heard Tahlia scream as a door banged open, and then Clyde emerged from Sharon's bedroom, dragging Tahlia by a clump of her orange hair in his fist. He took gigantic strides down a hallway that seemed too small for his frame. Tahlia squealed and dragged her heels, making tracks on the carpet while also trying to free her hair. God, it looked like he was trying to rip out her follicles like yanking on a stubborn tuft of weed.

'Let go of her!' I yelled, charging up the hallway. Clyde stared at me. Amusement flickered in his black eyes as this skinny little runt of a thing challenged him. I tried to grab his hand – the one that clutched her hair – but it was no use.

Tahlia clung to my shirt, hyperventilating. 'Don't let him take me; *please*, don't let him take me!'

'Get off her!' I screamed, but he grabbed my face with his free giant hand and shoved me backwards with such force, the part of my shirt Tahlia had grabbed ripped off, a chunk of fabric flapping about in her white-knuckled fist. The back of my head slammed against the floor when I crashed down, my elbows smarting from carpet burns. I won't bullshit and say I saw stars before my eyes, but it sure knocked the wind out of me. He removed his gun from his holster, and that's when a hot stream of urine ran down the legs of my pants as I lay on the carpet. He pointed the nozzle at Tahlia. She froze with an open mouth, her face deathly white.

'Shut up and listen,' Clyde said.

What chilled me was how calm and collected he was. I always thought raised voices and angry screaming were the worst, but this took the cake. He spoke like a kindergarten teacher would to calm kids down before storytelling time.

'Get your arse in the car with me now, or I'll be forced to use this.' He waved the gun in front of her ashen face, her wide eyes trained on the moving nozzle like a kitten following a red laser beam. 'Are you with me? Are we on the same page here?'

Tahlia nodded vigorously, then looked at me through pleading eyes before stumbling out the front door, sobbing. Clyde turned to me, his black moustache wiggling as his lips twitched. He holstered his gun and, moments later, I heard a car door open and then slam shut. A part of me had hoped Tahlia would use this opportunity to run away as fast as she could.

Clyde now loomed above me, hands on his wide hips, and inhaled while shaking his head. He crouched to his knees and they cracked like a frosted branch. 'I'm sorry about your friend in the living room, but the only thing a woman needs a big mouth for is sucking cock.' He brushed damp hair away from my terrified eyes. Anyone looking on would have seen it as a sweet, fatherly gesture. I wanted to bite off his goddamn fingers and then spit them back in his smug face.

He removed his fingers, but appraised me as his hands dangled between his open tree-trunk thighs. 'Now, you are not going to be telling anybody about this, right? Because if you do' – he patted his gun – 'and it won't end well for a bunch of snot-nosed teens.' His thick brows rose as I continued shaking all over. 'Okay? Are you with me?' He bent low and I flinched when his prickly moustache grazed the side of my cheek as he leaned in to whisper in my ear. 'Because if you tell, I'll end up doing to you what I did to that little whore, Nicole Sullivan.'

Chapter Thirty-Four

I DIDN'T TELL A soul about what Clyde had confessed to. Yet. I didn't tell my parents what was going on in this town, and I didn't tell any of my teachers – or even Ralph Ferguson. To me, this town had turned into the adults versus the kids. I look back now and think maybe there could have been another way, but tell that to my fourteen-year-old self. In my heart and mind, I believed there was only one person I could talk to.

All that Sunday, I stayed in bed. In the wee hours of the morning, I'd snuck back in through my bedroom window and shut the blind most of the way, watching the police cruiser roll by with Tahlia in the passenger seat, head in her hands, guilt rolling through me that I hadn't done more to save her. With shaky fingers, I'd whipped off my torn top and removed my urine-stained pants to throw them in a spare plastic bag. I had to avoid answering 'those' types of questions from Mum, so putting them in my normal bin wouldn't do. I swear my mum snooped through my stuff while I was at school.

I didn't need to be a Diane Keaton protégé to convince my folks I was feeling crook that day, and that's why I hadn't emerged from my room. I *was* sick. I was so sick, I'd wondered if I was going to die. My mind was sick, my stomach was sick, my eyes were sick of crying.

I wondered what had happened to Tahlia, and there were moments when I considered taking Helen's advice and going to the cops. But I didn't. Deep down I believed Trix would fix Clyde up, so if we made ourselves known to the police, and that we had issues with him, if Clyde were to disappear, they'd come straight for us. It was 'easier' to go on acting like we knew nothing. That didn't change the way my stomach kept cramping with anxiety or the way I kept shivering, teeth rattling inside my skull. I had all the symptoms of a fever, without actually having one. Subconsciously, I knew that when I told Trix, he would want to kill Clyde. Perhaps at this point he was only thinking of maiming the scumbag. But it was deeper than revenge now: Trix *needed* to know who had impregnated Nicole Sullivan. I had a lot of time to think about the scenario that Sunday when I didn't leave my room unless it was to pee.

I pictured it as this: Clyde is driving around the town one Friday night on patrol. He sees a young blonde girl at the kerbside, so he pulls over and asks if she's okay, or maybe even to book her for being drunk and disorderly. I could picture Clyde hopping out of the cruiser and walking over to Nicole as she's swaying from the booze, struggling to keep her head up. He picks her up and places her in his car. He probably sits in the driver's seat for a while, pulling on his bottom lip between his thumb and forefinger while thinking about his options. When he looks in the rear-view mirror, he sees a pretty blonde thing passed out, her thighs open and her boobs pushed up – not knowing that she is, in fact, a virgin. Clyde glances in his side mirrors, then eases the cruiser out and takes her to a deserted place – he'd know all the good ones in town. He probably scans the area one more time before hopping out of the car, opening the back door, then unbuckling his belt. He rapes her and ejaculates inside her. After he's done, he either dumps her off where she is, or he takes her back to the kerb where he'd picked her up in the first place – blood smearing her thighs. He finishes his shift and then drives to Lorraine Ashcroft's place to settle in for the night.

Six weeks later, Nicole discovers she's pregnant. And who was the last person she remembers being with before she passed out? Why, that wild boy over at Orange West High – it's the only thing that makes sense to her when she's staring at the confirmed pregnancy report while sitting inside the doctor's office.

In some ways, I now felt sorrier for her than anyone. In her mind, it was the *only* thing that made sense – she wasn't spreading rumours; she was simply misinformed. But because of that, Trix had almost died at the footy final, Rodney would surely spend time behind bars (even if it was a juvie prison), and our freedom had been taken away – seemingly never to be trusted by the adults again.

I'd mulled over everything in bed, and by the time Monday rolled around, I told Sharon to tell Bobby to tell Trix to meet me at Lickety-Split at eight p.m. I had a legitimate four-hour shift there (my mum could call and confirm), and if there was one adult in this town I could trust to at least keep quiet about my rendezvous with Trix, it would be my good friend and stalwart ally, Ralph Ferguson.

Chapter Thirty-Five

'One Way or Another' by Blondie was winding down on the jukebox when I entered Lickety-Split. Laverne DuBois and Eileen Bradbury were at the front counter serving the influx of schoolkids and parents of those students, too busy to notice me. When I opened the side door leading to the kitchen, I saw Ralph at the sink, bopping and humming away to his own rhythm. The sudsy water gave off tiny popping sounds as he lowered in milkshake jugs, silver ice-cream scoops and glass sundae boats, the remnants of crushed peanuts and melted ice cream sliding off and into the water.

He looked over and showcased his impressive choppers. 'Hey! There's my little Sunset! Slap me …' He held out a hand, so I gave him a five, and he spun around and held out wriggling fingers.

Despite everything, I laughed. Ralph was like sunshine on a rainy day, the light at the end of a tunnel, and a bunch of other clichés I could think of. But it was true. I never saw him cry, or get stressed, or get angry … which meant some kids made up rumours about him: he was an alien sent from Mars to spy on us before Martian global domination. Yep … I think some kids played a bit too much of Space Invaders.

He wiped his hands on the front of his white apron. 'How was school, little miss?'

'It was okay.'

He stared at me, squinting. 'What's wrong?'

'Nothing.' *Everything!*

He leaned against the sink, folding his arms in a manner that said he wasn't leaving until we spoke about it. 'Nuh-uh, something's the matter.'

'Ralph, can I ask you for a favour?'

'You know you can; anything you goddamn well like.'

I exhaled a gush of hot air and licked my dry lips. 'I've asked Trix to meet me here when we close the shop tonight.' He eyed me, staying mum while the fluorescent lighting bounced off his bald head. 'I can't tell you what it's about, but I hope you won't tell my parents, or even Keith.'

His dark-brown eyes tried to analyse me as the seconds peeled away. 'Are you in some sort of trouble?' His eyes lowered to my belly for a brief tick. 'Those older boys aren't good news.'

Hearing that made me want to cry for two reasons: first, Ralph was always optimistic and tried to see the good in people; second, the rumours of Trix had spread far and wide, so there was no way I could corral everybody and let them know they were falsified.

'But they are good,' I said. 'At heart, they are good.'

'Pig's arse!' He rubbed his shiny forehead, looking away. 'Did you read about the biffo at the footy oval in the papers?'

'I was there; I saw everything. The Orange East boys started it, I swear to God.'

'Ralph!' Laverne yelled. 'More boysenberry, please!'

He cupped the side of his mouth. 'Coming right up!' He looked at me, lips twisting.

'Please, Ralph,' I whispered.

He eyed me as his mind ticked over. 'And you can't tell me what the John Dory is?'

Closing my eyes, I shook my head. 'No. It's a secret.'

Silence.

Sneaking a peek, I eyed his hand held up and he sighed heavily. He'd dropped the proverbial towel. Ring-a-ding-ding!

'Fair enough. I won't tell a soul.' He then waggled a finger. 'I just hope you know what you're doing with that boy.' He walked away to the freezer to grab Laverne more ice cream, muttering something about he didn't come down in the last shower.

I felt like doing a Snoopy dance around the kitchen. Instead, I opted for a dorky grin – I knew I could count on him! At the sink, I donned yellow rubber gloves as Ralph hurried out the front and started helping Eileen and Laverne with the customers.

Ralph didn't question me for the rest of the night. Being a Monday, it slowed down at around five p.m., so Eileen went home first, then Laverne at six. After that, only two people were working: Ralph out the front serving, and me in the kitchen cleaning up. As I've said, it was easy work, but the shift felt like it had increased from four hours to eight. I kept eyeing the wall clock, watching the second hand tick slowly, my mind racing with a thousand different ways of telling Trix that Clyde had raped Nicole. Song after song played on the jukebox, and I must have scrubbed every square inch of the kitchen to keep distracted, until finally, Ralph switched off the outside neon sign and locked the front door.

After he'd turned off the jukebox halfway through 'Heroes' by David Bowie, he opened the side door and appraised the kitchen. 'All done out here?' He stepped tentatively over the wet floor I'd just mopped, with the cash register drawer under his arm.

'Yes,' I said, hanging up a damp yellow cloth on a silver dish rack. 'Trix will be here any minute.'

'Okey-doke. I'll be in the office counting up. If you need anything, let me know.'

Grinning, I gave him the thumbs-up. 'You're the best, Ralph.'

'Don't mention it.' He took off to the back office and closed the door. Not long after that, I heard the money-counting machine whir as it sorted out the coins. Then there was a knock at the front door. I walked out to the seating area just as Trix raised his knuckles to the glass door, ready to knock again. He was neither smiling nor frowning, his face its usual blank canvas.

Nausea rolled through me. I unlocked the door and let my dry tongue scrape over my equally dry lips. His wild hair smelled of shampoo, but his poor face was still battered and bruised, now with yellowish contours around the purply splotches. At least the stitches in his lower lip had been removed. 'Hi. Come in.'

He surveyed the empty seating area. 'Are you sure Ralph is cool with this?'

I pointed towards the back. 'He's doing the banking. He won't disturb us.'

He nodded once, then ambled inside, still looking around. I shut the door and locked it before facing him. 'Would you like a drink or anything?'

'No. But thanks.'

Exhaling, I led the way past gleaming tables smelling of lemon disinfectant, to sit in the last booth near the blank arcade games, sliding along the bench as he sat opposite me.

'How are you feeling?' I asked, taking in his injuries without trying to hide it.

'I don't know how to answer that,' he said, staring at me.

Dry swallowing, I nodded. 'Fair enough.'

He eyed me for a moment. 'Bobby said you need to tell me something.'

'I do.' Tears had already surfaced, my sweaty fingers intertwined. 'There's something you need to know.'

He sat back, fingertips at the edge of the table. No doubt he'd worked out it wasn't anything good I was about to divulge. I'd spent all day trying to work out how to say it, so in the end I took a leaf out of Sharon's book and just came right out with it.

'Clyde raped Nicole Sullivan. *He* was the one who got her pregnant.'

The only visible reaction was his chest swelled. He neither gasped, nor frowned, nor banged the table with his fist. He always wanted people to take the lead, but I'd said the hardest part. Now it was up to him.

His eyes darted towards the arcade games and I saw the veins in his flushed neck stick out as thick as rope. 'How do you know this?'

'Clyde told me.'

His head swung back to me. 'Clyde? Why would he voluntarily tell you that; when did you see him?'

'It was just after you'd dropped me off at my house.' I told him the entire story of what went down inside Sharon's house – the only thing I left out was the fact I'd peed my pants. Then it occurred to me maybe Trix would think I was making it up to make him feel better, or that I wanted to sweeten the deal of him getting rid of Clyde. He owed us nothing – we weren't related; he wasn't a boyfriend to any of us

– he didn't even know our birthdays. I held up a hand as if swearing under oath. 'I swear he said it, Trix; I wouldn't lie to you.'

He shook his head, dispelling my worries. 'No, I believe you. It all makes sense now, because *some*one got her pregnant and, in a way … in a sick, sad way, I can't blame Nicole now that I know. She was probably passed out during it all, so in her mind, I *was* the last person with her. Either that, or she was awake for the whole thing and when she found out she was pregnant, she went to Clyde and he blackmailed her, or threatened to kill her if she told anyone. Given she couldn't hide her pregnancy, she had to tell people who the father was, so she picked me. Easy target.' He leaned against the booth, closing his weary eyes.

'But the only problem is, if she knew it was Clyde, why did she have a rape exam done? If she was scared of him, she probably would have kept her mouth shut.' I shook my head. 'No, I believe Clyde did it while she was passed out, and in her heart she honestly thinks you did it.'

He leaned his head back against the wooden ledge, Adam's apple bobbing as he swallowed. 'If only I could go back in time and not have driven her at all.'

'You weren't to know what would happen – you said yourself she tried to touch you and she pulled her top down. I don't blame you for dropping her off at the kerb, Trix. This isn't your fault!'

His eyes popped open. 'Isn't it?'

'No! *Clyde* is the one going around raping virgins and molesting young girls!'

Trix stared at me for a moment and inhaled through his nostrils. 'You're right. I'm not the filthy scum.' He looked back over his shoulder to make sure Ralph wasn't within earshot. He wasn't; he was still in the back counting the day's earnings. Trix looked at me with a hardened expression. 'I'm going to kill him.'

My stomach lurched at how chilling this was, hearing the word 'kill' for the first time. 'I know.'

He leaned forward. 'No. Really. I am going to end his life.'

Heart rate on a steady incline, I leaned forward too. 'I know. And I am going to help you.'

He shook his head, a flat hand resting on the table. 'No fucking way. This is me. This is personal.'

'Trix, you cannot do this by yourself. I want him dead too.'

Shaking his head again, he said, 'Kylie, there's no way you're going to help me with this, so you may as well forget it now. It's my score to settle.'

We stared at each other, neither one of us budging in our stance – like two opponents facing off in the dusty streets of the Wild West. 'How are you even going to do it?'

'I'm still working things out. But I will do this.'

'Do you have a gun?' I whispered.

'No. God, no.'

'You cannot do this without our help.'

His dark eyebrows knitted together. '"Our" help?'

'Us girls.'

His eyes widened. 'What? No chance in hell are yo—'

'Trix. Listen to me. We know Clyde, we know Lorraine, and we know Tahlia. You cannot do this by yourself; you'll need our help.'

He shook his head, turning away from me. 'No. Too many people involved; someone is going to talk. My bet is Helen; she's the weakest link.'

'She won't. We're all loyal to each other.'

He placed his other hand flat on the table and stared at me. 'Kylie, have you ever killed a person? Ever been responsible for someone's last breath here on earth?'

'Have you?'

He sat back, his resolve slipping as his battered face softened. Of course he hadn't killed a person. None of us had. And I believed (and hoped) none of us would ever have to again. But this was personal; Trix was right about that. Given I'd never shown a propensity for violence, I was having a hard time myself believing I could speak about this with such vehemence. But the fierce rage I felt overrode any other emotion. I may have been a lot of things: bratty, selfish, immature ... but where my friends were concerned, I was a lioness protecting her cubs at any cost. Tahlia Ashcroft – as pure as virgin snow, with a heart of gold – was my best friend. Enough said. I truly believe anyone is capable of anything given the right circumstance. We're so fond of saying, 'I would *never* do such a thing!' But how do we know unless presented with a situation where we're forced to make a choice? How do we *know*?

'Tahlia can do things on the inside that you can't; she knows Clyde's work roster, where he keeps his gun when he's in the house ...'

'I've thought about this. I've thought of nothing else *but* this. And I will do it, but you need to know something before it happens.'

'What?' I whispered, staring into his eyes.

'After it's done, you'll never see me again.'

Chapter Thirty-Six

TRIX'S WORDS HUNG IN the air between us like spent gunpowder. His battered face became blurred as a barrage of tears spilled out through my stinging eyes. I sat back against the hard ledge, wrapped my arms around my stomach and whimpered. Warm tears skated down my contorted face.

'Kylie,' he whispered, 'I need to get out of Orange. This was always going to happen – with or without Clyde – but now it's sooner than I thought.'

I rocked back and forth, eyes clenched as pain ricocheted off every bone and muscle in my body while I struggled to breathe.

'Why do you think I've been selling drugs? I've been saving up the dough to get me out of here; to start a new life somewhere else – someplace where people don't know my name.'

Wet lips sucked inwards, I shook my head and hooked air through my flared nostrils. 'I don't want you to go.'

'I have to,' he said softly. 'There's no future for me here. Nothing is keeping me in Orange. Not my father, not my friends, not my education. I want to make something of myself while I'm still young. If I stay here, no good can come of it. I'm going to fucking end up like my alcoholic father.' He shook his head, tongue running along his lower lip. 'No. That's no life for me. I want better than that. I will not let my so-called grandfather win by taking away my freedom and future. This is for all the Clydes and Warrens in the world; for me to become successful and triumph against bad odds.'

After I'd grabbed some napkins and wiped my face, I looked up. 'I can't not have you in my life.'

He closed his eyes, jaw clenched, and his swallow looked painful. 'You have been one of the best things that's ever happened to me – you've shown me there is still light among the dark.' He opened his eyes again. 'But this has been in the works for years. Drug money is easy money and when I leave, I am forgetting about all that shit. I doubt you'll believe me, but I only smoked weed around the boys to keep up appearances. Never any time else. I knew, years before when things weren't going my way, that I had little option left. I've flunked high school, but that doesn't mean I can't have a future. I've been working towards leaving Orange for the past few years, and nothing is going to change that.'

Including me. 'But what about your friends?'

He shook his head. 'Friends are what drag you down; I cannot succeed with them in my life. What future do they have? Rodney is already locked up, and it'll be the same for the rest. I can almost guarantee it.'

'I don't believe that. How can you say that? They stuck up for you!'

'They'll survive without me.'

'But ... they're your friends. How can you do this? Don't you care?'

'Friends are crabs.'

'Crabs?'

'Have you ever heard of "crab mentality"?'

'No ...?'

'If you put a crab in a bucket by himself, he'll be able to climb out. But if you put a bunch of crabs into a bucket together and one of them tries to climb out, the others will pull him down. No-one ends up escaping – because if I can't, you can't – understand, Kylie? I cannot do anything in this lifetime if I'm in a group. I need to go solo, so I can make it out of here without people trying to pull me down.'

'But I don't think *I* can handle it. I don't want you to go.'

'I have to.' The corner of his mouth lifted in somewhat of a soothing, every-thing-will-be-all-right smile.

'And nothing I say will make you change your mind?'

His eyes softened. 'My bags are already packed.'

'Then unpack them!'

He smiled again softly. 'I don't mean literally.'

It wasn't until years later I understood what he meant by that. I'd never experienced love and heartache the way I did with Tristan Douglas Walker. I don't give a damn how young I was; I knew then I loved him like he was my soulmate, and I still do now. Even at fifty-nine, despite being married, despite the numerous relationships in my twenties and thirties, I still believe in my heart that if Trix and I had met in different times and in different circumstances, we would have been together forever. My heart was breaking in a way I'd never felt before. I thought I knew what sadness was – like when *The Partridge Family* aired its final episode on 23 March 1974 (I remember it well) – or when Joe Perry, the guitarist of Aerosmith quit the band after an argument – that was *nothing* compared to this heart-ripping-out-of-my-chest sensation as I stared at the first boy I ever loved, knowing I would never see him again after Clyde was taken care of.

Trix leaned over and held out his palms for me to hold. When he'd clamped his thumbs around my hands, my tears were again uncontrollable.

'It's gonna be okay,' he whispered, brushing his thumbs over my flesh.

Even being so young, I knew it wasn't going to be okay – not by a long shot – but what more could I have said? I don't think all the money in the world could have persuaded him to stay in Orange, and looking back now, I couldn't blame him. But my fourteen-year-old-self took offence that he didn't want to stay because of *me*. It was on the tip of my tongue to say 'Take me with you!' but he was too much of a gentleman to say yes. Trix foresaw (as I admitted to myself years later) that I would end up regretting my decision on such a whim. He wanted me to have an accomplished future, and a strong relationship with my parents – something he never knew with his own family. He wanted me to succeed, to be happy, and to create my own family. Him rejecting me was the most selfless thing he could have done.

During our talk, Ralph popped his head through the side door near the front counter. He didn't approach us, but he cupped a hand to his mouth and asked if we were okay or if we needed anything. Trix replied for me, as I was still bawling. Ralph then said he was going out the front for a quick fag, and that we had fifteen more minutes before he would kick us out. When the front door closed, Trix looked at me and inhaled.

'Okay,' he said, holding my hands tighter. 'Here's what we're gonna do ...'

Chapter Thirty-Seven

THE FOLLOWING DAY, I hurried into school with the niggling sensation that those in the quadrangle were watching me with eagle eyes, as though my plans were thought bubbles sprouting out of my head like Medusa for all to read. I knew it was paranoia, but it didn't stop the queasiness in my stomach as I rushed over to the girls. Despite mental fatigue, the fact Tahlia was present overjoyed me; I thought she'd be kept home from school. But by now, I figured Lorraine and Clyde knew it would cast suspicion over them if she kept missing classes. I didn't know for sure, though; it was hard to say how those two cold-blooded monsters operated. There were only so many times Lorraine could tell Headmistress McCarthy that Tahlia wasn't feeling well before she'd get suspicious and maybe send somebody over to check on Tahlia's wellbeing – perhaps even go herself? McCarthy *was* pretty scary.

I told the girls we had to meet in the library at lunch; that it was important and no-one could skip it. The general vibe pervading the air like phosphorus gas was dispirited and melancholy and, of course, we asked Tahlia how she was, but none of us truly expected her to open up about her feelings right before we had class.

Like the night before when I worked at Lickety-Split, waiting for Trix, time seemed to move backwards. My last period before lunch had been History, so I was the last to enter the library, as the block I'd been in was farthest away. Sharon, Helen and Tahlia sat around a square white table, far away from any other student – not that there were many; most kids preferred to bask in the sunshine during lunch, or play handball or touch footy.

I plonked down beside Sharon, and Helen and Tahlia sat on a two-seater opposite. After I'd thrown my schoolbag on the carpet and surveyed our surroundings once more, I did a 'Sharon O'Rourke' again: I got right to the point; there wasn't a minute to spare.

'Sunsets, I have something to tell you, but you all have to swear to me on the life of everyone you love that what I'm about to say doesn't go any further than this room.'

They all looked at each other, swapping frowns, but in the end everyone nodded. I turned to Sharon next to me. 'This includes Bobby. Swear to me on The Sunsets that you will not say a single word about this plan I'm going to share.'

She placed a hand over her heart. 'I swear. You girls will always come first – including over Bobby and my mum.'

I then eyed Helen. 'You, too, Helen – you cannot tell a soul.'

She nodded, but apprehension glossed over her eyes like cataracts. 'I promise.'

After taking one last quick look around, I leaned forward, as did they. 'Trix and I have worked out a plan to get rid of Clyde.'

Tahlia's eyes widened and she glanced all around, fearful if someone overheard.

'Get rid of Clyde?' Helen whispered, frowning deeply. Bless her heart, she probably thought we were going to send him on a vacation.

'We're going to kill him.'

Helen sat back in her chair, her face drained of colour.

'How?' Sharon whispered, and then looked around our area before turning back to me.

'First ... Trix wants me to say that none of you have to be involved if you don't want to be. He even tried to talk *me* out of it' – I shook my head – 'but I told him no way; I wasn't letting him do this alone.'

'I'm in!' Sharon whispered, raising a hand, even though I was sitting beside her.

I turned to Helen; she seemed off in her own little world, unblinking eyes on the table in front. 'You don't need to be part of this, but it still doesn't mean you can tell anyone.'

Helen swallowed, frown lines raking across her forehead. 'I-I don't know what to say or do.'

I then eyed Tahlia. 'Are you in?'

Tears formed in her brown eyes before spilling over. Her lips shrivelled and her face turned puce. 'Yes,' she said through clenched teeth.

'Good, because this plan involves all of us.'

'How?' Sharon whispered.

'Trix has come up with a plan. And after it's done, he's going to leave town for good.'

Sharon grabbed my arm. 'Oh my God, *what*? Are you okay with this?'

I swallowed deeply, lubricating my aching throat. 'He was always going to leave, but this is giving him the push he needs. He's been planning this for years – not even Bobby knows – none of the boys do.'

'What's the plan?' Tahlia whispered, tears clinging to her chin before yielding to gravity.

'Yeah, how are we to be involved?' Helen asked, clutching the hem of her navy-blue skirt.

'Tahlia, does Clyde have a usual rostered shift at the station?'

'Yes, he does mostly days, but sometimes nights too.'

'Do you know when he has a night off next?'

Her teary eyes drifted skyward as she ruminated. 'I overheard Mum and Clyde talking about it. This Friday and Saturday night he's working. He has Sunday off, then he'll work on Monday and Tuesday daytime.'

Expelling a sigh of relief, I said, 'Great. That's perfect. Trix doesn't want it to be on a busy night.'

'But how is he going to do it?' Helen said.

'Tahlia, you're going to need to be the insider for this to work. Are you cool with that?'

'Yes,' she pushed out through gritted teeth.

'Good. Do you usually have family dinners together?'

'Yes, all the time when he's not at work. He pretty much lives with us now.'

'And does he have a drink with dinner?'

'He's always drinking beer, even when he has a shift the next morning.'

I glanced around, making sure no student or librarian ambled by, even in the near vicinity. 'Groovy. Trix is going to give me some crushed sleeping pills sometime this week. I'll give them to you. All you need to do is slip them into his beer bottle or glass. And into your mother's drink too.'

'My mum?' She shook her head, her eyes wild and frantic. 'I don't want her to die.'

'No, I promise she won't. I *promise*! But she needs to be asleep too.' Tahlia sucked her lips inwards. 'Trix says the ones he'll give me will take a while to work. Do you have a torch inside your house?'

'A torch?' Her eyes roamed the table in between us as she thought about it. 'Yes.'

'After they've gone to bed, you're going to go into their room and say you heard something outside.'

'Why?' Tahlia whispered.

'You'll need to make sure they're both fast asleep, that's why. If you go into their bedroom and say you think someone is breaking in, Clyde would get up with his gun and check, right?'

'Yes, he would.'

'Exactly. If neither of them stirs, and if they're both snoring, then the pills have worked.'

'Okay. Then what?'

'Do you know where Clyde keeps his keys to the police car?'

Tahlia considered for a moment. 'I'm pretty sure in the bedroom, beside his gun and wallet ... on the nightstand.'

'Once you're sure they won't be waking up, you grab the keys and everything else he brings over. None of his personal shit can be left behind. Not his clothes, not even his toothbrush.'

Tahlia used both hands to wipe the tears from her flushed cheeks. 'Okay.'

'Then you go to your lounge room because it faces the front yard. Do not turn any lights on, but go to the window and flick your torch three times. Trix and us girls will wait outside for the signal. After you flash the torch at us, you unlock the front door and let us in.' I turned to Sharon. 'This is where you girls are needed.'

Sharon nodded, no hint of anxiety on her face. She wanted this to happen as much as I did.

'We all need to help carry Clyde out to the police car. Once he's in the boot, Trix will drive it over to the private lookout above Lake Canobolas. We all get out of the car, Trix will put it in neutral, then we all ... push the car until it goes over the cliff.'

'Are you sure it'll go in the water?' Helen whispered, her lips white around the edges.

'We roll down every window to make sure water gets in quick, taking the car under so if someone *does* hear the splash, by the time they wake up and turn the lights on to check, the car will already be sucked under.' Even uttering those words, my mouth dried up and my breath quickened.

'Are you sure this is going to work?' Tahlia said, her forehead pinched.

'The lake is deep enough that no-one would ever see his car at the bottom. Trix checked all this information out before he saw me at Lickety-Split. He drove his car over there on Monday morning before sun-up and checked the top of the lookout to make sure it could happen. It can. Trix is a planner and he is sure this will work, but ...'

The three girls leaned in closer.

Sharon raised an eyebrow. 'But?'

'But this is a secret we take to our graves. Even if decades later we have families of our own and you want to tell your husband ... no. Is this cool? Are we all in?'

'Wait!' Tahlia said. 'What happens afterwards? What happens to my mum and the other officers? They'll know he is missing as well as the police car; they'll want him – and it – back.'

'Trix has a plan, but this involves Helen.'

Helen pointed to her chest. 'Me?'

'You have the nicest handwriting out of all of us.'

Helen's upper lip fish-hooked. 'What does that have to do with it?'

'You're going to write a note pretending to be his wife.'

'His wife?!' Helen screeched.

I turned to Tahlia. 'Trix told me Clyde is married and he has a son.'

Her eyes widened to the diameters of dinner plates. 'Huh? Are you *serious*?'

'She's not from Orange, but he is still married; they haven't divorced yet.'

'Oh my gosh!' Tahlia clutched her ashen face.

'What a fuckin' scumbag,' Sharon said, biting her thumbnail. 'Imagine having a dad like that, deadset. Yuck!'

'Agreed. Helen, you need to write Lorraine a note telling her you know what's been going on. Trix wrote me a note so you can copy it down yourself. Are you ready?'

Helen, whose pallor now bordered on translucent, bobbed her head. I leaned down to my left and opened my schoolbag. I pulled out a folded piece of paper and spread it before the girls on the white table between us, looking all around once more, making sure we were still alone. Then I turned back to the paper with Trix's handwriting.

Dear Lorraine Ashcroft,

You and I have never met, but I am Clyde's wife. Yes, you little tramp, Clyde is a married man, and we have a son. How does that make you feel? He's come back to us – his family – and I found out all about you. I only think it's fair to let you know, you and he are through, and if you ever try to meddle with our relationship again, I will let everyone in Orange know what a trollop you are – sleeping with a married man. Shame on you! He won't be coming back; you need to move on with your life and leave married men alone. You have a beautiful daughter; perhaps you should start thinking about her?

Yours truly,

Mrs Hanratty

Sharon was the last to finish reading the note, but when she had, she faced me. 'Wow! He has nice writing; why can't we just send this one?'

'Yeah,' Helen said, fingers intertwining, then fidgeting in her chair. 'This is perfect.'

Shaking my head, I said, 'No. Don't forget: Trix is going to leave town right after this is done. If the police suspect something, Trix reckons they could put two and two together. They may even investigate the wife, and she won't have a clue about where Clyde or the police car is – she'll deny writing the note. If Lorraine goes to the police with the note, they could match up Trix's handwriting to school paperwork. We can't let anything go.'

'What if they suspect *me*?' Helen said, a palm against her heaving chest.

'That's the thing ... who would think that four young girls could be part of this?'

Sharon smiled as though reminiscing about a pleasant childhood memory. 'They won't. No way would they. Who would?'

'Exactly. But they could suspect Trix.'

'Does he have anything to do with Clyde?' Tahlia asked.

'Clyde has arrested him before, yeah.'

'Why won't Trix wait around after it's done, then?' Sharon said. 'Why does he need to leave now? That's only going to make it look more suspicious.'

'Agreed!' Helen said, scrunching her eyes.

'Trix never actually said it, but I think he's worried the Orange East boys are still after him. He wouldn't want to keep looking over his shoulder if more trouble is coming.'

Sharon sighed, slumping in her chair. 'Man, this won't ever stop, will it?'

'Nope. I don't think so. And I think Trix knows it too. Maybe this time they won't come after him at a public event where people are there to break it up; they'll get him when he's alone.'

I let that settle in before asking what they were thinking. Helen stared off into space. Sharon seemed the most unfazed. Tahlia appeared consumed by her thoughts, a fist covering her mouth as she eyed the note on the table.

'I need to tell you one more thing, but promise me you won't tell a soul.'

'Promise,' Tahlia said, looking up from the note.

Helen bobbed her pasty head and Sharon gave me the thumbs-up.

'Clyde was the one who got Nicole Sullivan pregnant.'

Sharon gasped, grabbing my right arm and squeezing hard. 'Shut the fuck up!'

'It's true. He admitted it to me.'

Tahlia cupped her open mouth. Tears oozed out of her red-rimmed eyes.

'Oh my *God*,' Sharon said, 'why didn't we think of this before?'

'It makes sense now, huh? And it makes sense why Nicole thought it was Trix. But I swear, Clyde told me.'

'How did he tell you?' Sharon asked, but then stopped as we waited on a teeny kid with a hearing aid wire dangling from his ear to walk by us as he searched the aisles. After he'd picked up a copy of *Interview with the Vampire* and marched off, I turned to Sharon.

'Remember on Saturday after you banged your head?' She clutched the back of her skull as though by me mentioning it, the wound throbbed again. 'When I was on the ground after he pushed me by the face, he whispered it in my ear. He said if I didn't keep my mouth shut, then he would do to me what he did to Nicole Sullivan.'

Helen sucked back air and stared at me. 'I only have one question left.'

I leaned forward. 'What is it?'

Helen's chest expanded, her nostrils flared. 'When are we going to do it?'

Chapter Thirty-Eight

Just before the shrieking bell signalled lunch was over, I pulled out another piece of paper. It may sound silly now, but I wanted each of The Sunsets to swear in writing that they wouldn't tell a soul about us breaking the sixth commandment. We didn't have a clue what actual legal documents were supposed to look like, but to me, this was as binding as any sworn statement. It was vital the girls understood this was more serious than a quick head nod or a 'yes'; by signing the paper, it made it more legitimate. Trix said my idea would work well – psychologically speaking. I hoped that if Helen, Tahlia, Sharon or even *I* ever reached the point of telling another soul what we did, then the memory of signing the paper would come to mind and put the kibosh on spilling the beans. I was relieved but not surprised when all four of us had signed that paper. I folded it in half and placed it inside my schoolbag.

The hardest part about this wasn't the fact we were about to snuff out a life – we *hated* Clyde Hanratty for what he had done – it was keeping this burden to ourselves. I loved Keith, and I loved Ralph Ferguson and, of course, my parents, but there was no way I could speak to anyone about this – not even David Cassidy. The difficult thing was also going to be acting normal. I hate the word 'normal' anyway, but normal for me was being a cheerful kid who loved to ride my bike while singing along to my transistor radio. Would I ever be the same again? Or was I selling my soul to the devil?

Paranoia is like a fever of the brain. As I rode down Sycamore Avenue that afternoon while people washed sudsy cars, or talked to other neighbours out the front as they collected their letters from the mailbox, I felt like their eyes lingered on me more than usual. Was Mr Willding ogling my schoolbag with X-ray vision and seeing the evidence against us? Was Mrs Lockhart with the orange casserole pot telepathically reading my thoughts like the children in *Village of the Damned*? Every part of me broke out in a cold sweat, so I pumped my scrawny legs as fast as they could go, only throwing a cursory wave at those who waved at me first. My bike shuddered as I bounced along, across driveways and over lawns. I almost clipped a toddler sitting in a small plastic fire truck, swirling around his driveway mimicking '*wee-ooh, wee-ooh, wee-ooh*'.

I'd never felt more relieved to be at my front door. I said hi to no-one and raced to my room, throwing my schoolbag on the bed before unzipping it with hands that shook like an exhaust on a motorbike. It's one thing to wish someone dead, but to know you will have a part in their last breath on earth is like comparing cats to catfish. Still, all I had to do to remain steadfast was close my eyes and envision the pain emanating from Tahlia when she'd sat on Sharon's bed and wailed, drawing back shuddering breaths.

This was going to happen. The moment Clyde first put his grubby hands on Tahlia was the moment he signed his own execution. I needed to get word to Trix and tell him that all four of us agreed to help, and Helen would write the note as instructed. I hid the paper with our signatures on it inside AC/DC's 1976 vinyl album *Dirty Deeds Done Dirt Cheap*. Poetic, don't you think?

As I collapsed backwards on the bed, my mind detoured to Trix and damned if I didn't start crying again. I'd put on a brave face for those girls in the library, but now it was killing me, robbing me of breath as though my lungs had a leak and oxygen was escaping faster than I could heave it in. Knowing I would never see that grin of his again; knowing he would not be the one who took my flower away; knowing I would never be in his godlike presence again ... I cupped my flushed face and screamed into my hands to relieve the pressure.

A minute later, my mum barged through the door. I was still mad at her for gating me over the footy incident, but right then, I did not care; I needed my mother – the equivalent of an elixir. When she rushed over and sat on the bed, I hugged her around the shoulders, braying into her neck. She didn't ask me what was wrong; instead, she held me, rocking me back and forth, letting me let it all out. And in that moment, I thanked her for being *her* more than anything. I thought I had a lot to complain about my mother and how uncool she could be, but then I thought of Cheryl O'Rourke, who flirted with the boys her teenage daughter brought home. And then there was Lorraine Ashcroft ... slapping her own daughter across the face when she told her she'd been fiddled with. In reality, my mother taking away my turntable, pink Princess phone and my TV didn't seem like shit.

It wasn't until I was a mother myself that I realised I was blessed to have the parents I did. Upon reflection, Mum was protecting her daughter the only way she knew how to, from a pitfall too many young women faced: pregnant as a teen, to a boy who'd run off and hump the next best thing when he could.

It also wasn't until I became a mother I understood that you see yourself in your child. Their failures are yours; their successes are yours. We are blessed with a second chance to redo life, to do the things we never got the chance to. It occurred to me how frightened my mother felt about Keith and me. I also understood that my mother was living her life through us a second time around. There is no way she could have foreseen herself as a stay-at-home mother, cooking and cleaning all day. Thinking was backwards – even in the '70s – where the woman stayed home and cleaned as the man went to work to make the dough. Her only enjoyment for the day was peering out the window with phone in hand, gossiping to a girlfriend: 'Did you *see* Marjorie's new bob cut? Her cat has a better hairdo!'

I'm sure that's not what my mother envisioned when she started dating Dad. She would have had her entire future planned out. She'd told me once she'd dreamed of being a famous tennis player like Billie Jean King. But as I've said, seldom do childhood dreams become reality.

As much as a hard-arse my mother was, I realised decades later when I held my firstborn that her anger towards Keith and me was borne of fear. For me, adulthood has been about reflection and understanding from experience. You can't put an old head on a young person's shoulders. A child will always be the greatest love of your life, but you will never be theirs.

At the time, I questioned whether Mum would still love me if she ever found out about my involvement in murdering a policeman. Either way, because of my unwavering loyalty to Tahlia Ashcroft, I thought it was worth the risk of finding out.

Chapter Thirty-Nine

It was Thursday before I saw Trix again. After my little crying episode in my bedroom, Mum returned my stuff on the proviso that, henceforth, I promised to be open and honest with her about where I was going and who with. While crossing my fingers of one hand behind my back, I looked her in the eye and gave her that promise. Even though the pink phone lay beside me on my bedside table again, I didn't want to risk speaking to Trix on it and having my mother pick up the receiver from the lounge room and listen in. Being a town gossip, it was not uncommon for me to come home from school and see her in the lounge room, phone to ear, one hand pulling the front curtain back a tad while 'keeping a watchful eye out'.

So I relied on Sharon to tell Bobby to tell Trix when to meet me at school and at what time. Bobby didn't ask any questions. She'd usually give him instructions after they'd had sex (which apparently *was* better the second time around).

I'd ambled into school on the Thursday morning and headed to where the girls had congregated on the benches. Helen, Tahlia and Sharon were seated, but no-one spoke. The understanding of what we were about to do weighed on our minds like a cement blanket and I grew anxious that one, or all, would back out.

'Are any of you having second thoughts?' I asked, looking at Helen, who was reading *The White Dragon* – well, more like staring than reading; her unblinking blue eyes never moved.

Tahlia shook her head and placed her water bottle on the bench beside her. 'No. He ... touched me again last night.'

Sharon embraced Tahlia and soothed the back of her head. Tahlia's orange hair still didn't have its usual vibrancy, but I promised her this nightmare would be over soon. Seeing her drooping jowls and red-rimmed eyes convinced me that we were doing the right thing. This *had* to end, for all our sakes; I couldn't sleep at night knowing at any given moment Clyde, penis in hand, could creep up on Tahlia as she slept.

'Are we still planning it for this Sunday?' I asked. 'Because Trix will be here soon and he'll want to know. I don't think I'll see him again after this is done.' Saying those words felt like a bellyflop onto concrete. I couldn't focus on the gut-wrenching pain of meeting someone so alluring, then never being in his seraphic aura again. The mark he'd left was sure to remain, the memory of Trix etched into my mind like a tattoo. But this was not about me.

Helen nodded meekly, slotting a lilac bookmark in her paperback.

'Good,' I said softly. 'Sharon? Tahlia?'

They both agreed this Sunday was the day. Trix wanted it to be on a quiet night, anyway. Lake Canobolas on Fridays and Saturdays morphed into lovers' lane, and although that was on the other side and down in the main car park, the noise of a car slamming into the water would surely grab anyone's attention – think of the echo.

Helen pointed behind me. 'He's here.'

I swivelled my head and saw Trix standing alone among the bushes flanking the student car park. To a teacher he could have been a peeping Tom, dressed in all black with dark shades, slinking into the bushes ... but Trix had told me to beware of who spotted us talking. He still had his doubts about Ralph Ferguson, despite my promise he was one of the good guys. When I turned back to look at the girls, Sharon was still holding Tahlia. 'I'll be back.' That strange bubbling cauldron feeling in my stomach returned as I strode past a cluster of students sucking on melting Splices. Could they read my mind? Did they know what we had planned? Was it tattooed on my face for all to see?

I made my way over, without rushing, without drawing attention to myself; I was just another student walking around the grounds.

I'd never seen Trix appear so foreboding, more intimidating, and it didn't help that the dark sunnies hid those enticing brown eyes.

'Hi,' I said, stepping over dried leaves and fallen bark to stand with him among the bushes, whiffing the earthy scents of eucalyptus leaves and warm soil.

'Hello, Kylie. Is it agreed upon?'

I moved beside him to stand shoulder to shoulder, so I too could peer about. Queasy stomach constricting, I focused on a sky-blue Kingswood in the parking lot. 'Yes. This Sunday.'

'Same time, same place?'

'Yes.'

He glanced around before speaking again. 'How is Helen?'

I held a small branch away from my face as my eyes roamed left and right. 'She's nervous, but she's in.'

'Has she written the note?'

'Yes.'

'Good. Keep it safe.' He pulled out two white envelopes from his breast pocket. 'This is flurazepam; they're prescription pills – my dad uses them. I've given you equal doses for both Lorraine and Clyde. With the amounts here, they'll start to feel woozy and light-headed within thirty minutes. Make sure Tahlia gives this to them close to bedtime.'

Sickness crept up my stomach lining and, for a moment, I thought I was either going to projectile vomit or pass out. We were doing this. We were truly going to commit murder.

'She knows what to do, yeah? Make sure it's mixed in with a fork. She'll have to bring the drinks out to the table or lounge room; she can't rely on Clyde turning his head and then slipping it in his drink, otherwise the crushed pills will float on the top.'

Vertiginous, my surroundings skewed out of focus. *Calm down; just breathe.* 'She knows.'

'Good. Make sure this is towards the end of the night – the whole dose. We can't risk it wearing off, even though it should knock them out for a good six hours or so.'

He handed me the envelopes and my jittery fingers pressed the bulge of the crushed powder. I turned to look at him as he surveyed our surroundings through the dark-green leaves.

'Trix?' He faced me. God, how I wished I could have seen some comfort in his eyes. 'Thank you.'

'This is just as much for me as it is for Tahlia.' He pulled me in for an embrace and I heard him dry swallow.

I closed my eyes as my cheek grazed his warm leather jacket. 'Have you changed your mind about leaving?'

'No.'

My chest tightened and it took an age for my aching throat to open. 'When will you go?'

'Monday morning. Dad leaves for work before the sun comes up. I'll pack my bags and money the night before – before I come and get you – then as soon as his car backs out of the driveway, I'll jump into my car, never to return to this shithole.'

Boy, I was glad he couldn't see my contorted face. 'I'm going to miss you so much.' I squeezed him tighter, my organs rearranging themselves to accommodate the abundance of pain.

He leaned away from me, holding me at arm's length. He brushed away my tears with the pads of his thumbs and, in that moment, I believed he was going to kiss me. But the shrill bell interrupted and he turned to look towards the quadrangle on his left. We heard students cheer and others laugh as a horde of shoes clobbered across the concrete in a mass exodus from the playground.

'Make sure no-one sees you giving this to Tahlia,' he said, pointing at the envelopes. 'She has to keep it safe.'

'I'll make sure.' We watched the last stragglers hurry through the front gates, and a dusty-white Statesman pull into the student car park, its greasy-haired driver blowing a plume of smoke out of the window before leaning back and plopping in eyedrops.

Trix nodded, then swallowed and cleared his throat. 'So ... I guess I'll see you on Sunday night.'

'Sunday night.'

He caressed my cheek again and left without another word, leaving me to stare at him walking away. It only occurred to me then that he hadn't brought his car along; he'd either parked it around the block, or he'd trekked all the way here, in the heat, wearing a leather jacket.

The boys were still suspended from school until the following week, and it felt weird not seeing them around. Mike Perkins could attend, but he'd chosen not to, to protest his friends not being able to attend their Year 12 formal. I wondered what the boys were doing during their spare time.

I felt bad that Trix would not tell them he was skipping town, but who could blame him? I understood why he'd trusted only The Sunsets to keep this a secret – and he was right: the more people who knew meant the more chance of word getting out. The last thing I wanted was for Trix to leave town for a better life, only to have the police track him down and bring him back here to stand trial. But with our plan, I didn't see how anything could connect him to the murder apart from circumstantial evidence – I didn't even know what that word *was* back in 1979, but it was in line with my thinking. There would be no witnesses apart from those involved, and unless the traitor wanted to be behind bars also, we would keep this to ourselves. But as Newton's third law goes: for every action, there is an equal and opposite reaction. The consequences of what would happen on Sunday night would be no different.

It almost seemed too heavy a price to pay.

Chapter Forty

When 2 December rolled around, I was too sick in my belly to even *look* at food, let alone stomach it. Mum had made her famous spaghetti bolognaise with garlic bread and a garden salad. Amy joined us at the table that Sunday night, and I was thankful because she and Mum spoke non-stop about the baby. What size clothes to buy; how does giving birth feel? 'My boobs already hurt ...'

No-one paid attention to the fact I plopped the tiniest bit on my plate; I didn't even have a slice of buttery garlic bread. Whenever I looked at the bolognaise sauce, all I saw was Clyde's blood. Dad was his usual, quiet self, muttering only a thing or two. I was glad Mum had now had a change of heart since her initial outburst when Keith had told her Amy was pregnant. But that was classic Mum. She was like one of her casseroles from the oven: too hot to touch in the beginning, but when it cooled down, it was beautiful.

When six p.m. rolled around, Mum suggested we all migrate to the lounge room and watch telly. Everyone agreed, so to avoid suspicion I joined my family on the dark-green leather couches and stared at the TV while *Countdown* came on the ABC. Ian 'Molly' Meldrum filled the TV screen, wearing a colourful light-pink shirt with red roses, forgoing his usual Stetson in favour of a baseball cap with yellow horns on either side, Viking-style. As Elton John belted out his rendition of Chuck Berry's 'Johnny B. Goode' in front of a bunch of women waving teddy bears, I mentally switched off from my all-time favourite TV programme.

I remember nothing after that because my own movie reel was playing before my unblinking eyes. I was packing shit. Not so much about ridding the world of a piece of filth, but of getting caught. Of Trix never being able to leave town, of what my parents would say if they found out I was involved in plotting a policeman's death. And yes, the notion of innocent teen girls orchestrating someone's demise may sound fucked up. But there was no way I could handle the thought of Tahlia being at home, going through this abuse night after night with no-one to help her. If Lorraine Ashcroft had been a decent mother, then I believe this could have been avoided – yet, some other unfortunate soul who found Clyde dreamy would welcome him into her home, and another child would have to suffer because of it. I didn't want that to happen; I didn't want that on my teeny fourteen-year-old conscience. To my mind, those who helped cover up evil were just as much a part of the problem as those who went out and perpetrated it.

I chanced a look at the wall clock as the others laughed at something funny Elton had said to Molly before Molly awarded him a platinum record for 'A Single Man'. When it cut to the music video of 'Video Killed the Radio Star' by the Buggles, I closed my eyes and shuddered. The sand in Clyde's hourglass was depleting rapidly, and as the second hand ticked on the clock, sweat broke out on my upper lip, and my skin felt syrupy. But if I wasn't with my family watching *Countdown*, where else would I be? Probably in my bedroom, throwing up in a plastic garbage bag. As Mum headed into the kitchen to make us popcorn, my mind drifted to Tahlia. How on earth was she going with her performance at the house? Would the guilt and panic overwhelm her and make her blurt the whole thing out? What if Clyde was on his way here right now to arrest me for conspiracy to murder? Again, that wasn't a part of my vocabulary back then, but I was so stressed, wondering whether Tahlia would go ahead with it. Yes, she wanted the molesting to stop, but she was so sweet and innocent that asking her to take part in murder was like asking a nun to help kill someone.

There I was, sweating like a piece of steak over a flaming grill, wondering if Tahlia's acting skills measured up. Would Clyde's copper instincts pick up on any strange behaviour? Would Lorraine? Every shadow moving outside the curtained windows that caught my eye spiked my heart rate. Clutching a glass of lime cordial, my hand quivered, swishing the green water around.

It felt like the '70s had rolled into the '80s by the time my parents and the others called it a night, when the few TV stations shut down and nothing but static played. I wasn't sneaking out until after midnight but still, I needed a moment of pure silence, praying to whoever the hell was listening. I wouldn't need to set an alarm in case I fell asleep; the anxiety pumping through me felt like I was one heartbeat away from collapsing. When the clock finally ticked over to 12:30 a.m., I was buzzing with adrenaline and fear I'd never known to be physically possible, and I must have gone to the bathroom a dozen times to relieve my weak bladder. My chin wobbled as much as my legs as I made my way to the window, mouth and throat as dry as hay. I'd dressed in all black, just as Trix had asked us to. I braced myself on the window ledge for a moment while crickets chirruped in the warm, still night, and then placed one rickety leg out of the window. Then I ducked, and my body and left leg followed through until I stood on the outside of my house. I'd crossed the threshold of no return. After taking a quick peek around, I made a beeline towards Sharon's place.

Chapter Forty-One

Sharon and I rounded the corner of Tahlia's street, sticking to the bushes and darkness like Trix had told me to. We hid beside a rusty Toyota Corolla, ducking low until we saw torchlight ahead flick once. That was Trix's signal to us that the coast was clear, that no neighbours were around, that no insomniac was out walking their pooch. My legs were shaking so badly I didn't think I could walk to Tahlia's house. But with the grace of God, I moved one foot in front of the other, stooping so low my lower back ached. When the tip of my joggers kicked a pebble and it skidded forward across a concrete driveway, I winced and turned to Sharon. She froze with wide possum-like eyes, but then waved a dismissive hand and pointed forward as if to say: *Don't worry, just keep going.*

Sharon and I had only seen two panel vans driving around since we'd got going. Houses were pitch-black, not even a porch light left on. We held sweaty hands and crept along front lawns, past wooden fences, and in between parked cars in driveways. Tahlia's house stood to the left and when we approached, Trix looked so blended in with the black surroundings that if it weren't for the whites in his eyes, we would have stumbled over him. When Sharon and I reached him, he motioned for us to hide behind the knee-high brick fence of the neighbour's house across the street. Being in someone else's front yard, hiding behind their fence terrified me, but it was a good vantage point. If the pills hadn't worked and Clyde emerged from the house to search for us, then we would be dead meat.

Trix had given me a verbal list of strict instructions that Monday night at Lickety-Split, including not to speak a word. He'd told me the clothes and shoes we should wear, and he'd suggested we work out hand actions for communicating. I hadn't seen why we would need to, but the girls and I had done practice runs at lunchtimes in the library. Turns out there's a lot you can communicate by using just your hands or facial gestures.

Trix swivelled around to the opposite end of the street and flicked the torch once. That one was for Helen, who'd come from that direction. Trix shoved his torch into his pants pocket, waiting until Helen tiptoed over, and when she did, he pressed an index finger against his lips to motion for silence. When she nodded, he pulled her down behind the brick wall next to us. When I gazed into her face, I thought she was either going to spew or pass out. Her pallor was as faint as the moonlight; she could have blended in like a headless ghost.

We dropped to our knees and our fingertips clung to the brick wall while we peered over the top to spy on Tahlia's house opposite. No lights illuminated – not even a blue TV glow; the cruiser sat in the driveway and not even a dog had barked. Everything was as it should be.

It couldn't have been more than ten minutes since we'd started eyeing the house, but goddamn ... Oh *Lord*, how I wished for this to be over. I clutched the jagged bricks until a trickle ran down the pads of my fingertips. I pulled my fingers away, but upon squinting in the moonlight I saw it was sweat, not blood. We were all drenched in perspiration while waiting for the signal.

Fear gripped every one of us that night – I could smell it in the air like bad BO. Not only did I feel like throwing up what little I'd eaten of Mum's spaghetti, my poor bladder was begging for mercy again; Sharon kept fidgeting next to me, and Helen was breathing so heavily through her nostrils Trix had to motion for her to stop by holding up a palm, and then pinching her nose. She nodded to say she understood, and he released her nostrils before facing Tahlia's house. Once again, I closed my eyes and prayed we wouldn't be caught, that everything would go according to plan and we could get on with our lives.

I think each of us shot out solemn promises that night, but mine was: *Dear God, I will never sin again in my life if You let us get away with this.* He and I both knew this was utter bullshit, but what else was I going to use to strike a bargain with God; Anzac biscuits?

My stomach made a gurgling sound similar to water spiralling down a plughole, and Sharon turned to me with a finger pressed to her lips. I wanted to retort: *Oh, yeah, sure, Sharon, I'll just control my bodily fluids*, but each of us was as nervous as the other; everyone was on edge. My full bladder pressed into other organs, my hair clung to my sweaty temples like papier-mâché, and Helen couldn't stop dry swallowing. While the minutes peeled away, I began to feel something was wrong. The plan would not go ahead; Clyde would burst out the front at any moment with his gun pointed, searching for us because Tahlia had confessed.

Just as I was about to turn to Trix to communicate with my eyes: *This is taking too long; something went wrong*, three flashes of a torchlight blinked from behind Tahlia's lounge-room window.

Chapter Forty-Two

After emerging from behind the brick fence, looking right, then left, Trix led the way across the street. He beckoned us with a 'come on' wave, so we followed: Helen, then me, and Sharon at the rear. We crept across the road, up the driveway, passing the police cruiser, then Lorraine's white Ford Capri. The front door opened and Tahlia stood at the threshold, snivelling back tears. None of us stopped to hug her, but she pointed Trix to where the master bedroom was, and we followed, but not before Helen taped the handwritten note addressed to Lorraine onto the front door. We tiptoed down the carpeted hallway, following the symphony of snores by both sleeping occupants.

Clyde, dressed in a singlet and shorts, was sleeping on his back, and Lorraine lay on her side facing the window, the moon's glare illuminating the translucent drool pooling from a corner of her open mouth. Trix approached the bed and tapped Clyde's shoulder tentatively – as one might when checking if a stove hob is still hot. Satisfied that Clyde was no more cognisant than a doornail, Trix grabbed his upper half. With jittery hands and pinpricks of light dancing before my eyes, I grabbed Clyde's left leg, Sharon took his right, and we picked up his beefy body as I fought the urge to puke. Helen supported Clyde's right shoulder when Trix lifted him off the bed. Even with the four of us holding his six-foot-three frame, it was like trying to lift a house. Oxygen exploded from my lungs as we took on his full weight, and Helen wheezed as she tried to hold on. Puffing and wincing, lower backs throbbing, we shuffled along, Clyde's body dipping at the waist as Sharon and I waddled backwards out the door first, Helen and Trix following. We'd waited for

Tahlia to run back inside and give us the thumbs-up, which meant the coast outside was clear. It'd been a shaky thumbs-up, but message received all the same.

The four of us shambled over to the cruiser, where Tahlia had already opened the boot and the car doors. I told myself platitudes so I could keep my shit together. *We're doing the right thing; he deserves this.* Clyde never stirred, he just snored and gave interspersed watery snorts. When we reached the boot, Trix and Helen placed his upper body in first, and the car dipped from the weight, the springs creaking. Once he lay half-crumpled inside, Sharon and I pushed his legs inside as Trix bent them at the knees. It was a tight fit, but we managed to get him into a foetal position. We knew our part in this as Trix had instructed, so before the boot was closed, we were already inside the car – Tahlia, with a plastic bag of Clyde's possessions in hand, kept a lookout up and down the road.

When Trix closed the boot, Tahlia raced up the driveway and hopped inside before he followed – the last one to enter the car. With quaking hands, Tahlia handed Trix the policeman's hat, and he slipped it on as we all ducked low in our seats. I sat in the passenger seat and Helen, Sharon and Tahlia sat in the back, huddling together. When the car rumbled to life, I thought I was going to pee my pants for the second time since becoming a teenager, but I kept it together, sweaty hands clenched while I prayed to God no-one would hear. The air grew hotter than an oven in the car. I couldn't work out if it was our rapid panting or body heat, but it was summertime and even at night it was that sticky humidity that steals your breath away.

Trix backed out of the driveway, the car rocking slightly until it settled on flat ground. He shoved it into first gear and took off before flicking on the headlights. He cruised down the street at the normal limit, then flicked the indicator and veered left. None of us spoke a word; there was nothing to hear except heavy breathing and the tyres treading the bitumen. Trix cupped the back of my sweaty head, caressing me, letting me know everything was going to be okay. But I could not open my eyes. Whimpers floated from the back seat – but I couldn't discern if it was Tahlia, Helen, Sharon, or all three. I doubted it was Sharon, though; she was as composed as a strong girl could be while committing a felony.

The whole time driving up to the clifftop I kept praying, kept talking to myself, kept convincing myself we were doing the right thing. After a while, Trix turned left again and the tyres left the smooth bitumen surface and travelled over rough terrain. He flicked off the headlights and I assumed he was rolling down the dirt path that led to the clearing.

He eased the car to a stop, flicked the interior dome light off, then opened his door and hopped out. I could hear his joggers crunch over the dirt and dried leaves, and then a metal chain *clinked* as Trix unhooked it off a pole to open a gate to gain access. Seconds later, he slid back into the cruiser, shut the door as quietly as he could, then rolled the car forward as the tyres snapped twigs and fallen branches. Tears welled as Mum's oily spaghetti swirled in my knotted stomach, and the whimpers from the back definitely sounded Helen-like.

When Trix finally pressed the brakes and the tyres squealed, I thought it sounded like a ghostly apparition pleading for us to stop; to just think about what we were doing, about the repercussions of taking the law into our own hands. My poor heart couldn't take any more. Was I having second thoughts at this point in time? Yeah. Now I was. Was there even the teeniest part of me that had participated to impress Trix, to show him I was as tough and brave and adult-like as he? Plausible. But was it too late to back out and form a contingency plan? Abso-fucking-lutely.

No-one said a thing when Trix killed the engine, pulled up the handbrake and hopped out again. When I sat up and glanced around, a horror panorama confronted me. Dark branches resembling witches' grasping hands and bony fingers loomed above us, the dark-blue horizon providing just enough contrast for me to make out the plummet metres ahead. The darkness seemed claustrophobic and I had to tug at my sweat-drenched shirt collar to breathe, desperately drawing oxygen into my lungs. Trix opened my door and offered me a helping hand to get out. Once outside, I closed the door and sucked in whatever fresh air I could as Trix opened one of the back doors. The girls stumbled out in single file: Helen, Sharon, then Tahlia. Still none of us spoke, but there were snuffles, and I heard someone gulping for oxygen as she tried to keep her emotions locked tight.

Trix surveyed our surroundings, although we couldn't see shit – no doubt he was searching for any signs of life, even though trespassing was illegal. When he was satisfied we were alone, he removed the torch from his pocket and flicked it on to help him see to unlock the boot using the silver key.

The lock clicked.

Trix lifted the boot.

And that's when Clyde opened his eyes.

Chapter Forty-Three

Helen's piercing squeal could have woken someone in a coma. My throat closed up like that same ghostly apparition was choking me, and Sharon covered her own mouth to muffle a scream. Tahlia froze and even Trix gasped. When Clyde opened his eyes, he was waking from a deep sleep, needing a second to get his bearings. He didn't open his eyes, jump out of the boot and start swinging punches like in a B-grade horror movie, but his head inched towards us, blinking rapidly in the bright stream of the torchlight. Drool pooled at the corner of his white lips. He raised an arm with the slowness of someone who has no gas left in the tank, and that's when Trix slammed the torch over Clyde's head. I don't know what was worse ... the sound of bone crunching, or the sound of the torch glass shattering upon impact. Clyde's head split open and his warm, thick blood spurted onto my face, clinging to my eyelashes as I quivered in disbelief. Helen squealed again, but Sharon rushed over, covering her open mouth with both hands from behind.

Clyde sounded like he was gargling wet clay, but he still tried to get up. Trix ripped off the policeman's hat and threw it on top of Clyde's body, just as Clyde raised a hand again.

'Tahlia, *now!*' Trix stage whispered. Chest expanding on a deep breath, I faced her, but she seemed immobile. Trix dashed to her within three strides, snatched the plastic bag full of Clyde's belongings off her, then rushed to the boot and threw it on top of Clyde's heaving chest.

Clyde groaned, and I helped Trix push his barrel-chested body down before Tahlia, Trix and I grabbed the boot lid and slammed it shut.

By the time Sharon and Helen had joined us, Clyde was pounding on the lid of the boot with a last surge of energy. It was a dull, metallic sound like a rubber mallet hitting a sheet of metal, but it made me dry-retch. It was sickening, hearing him trying to pound his way out of his situation, although I'll bet he couldn't have foreseen what was going to happen, or how his rotten life would end. Trix ran to the driver's side door and slid inside. He then released the handbrake and put the car into neutral. Helen stood and sobbed next to me while Sharon shushed her.

'Stop it!' Sharon whispered harshly. 'Someone will hear you!'

I was too emotional to utter a word. Tahlia appeared zoned out, but she stood with both quaking hands on the boot, ready to push. When Trix closed the driver's door after he rolled down the window, The Sunsets started pushing against the car. Even when Trix squeezed in the middle and began giving it all he had, the damn thing took ages to budge over the bumpy terrain. My sweaty palms kept slipping off its sleek surface. My joggers skidded in the dry dirt, but I gained traction and we strained, putting all our weight into it. When the tyres started rolling, I almost cried in relief; I wanted this to be over and done with for the sake of my hammering heart. The worst thing was, we could hear Clyde banging on the boot, moaning out nonsensical words, but on we pushed and soon Sharon and I turned around and used our backs and thighs to help throw our weight against the car, our shoes skidding on the terrain.

Once the car picked up momentum, it seemed as light as moving a bunch of pillows. Twigs and dried branches snapped around us as the tyres crushed them, and when Trix said, 'Now!' we let go of the runaway vehicle. Sharon and I stumbled backwards, but Trix helped me up with the reflexes of a ninja, and Tahlia grabbed Sharon. Believing I was one pant away from fainting, I spun around just as the silhouette of the car in the dark-blue horizon plunged over the side of the cliff, and the sound of Clyde's pounding stopped.

Chapter Forty-Four

We waited with bated breath until we heard the sound of the car break the water's surface. In the silent night, the crash sounded to me like earth's mantle splitting open. Helen screamed loud enough that birds took flight, then threw up her father's barbecued lamb chops in three noisy hurls. Sharon grabbed her again.

'Stop it!' Sharon slapped Helen across the cheek. 'You'll get us busted!'

Helen cupped her face and whimpered, but out of Helen's scream and the car hitting the water – the latter was far louder. But we were scared shitless that night, as you can imagine. I had a vision of Clyde somehow opening the boot, swimming to the surface as his cruiser plunged deeper, and then him waiting for me at my house, clothes dripping wet, blood spurting out of his head, stumbling towards me with his arms raised like a zombie and his eyeballs popping out like yo-yos.

Of course, nothing of the sort happened. I tried not to think about Clyde drowning in his own beloved police cruiser. I kept telling myself we had rid the world of evil; we'd sent Clyde Hanratty to the bowels of hell where scum like him belonged.

None of us spoke another word. On numb legs, we ran as fast as we could in the opposite direction, back towards the gate. Trix picked up the metal chain with a DO NOT ENTER sign attached and hooked it around the circular metal attachment. We stumbled on, some of us snivelling and some of us breathing in short bursts until we were back at the tree-lined road. None of us stopped to hug or whisper soothing words. We piled into Trix's Pontiac and he took off into the night.

The rancid smell of vomit clinging to Helen's breath blew around the car as she panted like an overheated dog. Clenching my fists and eyes, I prayed that no-one spotted us, and that no other policeman would pull us over, because if that happened, I felt certain Helen would spill her now-empty guts and scream: *They made me do it*!

But one by one, Trix dropped us off at our houses. Helen first, Tahlia next, then Sharon. None of us spoke words of farewell or even looked at each other. When Trix pulled up at the end of my street, I asked him to wait five minutes. At first, I thought he was going to say no, that he wanted to get back home as soon as possible. He must have been exhausted; he'd driven his car to the lookout hours ago and trekked all the way to Tahlia's house. But he assured me he'd wait, so I took off, running back up the road, and climbed through my bedroom window. I felt sure my erratic panting would wake someone up, but no-one stirred. Mum had knackered everyone by pumping them full of pasta and buttery popcorn. I snuck into the bathroom and finally relieved my balloon-sized bladder. My hands resting on my pale thighs shook. Ghastly images tried to poke through my defence shield like a game of Whac-A-Mole: dark blood dripping down Clyde's face, Helen puking, what felt like acidic blood burning away my eyelashes.

I did not turn on the light or flush the toilet, but ran to the sink to wash my hands, and then used my toothbrush and toothpaste in case any of Clyde's blood had landed in my mouth when Trix had hit him with the torch. I gargled mouthwash as soundlessly as I could, and then chucked the toothbrush in the bin. Mum always kept spares. Using a damp washcloth, I rubbed my face and eyelashes, then took the washcloth with me.

I tiptoed back into my bedroom, ducked out of the window and stepped onto my front lawn, praying Trix would still be there. Thank God, he was. His Pontiac was just another car in the street, nothing conspicuous here. I dashed towards his car, glancing back over my shoulder to make sure no-one was watching me or driving down the road. Although at this ungodly hour, who would?

After throwing Mum's washcloth in someone's bin sitting in their front yard, I climbed into Trix's passenger seat and faced him.

'I would ask how you are feeling,' he whispered, 'but it seems redundant.'

'We did the right thing, Trix.' My hammering heart knew it to be true, but still, I felt I was a millisecond away from chucking up my guts – the sound of the cruiser slamming into the water a perpetual echo in my frazzled mind.

He faced the front and then glanced into his side mirrors. 'You think the girls will keep quiet?'

'Honestly? Yes, I do. They might never want to speak of this again, but they'll keep their promise.'

'Good. I hope they can live with it.'

'Can you?'

'I've lived through many things I never thought I could. What's one murder on top of everything else?' He didn't smile, and I didn't laugh. He turned to me, exhaling harshly. 'I'm not great with goodbyes.'

That did it. I shielded him from seeing my ugly-cry face with trembling hands. Our paths would never intertwine again. I refused to believe his sole purpose for entering my life was just to help me get rid of someone in such a traumatising way. How would I be able to breathe without Trix? I was suffocating as it was.

Conscious of time getting on, I lowered my wet hands and sniffled back the tears. 'I know you won't change your mind ... but I don't want you to go. Please stay with me.'

He cupped the sides of my face. 'Perhaps in our next lifetime it's meant to be. But for now, I have to go.' He shut his eyes as tight as he clenched his jaw. 'But I want you to know that out of all the people in Orange, you're going to be the person I miss most.'

His forehead connected with mine, and my heart fucking *snapped*. He held my face, our foreheads pressed together as my body shuddered with sobs. None of what we had just done entered my mind in that moment. Not the murder, not the God-almighty splash the car had made when breaking the surface, not Helen's piercing screams. Nothing mattered to me; I'd compacted everything like the back of a shovel patting down earth. To survive this ordeal, I had to.

My heart pounded, kicking me into action. 'Take me with you! Let's go, right now! I don't care what anyone will say. Please!'

He leaned back, brushing my damp hair away from my temples, but was close enough that our breaths mingled. 'You have a bright future ahead, and I wish nothing but wonderful, beautiful things for you. One day you're going to marry someone who adores you, and have many cute babies. You're going to be the pride of your parents, and you're going to thank me for not taking you with me. Trust me. It might be years from now, but you will. And I will *never* forget you.'

He brushed his lips against mine and I clung to him, kissing him back as my overflowing tears slid over our mouths. It wasn't a passionate, I-want-to-rip-your-clothes-off-and-fuck-the-shit-out-of-you kiss, but it was, to date, the most beautiful kiss in my life. No tongues, no groping, just two people who'd met at the wrong place and wrong time saying goodbye forever.

When he pulled away from me, his eyes glimmered in the moonlight. 'I have something for you.' He cleared his throat and reached into the glove box to pull out an envelope. 'Take this. And also ...' He removed his silver thumb ring from his left hand and placed it in my flat palm. 'As much as I want to stay here with you, I need to get going before someone sees, and before Dad wakes up.'

My heart splintered even more to hear him say it, but I understood this was always going to be the outcome, and I couldn't do a damn thing to change that.

The weight of the envelope had me wondering what it was. The last envelopes I'd held contained crushed pills. Surely nothing like that. Nodding, I wiped my face, but it was useless; new tears replaced the old like a relentless stream.

'Trix ... I-I love you.'

He brushed my cheek with his thumb. 'I love you, too, Kylie. And don't cry anymore, okay? Things will be better tomorrow morning. I promise.'

Technically, it already *was* Monday, but I knew what he meant was when the golden sun would laminate the land and the day would become bright again, giving hope for the future, boasting of a new beginning.

'Take care of yourself,' he whispered.

'You too.' I licked my lips, tasting salty tears as I tried to burn his image into my retinas forever. 'I don't know what else to say ...'

'You should say *au revoir* for now, and promise me you'll get on with your life.'

'I-I promise. I promise I will.' As I reached for the door handle, I whimpered again and turned to him once more, knowing this would be the last time I'd ever see his face. He appeared so sad sitting there looking at me. He didn't cry, but his neck was taut as though it took great pains to hold the emotions in, clenching his jaw.

'*Au revoir* for now, Trix. Thank you for everything.'

A ghost of a smile played over the strong planes of his face. 'Goodbye. Kylie Gardner.'

I hopped out on hollow legs, closed his car door gently and didn't look back. With a heavy heart, I sprinted as fast as I could, swiping away hot tears as my legs trampled over grass, over concrete, until I reached my house. Swallowing past a congealed throat, I slowed to a walk, tiptoed over my front yard and climbed in through my bedroom window. I didn't shut it for fear it would wake someone up, and in the distance, I heard the Pontiac's engine start, and the sound soon faded away until the night was once again silent – save for the crickets. How I wanted to fall to my knees and wail, but all I could do was crumple on my bed and heave silently into a pillow while clutching Trix's ring, his residual body warmth offering little solace.

When my tear ducts finally stopped manufacturing for the time being, I hopped up, envelope in hand, and turned on the ceiling light. Through stinging, puffy eyes, I opened the flap and stared at a wad of fifty-dollar notes. It took until weeks later before I found the courage to count it, discovering he'd gifted me a thousand dollars. To a teenage girl in the '70s, that was worth about a million vinyl records. But it wasn't about the amount; it was his grand gesture of letting his actions speak.

His silver thumb ring was too big for any of my fingers. Instead, I found an old necklace and threaded it through the chain, so it could comfort my shattered heart.

Chapter Forty-Five

We hear of people going through shocking, life-changing events: a soldier returning from war, a mother burying her child, a driver accidentally killing someone who ran out in front of their car ... and we see the effects these have on the body and mind. I never knew it to be true until I saw Helen Baldwin the next day at school. I won't say her hair had turned white and her face resembled a haggard witch's, but overnight she looked thirty instead of thirteen. Seeing her pallid complexion and the dark crescents under her unblinking eyes made me wish I'd kept her out of it. We'd all agreed Clyde Hanratty deserved what he had coming – no two ways about it – but it was different being involved – like a person who eats meat seeing a cow slaughtered before their eyes.

When I approached Helen and Sharon the next day at school, Helen didn't utter two words. Anyone with half a brain could deduce she'd gone through trauma and was in shock. She clutched her schoolbag in front of her chest and Sharon looked at me with eyes that said: *She's going to crack and tell someone.*

But Helen never did. None of us did. We kept that burden to ourselves all our lives, and although it surfaced through dreams subconsciously, we learned to live with it and get on with facing the future.

I was more surprised Tahlia wasn't at school that Monday. Maybe she was too exhausted to come in? Lord knows I felt buggered, as did the others, I'm sure. The few hours I'd lain in bed couldn't be constituted as sleep, for whenever I'd closed my eyes I saw Clyde's expression as recognition dawned he was about to die.

Speaking to Helen was like interacting with an inanimate object, and when the bell rang for first period I touched her shoulder, but she flinched and took off. I turned to Sharon and asked her where Tahlia was. She said she had no clue.

First period was English. I kept staring at the door, hoping Tahlia would walk in at any moment. Perhaps she'd told Lorraine what had really happened. By now, I was sure Lorraine had read the note Helen had pinned to the front door. No doubt she'd woken up (probably with a whopping headache) in an empty bed, wondering where her lover was. She'd probably opened the door to see only her car in the driveway until the note caught her attention. She would have read it and probably burst into tears, wondering how a man could do such a cruel thing to her.

As usual, Willie Miller rhapsodised about prepositions and other uninteresting grammar terms from behind his desk. I'd chosen a seat next to the window; Helen sat at the back, far away from Sharon and me. At least Sharon seemed to be keeping it together; she was even wearing ice-pink lipstick.

Through drooping eyelids, I kept glancing out the murky windows, visualising Trix breezing through the grounds with that devil-may-care swagger I'd fallen in love with. It was hard to believe that had happened only a few weeks ago, but as I learned later on, things are always changing; life never stays the same, and good things happen when you least expect it.

Where is Trix right now? How is he feeling? Will he always remember me?

Picturing Trix put a smile on my face, but it also conjured tears. Our time together was over as quickly as it had begun.

When the bell rang, Helen packed up and raced out the door before anyone else.

'She's not handling this too good,' Sharon whispered, zipping up her schoolbag.

I eyed the other students around me before looking at her. 'I know, but where is Tahlia?'

Sharon shrugged, yawning and then swallowing. 'Beats me. Maybe her mum is taking it out on her? God, I hope not. I'll call her this arvo and make sure she's okay.'

'Okay, and let me know too.'

'Will do.' She shouldered her schoolbag. 'See ya at recess.'

'Love you.'

'Love you, too.' She grabbed my arm and leaned in close as students shuffled by. 'We did the right thing.'

When lunchtime rolled around, I exited the History classroom, rubbing my tired eyes as students rushed past. However, there was none of that usual exuberance kids displayed at lunchtimes; some seemed downhearted as though they were headed into yearly exams, or they ran off to find their friends, as if to tell them something urgent. I heard whispers – 'Can't believe it' – and that's when my food from recess resurfaced, coating the back of my tight throat. Staring at the whispering kids, I believed that somehow, some way, Clyde's police car had floated up to the lake's surface, and the police were investigating his murder right now.

A redheaded girl sobbed as her ashen-faced friend draped an arm around her drooping shoulders; teachers hurried by, some shaking their heads in disbelief, others with sad expressions on their insipid faces.

As my heart rate rose steadily, I had to stop my textbooks from slipping through my sweaty hands. With a parched mouth, I darted past groups of pupils clustered together and rushed out of the exit. Pinpricks of light dotted my vision. The energy in the halls and outside was kinetic; it took me back to the Monday morning after the footy incident, when there was a buzz in the air as everyone gossiped about it. Eyes and ears on high alert, I swallowed down scaring bile and dashed through the quadrangle. I understood then that this was far more serious than chatter about that footy brawl. Kids were not playing handball. The canteen lines were shorter. The murmurs among the pale-faced students sounded like a dull humming from a swarm of bees. I ran on wobbly legs while people stared at me. My heart fluttered. I broke out in a cold sweat. The world around me felt off-kilter. When I reached the benches where The Sunsets usually sat, it was vacant. Frowning, I spun around and looked towards the student car park to see Bobby hugging Sharon.

Oh my God, something happened to Tahlia!

Trepidation hurtled through me. I dropped my bag on the aluminium bench, papers and textbooks flying to the ground, and sprinted towards my friends. When I reached them, Sharon was wiping her eyes, but Bobby's eyes were glazed over too. His chin quivered.

'What happened?' I asked, panting while panic reached up like a claw ready to strangle me.

Sharon sniffled and she made her way over, throwing her arms around me. I didn't return the hug; I needed to know what the hell was going on and my anxiety had rendered me frozen stiff.

'It's awful,' Sharon said, whimpering. She leaned back and grabbed my upper arms. 'I'm so sorry, I'm just so *sorry*.'

A coil of dread tightened in my stomach. I managed to push Sharon away by her shoulders and, in a daze, I made my way over to Bobby. He raked his hands through his sandy-blond hair, turning this way and that on his feet as though he didn't know if he was coming or going. This wasn't about Tahlia.

'Bobby,' I whispered, a shudder twisting up my back, 'what happened?'

He finally faced me as he sniffed hard, holding back threatening tears. 'They fuckin' shot him. They fuckin' killed Trix in his driveway this morning.'

Chapter Forty-Six

My knees gave way and I crumpled to the ground, numb legs splayed out beside me. Sharon squealed and ran to me as my whole body felt like it was pumped full of anaesthetic. I didn't cry, I didn't scream; my body had erected a barrier to stop me from absorbing the immense pain.

Sharon held me, but her words of condolence sounded as distant as the lake. Bobby sniffled as he struggled to hold back his emotions, and that's when I collapsed backwards, weightless arms and legs spread out as I stared at the cerulean sky. The burning sun was to my right, but I did nothing to block the intense glare. All I saw in my peripheral was Sharon's red face, her crying and asking me if I could hear her.

I don't know how long I stayed there, feeling paralysed, but breaths rushed out of my mouth and swirled around my ears. Sharon kept shaking me, her lips flapping. Words floated around me in gentle oscillations as my mind's eye played the reel of what had happened only hours earlier.

When Sharon pulled my limp body into a sitting position, Bobby bent down and hugged me tight. 'It's fucked! They're gonna fuckin' die, the lot of them!'

I didn't need for Bobby to tell me who 'they' were. The Orange East boys had paid their debt to Trix, as they said they would. I closed my eyes to block any more pain. Sharon rocked me back and forth, my mind swirling, my neck pulse throbbing, unable to feel the ground I sat on.

'It's horrible, *horrible*!' Sharon chanted over and over.

Swallowing hard, I opened my eyes to peer up at Bobby. 'In his driveway?'

He wiped his wet cheek on his forearm, his crumpled face and jutting chin suggesting he was about to explode in a tyrant of verbal abuse. 'Yeah, the *fuckin'* dogs. He was hopping into his car early this morning and they were waiting for him. His old man told me Trix had suitcases in the car, so I don't fuckin' know where he was going, but they shot him in the back just as he was climbing into the car – one leg was still inside the car when the coppers arrived.'

'It's horrible!' Sharon said again, shaking her head, hugging herself as she remained on her knees. 'I can't believe it! I'm *so* sorry, Kylie.'

'They're gonna pay! I've already spoken to Ed and Mike about this – they're fuckin' going down!' Bobby stood up, rubbing his face as he screamed. 'Fuckin' dog *cunts*!' He started crying again, raking jittery hands through his hair.

'Come on,' Sharon said gently, helping me to stand by grabbing my defunct arms. I was upright, but I swayed from left to right, thankful that Sharon was propping me up. 'You should go home. They can't get mad at you – screw McCarthy; we only have a few weeks left of school.'

'My ... stuff,' I whispered, blinking slowly, an arm wrapped around my hollow stomach.

She turned around to our usual spot, then back to me. 'I'll get it. Stay here. Bobby will drive us home.' She sprinted towards my school shit, her blonde hair splaying out behind her.

Bobby wrapped his arms around me. When I hugged his trembling body, my wall of suspended disbelief came crashing down and my kneecaps dissolved again.

I have no recollection of anything after that. I'd imploded in a tangled heap. I don't recall Bobby driving me home in his father's car, or of me stumbling inside my house, bumping into walls. I have little memory of Sharon at my doorstep, telling Mum what had happened and why I was home from school (although I suspect Mum already knew, given her gossip connections in town). I have no recollection of the rest of that week; I stayed in bed, too numb to move or even sit at the dinner table. I can barely remember hearing Mum, Dad, Keith and Amy talking about it over dinner the night it happened. I have no recollection of the number of times people tried to call me on the phone, or popped over for a visit, or of the times Keith tried talking to me as I lay curled in bed, unable to speak.

But there was one thing during the aftermath of Trix's murder that stood out in my mind, breaking my paralysis, and that was Sharon rushing into my room, sobbing her heart out. She sat on my bed as I lay there with my eyes closed. The doona was pulled up to my chin (despite the warm weather), and I reluctantly shuffled over to make room for her – my eyes still shut.

Sharon crumpled over my body, heaving as she clung to me. 'Kylie, we miss you so much. Please come back to school.'

'Can't,' I croaked through rusty pipes.

'Trix wouldn't have wanted this. He'd want you to be happy and to finish your year with good marks.'

'It's too ... *hard.*'

'I'm so sorry this has happened. He was a good guy, Kylie. He really loved you.'

Hearing that only started the waterworks again, but yes, I believe deep down he loved me as much as I loved him. Over the years, when hard times befell me, I developed a thicker skin. Sure, other ordeals still made me cry, but I don't think I've ever experienced pain as excruciating as that, because I fell in love only as a teenager can: wholeheartedly. They say the first cut is always the deepest, and the wound inflicted became more like an impediment until, over time, it filled itself in, like a hole in the sand during high tide. In a way, his death prepared me for other torments later in life. If not for Trix, I may not have survived them. The poet, Dylan Thomas, wrote: 'After the first death, there is no other'. Couldn't have said it better myself.

'How's Tahlia?' I asked after a bout of sniffling, wiping my snotty nostrils on the doona.

'She's okay. Helen is the one who's all weird now. She doesn't sit with us any-more.'

'Really?' Even when I mumbled it, it wasn't a surprise. Seeing Helen the morning after had made me feel like we'd killed two people that Sunday night.

'Yeah. She's become a total loner; doesn't sit with anyone – not even Melinda. I think she spends recess and lunch in the library.'

'How's Lorraine?'

Sharon scoffed. 'Tahlia told me she's a mess. Like, a total fuckin' mess. When she read the note on the door, she became like you: cried all day in bed, and Tahlia had to make their meals. Apparently, Lorraine is too scared to walk out of the house, packin' shit that Mrs Hanratty is waiting there for her, or that the people of Orange know she was screwing a married man. What a deadset moll.'

'What do the papers say about him and his missing car?'

'Nothing yet. The cops went to see Tahlia's mum, and she showed them the note, calling him a lying pig and all sorts of stuff. But they must have believed it, because there's nothing about his disappearance in the *Central Western Daily*.'

'Do you realise people swim where Clyde's body is?' I whispered, swallowing past a knot.

'Yeah ... of course I thought of that. But we didn't have a choice; where else were we going to bury him and get rid of the car? We needed to make it look like he skipped town, taking the car with him.'

'We can never go back there.'

'Fuckin' oath. The thought of swimming in that water ever again ...' Her body shuddered, and the motion rocked my bed.

'What do the police say about ...?'

'About Trix?' she whispered.

I nodded, but opened my scratchy eyes for this, focusing on the yellow wallpaper.

'I'm not gonna lie, babe, it's been front-page news in the papers ever since. They say the cops are investigating leads, but nothing has happened. But we all fuckin' know who was behind it. Bobby wants to kill the Orange East boys, but we don't know for sure who ... shot him.'

'But the police know?'

'One article said a witness saw four boys dressed in all black, running away from the scene shortly before Trix was found. That's it. Four boys, dressed in black. It could be any of them.'

Clenching my teeth, face bunched tight, I pushed out, 'Who found him?'

'A next-door neighbour. After the sound of the gunshot, he crept outside and saw Trix half inside his car but lying on the ground – if that makes sense?' She cleared her throat. 'I know this won't make you feel any better, but he didn't suffer, Kylie. It was quick and painless.'

That. Was. It. For. Me. I pulled the doona over my contorted face as a deluge of tears came barrelling out and my pretzelled stomach heaved. Picturing Trix lying in his driveway surrounded by his own blood did a number on my mental state. Oh, God, why did he have to die? After everything he'd endured in his short life, why did he have to go out like that? I cursed God because I didn't know who else to blame. *He* should have been watching over Trix, because He knew no-one else was.

Sharon knew I'd heard enough, so she rubbed my closest thigh and whispered a few things to me, telling me she wanted me to come back to school. That was the last place I wanted to be; I visualised students and teachers talking about it, whispering things behind my back as I passed by. I couldn't stand the thought of facing that, but Sharon had said one thing to me that rang true: Trix would want me to go on with my life. If he was looking down at me, he'd hate the sight of me spending my days in bed, crying, eating up oxygen, not even having an interest in listening to music to pull me out of the torpor I now wallowed in. Unfortunately, I could not shake off my profound grief like a dog expelling bathwater. Considering Sharon came over on the Friday, I vowed I would return to school the following Monday and try to get on with my life. It would not be easy, but sooner or later I had to go back to Orange West High.

I was surprised my mum was as cool and understanding with it as she was. I expected she would let me take that Monday off, then send me back to school on the Tuesday, bright and early. But both she and Dad knew my heart had been frozen, then smashed to pieces by a sledgehammer. It would eventually mend itself, of course. Day by day, little by little, after Trix's death, my heart healed.

Isn't the human body the most miraculous thing? I've no doubt Trix's death caused a fracture in my heart – a place where it doesn't quite match up to the rest. Over the course of a lifetime, pain and heartache remove tiny chunks from your heart that don't heal – and you can never get them back. But you move on with this new, reassembled version of 'you'. You eventually learn how to smile again and to give what's left of your heart to other people, but if you could run a hand over it, you'd feel the battle wounds it's suffered over the years.

Hearing Sharon sobbing made me realise there were still people in this world who loved me, and I needed to be strong for them. It also occurred to me that while I wallowed in mourning, others were also suffering. Helen and Tahlia, for instance. I needed to toughen the hell up and be there for the girls, and I would do that, but after the weekend. After I'd let it all out so that nothing but a human-shaped casing remained.

Chapter Forty-Seven

Monday was as tough as overcooked steak, as expected. Students avoided eye contact with me, or just stared with mouths agape. I tried hard to put on a brave face as I ambled into the school grounds, but I wasn't deaf and wherever I went, Trix's name floated in the air like pollen during spring. I'd deliberately avoided looking at newspapers lying on front lawns as I'd pedalled to school that morning, but I couldn't tell people not to talk about it – this *was* big news. Links were already being made between the footy final and his death. Some students – who knew neither me nor Trix – vowed to get back at those 'spineless poofters' at Orange East High to avenge what they did to him. But no-one ever rose to the challenge.

The last time Orange had seen a murder was before I was even born, so you can understand the furore. In the space of a few weeks, the citizens of Orange had seen an unprecedented, violent footy brawl and now, a murder. I heard later on that some people even moved out of town as a result. To me this seemed far-fetched, but there were those who thought Orange was no longer a safe place for the kids: 'It ain't what it used to be when we was growin' up!'

That may have been true, but I can only tell you about my experience of growing up there and, despite what happened in the summer of '79, if I'd had a choice, I wouldn't have changed a thing about Orange, even though at the time I thought it could be totally uncool.

These days you don't see kids on bikes, or kids playing marbles or hopscotch – everyone's always inside (including the adults) playing video games or watching TV, and I think this is such a shame. Why has everyone gone from being so outward, to inward? When people see an incident where they could render help, instead they pull out their mobile phone to video it. I mean ... why? Has society deteriorated, or am I just jaded?

I know I'm showing my age here, but you can see the stark contrast to when we were kids. I believe, however, that if kids in the '70s had had mobile phones, then they would have busily captured me entering the school that Monday for the first time since the murder – we're all a product of our time. They would have videotaped the footy brawl, they would have snapped pictures of Trix lying on his driveway after being shot, and they would have uploaded them all to social media – probably with hashtags.

As soon as Sharon saw me trudge into the grounds, she waved me over, even though I was already heading in her direction. We hugged fiercely, then I turned to Tahlia and embraced her too. It was the first time I'd seen her since ... what we did.

'How have you been?' I asked Tahlia, sitting down beside her. Her orange hair already looked like it was making an encore, and her cheeks again resembled the colour of Pink Lady apples.

She played with her fingernails, staring at them. 'I feel better about one thing, but worse about the other. Mum's totally bummed out; she won't even talk to me.'

'I'm sorry; that sucks.' I placed a hand on her nearest shoulder, thinking Lorraine Ashcroft deserved every bad thing coming her way. I'd never forgive her for slapping Tahlia or for covering up the abuse inside her own home. Too bad there hadn't been room enough for two in that boot.

'Yes, it does suck. I don't know what she's thinking or feeling, but she's been drinking more wine.'

'She'll get over it,' Sharon said, flicking hair behind her shoulder. 'Oh, hey ... there's Helen.'

I spun around as Helen plodded through the quadrangle, but instead of heading towards us, she cut straight down the middle, textbooks and folder clutched in front of her chest as she passed some kids chasing one another. That's when I thought it made sense, Sharon beckoning me over. She thought I would probably 'chuck a Helen' and keep on walking. My heart constricted watching her stroll away from us. Out of The Sunsets, I'd wondered if Tahlia would have the worst time adjusting to and accepting what we did, but clearly she'd handled it better than I expected. No longer did she have to worry about being raped or molested, or being slapped across the face by her own mother because of her 'accusations'. She could sleep well at night without having to feel that sheer panic, wondering if this was going to be the night the knob of her bedroom door squeaked and turned, or waking up to find Clyde looming over her bed, stroking himself while staring at her. That piece of shit was gone, and Tahlia was holding up about as well as Sharon and I were. But Helen ... I couldn't tell whether she was avoiding us solely because of what we did, or whether she was upset at Sharon for slapping her, or ... there could have been a myriad of reasons she was avoiding us. But it hurt to witness Helen walk away from us without even a glance or a wave.

'Helen hasn't sat with you guys at all? Not even in English?' I turned away from the sorry sight of her to look at Sharon and Tahlia.

'Nope,' Sharon said, shaking her head. 'I don't know if she will ever talk to us again.'

'That's crazy! We're still her friends.'

'Maybe she thinks that's all we're going to talk about and she'd rather forget it?' Tahlia said.

I wasn't sure if she was hinting something to us as well: *Sunsets, let's never mention his name or what we did again.*

'I'm happy to see you here,' Sharon said, giving me a tender smile, then it faded. 'The funeral is on Friday; the medical people have finished with his body.'

I eyed my clenched hands in my lap, stomach churning as tears welled. 'Are you girls gonna go?'

'Of course!' they said in unison. Then Sharon put her arm around me and Tahlia followed suit.

'I love you,' Sharon whispered.

'Yes, me, too,' Tahlia said, squeezing my shoulder. 'You girls are my bestest friends in the whole entire world. No-one else would have helped me like that. *No-one.*'

I wiped my eyes, sniffled back the tears and looked at them both. 'I love you girls, too. Very much.'

'The Sunsets,' Tahlia said, smiling as her own tears spilled.

'The Sunsets!' Sharon and I chorused.

Then the bell rang and pupils groaned as they began the pilgrimage towards the numerous building blocks around Orange West High.

As I slid my schoolbag strap over my shoulder, I glanced towards the student car park. Trix stood there with a halo around him, as bright as a solar lamp. He waved at me with that cheeky grin he'd given me the first time we'd laid eyes on each other in the corridor.

I raised my hand, smiled through the tears, and then whispered, 'Goodbye, Trix. And thank you. For everything.'

Chapter Forty-Eight

As my English teacher, Willie Miller, once said, every story has to have a beginning, a middle and an end. But I came to discover the three-act structure also works with friendships as well. Aristotle once wrote about there being three basic types of friendship: friendship of utility, friendship of pleasure, and friendship of the good. I still don't know which one each of us Sunsets served towards the other.

The school year finished and I received average marks. My parents were lenient with me on account of what had happened near final exams, and I promised to do better next year. When the school break arrived (and not a minute too soon), I vegged out and listened to my records – although, after Trix's murder, I found it hard to glean joy from anything. Music, food, even *Countdown* had become as bland as dry toast. Still, I had to find distractions, even if they seemed mediocre. Swimming at the lake was out of the question; I didn't even want to *think* of that place or what we'd done. So, it didn't leave many options.

During the second week of the school break, I was sitting on my bed listening to a song that became the soundtrack for most of my remaining teen years, 'Comfortably Numb' by Pink Floyd. I heard someone bang on the front door, so I turned down the volume and could hear my mum talking, but I could also hear someone crying. I opened my bedroom door ajar, wondering who on earth it was.

Sharon barrelled around the corner dressed in a rainbow-pattern A-line dress, a baby-pink scarf pushing back her blonde hair. Tears were gathered at the tip of her red nose. She grabbed my upper arms before I had a chance to ask her what was wrong. 'It's terrible, Kylie, so terrible!'

'What?' Panic clogged my airways, forcing me to swallow. 'What happened?'

'Lorraine moved out of Orange, and sh-sh-she took Tahlia with her!'

Wide eyes roaming hers, I held onto her arms. '*What*? When?!'

She turned around to face my mother. 'We'll be back soon, Mrs Gee.' Sharon dragged me behind her as she sniffled and wiped her nose with the back of her hand. We rode our bikes all the way over to Tahlia's house. When we arrived, my stomach lurched to see a FOR SALE sign planted in the front yard. We threw our bikes on the lawn and sprinted to the house to peer inside the lounge-room window. It was as bare as a *Playboy* centrefold; Lorraine had packed everything, including the pictures on the walls.

'I don't understand!' I said, my panting causing the windowpane to fog up. 'Why wouldn't Tahlia tell us?'

Sharon faced me, wiping her tear-streaked cheeks. 'Because Lorraine didn't even tell her; isn't it obvious?! She just up and left! Tahlia didn't have a chance to tell us.'

'How do you know?'

'Their neighbour told me! I rode here before coming to yours, and the old woman told me Tahlia was dragged out of the house yesterday, kicking and screaming! Then the removalists and family friends came and packed everything on Lorraine's behalf. She'd been planning this for yonks!'

'Where did they go?'

Sharon shook her head, swallowing. 'The neighbour said Lorraine didn't tell anyone – not even her. No-one knows. They just vanished – like Harold Holt.'

I'd had no idea the last day of school would be the last time I'd see Tahlia Ashcroft again. Decades later, when this new craze called social media emerged, I downloaded Facebook. The first thing I did was search Tahlia's name, but nothing came up – well, not *my* Tahlia. The odds of her having married and changed her surname occurred to me, and without her reaching out to me, I had no way of finding out what happened to Tahlia or her mother.

At first, I couldn't grasp why Tahlia hadn't at least written a note, or made one quick phone call to explain how it all went down. But something told me that perhaps she eventually welcomed the change. By forgetting about us and Orange, it would allow her to start anew someplace different – like a snake shedding its skin

– only in her case, leaving behind a traumatised past. Whatever the reason for her silence, I hoped with everything I had she'd made something of herself. She'd always longed to be a schoolteacher, but after what happened, I wasn't so sure – maybe being in a school environment would only dredge up forgotten memories.

A week after Sharon and I had ridden our bikes to Tahlia's empty house, Sharon phoned me. Weeping hysterically – like my mother had when Elvis Presley had passed away suddenly back in '77 – she told me Bobby had dropped her for another girl. I could have seen this coming, but to Sharon O'Rourke, the news was both shocking and unexpected. Sharon blurted out, 'Good luck to the moll; he can't even keep his teeny dick hard!' And then, 'I love him so much!'

Talking above 'I Was Made for Lovin' You' by Kiss playing on repeat at Sharon's end, I tried to console her as best as I could. I even tried to visit her a few times afterwards. But ... things change, as they always do. The first time, no-one was at the house and I'd assumed maybe she and Cheryl had gone somewhere on a holiday. I gave it a few days and rode my bike over there again, and saw Sharon standing out the front with a group of older girls. The type of girls who loved themselves more than anyone else; the type who thought *Countdown* was lame-o; the type who would never amount to much more than baby-makers. Harsh, but true. Sharon wouldn't have ignored me like Helen did, but it was clear she was searching for something bigger and better than I could give her. She'd always yearned for something to fill the void, on the lookout for people to tell her she looked fab and that they loved her. It appeared my friendship with her didn't cut it anymore. I still have no idea how she became friends with those plastic Barbies in the first place. Perhaps she went out one night, heartbroken over Bobby dropping her, and met them at Lickety-Split or the Cherry Inn. Who knows? I was happy for her because *she* thought she was happy, but sad that our friendship would never be the same. Sure, I could hang around them if I wanted to, but talking about sex and make-up and ditching school was not my jam. And Sharon knew that. Nothing bad actually *happened* between us, but I've learned friendships can be like your favourite pair of Levi's: you eventually outgrow them.

When school recommenced in early 1980, Sharon and I still waved to each other in the corridors in between classes, but then it segued to us walking right past each other as she laughed and gossiped with her group of older friends. Her make-up increased from ice-pink lipstick to fake lashes, and she wore her navy-blue skirt shorter to show off her smooth, tanned legs. Our days of sleepovers and discussing music and heartthrobs had come to an end in the summer of '79. We'd called ourselves The Sunsets, but you can't have that without the sun, and Tahlia had been that bright, shining light for all of us. It would never be the same without her.

We'd lost Helen the night we pushed Clyde's car off the cliff. She didn't even do the polite thing and wave to either Sharon or me, and soon Helen Baldwin was another face that became a distant memory.

When I downloaded Facebook, I also tried to search for Sharon and Helen – for old times' sake, ya know? Friendships are never the same as the ones you have growing up – there's something raw and magical about those – you cannot replicate it, because in childhood you don't need to give a shit about anything. You don't worry about work, or bills, or having to put food in the cupboards. Our biggest dilemmas used to be picking a time to go hang, or what song to listen to on the turntable. We didn't have a care in the world. Except a care for one another.

I found Helen on Facebook quite easily. It appeared she hadn't married and, unfortunately, she wasn't a famous author like Agatha Christie – ironic considering she'd once loved cosy murder mysteries, never knowing her life would involve one. She was a fairly private person, and it looked like she worked at a Holden car yard as an accountant. From what I could gather, not only did she not have a husband, she also had no kids. Her profile picture was of three black-and-white cats sitting in a clothes basket.

When I contacted her through Messenger, I half-expected her to ignore me. But what I got back was worse. She told me we had nothing in common anymore, and to never contact her again.

I complied with her request.

Sharon was listed under 'O'Rourke', but that was because she was in between husbands. When I reached out, she seemed genuinely thrilled that I had – and why not? We hadn't argued or had a nasty split. We spoke for a few days, sending messages back and forth. She told me she'd been married three times, and joked she was on the lookout for husband number four. Looking through her photos, I saw she'd done what many women who pride themselves on their good-looks end up doing when gravity takes hold: lip fillers, Botox, pencil-thin tattooed eyebrows, an orange Oompa Loompa fake tan, a Pamela Anderson boob job. She was only in her forties, so I wondered what the fallout of all this cosmetic enhancement would do to her in her later years, considering it would only expedite what she feared most: growing old and losing her youthful looks. Maybe it was because that's the only thing she felt she had to offer, or was made to believe was her form of currency in this world. A gene-blessed meal ticket from a pureblood pedigree.

She worked part-time managing a local tavern, ordering stock, dealing with hostile pokies players. She'd moved out of Orange in the mid-'80s after she fell in love with a hunky mechanic. They got married after knowing each other for only seven months, and she'd been three months' pregnant by the time they tied the knot. Her first was a son named Kieran. Two years later, she welcomed another son, Patrick. Sharon filed for divorce when Patrick was four, after she caught her husband in bed with the next-door neighbour – and the lady's husband.

Years later, Sharon married an older dentist with kids of his own, and all seemed to be going well until he suffered a fatal aneurysm. Husband number three came not long after, but this guy was younger. Two days after their daughter, Amelia, was born, it turned out the twenty-something tradie realised he was not fit to be a daddy. Sharon arrived home from the hospital with Amelia in a carrier to find the house empty of his belongings.

Sharon sent me about a hundred pictures of her kids, but over the span of the four days since we'd made contact, it occurred to me the conversation orbited *her*. There was the initial 'OMG, how are you?!' but then it tapered off into her life and her woes. It also occurred to me *I'd* been the one to go searching for those three; any one of them could have found me on Facebook just as easily. But I let it slide. I was honestly happy to speak to Sharon again; it'd been too long.

I asked her if she found out what had happened to Tahlia or Lorraine and she told me no, she hadn't heard a thing; Tahlia and her mother had dropped off the face of the planet. I also asked Sharon if she'd spoken with Helen, but as expected, she said she hadn't bothered reaching out because she knew she'd have more luck winning *Wheel of Fortune*.

At the end of our conversation, Sharon said we should get together for a drink sometime, as she only lived an hour's drive away.

Years later, I'm still waiting for that drink.

Chapter Forty-Nine

Rumours spread between adults just as much as they do among kids, and what I am going to tell you about some other people from Orange is pure hearsay.

When Headmistress McCarthy retired in the mid-'80s, Willie Miller took over as head. From what I heard, he did a bang-up job and turned things around, including renovations and expanding the library. Of course, during the '80s, drugs became about as popular as Guns N' Roses. There were problems within the school and violence increased, but Willie was fair with his discipline, and most parents agreed he did a better job than McCarthy.

Years later, I bumped into Willie in Sydney, on 26 January 1987, at a concert called Australian Made – where local acts like Jimmy Barnes, Mental As Anything, and INXS performed live. (My love for David Cassidy expired when I discovered Michael Hutchence.) Willie and I shot the shit and spoke about past students and teachers, and I asked him about Mr Evans – you remember, my Science teacher who was rumoured to have been into kiddie porn? All Willie said was, 'Whatever you believed to be true, probably was.' They'd fired Mr Evans, and no-one knew what ended up happening to him.

During the late '90s, Ralph Ferguson sold Lickety-Split and lived a quiet, happy life with his wife until he passed away at the age of seventy-eight. His funeral was one of the largest in Orange, and the local council even commissioned a plaque. Years later, the ice-cream parlour was knocked down after a decline in sales and an increase in VHS tapes, and became 'Café Olé'.

Speaking of funerals … no-one was ever arrested for the murder of Tristan Douglas Walker. We all know who orchestrated it – Nicholas Sullivan, Nicole's twin brother from Orange East High. But no-one was held accountable. The ballistics team deduced a shotgun was used, but given the rural town had many farmers and hunters who liked to go boar hunting, it wasn't an uncommon item for a local to possess or at least gain access to – not to mention there was a firearms store called Flynn's, which sold everything from .22 rifles to Winchesters.

Trix was buried at Orange City General Cemetery and I visited him often, including the day I left town. Like with Ralph Ferguson, his funeral pulled a massive turnout. It was the first and only time I saw his father up close. Bill Walker had that dimply, bulbous red nose one only acquires through years of hard drinking. He sobbed heavily as Trix's coffin was lowered into the ground, but I could smell the booze on Bill's breath from a mile away. As promised, Sharon and Tahlia stood by my side that day, hugging me while also shedding tears. Trix's mother never made an appearance for reasons unknown. Ed, Mike and Bobby also attended, and I'd never seen them look finer: fresh haircuts, crisp suits, and all of them wore black sunnies – not just Mike. Bobby was the most distraught, but neither he nor the others ever sought revenge against those who murdered their best friend. There's still bad blood between Orange East and Orange West, but nothing has ever come close to what happened in the summer of '79.

Bobby Dean and Mike Perkins are the only ones still living in Orange to this day. Last I heard, Mike ended up doing an apprenticeship and became a qualified mechanic – he now co-owns an auto shop with his brother on the outskirts of Orange. Bobby and Mike still catch up on the weekends, hitting up the local bowling club, playing darts, drinking beer, and getting involved in fights. Bobby and Mike both have kids, but they're not with the mothers of them. How do I know all this? Through conversations with Sharon, various town locals, and Willie Miller when I saw him at that concert.

No idea what ended up happening to little Ed Rickard, as he and his family moved out of Orange before I did, and although I tried to search for him on Facebook for old times' sake, I couldn't find him.

For Rodney Saliba's involvement in the footy brawl, and the fact he stabbed multiple people, he served eighteen months in juvie. Shortly after his release, he was sentenced to an adult prison after someone started on him at a pub – taunting him, calling him a chickenshit pussy. Rodney tore the guy's face to shreds with a broken beer bottle. He did more time, got released, but then found himself at home with a gang – stealing cars, dealing drugs. The last I read in the papers was that Rodney (now heavily tattooed, but still bald) was given twenty-five years for the murder of a grocery clerk whom he'd tried to rob, and ended up shooting dead in the struggle.

It seems Rodney's life ended up having a gigantic snowball effect. If he'd ever ended up marrying and having kids, what would his offspring have turned out like? Where does the buck stop, and with whom? Some people should never have kids to begin with.

Speaking of shit mothers ... when I contacted Sharon through Facebook, I asked her how Cheryl was. She told me her mother had married again – to someone only a few years older than Sharon. I have no clue if Bobby and Cheryl ever got it on, but honestly, nothing would surprise me about that woman – Sharon certainly didn't mention anything.

Later in life I asked myself, if Lonnie O'Rourke hadn't died in Vietnam, would Sharon have turned out different? Would Cheryl have?

The marriage never lasted – shock-horror! – but Cheryl was doing fine living by herself, not having much to do with her own grandkids; instead, preferring to spend her time getting perms and fake nails and strutting her wrinkly stuff down the streets of Orange in search of her next prey.

Youth ... sometimes I think it's the most precious thing we are blessed with.

Chapter Fifty

It turned out to be a tough year, 1980. Not only did I not have Trix, but The Sunsets had disbanded quicker than the Knack. I made new friends, of course, but it was hard. I missed Sharon and the others terribly. Not only that, I'd hoped we could go through the aftermath of the murder together. Console each other. Convince each other. Assure each other. I wondered if the others slept with a night-light on too. Did they also wake up in a cold sweat? Did they also hear the echo of the car slamming into the water late at night? Were their dreams also hijacked by haunting nightmares? I could only imagine so.

When I turned fifteen, I got braces. The other students loved that one, all right; I was like a fish being shot at in a barrel. I cried at the teasing in the beginning, but soon the bullies found other unfortunates to laugh and joke about. It was a struggle for me to concentrate at school when all I could think of was Trix – his spirit omnipresent.

But time helped me heal, as Mum promised it would. It got to the stage I would no longer cry when thinking about him, and soon his memory faded as other things pushed to the forefront of my mind. Keith and Amy welcomed a baby girl in August that year. At the hospital, after Keith had called to say all was well and we could come down to meet their daughter, Mum forgot all about being pissed off, and she cried and gushed when she held Emma for the first time. Dad patted Keith on the back for a job well done, and that was about as good as it got for praise from Dad. He was a quiet man, but he was a good man.

I celebrated my sweet sixteenth at home. There was nothing fancy about it – no friends sleeping over, no ten-pin bowling or going to the movies; Sharon didn't even drop a card in the mailbox, despite the fact I'd done so for her a few months earlier. Mum made my favourite meal – roast pork with all the trimmings – and she baked a gooey chocolate cake. After donning conical party hats and doing the birthday cake routine, my parents, Keith, Amy and Emma watched as I unwrapped some new vinyl records, and then we sat together and watched *Young Talent Time*. My life was average at that point; nothing memorable to note. Comfortably numb, remember?

It wasn't until 1983 that I experienced my second biggest heartbreak. By then I was in Year 12 and only a few months shy of graduating. My braces were yesterday's news, but pimples had pushed their way through the oily surface of my face like dormant volcanoes, and I had a boyfriend. Yep. I'll get into that in a moment.

I arrived home from school on a Thursday afternoon to find Mum and Dad at the kitchen table. To see Mum crying wasn't unusual, but to see Dad with his head in his hands, tears spilling over the edges of his jittery fingers ... I knew something fucked up had happened.

With a pounding heart, I plonked my heavy schoolbag on the linoleum floor and made my way over to them. 'What's happened?' I whispered, dreading the answer.

Without them speaking a word, my own tears developed; the palpable sadness was contagious. I took a seat at the table and waited for someone to tell me what was going on. Mum raised her head and kept dabbing her leaking eyes with a tissue – her face the colour of rhubarb. Dad kept gasping as though fighting to breathe.

Mum inhaled deeply, a fist went to her heaving chest. 'Keith ... had an accident, honey. His car lost control and slammed into a ... into a ...' She waved her hand as if to say she couldn't continue, and then sobbed into her tissue.

Dad wailed as I'd never heard him do before, and never did again.

What Mum couldn't verbalise was that Keith was travelling home from work when his beloved Monaro lost its steering function. He had slammed into a tree doing eighty kilometres an hour. The toxicology report proved no drugs or alcohol were present in Keith's system; mechanical car failure had caused his untimely death. Amy had been feeding Emma at their place – a rental house a few streets away from us – when the police came to deliver the news.

I will not blame Keith's death as a cause of my parents' divorce. As you may have gathered reading this story, their distance and lack of love for each other was the writing on the wall. I used to think the worst thing in the world was having parents who argued all the time, but I was wrong. With arguing parents there is something there: passion, jealousy ... whatever, but at least there is *some* fire in the belly. My parents didn't speak a word to each other, couldn't stand the look of the other. There was nothing left to salvage, and there hadn't been for some time.

Mum and Dad separated about eight months after Keith passed away. When she told him she wanted out, he nodded meekly as though she'd just told him supper was on the table, and then resumed watching his train going round and round the track. I'd been spying on them from my bedroom door, peering down the hallway, and my heart snapped in two. It was as if the sun had disappeared behind a cloud forever. She'd stared at him from the doorway, waiting for him to say something, *any*thing! But he stayed in his den until one a.m. and then slept on the couch. He'd been expecting the divorce, but did nothing to prevent it. My dad was a hollow man after Keith passed away, and when Mum told him she wanted him out of the house, he packed a few bags and found a rental on the other side of town.

I would ride my bike over to visit him after school and on the weekends. But there was nothing for us to talk about. No common interests, and he certainly didn't ask me how Mum was doing, nor did he want to talk about Keith. When I bought a second-hand Toyota Corolla, I'd sometimes go over and cook us dinner and then we'd watch *The Benny Hill Show* together, but it was awkward as fuck. After Keith died, I believe Dad hoped, every new day, that *that* would be the day he could join Keith in the sky.

When Dad passed away in 2009, I felt sad, of course, but I wasn't heartbroken. That may sound harsh, but it is true nonetheless. In a way, I was at peace knowing Dad could finally be happy with Keith. Mum made all the funeral arrangements, and she certainly shed a tear at Dad's graveside, but I think it was more about remembering a time when they were crazy in love with each other, before the hardships and monotony got in the way. We laid Dad to rest beside Keith, and I know if Dad was looking down, he'd have been happy as heck she did that for him. There wasn't a better place for my father to be.

Chapter Fifty-One

IT WASN'T UNTIL I'D left high school that I had sex for the first time. I was eighteen and rebelling against life. I'd lost Trix, I'd lost The Sunsets, I'd lost my brother, my parents were living apart.

Jared King was good-looking in a goofy sort of way. My adult self wonders how I could have lost my virginity to him, but at that fragile stage in my life, I needed him more than ever.

We were at one of his friends' places, drinking heavily. Mötley Crüe blared from the speakers as we all gathered around a blazing bonfire, smoking dope and laughing too hard. I'd knocked back a bit more Brandivino than I could handle, and began making a goose of myself by stumbling around, laughing at things that weren't there – but boy, were the effects numbing.

With his arm around my waist, Jared led me over to his Holden Camira and we slid into the back seat, giggling while stoned off our brains. We could see the vast property before us, watching the others jamming away to 'Too Fast for Love', or running around chasing one another, and we could hear people nearby cackling (or throwing up).

And that's when he started kissing me. We moaned and waggled our wet tongues together until Jared slipped a hand inside my shirt, over a bra-cup and fondled one of my breasts. He soon found my nipple and pinched it too hard. I slapped his shoulder, crying out, and he gave me this big, cheesy grin.

'You wanna?' he drawled, braces glimmering in the moonlight as his shaggy eyebrows jiggled up and down.

And in the words of Sharon O'Rourke, I said, 'Hell yeah!'

He pushed me onto my back and his jovial face turned to one of seriousness, like he had to concentrate on this task before him or there'd be dire consequences. He ripped off his striped shirt in a frenzy, then started on my Levi's. My head spun like a vortex, but I cackled as, in a serious tone, he told me to be still so he could unbutton my jeans. I opened and closed my eyes as various images crossed my hazy mind's eye: Trix, Keith, my ex-best friends. Would Trix have approved of this? Me being in the back seat of a Camira while people chundered in the foreground? Warm tears gathered in my stinging sockets, but I wanted this; I *needed* this physical contact more than anything. I heard foil being ripped open as he placed a rubber over himself, and he asked me if I was okay. I answered that by spreading my legs wider, and he nestled in between my thighs. I dared open my eyes, and boy was he determined to make it last and do a decent job of it!

'It'll be good, it'll be good,' he said, but I wasn't sure if Jared was talking to me or trying to convince himself. When he grabbed his tallywhacker to get ready to enter me, he gasped sharply and shuddered, clenching his eyes shut.

Because he was taking this so seriously, I couldn't help but giggle. When he thrust into me, however, it was nothing special or tender, or how it's depicted in books or in movies with cherubic harp music playing. Despite the booze and drugs, it hurt like a bitch. A giggle died in my throat, and my watery eyes popped open wider as a searing hot poker entered my vagina.

He gasped again and looked at me through frantic eyes. 'Are you okay? Are you okay? Are you okay? I'm sorry, I didn't mean to—'

Tittering, I slapped his sweaty shoulder again as my muscles relaxed and expanded to accommodate the foreign object. 'Shut up and let's do it.'

He panted for a minute, his sweat dripping onto my face. 'Okay. Okay. I can do this.'

And he did do it. Three pumps later and he was hollering Hail Mary. At least it was good for him.

Jared King and I broke up a year later. I'd graduated from Year 12 and went on to study a Bachelor of Business at Mitchell College in Bathurst, and he attended the

University of New England in Parramatta. We promised to keep in touch but, as is often the case, it didn't last. I finished with an honours degree and became an event organiser. I never became a music producer like my idol, Ian 'Molly' Meldrum, but I did work on major events in Sydney for high-profilers.

And that's when I ended up moving to Sydney. It was chalk and cheese compared to Orange, and it took me aeons to adjust to city life. But I managed and I made friends. I dated a few guys and eventually fell in love with Antonio Romano – we met at a music festival I was managing. He worked as an entertainment reporter and he was covering the band 'Nut Sax'. After the concert, he approached me and we started talking, each finding out things about the other.

What can I say? We fell in love, the sex was crazy, and we ended up marrying a few years later. Antonio and I bought a two-storey house in Sydney near the Alexandra Canal. Our son, Tristan, was born twelve months after we tied the knot and our daughter, Tahlia, was born three years after that – at least I could protect the innocence of these two.

Twice a year we made the pilgrimage to Orange to see my mother. Amy Jung stayed in Orange with Emma for a while. It was good of her to pop around and let Mum see her grandchild, but as is the natural way of life, Amy fell in love with an accountant and they moved away after the marriage. It broke my mother's heart. No son, her only daughter and granddaughter had moved hours away, and now she was alone in the house.

When I discovered Mum had developed Alzheimer's, I told my husband she would be moving in with us. I hired a full-time carer, but towards the end, Mum didn't even know who I was. When she passed away in her sleep, it was a relief. Again, this sounds harsh, but I felt more at peace knowing she no longer lived in a world that must have confused and scared her. She'd needed help with eating and going to the toilet. I don't think there's a child on earth who would wish their mother's agony to continue like that. It was depressing and I felt like we were torturing her, so in the end I prayed she would go peacefully – to be reunited with Keith and her own parents, who'd both died when I was young.

I don't think about the summer of '79 much anymore, but when I do, I smile at the fond memories. I still have Trix's silver thumb ring; I just don't wear the chain around my neck. I still have that photo of The Sunsets – the one at Sharon's house, where we sat on the front steps and Cheryl snapped it without any of us being ready. Sometimes those are the best moments in life, when you're not ready or looking your finest. Hell, *I* wasn't looking for a husband, and then – *BAM*! Married with two beautiful kids, who in turn gave me adorable grandchildren.

I've never regretted what we did to Clyde, but I was sad I never got to say goodbye to Tahlia, and that Helen viewed us as though we were nothing. It saddened me that Sharon moved on to cooler, older girls, and I was never able to enjoy my time at the lake again.

To the best of my knowledge, no-one knows the police car is down there. I'm sure the cops investigated where Clyde was, and the missing car that belonged to the station, but I never heard about it. By now, there would be next to nothing left of Clyde Hanratty. He would have been food for the fish, and I'm sure the water would have dissolved his clothing. I think about how people to this day go swimming there, and the thought of them accidentally swallowing the water makes me shiver. But what option did we have? The murder induced many nightmares, especially when I pictured the moment of realisation in Clyde's eyes that his life was about to end. I lost my friends because of it, but how can I regret that we rid the world of filth?

It sickens me when I read about rapists going away for a few measly years, only to be released back into society, and when they reoffend, those at the Mental Health Review Tribunal are shocked by it. Shocked! Like it's a genuine head-scratcher. A sordid person like that will never change; it's ingrained in their psyche. And let's not forget the major thing about Clyde Hanratty: it was because of *him* that Trix was murdered. The boys from Orange East High believed Trix was the one responsible for impregnating Nicole Sullivan by force, and they wanted revenge. How could I tell anyone that Clyde told me the truth? As if a bunch of kids would believe that a policeman raped one of its citizens. They'd have laughed in my face, probably spat in my face, and said I only made it up to protect my 'boyfriend'. Trix was *so* close to starting his new life; he'd been sliding into his car – boot and back seat loaded with his prized possessions, and they'd shot him from behind. No, *fuck* you, Clyde Hanratty, I hope you're burning in hell.

I have no clue if I actually saw Trix that Monday at school, waving at me before crossing over. I like to believe so, and I like to believe Trix has watched over me all these years. My short time with Trix left a mark; it was like I had some sort of celestial experience from a divine visitor, which I cannot properly put into words. Sometimes I think I dreamed the whole thing. I've never seen a ghost or apparition since, but I have received signs.

Years later, on the anniversary of Trix's murder, I was driving home from work one afternoon when 'You'll Never Walk Alone' came on the radio. I burst into tears and pulled over, cupping my face and weeping like I hadn't done in years. I could smell the richness of the warm soil at Lake Canobolas, I could see Ed's red face giving it all he had while belting out the lyrics, and I could hear the rest of the townsfolk around us join in like one magical choir. No-one can take these memories from me. They were some of the best times of my life.

Now that I've covered pretty much every darn thing, I guess you want the big reveal – as in whose funeral it is I am travelling to. Well, as I said in the beginning, I'm still coming to terms with it myself, but the funeral is my own.

Chapter Fifty-Two

LAST YEAR, WHILE WASHING myself with a loofah in the steaming shower, I felt a lump under my breast. I hopped out, conditioner still in my hair, and asked my husband to take a look. Antonio adjusted his glasses, squinted and felt around, and when he straightened, I could tell by the dismayed expression amplified by his lenses that it wasn't good.

I saw my GP the next day, and after tests and prodding and poking, the results came back: I had aggressive breast cancer. There was nothing they could do.

Afterwards, in a daze, we sat around the dinner table and I told my husband and our two children that the docs had given me a use-by date of six to twelve months. Boy, I tell you, there isn't a bigger kick in the gut to know your time here on earth is counting down. It always is, though; from the time we're born, we have the clock ticking against us. We all know we have a precious amount of borrowed time here on earth. But to actually *know* when your expiry date is ... well, it's bloody terrifying. But from the time I found out, I did not cry once. Can you believe that? I think it was the shock of finally facing my mortality. Or maybe I accepted what was handed to me with quiet dignity, knowing there wasn't a damn thing I – or the doctors and science – could do to change the outcome. I'd chalked the fatigue and weight loss up to my gruelling work schedule. And the fact that I was simply getting older. More fool me.

My family sat around me at the dinner table and they cried – my son the hardest. I wanted to be as open and honest with them as possible; I didn't sugar-coat a thing. In some ways, I would have preferred not to know the amount of time I had left.

It dampened everything, tainting any possible joy. I wanted to bow out like my mother, just close my eyes and drift off in the middle of the night.

Instead of enjoying our last Christmas together, we'd spent it sitting around the flashing Christmas tree, everyone (except me) bawling. I'd made sure to give my children, my grandkids and my husband the best presents money could buy, and later on I wrote a personal letter to each of them, only to be opened once I crossed over. However, knowing I was going to die allowed me one thing: to prepare. I made sure my money would go to the right people; I made sure my husband knew what the funeral arrangements were to be – my mother wanted us all to be together in Orange City General Cemetery – and it gave me time to draw up a proper will. I also told my husband I wanted him to move on with his life, to marry a lovely woman who'd take care of him in his later years. Antonio sobbed his heart out and said, 'How can you think of such things?!' But I wanted to reassure him he should feel no guilt for wanting to be happy.

Towards the end, I could barely keep my head up. I wanted to die in my own bed, to have the comfort of my surroundings, but I grew too sick for my husband to manage. When I slipped into unconsciousness, Antonio had to call an ambulance to rush me to the hospital. Thanks to fluids and the tireless efforts by hospital staff, I rallied, but we all knew it was the end. We were only delaying the inevitable, squeezing every possible last drop out of my timeline before we said our goodbyes forever. I remained in hospital for one month exactly, until 21 April this year. I'd lasted seven months from the time they'd discovered it was too late. Seven.

If there is a moral to my story, then it is this: enjoy your time here while you have it; don't take for granted what you have been given. If you go through life accepting there are things you cannot change, the better off you'll be. Life has ups and downs; it can be cruel and knock you with savage blows, but don't let it get the better of you. Stand tall, stand strong, and know you'll never walk alone.

Thank you for following me on my last journey. You don't cross to the other side as soon as you take your last breath – I promise you that. You linger with unfinished business. So, now that I have unloaded everything off my chest, I have arrived at my destination: Orange City General Cemetery, to be buried alongside my mother, my father and Keith. Kind of poetic, don't you think? We've come full circle. I was born in Orange, now I shall reside here forever.

I'd always wondered whether by doing what we did in '79, it would prevent me and The Sunsets from going to Heaven when our time came. I'm pleased to say there is a white door before me, with brilliant light all around it. On the other side of that door, there are many people waiting to see me: my parents, my brother, my grandparents and, of course, Trix. I suspect we'll have many things to catch up on. So, I'll step through the door now and enter another phase of my existence.

Take away from this story what you will, judge me however you want to, hate me if it pleases you, but always remember this: I regret nothing.

Farewell, my friend. I'll see you on the other side ...

Acknowledgements

A commonly asked question I receive about my books is 'Where do you come up with your ideas?' Sometimes I remember the answer clearly, such as a segment I heard on the news; other times, it's a mishmash of thoughts and ideas merging into a compacted novel. In this case, it was the latter. I'd always wanted to write a story based on my childhood adventures. Growing up in the '90s, when Spice Girls and Aqua dominated the charts, leaves me with a profound sense of happiness whenever I am taken back to the past. I've always enjoyed novels revolving around a group of teens – navigating life together, going through the ups and downs of what puberty has to offer. One of my favourite movies growing up was *Now and Then* – starring Christina Ricci and Melanie Griffith. While drumming up ideas for a story based on friendships, I took inspiration from that storyline and then thought long and hard about how to build an original story from that.

Enter *Rumours and Repercussions*. Although it is not a replica of the movie (that would be plagiarism!), I wanted to venture out and create an 'adult version' of a story that is close to my heart. Although I think *Now and Then* is an all-round great movie, I'm fond of it because it transports me back to the '90s – being with my best friends in Toongabbie, heading down to the creek to search for tadpoles, riding my bicycle with pink streamers on the handlebars. Okay, maybe not so much the streamers, but the rest is true.

I'm partial to turning tropes upside down and exploring that in great length. Typically, we're exposed to the mindset of teen boys doing all the dirty work. I certainly can't remember the last time I watched a flick or read a story where a bunch of teen girls take the law into their own hands – I'm not saying one doesn't exist, I just haven't stumbled across it *yet*.

I am a pantser by nature – for those who don't know what that is, it's basically a writer who has no idea what the heck they're doing; we fly by the seat of our pants and make it up as we go along. That is a rush for me; pure excitement as I sit down in front of my keyboard and let the story unfold naturally. Just to be clear: there is indeed a town called Orange, and there is a Wade Park, a Cook Park and a Lake Canobolas, but for the sake of my story, certain locations, dimensions, terminology and layouts needed to be altered (including third form, sixth form etc.). For those familiar with Orange, forgive my poetic licence! And to the best of my knowledge, there are no bodies hiding deep below the lake's surface, but if you feel something tickling the underside of a foot as you take a dip, then swim like hell and don't look back!

Rumours and Repercussions was an absolute blast to write, and I hope you've enjoyed following the journey of its characters.

Even though writing is a solo journey, the act of getting it ready for publication is not. Throughout the course of editing and rewriting, I had a plethora of people come to my aid and point out mistakes or give me general advice, which I have to say, I gladly took on board. You've all helped shape my novel, so here are my thanks:

To Ruth McIver, author of *I Shot the Devil*, thank you for your encouraging words and for giving me broader insights into what it was like growing up in Australia back in the day. You've inspired me to push myself harder as a writer, and thank you for being my first author friend – saving your number in my phone felt like a milestone!

To Stacey Thomas Roth from Last Look Beta Reading over in the US, thank you for your structural advice. Because of you, I tightened up my novel to improve the flow, resulting in the story we have today. Your quick service and comprehensive feedback did my story wonders. I cannot wait to work with you again in the future.

To Sally Asnicar from Full Proofreading Services, once again, you've tightened up the nuts and bolts of my story – pointing out inconsistencies I would have slipped past if it hadn't been for you. You've been with me since day dot, and I appreciate your time and for answering the influx of emails from me asking those pesky questions. For any writer out there looking to hire an editor, you'll do your novel a great deed by employing Sally's services.

To Julie and Mick Willding, thank you for being my Orange consultants. It certainly helps that you were both living in Orange during the period my story is set, and I know you're going to enjoy your retirement there. It truly is a remarkable place. Much love to you both for the years of friendship and support.

Thank you to all the readers out there who've bought and read my books, as well as left glowing reviews on Amazon and Goodreads. I appreciate your support more than you'll ever know, and I'll continue to pump out novels for as long as you'll have me.

Mum, thank you for being the positive light in my life. These past few years have not been easy, but you and Brendan have truly been the crutches I've hobbled on. I love you both dearly.

To my wonderful friends: I couldn't have come this far without your love and guidance. Thank you. All of you.

And to Dad watching over me from above, I still work on every novel with you in the forefront of my mind. There aren't enough words to express just how much I love and miss you, but I promise to try to make you proud until we reunite down the track.

Until next time, book lovers, and for anyone who needs it ... remember: you'll never walk alone.

Stephanie L. May

About the author

Stephanie Louise May is an award-winning international actress-turned-author. After spending years in the acting business, she has turned some of her focus and energy to entertaining people through writing. Stephanie has written novels in genres ranging from romance to horror, and is currently working on a cookbook. Her pastimes include exploring rural Australia, reading Stephen King novels, and cooking Italian or Mexican cuisine while crooning to hits from the '60s and '70s. To keep up to date with her journey, please visit http://www.stephaniemayofficial.com

instagram.com/stephaniemay_90

goodreads.com/author/show/17145351.Stephanie_May

facebook.com/stephanielouisemay

https://x.com/StephanieMay14

Also by

'A heartfelt coming of age story, while inside the usual motifs has its own unique flair that has you laughing, shaking your head and exclaiming loudly on the train "Oh, Cherry!" Not my usual style, but found myself unable to put it down!' Goodreads reviewer

https://mybook.to/yQ0s5EA

'I am not typically one for romance, but this book was amazing and a must-read if you are a fan of historical fiction. The format reminded me somewhat of Nicholas Sparks' *The Notebook*, with flashbacks to the 1960s-1970s and the story of true love impacted by the perceptions of others and social class/status. I would love to see this made into a movie!'

Goodreads reviewer

'From the turn of the first page, *Memories of Then* draws you in, making it impossible to put down. This beautifully written piece takes you on an emotional journey, capturing the essence of each character. The author's vivid word imagery takes you into every moment, captivating from beginning to end. I highly recommend this book.'

Amazon reviewer

https://mybook.to/asWseUf

'Suspenseful. Riveting. Thrilling. A twist-ending that has left me reeling in shock. And as an avid reader, it's not very often I say something like that. Loved the depiction of Australia during the '80s. Believable characters. A walk down memory lane. I cannot wait to read Stephanie's next instalment.'
Amazon reviewer

'Wow, this was honestly such a good read! This cat-and-mouse thriller will keep you on the edge of your seat! Definitely a must-read for thrill-seekers.'
Goodreads reviewer

https://mybook.to/t7zrBT1